ATTILA

THE GATHERING OF THE STORM

Also by William Napier

Julia

Attila

ATTILA

THE GATHERING OF THE STORM

William Napier

First published in Great Britain in 2007 by Orion Books,
an imprint of The Orion Publishing Group Ltd
Orion House, 5 Upper Saint Martin's Lane
London, WC2H 9EA

1 3 5 7 9 10 8 6 4 2

A CIP catalogue record for this book
is available from the British Library.

ISBN-13: 978 0 7528 6113 5 (hardback)
978 0 7528 7433 3 (export trade paperback)
ISBN-10: 0 7528 6113 1 (hardback)
0 7528 7433 0 (export trade paperback)

Typeset by Deltatype Ltd, Birkenhead, Merseyside

Printed in Great Britain by Clays Ltd, St Ives plc

The Orion Publishing Group's policy is to use papers that
are natural, renewable and recyclable products and made
from wood grown in sustainable forests. The logging and
manufacturing processes are expected to conform to the
environmental regulations of the country of origin.

www.orionbooks.co.uk

To Iona

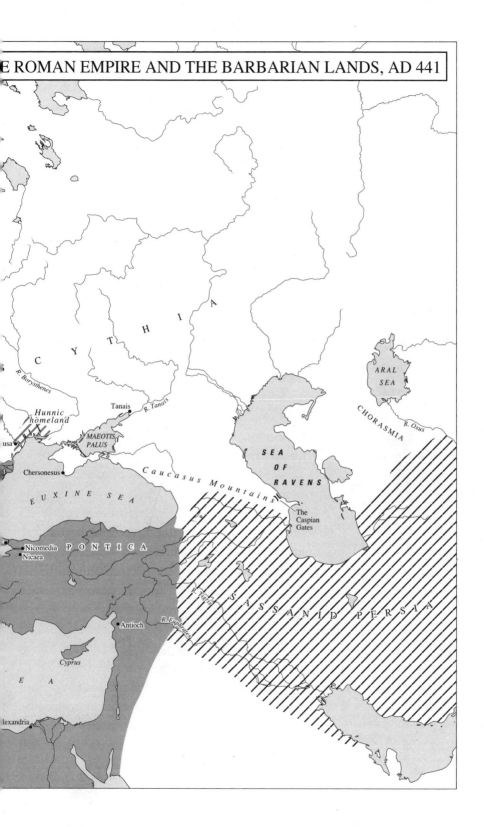

C Y T H I A

R. Borysthenes

Hunnic homeland

usa

MAEOTIS PALUS

Tanais

R. Tanais

Chersonesus

E U X I N E   S E A

Nicomedia   P O N T I C A

Nicaea

Antioch

R. Tigris

R. Euphrates

Cyprus

E   A

lexandria

Caucasus Mountains

SEA OF RAVENS

The Caspian Gates

ARAL SEA

CHORASMIA

R. Oxus

S A S S A N I D   P E R S I A

LIST OF PRINCIPAL CHARACTERS

Characters marked with an asterisk were real historical figures. The rest might have been.

Aëtius* (pronounced Eye-EE-shuss) – Gaius Flavius Aëtius, born 15 August, 398, in the frontier town of Silestria, in modern-day Bulgaria. The son of Gaudentius, Master-General of Cavalry, and himself later Master-General of the Roman Armies of the West

Aladar – Hun warrior, the son of Chanat, and one of the eight chosen men

Amalasuntha* – only daughter of King Theodoric of the Visigoths

Athenais* – daughter of Leontius, a Professor at Athens, and later the wife of the Emperor Theodosius II

Attila* – born 15 August 398. The King of the Huns

Bayan-Kasgar – general and later king of the People of Oroncha

Bela – Hun warrior, one of the eight chosen men

Bleda* (pronounced BLAY-da) – Elder brother of Attila

Candac – Hun warrior, one of the eight chosen men

Chanat – Hun warrior, one of the eight chosen men

Charaton (pronounced Karaton) – chief of the White Huns

Checa* – Queen Checa, first wife of Attila

Csaba – Hun warrior, one of the eight chosen men

Dengizek* – eldest son of Attila

Ellak* – second son of Attila

Enkhtuya – a witch of the Kutrigur Huns

Galla Placidia* (pronounced Galla Pla-SID-ia) – born 388. Sister of Emperor Honorius, mother of Emperor Valentinian III

Genseric* – born 389 near Lake Balaton, modern-day Hungary. King of the Vandals from 428

Geukchu – Hun warrior, one of the eight chosen men

Honoria* – born 422, daughter of Galla Placidia, sister of Valentinian III

Honorius* – born 390. Emperor of the Western Empire until 423

Juchi – Hun warrior, one of the eight chosen men

Kouridach (pronounced Kuridak) – chief of the Hepthalite Huns

Little Bird – a Hun shaman

Mundzuk* – older brother of Ruga, and briefly King of the Huns

Noyan – Hun warrior, one of the eight chosen men

Orestes* – a Greek slave by birth, and lifelong companion of Attila

Pulcheria* – sister to the Emperor Theodosius II

Ruga* – younger brother of Mundzuk, and later King of the Huns

Sky-in-Tatters – chief of the Kutrigur Huns

Theodoric* – son of Alaric, and himself King of the Visigoths, 419–451

Theodoric the Younger* – the first of Theodoric's six sons

Theodosius II*, nicknamed 'Kalligraphos', the Calligrapher – Emperor of the Eastern Empire, 408–450

Tokuz-Ok, 'Nine Arrows' – God-King of the People of Oroncha

Torismond* – the second of King Theodoric's six sons

Valentinian* – born 419, Emperor of the Western Empire, 425–455

Yesukai – Hun warrior, one of the eight chosen men

PROLOGUE

Thirty years passed after the Hun boy, Prince Attila, was sent into exile, and the world knew an uneasy peace. What he experienced during that exile in the unimaginable wastes of Scythia, with only his faithful Greek slave Orestes for company, none can tell. But one can surmise well enough. For scripture warns us that man is born to sorrow as the sparks fly upward. And exceptional men are born to exceptional sorrow.

In the first volume of my chronicle, I, Priscus of Panium, told of Attila's boyhood as a hostage in Rome, of his escape and flight through an Italy ravaged and laid waste by the Goths, and of his doomed return to his Hun homelands. In this, my second volume, I shall tell of what came thereafter: of Attila's return from the haunted wilderness, and the blood-darkened day on which he made himself king; and of how he gathered all the tribes of his own and kindred peoples and welded them into an army vast and terrible enough to fulfil his final ambition. To turn upon the Empire of Rome, that hated Empire which had tormented his boyhood, destroyed his youth, and humiliated his people during the long years of his exile. To make all ready for his long-meditated and apocalyptic vengeance.

Then let our story resume.

Part I

THE COMING OF THE KING

1

THE STONE HORSEMAN

The steppes of Scythia, near the River Borysthenes,
autumn, AD 441

The old Hun warrior pulled his mount to a halt and squinted eastwards. The strange horseman was still there. He had been there for a day and a night under the hot sun and the cold moon and he had not moved. There was something about him not of this world and the old warrior shivered.

It was the Month of Storms, though no storms had come yet, and the sky was growing dark with waiting. The wind gusted hard through the brown and dying feathergrass, and in the watercourses of the steppes, dried by six months of summer sun, it whipped up spiral devils of forlorn dust. Grey clouds shifted restlessly in the sky, the horses in the corrals were skittish and high-tailed, and the dogs cocked their ears and whimpered uneasily under the wagons. It was a day of expectation, of pent-up energy. Behind the curtain of the world the spirits were once again stirring and awakening, considering in their minds some fresh irruption of their limitless power and playfulness into the world of men, which men might wonder at and worship but never understand.

Some said later, after the dreamlike events of that day, that they had seen lightning come sheer out of the sky where no thunderclouds were. Others had seen the shadow of a gigantic eagle pass over the earth, near the gravemound out on the plain.

The unknown horseman sat his squat little skewbald stallion on top of the long grave-mound of Mundzuk, the brother of old King Ruga, who had died thirty years ago or more. The songs of the tribe used to say that Mundzuk had not died, but had been miraculously snatched away into heaven by a giant eagle, Astur himself,

5

the Father of the Gods. They said that Mundzuk was taken off, with hecatombs of slain horses and all his most beautiful wives and slavegirls, in the noonday of his strong manhood into the Eternal Blue Sky, to live with his ancestors for ever, fighting and feasting until world end. Mundzuk never passed through the portals of death like men of mortal flesh.

But after a while King Ruga began to tire of hearing the people sing Mundzuk's praises, and made his displeasure known. Nowadays few in the tribe remembered so much as Mundzuk's name. Three decades was a long time among a people where a woman, so they said, was old at twenty.

The aged warrior remembered, gazing out across the plains towards the grave-mound. And although his old, watery eyes, squinting into the dry steppe wind, could make out little of the strange horseman's form or features, something about the way he sat, so still and strong, made him shiver. As still and strong as a stone. Time was when the Hun warrior would have kicked his horse forward without a moment's hesitation and galloped over to the intruding stranger, pulling an arrow from his quiver and knocking it to his bow as he rode. Who was this lone spectre from the steppes who came and sat his horse on the very grave-mound of one of the dead Kings of the People and asked no leave? Chanat was old now, and he hesitated to pull back that powerful bowstring. He would ride back to the camp and tell what he had seen. Soon enough he would die in battle like a man. He prayed to the gods for such a death every night. But not today. Not in a lonely skirmish out on the steppes with an unknown horseman, and none to witness or hymn his passing.

On the mound, the horseman turned his head a little, and seemed to stare fixedly towards the old warrior. Chanat couldn't see his expression. His eyes were old and weak. But the horseman bristled with a fierce, still energy, waiting to be unleashed. The wind ruffled his horse's cropped mane, and the horseman's dark hair whipped back and forth across his face. There was energy even in the way his fist held his rope reins bunched. Even in the way he gripped his horse's flanks between his thighs. There was something in it of stone and iron, and nothing so soft as flesh.

The stone horseman raised his right arm and flicked his hand, just once, in a gesture of unmistakable command. He let his arm drop again and looked away, waiting. The old warrior could do no other but the stranger's bidding. He who had obeyed no man's word but King Ruga's for thirty years or more, heeled his pony and rode towards the mound.

The stone horseman turned back as he approached and looked down at him evenly. The warrior came to a halt before him. He looked up into the horseman's face a little while, fighting against belief. But no! It could not be!

The horseman was perhaps in his middle forties. He wore a short fur cloak knotted at his throat with a knot of rawhide. The cloak must once have been as glossy and dark as a mink's pelt, but was now grey and dusty with the dust of the plains. On his head a pointed felt kalpak, a cap in the Hunnish style, was drawn down low over his wide brow. His hair fell thick and dark and streaked with grey over shoulders ridged with muscle. His dark eyes glittered beneath his brows, but any humour there was of the fiercest and most sardonic kind. His nose was strong and bony, and told of beatings and batterings received over many long years. His mouth was set extraordinarily hard, and his chin was covered in thin wisps of greying beard. He wore bright gold rings in his ears. His copper-skinned arms appeared beneath his cloak, bare to the shoulder but for two bands of silver, high round his biceps. His muscles were large and as hard as stone. His forearms were corded with thick veins and bunched with more sinew, as strongly shaped as a black-smith's but a good deal more scarred. His right arm, especially, was as lined and crosshatched as a butcher's chopping board.

Beneath the dusty cloak he wore only a battered jerkin of black leather, knotted down the front, and below that crossgartered breeches and tattered deerskin boots. From a thick leather belt round his waist hung a Hunnish chekan, a short hatchet with a curved and spiked iron head, and a blackened rope lasso. At the other side hung a fine sword, more of Persian or Byzantine than of Hunnish make, with elaborate gold scrollwork in the handle and a scratched leather scabbard that betrayed a shape something like a Spanish blade, with a sinuously swelling then tapering blade and a long, lethal point. Crossways on his back he carried a leather quiver of arrows and the short, lethal sprung bow of the steppes.

His hands were bunched into fists on the pommel of his crude wooden saddle, knotted and gnarled with thick veins, the hands of a very strong man. The skin was as weathered and aged as the wind-furrowed skin of his face. All told of a man who had endured years of ice storms and bitter desert winds and maddening noonday suns, and ridden on unbeaten, unbowed.

'So,' said the stone horseman, his voice a soft rasp. 'Chanat. Still alive.'

Chanat said nothing. For an old man, it was true, was nothing but a burden and a shame to his people; he should have died sword in hand on some bright, bloody battlefield long ago.

'I, too,' said the horseman. 'Still alive, and come home to claim my own.'

It was him after all. Chanat looked up again. It was him.

There was another horseman approaching from the east. This other was about the same age, perhaps a year or two younger. He rode a small bay mare. Battered and travelstained as the other, but lighter in his saddle, his eyes keen and darting, his head bare and his narrow, almost monkish skull balding on top, the fair hair cropped close at the sides. His stubbled cheeks and chin as well as his colouring said that he was no Hun, but he too carried a short Hunnish bow and two quivers on his back, cross-strapped. Even after all this time, Chanat thought he remembered him. The slave-boy, a Greek, one of those fair-skinned Greeks. His master's faithful servant through all those exiled years of who knew what mysteries, horrors and griefs. The servant bowed his head to Chanat. Chanat nodded back.

'Chanat,' said the stone horseman. 'Go to the camp. Bring us a spade.'

Chanat frowned. 'A spade, Prince Attila?'

'Attila Tanjou,' he replied. 'King Attila. King.'

Twice Chanat was questioned as he rode out of the camp carrying the spade across his saddle. Both times he ignored the questioners and rode on haughtily. In his heart, in his whole chest and throughout his stiff old frame, he felt the burn and surge of such excitement as he had not felt in years. His master had given him his orders. Nothing else mattered. A master who commanded respect with the crook of his little finger. Such a master as he had longed to serve all his life. Not that guzzling old degenerate back there in his royal tent, in his tunic of soft white Anatolian wool and his gifted purple robes of Byzantine silk. His ironbound chests full of Imperial solidi: massy gold coins stamped with the legends of alien religions and the heads of foreign kings. With wine stains in his beard, snoring with his head in some captive young girl's lap, while the swords and spears hung rusting from the tent-posts. There atop the grave of Mundzuk sat a true commander of men, haughty and unhesitating in his pauper's vestments of beaten peltry and dusty hide: a Tanjou. A King.

Chanat rode out past the bored and curious watchmen, for all the world ready to thwack them across the skull with the flat of the spade if they should dare to try and stop him. They didn't. The lean, grim-faced old warrior still commanded respect in this sleepy camp of the Huns.

He held the spade out to the King. His King. How many more offerings he would willingly make to him, not excluding the spilling of his thin and ancient blood.

'Orestes,' said the King.

The fair-skinned Greek took the spade from Chanat and slipped gracefully from his horse.

Attila rode down from the mound on the eastern side and looked back. 'Dig there,' he said, with a jerk of his capped head.

'You are going to break open one of the mounds of—'

Under the King's sudden, ferocious glare, even Chanat stumbled for a moment. But then he pressed on. This was a King who would not resent a man speaking his mind, if his mind was true.

'One of the mounds of the Buried Kings?'

'The mound of Mundzuk,' said Attila. 'The mound of my father.'

A shadow passed over Chanat's face but he said nothing. They sat back and watched until Orestes had dug through to the heart of the mound, clearing the black chernozem earth from around the heaped burial stones. Attila himself dismounted and knelt beside the long cairn of stones, and removed them one by one with utmost delicacy. He paused for a long while before reaching in. Brushing aside the fallen earth within, he laid his warm palm flat on the cold bone forehead of his father and prayed for his forgiveness and understanding. He knelt a long while, then reached his other hand in, and seemed to be tugging at the forlorn and soiled skeleton itself. At last with a gasp he pulled free, got swiftly to his feet and vaulted back onto his horse. The two men, the tough Greek servant and the wiry old warrior, took it in turns to replace the stones and heap the earth back into the gaping wound that had been rent in that sacred earth and then laid back the turf. Finally, they tamped it down with the flat of the spade and all was as before.

They remounted and drove their horses up onto the long barrow. The King held his right arm up over the mound, and in a low keening voice repeated a part of the great Hunnish prayer for the burial of the dead.

Then they heeled their horses and rode forward, down the steep slope of the grave-mound and towards the quietly smoking camp of the Huns.

Nearing the camp, Attila reined in his horse and his two men stopped beside him.

He turned to Chanat. 'He was buried without his horses, without his wives or his slavegirls.' His voice grew in intensity. 'Without one gold ring for his journey.'

Chanat could not look him in the eye.

'Speak,' rasped Attila.

With a look of pain, Chanat said softly, 'Oh, do not ask me, Tanjou. Do not ask me about the dead.'

Attila looked to the far horizon. As if he would cut the throat of the horizon itself. Then they rode on.

2

THE BURNING TENT

The Hun camp lay near a bend of the wide River Dnieper, which by the Greeks is called the Borysthenes. Its headwaters rise far to the north among the frozen mountains, and even at the end of the burning summer it still flows wide and serene through the grasslands towards the Euxine Sea. There the Huns had lazed all summer long, drying and salting perch, feasting on the great sturgeon of the river, shooting wildfowl, and hunting the plump grass-fed saiga antelope as they came down to the water at dusk to drink. Once the summer had been the season for war and the winter for peace. Now it was a long time since the Huns had been at war, even with their tribal neighbours, and peace lasted all the long year round.

At the entrance to the huge sprawl of the camp, the watchmen looked uncertainly at Chanat and his new companions. One of them reached out and seized the rope reins of Orestes' horse, and the Greek halted without protest. But Attila rode on in, and when he fixed his eyes upon the watchmen none dared stop him. He came to the Royal tent and lowered his head, kicked his horse and rode straight on in between the tentflaps, appearing in the great outer chamber still mounted. Two warriors levelled their spears at him and one demanded his name.

'Nameless-under-a-Curse,' he said, swinging one leg forwards over the head of his horse and slipping to the ground. He made towards the curtained inner chamber. One of the two warriors stepped before him and then doubled up in an instant, bowed over Attila's bright sword-blade in his stomach. He lurched backwards and sat down, bleeding heavily. The other warrior came at him with his spear held low but Attila broke the spearhaft in two with a ferocious sideswipe of his sword, stepped in close alongside the warrior and drove the blade underarm between his ribs. He walked on, never pausing, wrenching the sword-blade free as the warrior fell dead behind him.

He grasped the curtain to the inner chamber, fine Byzantine silk, and pulled it to the ground and trod it underfoot. There was King Ruga, stumbling up from his couch, a young girl kneeling at his feet. The king stared blearily at the newcomer. He had grown fat in the intervening years, but was still an impressive figure in his early sixties, with his full beard so unlike the typical Hunnish, and his powerful, rounded shoulders. But his snub nose was as purple as vintage wine and his eyes were puffy and bloodshot. He glanced down at the girl and gave her a kick, sending her scurrying away, then looked up again at the figure before him. For all his wine-sodden trembling, he showed no fear.

'Who sent you?' he demanded roughly.

'Who sent me?' Attila smiled. 'Astur. Astur sent me.'

Ruga stared.

The stranger reached up and pulled his kalpak back from his wide, sunburned brow, and the old king saw three faint, reddish scars. The scars on the stranger's cheeks were blue-dyed and delicate, done in babyhood by his mother no doubt. He was clearly one of the people. But the scars across his forehead were not of the custom of the country. Except for traitors condemned to exile and death.

Attila stood in stony silence before him, his sword-blade dripping. Ruga seemed oblivious, baffled, and then, astonishingly, joyful. He stepped forward and threw his bearlike arms around him. 'My boy!' he cried. 'After thirty years, you have come back! Surely Astur sent you. Surely Astur watched over you and sheltered you under his wings for thirty years!'

He let go and stood away from him. He began to babble. 'I never believed I should see you again, when I sent you away according to the law and custom of the tribe. For not even a king may overrule the law of his people. Remember that, my boy, when you come into your kingdom. But oh, Attila, I would have given you everything—'

'You slew my father,' said Attila. He held out his left hand and opened it palm upwards. 'Here is the arrowhead I took from his skeleton today. From his miserable and unaccompanied grave.'

Ruga stared at him, blear-eyed, faltering. Finally he turned and sat on the couch. 'Sit beside me,' he said.

Attila stood before him.

'Attila,' said the old king. He reached out a plump, palsied hand as if to touch his face, his traitor's scars, but let it fall again. He took a deep breath and exhaled. 'Mundzuk was not a man to revere. He was killed, yes. And there was none to dispute the killing with me.'

Attila's eyes blazed but he could say nothing.

'Memory is strange, and imagination often mimics it.' Ruga shook his head almost with sorrow. 'You know the law of the tribe. After Bleda, your elder brother, was born, Mundzuk never lay with your mother again. In the grave-mound his bones now lie alone. Yes, embrace me, boy. For I—'

Attila fell forwards upon the king's neck and threw his arms round him.

Ruga wept at such a homecoming, such an effusion of grief and happiness. 'My boy,' he said, 'my boy ...' His voice, broken with emotion, caught in his throat. Then it stopped altogether and nothing came from his open astonished red mouth but an empty gasp.

Attila pulled back and set his hands round the old man's neck, the arrowhead that killed Mundzuk still clutched in his left hand. With a grip like the jaws of a wolf he forced the arrowhead slowly into the gagging king's throat.

'You lie,' he said softly.

Ruga's mottled hands fluttered over the hands that bulged with muscle round his neck, but they were as ineffectual as moths. His slippered feet scrabbled upon the reedmat for purchase, and his eyes turned upwards beseechingly. Attila pressed harder, the arrowhead pushing through the king's fleshy wattles and penetrating his windpipe, blood oozing between his murderer's fingers, frothing with bubbles that arose from collapsing lungs.

'My boy,' wheezed the dying king. 'My son ...'

Attila laid one hand across Ruga's forehead and pushed his head back, and with the thumb of his other hand he pushed the arrowhead deeper into the gory throat. The tip of the soiled and rusting arrowhead grated against the spinal column, and then with a final vicious shove it broke through and the old king was dead. Attila shucked his thumb free from the garish hole. Blood gouted out after it, then slowed to a trickle and ceased.

Attila stood back, perspiring, his hands glistening with blood, his eyes fixed on the dead man before him. His chest heaved and he looked like a man who was still locked in combat. He shook his head violently. Drawing his sword, he grasped a hank of the old king's faded hair and sliced his head off.

He walked out into the main audience chamber, remounted his horse, which had stood waiting and watching patiently this butchery, pulled it round and rode back out of the tent.

Outside, in the natural arena formed by the circle of tents of the chief Lords of the Tribe, at the very centre of the camp, he cast the severed head with its astonished open mouth into the dust and sat and waited. Slowly the horrified people gathered. Men with soft stomachs and open mouths like the dead king's, women with big, frightened eyes nursing infants, grubby children crawling forward between their parents' legs to see. No more than a few hundred people in all, and many more men than women. For childbirth had winnowed the women year by year, but for a generation now there had been no wars to winnow the men. A ragged, dusty, peaceful, gentle people.

As he looked out over them, a voice, the voice of Chanat, called out, 'Hail, King Attila!'

As one, the people echoed, 'Hail, King Attila!'

Still Attila looked out over his people, unsmiling.

After a long, uneasy silence, he summoned Chanat to his side. 'Bring me a brand.'

Chanat rode over to the ranks of standing tribespeople and they scurried away to do his bidding. No fewer than eight smoking rush torches were soon being offered to him. He chose the one that burned brightest and returned to his king. Attila took the torch, in his right hand, pulled his horse round, rode back to the royal tent and cast the flaming brand against the white felt walls. Immediately the flames began to devour them and the wooden posts they hung from.

'My lord,' said Chanat coming up beside him. 'The girl ...'

'Hm,' said Attila, looking back at him and stroking his thin beard unhurriedly. 'And the gold.'

He drove his heels into the flanks of his horse, and the terrified beast rose up on its back legs and whinnied, the stench of greasy burning felt already foul in its nostrils. Attila pulled his looped lasso from his belt and thrashed the poor beast mercilessly across its rump, his other hand bunched so tightly in the rope reins that the horse's muzzle was pulled right in to its neck. His heels drove into the creature's heaving flanks as it reared again and screamed a final protest from its half-throttled throat, and then plunged forward and through the flaming door of the tent.

The people stared. Not for a generation had they seen such things. And this, they knew, was only the beginning.

Behind the ranks of watching people, another watched. The silent Greek servant of the new king. The people watched the flaming tent. The servant watched the people. One fellow, a youth of no more than twenty, took a step forwards towards the tent, as if willing to go after his king. Orestes smiled almost imperceptibly to himself.

One wall of the tent collapsed as the wooden supports within gave way, and the roar of the flames grew more furious. People stepped back from the intense heat. Some looked to Chanat but he did not stir. Flames gouted high into the louring shield-grey sky, sparks erupting still higher, ash and scraps and tatters of blackened felt spiralling up to heaven like some deranged offering to the gods. The tent was an inferno. No man could survive it. Surely today the tribe had been visited not by a murderer or a usurper but by a simple madman.

And then horse and rider came rearing back through the flaming tatters of the tent, galloped free and skidded to a halt in the dust before the crowd. The people stared. The horse's coat was actually smoking, and the stink of burned hair was foul in the air. The horseman's face was blackened and his eyes blazed red from his face. A bolt of lightning came out of the sky, out of the outraged heavens, and struck the last standing tentpole of the royal tent and dashed it to the ground. The new king did not even look round, and his panting, smouldering horse did not stir. The lightning came with no thunder, they later swore, and no first few hesitant drops of rain that might extinguish the monstrous pyre behind. The collapsed tent blazed on into oblivion. The gods willed it.

Against the awesome backdrop of blood-orange fire, the blackened horseman sat and looked out again over his people. Then he pulled free the bundle that lay across his lap and dropped it to the ground. It was the young girl whom the dead king had so favoured, wrapped in a rug to save her pale skin from burning. She stumbled to her feet and stepped backwards, away from the terrifying vision of the burned horseman. He half turned and hauled on his lasso, and the people saw that he had also dragged free of the inferno the dead king's great treasure chest. Their eyes gleamed, and not from the fire alone.

The deranged horseman, the burned king, whoever this being was, flicked his lasso and it came free of the handles of the chest. He nodded to Chanat, and the old warrior dismounted, went over to the chest and gave it a mighty blow with his axe. Something cracked inside it. He grasped the heavy lid and lifted. The chest was full to the brim with gold coins.

The smouldering horseman began to ride back and forth before his people, as a general might before the standing ranks of his men before a battle. In a strange, singsong voice, he recited:

'What force or guile could not subdue
Through many warlike ages,
Is wrought now by a coward few,
For hireling traitors' wages,'

They shifted uncomfortably.

His voice grew harsher. 'But no more. A people who were once great warriors, feared from the Altai mountains to the Sea of Ravens, and to the very banks of the Danube, shall be so again. The gods are with us.' He fixed his blazing eyes on his chosen people, and they looked back at him and seemed to feel something ignited in their souls.

'As for the gold,' he said contemptuously, glancing at the chest, riven-open where it lay. 'you can have it. No true warrior glories in mere gold.'

He stopped and looked over them again and seemed to sit

taller in his saddle. 'I am Attila. I am your king. I am the son of Mundzuk, the son of Uldin, exiled for thirty summers by the word of a dead man.' He looked at the remains of the burning tent, and then back over the faces all spellbound by this vision. Some bowed their heads as if in collective shame. But his voice surprised them, growing gentle.

'I am your king, and you are my people. You will fight for me, and I will die for you. And we shall conquer to the shores of the western ocean, and to the islands in the Middle Sea, and none shall stand against us.'

The people with one voice gave a great cheer, and at last it began to rain.

Attila's eyes glittered with something like amusement. Behind him, the blackened ruins of the royal tent began to hiss and smoke and settle under the heavy, battering raindrops like some great animal breathing its last.

3

THE CHOSEN MEN

He took a lance from one of the attendant warriors, speared Ruga's severed head where it lay gaping in the dust and held it aloft.

'Orestes,' he said. 'The chosen men.'

The Greek slave came riding to the front of the crowd and, as if at random, picked eight men from the crowd. One of them was the youth he had seen step forward. The other seven he had observed just as closely.

They stood expectant.

'Your horses,' said the king.

They ran to get them from the corral.

Attila's gaze roved round the circle. He nodded at a fine blue tent opposite, with carved wooden tentposts and a colourful pennon fluttering from the summit.

'Whose tent?' he demanded.

After a pause an old man stepped forward, with wrinkled visage, soft white hair and cunning, wary eyes.

'It is mine,' said Attila. He nodded down at the young girl he had brought out of the flames, who was standing anxiously nearby. 'She is yours.'

A low ripple of laughter ran through the crowd. For it was well known that the old man, Zabergan by name, was an atrocious miser who cared only for the size of his herds, for his nurtured hoards of hacksilver and his oddments of gold, and his fine blue tent. As for wives and women, he had never seen reason to go to the expense of having more than one: his old wife Kula, a terrible baggage but cheap to run. And though this gift of a young girl was coltishly long-legged and pretty, the people knew that old Zabergan would far rather have cold bars of silver in his bed than a warm young body. Dourly the old man thanked the king and glared at the poor girl as she shuffled close to him.

Attila grinned and commanded the people to depart.

The eight chosen men returned, mounted now.

The grin faded.

The men shivered under the glare from those leonine eyes.

'And your bows,' he rasped.

His voice scoured the air between them, and some wanted to protect their ears with their hands at the sound. Then they broke and trotted bemusedly back to their tents, their horses almost tripping each other in their riders' hurry to bring forth their bows. They returned with faces flushed like scolded schoolboys'.

Attila lined them up and demanded to know their names.

'Yesukai,' said the first, bright-faced, eager. He was the young man Orestes had seen move towards the burning tent after Attila. Attila regarded him. Even now, as he gave his name, he looked as if he wished to step forward, impatient with youthful energy. Hurried, impulsive, courageous, loyal. Attila nodded. He would die young.

Attila stepped his horse sideways.

'Your name?' he rasped again.

The second was Geukchu. He had cautious, intelligent eyes, a slightly crooked mouth, and was about the same age as Attila. Untrustworthy, certainly; but one who could use his brains.

There were three brothers: Juchi, Bela and Noyan, the three sons of Akal. Young and powerfully-built, expressionless, shy. They would never command armies, or the love of beautiful women; but they would fight and die for each other in battle. They were strong together.

There was Aladar, the tallest there, on the tallest horse. Lean but muscular, grave and handsome, with his long black oiled hair and his fine moustache. The women would go crazy over him.

'How many wives in your tent, man?'

Aladar smiled faintly. 'Seven too many.'

He would never have peace from women, this one. But there were enough scars on his arms to tell his king that this was no mere

19

tent-lounger, wanting only to lie all day and all night with his seven wives while they covered him with their kisses, caresses, and fatal invisible chains.

There was Candac, a little plump around the middle but with powerful arms and a certain resolution in his round, well-fed face. This one might after all have the trick of command. He would die old.

And there was Csaba, who looked frail and dreamy and no doubt liked poetry and played a lute he had had since childhood. Probably just the one wife, whom he adored beyond embarrassment, kissing and embracing her even in public view. Attila knew the type. One moment he might be singing lullabies to a kitten. The next he would be going berserk on the battlefield, the limbs of his enemies flying, his head full of quite another kind of poetry. Half mad, for certain. But the half mad could fight, strong scarred arms or not.

Attila nodded again. Orestes had, as always, chosen well.

They rode out onto the plains under charcoal skies and beating rain. It was still only mid-afternoon on that tumultuous day, but it was as dark as a winter dusk. Some of the men looked askance at being led out into such a downpour, some of them bare-headed. But their leader showed no sign of hesitation. With his burned horse steaming in the rain, his face barbarically streaked with rain and smuts from the fire, he had ridden into and out of, like some creature protected by heaven, his sardonic eyes glittering under the dripping brow of his black felt kalpak, none felt inclined to question his leadership.

His silent foreign manservant slave rode uncomplaining just behind him, head bare and half bald, his skull shining wet. And then Chanat, the aged warrior of the tribe, his long hair a coarse grey mane still streaked darkly here and there, his long moustache luxuriant, a darker grey over his wide, set mouth. He was now in his seventh decade, perhaps, his eyes weakening, his hearing not so sharp as it was, but his body as lean and wiry as ever. His broad forehead bore deep wrinkles. All aged fast in the bitter cold of winter and the blistering heat of summer on those steppes, where the winds blew forever across the swaying and shimmering grasslands. But Chanat's deepset eyes burned bright with inner fire again, and brighter than ever now as he rode proudly behind his new king. His big fist clutched his bow without a tremor, and he no longer doubted that he could draw it as well as any there. The copper torc still held tight around his muscular throat and nothing about him showed the slackness or defeat of age.

Attila pulled back beside him. 'The one called Aladar. He is a son of yours.'

Chanat smiled proudly. 'How did you know?'

'He's almost as handsome as his father.'

'Almost.' He ruminated. 'That was a good night when he was begotten.'

'I don't doubt it,' said Attila.

The king rode with the long lance over his shoulder, the mangled burden of old king Ruga's head impaled on the end, dripping pink rain. At last he stopped and twirled the heavy burden around as if it were no more than a straw, and stuck the butt of the lance into a marmot hole in the ground. The severed head with its gaping mouth, its fine earrings still hanging from its lobes, its remnants of hair plastered flat to the great skull, silver raindrops beaded in its beard, stared back at them through the grey bars of rain.

Attila pulled his horse round and hazed them back fifty yards or more.

'Now!' he bellowed into the wind and the rain. 'A tenth of the gold in the chest to the first man to hit the target!'

With reluctance and even dread at first, but then with increasing, yelling competitiveness, their blood stirred by the barbarity and goldlust of the scene, the men milled around and took turns at trying to hit the head. None could do it. The wind played havoc with the flights. While they milled and fired, their arrows flying far to left or right or slithering through the wet grass and lost, Attila pulled back and observed.

After some minutes he rode forward, pushing his horse between the others. He seized a bow and a single arrow from Candac, the plump but tough-looking man on a white gelding. The eight chosen men fell back and watched as the king nocked the arrow to the bow and in one smooth, rapid movement, barely pausing to sight along the shaft, let fly. The bowstring hummed and the arrow flew askance then curved slightly in the prevailing wind, veered inwards and punched straight through the ghastly head on the lance, fell out and curved down into the sodden grass beyond.

The men stared.

He tossed the bow back into Candac's lap.

'One day, you will all shoot as well as that,' he said. 'One day soon.'

Then he wheeled and turned back towards camp.

The head would remain impaled on the lance out on the plain, as a lesson for men and a breakfast for the crows.

When the storm had abated and the clouds broken apart to show the blue sky again, he drove them out onto the plain once more. One of the wives called out that her husband would be no good for honouring her as she deserved that night: he would be tired out.

He called them to a halt and looked over them. Then he heeled his horse furiously and galloped back and forth, like a commander before a battle rousing his men, hurling his bitter words into their faces.

'How do the Chinese call us?' he roared. 'How are we known in their records? How do they name us in their ancient annals?' He pulled up violently before them and spat the words of insult full in their faces. 'The Waste Wanderers! The Milk Drinkers!'

The men flinched and their faces darkened. They knew how despised they were in the cities of the civilised world, in the golden heart of China: that country whose very name it was ill fortune for any Hun to speak. Or far away in the mysterious empires of Persia and Rome, of which they had heard such strange tales.

'In Rome,' he roared, 'how are we described in the histories of those swollen-headed tyrants of the western world? "A vile, ugly and degenerate people" – in the books of one Ammianus Marcellinus. Were he not dead already, he would be the first to be skewered lengthwise on a stake when we enter Rome!'

The men muttered their approval.

'To the Chinese, we are "the Stinking Ones". We drink nothing but milk and eat nothing but meat, they say, and we stink like animals and they wrinkle their delicate noses at us. In Chinese, our very name is traduced! And we Huns, we Hunnu, we the People, become the Xioung Nu. And what does this make us in the language of the Chinese? The Bad Slaves!'

Their blood boiled within them. Their horses champed and whinnied, stepping their forefeet nervously in the long wet grass. Voices rose from the huddled men in an angry, buzzing murmur.

He rode in dangerously close to Csaba and fleered in his face, 'Are you a slave?'

Csaba yelled back at him in defiance.

'O Stinking Ones!' Attila roared out over them. 'O Accursed Wanderers of the Earth, despised outcasts from the Great Wall to the Western Sea. Offspring of the Devil, Spawn of Witches and the Demons of the Wind, know how deeply you are hated! And how is that immemorial hatred to be repaid? With nice politicking, with polite debate?'

The men scowled their response.

He goaded them. 'With gifts of silk and gold to our natural, god-ordained masters in Byzantium, perhaps? With solicitous, smooth-tongued embassies? With meek and slavelike acceptance, with humble abasement, as befits such stinking slaves as we?'

Already swords were unsheathed from their leather scabbards and raised aloft, blades flashing in the blue air.

'How is this lofty contempt best countered, my beloved people? My Stinking Ones?'

Even as he spoke, he snatched his recurved bow from his shoulder and nocked an arrow to its string faster than the eye could see, and loosed it into the startled midst of them. His aim was sure and the arrow flew straight and struck Geukchu squarely on his buckler. The warrior looked down startled, but it was a light draw and the arrow did not make headway.

Attila pulled himself up in his saddle and roared out over the heads of his men, weapon held high, 'By our horses and our bows the world will know us!'

The men chorused back the ancient Hun war-cry, and the earth trembled under them as they curved and galloped away over the steppes in the rush of their fury.

He brought them back to him and marshalled them and drilled them for the rest of that day and on into the dusk, telling them that soon they would be drilling warbands of their own. He mocked them and poured scorn upon them, goading them into ever more competitive zeal. He commanded them to see how fast they could fire a dozen shots. The chosen men snatched and strained back at their quivers, fumbling for single arrows, eyeing the nocks in the ends of the arrows before fitting them carefully, sighting along their arms, drawing back the bowstring steadily. Most took two or three minutes to fire their dozen arrows. At standstill.

At last in his impatience he surged forward. One hapless warrior, burly, sausage-fingered Juchi, was still struggling to fire his last arrow. Attila struck out with his fist and dashed arrow and bow together to the ground. Juchi's horse flared its nostrils and trotted backwards into the mass of warriors behind. They laughed. Juchi scowled.

Attila seized twelve arrows in his left hand.

'Now watch,' he said, suddenly going quiet. 'Orestes,' he called over his shoulder.

The Greek rode away some distance, thrust his long spear into the ground and hung his buckler loosely by its leather strap from the butt.

All watched, transfixed.

Attila took his bow in his left hand, the dozen arrows still bunched up in the same fist. He turned sideways on to them. He did not eye the arrows, he seemed only to touch them, to feel the nock with his thumb. He drew each arrow out of his fist and into the string, and straight back against the straining curve of the bow in one long, easy movement. He let fly, and was already drawing the second arrow from his fist and nocking it afresh. The first arrow struck the tossing buckler dead centre. He wasted no time pulling the string back to his cheek and trying to sight along the arrow, but held the bow at an angle nearly sideways and pulled the string into his chest. To his heart. Drawing the bow thus meant no chance of it getting caught or bumping into his thighs or saddle.

'At what point does a galloping warrior loose his arrow?'

They stared back dumbly.

'Only when all four of his horse's hooves are off the ground. Only then does he inhabit a tiny moment floating through the air, smooth and free, when the arrow flies true. Loose an arrow when your horse is bumping over the hard ground and you are jolting in the saddle, and you will miss.'

The men looked at each other. Some grinned. Now he was testing their credulity.

Then suddenly he was at a gallop, circling the buckler on the spear at a furious pace, his horse low and straining into its bit, ears flat back, teeth bared, and their king in his animal fury likewise. They saw as he blurred by them how he continued to pull and loose the arrows in swift, easy movements and how each arrow flew and struck the swinging buckler on its strap. Some, staring closely as he fired, could have sworn that what he said about firing in that split second when his horse was entirely in the air, free of the hard ground, was quite true ...

He pulled up and looked back. The buckler was stuck with eleven arrows. The twelfth had split the spear-haft.

From drawing the first arrow to firing the last had taken perhaps thirty seconds. No, even less – their faces were blank with disbelief. He had fired an arrow every three seconds or so, at stand and at full gallop, it made no difference. It seemed an almost supernatural performance.

He looked over them, his chest heaving, a wide smile on his face now. 'Oh my Stinking Ones,' he said gently, 'you too will learn to shoot like that. And you will be the terror of the earth.'

'My brother Bleda?' Attila said to Chanat as they rode back.

'In his tent.'

'Bring him to me.' They rode on. 'And Little Bird?'

Chanat shook his head. 'He still lives. He's not been seen all summer. But he'll be back.' He nodded. 'Now he will be back.'

Bleda had grown fat, and most of his hair had fallen out, but his expression was the same as ever. Greedy, sleepy, conniving, resentful, sly.

Attila embraced him warmly.

'My brother,' slurred Bleda. He was already drunk, for it was after sundown. 'A great return. I always longed to see that traitor slain.'

'And now we rule together,' said Attila, holding his arms tightly and shaking him. 'We two brothers, we two sons of Mundzuk. We shall rule the people together, for there is much to do.'

Bleda looked into his younger brother's burning eyes, and it crossed his mind to say that he didn't want to rule the people. He would rather stay in his tent with the new young girl he had bought recently with a gift of gold from Ruga. Circassian she was, and her body was so smooth. When she—

'But first,' said Attila, striding away from him and then back again, clapping his hands together. 'Organisation.'

Bleda sighed.

After dark, and a few mouthfuls of meat but no wine, Attila walked out with Chanat among the tents of the people. The king wore no crown or diadem, no rich Byzantine robes of purple silk, but only his battered leather jerkin and crossgartered breeches, his rough deerskin boots.

'My lord,' began Chanat. 'Your slave, Orestes. He addresses you by your familiar name. I have heard him. It is not right.'

'Slave?'

'Your ... servant.'

Attila shook his head. Orestes was not his slave any more, nor his servant. Even the words 'friend' or 'bloodbrother' were inadequate. There was no word for what Orestes was to him.

'Orestes can call me what he likes,' he said. He glared at Chanat. 'And only he.'

The old warrior could not approve, but he said nothing.

Towards the edge of the great circle of tents they pulled up and looked over the corral of the horses. There were perhaps a thousand of them; squat, ungainly beasts, with huge heads and thick necks, barrel chests and short, sturdy legs. As fast as deer, as tireless as mules.

'There lies the strength of the Huns,' murmured Attila.

'By our horses and our bows the world will know us,' said Chanat.

The horses whinnied and snickered in the corral, snuffing the night air, the low moon of the first hours of darkness casting a low silver light along their backs and over their coarse, cropped manes. Attila turned his face to the sweet horse smell of them and inhaled.

A voice came to them through the night air, and on such a night as this, of promise and expectation, it struck Attila as a dreary and mournful song. He turned and stepped nearer the tent where the music came from. It was a woman's voice, soft and low. He moved silently though the darkness and saw her sitting in the entrance of a humble tent, an infant asleep in her arms. Another child of two or three lay asleep on some blankets close by, and three or four other women sat behind and around her in a semicircle. She sang:

> 'Though the grass will shoot from the land
> He is not grass, he will not come to my calling,
> Though the waters will rise from the hills,
> He is not water, he will not come to my calling
>
> Oh the jackal lies in your bed,
> The raven broods in your sheepfold.
> Only the wind plays the shepherd's pipe,
> Only the north wind sings your song,
> Oh my husband …'

The woman's voice faltered and stopped and her head fell in sorrow onto her breast and her infant looked up wide-eyed at her. One of the others close by reached out her hand and laid it on the singer's shoulder.

'Who is she?' whispered Attila.

'The woman of one of the two guards you killed in Ruga's tent.'

Attila frowned. He had forgotten them.

He went up to the tent and stood silently. After a while the women looked up and some of them started. But not the widowed woman.

Attila gestured over his shoulder at Chanat.

'Woman,' he said, 'here is your new husband. Be content.'

She stared up at him through tear-bright eyes. Then she slowly got to her feet, her infant still in her arms. She stepped in front of him and spat on the ground almost between his feet.

She said, 'You slew my husband and burned his body to ashes without burial. You left me a widow and my children helpless orphans. My heart is broken like an old pot, it is in a hundred pieces on the hard ground. My tears have all cried out and dried and still my sorrow within me would cry out a river. Now you treat me as you would a cow, and give me to this ancient bull here with his old dog's breath and his wrinkled ballbag. But I am not to be so easily given. Leave my tent and go back to your own bed, with your bloody sword for company through the cold night. And may the gods judge you harshly.'

Chanat stepped towards her, but Attila held his arm out across the warrior's chest.

The woman stared a little longer at the king, contemptuous and unafraid. 'How many more will you slay likewise, my lord widow-maker? I know minds and hearts such as yours, and they are no mystery to me. O great Tanjou! Khan of all the kingdoms under heaven! Great king of everything and nothing!'

She spat again, then turned swiftly and went back into the tent and pulled it closed behind her.

'My lord!' protested Chanat, but Attila shook his head.

'Words, words, words,' he said.

They walked on.

'In the face of desert storms, the lion's teeth, armies of tens of thousands,' Attila said, 'one may ride without fear. But in the face of a widow's anger ...'

'Such a woman would be a good hot ride,' said Chanat. 'And a good mother of warriors. A pity her desire was not stirred by the thought of my wrinkled ballbag.'

'A pity indeed,' said Attila.

Passing another tent nearer the heart of the camp, they heard a young girl's screams and an old man's impotent bellowing. Then the girl herself almost fell out of the grubby, mean-looking tent at their feet. Her hair was torn out in clumps, her face beaten and bruised, and her tunic half ripped from her back. After her stumbled an old man, gasping with fury, his eyes bulging, and spittle in his skimpy beard. He stopped and pulled up when he saw the king.

'How did you come by her?' rasped Attila. 'I gave her to Zabergan.'

'Zabergan sold her to me,' said the old man. 'He is my cousin. I gave a good price.'

'And now you beat her?'

The old man smiled conspiratorially. 'The more it is beaten, the tenderer the meat.'

'How do you beat her?'

'With this,' said the old man, brandishing a knobbly stick. He came closer to them, and his breath was hot and thick with koumiss and lust. 'On her back,' he said, almost whispering, 'on her firm young buttocks, and on her soft young thighs—'

'How? Like this?' said Attila. And in a blink of an eye he had snatched the stick from the old man's grasp and hurled him to the ground. Chanat thought he heard something old and brittle crack as he hit the hard ground. Then Attila was standing astride him and belabouring his skinny, bony back with all his might. Under the rain of blows the man could do nothing but curl up and whimper for mercy. Attila stood straight again, snapped the stick over his upraised thigh and dropped the two halves into the dust.

He pulled the girl to her feet and looked her over briefly. 'Go to the Compound of the Women. Tell them I sent you. They will clean you up well enough. You are mine now.'

The girl stared at him, rabbit-eyed.

'Go,' he said, giving her a shove.

She went.

'Sorting out my people's domestic troubles!' he growled, looking after her. 'I had my mind on higher things when I dreamed of being king.'

Chanat guffawed. 'You are kind to women.'

They walked on, leaving the old man in the dust.

'Kind?' Attila grunted. 'Kindness has nothing to do with it. I want good warriors out of that one's womb.'

In the morning, a widow in a tent at the edge of the camp near the corral of the horses, her face etched and exhausted with grief, came to her door to find the silent Greek on horseback, holding out a fine silver vase. She took it and looked inside. There were some ashes. She turned without a word and vanished back into her tent.

At dawn, Attila and his chosen men were already out on the plain for target practice.

'You will learn how to shoot as well as your king shoots,' he told them, 'or your fingertips will bleed away in trying.'

He left them and rode on with Chanat and Orestes.

Orestes' big hare eyes darted left and right across the steppes, as if expecting the shadow of the Erinyes themselves to come up over the horizon: those clotted avengers from Tartarus with blood spilling from their eyesockets and snakes twined in their hair, as they had come to another older Orestes. Come as before to avenge the murder of parent or uncle by the outraged prodigal child.

But then Orestes always looked guarded and uncertain. Or certain only of the uncertainty of the world. He had come back from his thirty years of wandering with his master through the unknown wastes like a man who trusts in the stability of nothing. Except of his own heart.

Finally Attila reined his horse in, and the three sat and gazed at the far horizon.

'My father ...' he began.

'Do not ask, I beg you,' said Chanat. 'Oh, do not.'

'Ruga had no sons or daughters.'

Chanat looked away. 'He was injured in his stones. When he was twenty summers or so.'

The grey sky of the steppes was paling and warming in the sun. From afar off came the high chatter of spotted susliks. Dust on the far horizon, perhaps a herd of saiga antelope. Perhaps only devils of the wind.

'Before that, Ruga and my mother ...'

'Oh, do not ask, my king.'

The sky lightened from shield grey to pale and then to daylight blue. Like the fine blue silken robes that King Ruga had worn when he gasped and died.

Attila turned and nodded to Orestes. The Greek already knew his mind, as always. They did not even need to speak in a private language, these two, as old friends do. They barely needed to speak at all.

Orestes heeled his horse and rode on, veering southwards towards the settlements beyond the low hills.

'Might I ask who, my lord?'

Attila gazed at him unblinkingly. 'My family,' he said.

In late afternoon two days later, after many miles of riding, Orestes came back into the camp, dusty and weary, with a strange procession of women and boys. The older boys, well into their second decade, rode horses of their own, but the younger, and the women, rode in a covered wagon, peering from the back at the unfolding camp.

The camp gazed back in curiosity and then in astonishment. There were arguments about how many there were, but general agreement was that there were six sons and as many daughters, and then again as many wives.

Attila commandeered two more fine tents in the heart of the camp, and into one trooped his six sons. Their ages ranged from seventeen or so down to four or five, and the youngest wept as he parted from one of the women. Attila sat his horse and watched them go. Into another tent trooped his women. In time, the people learnt that they comprised five wives and eight daughters, and they marvelled anew. For a king to have five wives was nothing. But for one who had been a vagrant in the wastes of Scythia for thirty years to have five wives, and to keep such a family together, defended from every brigand that passed by, was scarcely imaginable. What strength must have defended them. What ferocity ...

As the stature of the sons and the beauty of the daughters well attested, the wives themselves were no cast-offs from some foul-smelling brigand's harem. The older were as haughty as queens, and the younger were as young as his eldest daughter. Surely their new king was a great king.

At the head of the wives walked one who was perhaps as old as her husband. Her step was graceful and serene. Her eyes were large and dark, her hair loosely braided. Her gown was a simple brown woollen robe, and her only decorations were two modest gold earrings, and a fillet of fine gold round her brow. She was tall and slender as a queen, but her fine, handsome face told of long hardship and desert wanderings, and no soft years in a royal palace for her. She already had many delicate wrinkles around her beautiful eyes, her skin was drawn across her wide, high cheekbones, and her long dark hair was greying at her temples.

The king called out, a word that none understood. The woman stopped and looked across at her lord and master, and smiled with a smile of covert triumph. She walked over to him, and into his fine blue tent behind. The rest of the wives – younger, prettier, still of childbearing years – watched her go. And then they went on into the new tent of the king's wives.

'What is the first wife's name?' Chanat murmured to Orestes.

Orestes didn't answer for a while. Then he said, with a small smile, 'She is called Checa. Queen Checa.'

Long after dark she lay on her back beside her husband, her face streaked with perspiration, her hands folded, a smile on her lips as playful as a young girl's.

'Oh great tanjou,' she whispered, looking across at him and widening her eyes beseechingly. 'Oh my great lord, my strong lion, my ravisher, my fierce king and conqueror. Did you miss me these last few days?'

'Hnh,' grunted Attila, his eyes closed.

Checa laughed.

When she awoke an hour later he was gone.

For his blood was up and his time had come and the strength and surge of his blood knew no bounds and his hunger for the world was limitless. He strode out onto the plains alone and unarmed and held his arms wide under the stars and prayed to his father Astur, who made all and watched all. He asked for nothing in his prayer. He had all he wanted for now, and all else that he wanted he would soon have, too. He closed his eyes and smiled up into heaven and his only prayer was to feel the presence and power of his father Astur and be bathed in the silver starlight that God made even before he made the earth from a clot of blood.

He returned and went into the tent of the women and pulled them to him. Among them was the girl he had rescued from Ruga's tent and given to Zabergan. Still bruised from the brute who had beaten her, she came to him shyly. And when dawn came up over the eastern steppes, five more concubines lay on their backs with their hands on their bellies and uncertain smiles on the lips, wondering if they might now be carrying a son of the new king.

The king was gone already. He had slept two hours that night and it was enough, more than enough. Sleep made him impatient. 'Time enough to sleep in the grave,' he growled, toeing Orestes grumblingly out of his blankets. Now, as dawn came up, they were already out on the plains, a dozen miles out from the camp and still at full and furious gallop, Attila yaa-ing and roaring, Orestes jolting in the saddle and laughing at the pitiless energy of his master, a fast-moving dustcloud of saiga ahead of them and the king with teeth bared like a wolf that was ready to devour the whole herd.

For he had waited thirty years to come into his kingdom. Riding the solitary grasslands and the dustlands and deserts farther east, shoulders hunched and head bowed against the scouring sands and the blistering loneliness. But one soul stayed with him through it all and would not leave his side, though at times he commanded him to and flung his loyalty back in his face with bitterness. Orestes stayed there by his side, no more to be cleaved away from him than his own shadow.

In some distant, hidden valley in the far White Mountains – so the story went among the fascinated and gossiping people who now called him their king – he had carved out a bandit kingdom, and drawn men to him. And wives. The wives had come with him, back west to his heartland in the pastures by the Euxine Sea. And the men – perhaps they still waited for him far to the east.

Now the three desert decades were over, and it was time for it to begin. He could not have returned earlier, all the tribe would have been against him. But he had served his traitor's exile, cut off from his people, his shamans and his gods, and now it was time. Time to come into his kingdom, and ride out against the world that had so belittled and humiliated him. He had survived scorn and abuse, beatings, half-killings, silence and contempt, as must any tribeless man with none to defend him or fight with him. He had been a mere bandit leader, though the son and grandson of kings. For the world is not a just place; or it is just only to the powerful.

When he rode out into the wilderness, a broken-hearted boy all those years ago, none had believed him truly a traitor. But Ruga's sentence that bright morning had expressed the will of the gods, and none might go against it. Had any in the tribe spoken with Attila or taken him in as their secret guest during years of his exile and ostracism, they would have been punished terribly. None would have so transgressed. Now he was back, an aura of miracle about him in that he had survived so long alone and tribeless in the wilderness, with only his silent, watchful, mistrustful foreign slave and his ragged, mysterious family for company. Surely the gods must have watched over him, for such survival would not have been possible otherwise.

There are many such tales among other peoples, of mad kings driven into the wilderness to live like animals: King Nebuchadnezzar of the Jews, who turned aside to eat grass like the oxen, and whose body was wet with the dew of heaven, till his hairs were grown like eagles' feathers, and his nails like birds' claws. Or one-eyed King Goll of the Celts, who fled from the field of battle not from cowardice, but maddened by that blood-red rage which grips men amid carnage. I heard a fragment of the haunting Song of King Goll sung long ago by a brown-eyed Celtic boy:

> And now I wander in the woods
> When summer gluts the golden bees,
> Or in autumnal solitudes
> Arise the leopard-coloured trees;
> Or when along the wintry strands
> The cormorants shiver on their rocks;
> I wander on, and wave my hands,
> And sing, and shake my heavy locks.
> The grey wolf knows me; by one ear
> I lead along the woodland deer;
> The hares run by me growing bold.
> They will not hush, the leaves a-flutter
> round me, the beech leaves old.

Attila was no such sorrowful king nor idle folk tale. He was a living myth to his people, dressed in flesh and blood, back from the wilderness to dwell among them, and they beheld his glory.

World-bestriding conquerors are furious in their youth, and as impatient as youths even if they make old age. Alexander had conquered the world by twenty-nine. Hannibal faced and destroyed the flower of Rome in the field when he was but thirty, and Caesar chafed bitterly at not having brought the world to its knees before him by the same age. Attila was one with these men of world-hunger. But he was in his forties before he even tasted power. Some say he could have exercised that iron will of his and deposed Ruga far earlier taking the crown of the Huns and setting it on his own broad head. One glare from those leonine eyes, and not a man of the tribe would have dared oppose him. But Attila was wiser than that. He knew that patience is the nomad's greatest weapon. He watched. He waited. And when he finally rode back into the camp of his people, it seemed that he not only had might but right on his side, having been preserved in the wilderness for so long. What trials and tribulations he must have faced there. And so his return only seemed the more extraordinary, the more miraculous. All the warriors of his tribe then believed in him, in a way they had never believed in Ruga, or even tough old Uldin before him. He was consort of the mountains, he was friend of the desert and brother of the waste places. There blew through him that same invisible wind that blew from heaven and coloured the shamans' dreams. With him at the head of their armies, none could oppose them. That was what they believed, and he knew it. 'An army that believes in something – anything – will always defeat an army that believes in nothing.'

His army would believe in him.

4

LITTLE BIRD

It was as Chanat had foretold. Hearing somehow – in the voices of the wind, perhaps – of the things that had transpired in the camp of the Huns, and the return of the Prodigal Son, come murdering his own uncle with his bare hands and a rusting arrowhead – Little Bird reappeared.

Impossible to say if he had aged at all, or how many summers his life had counted now. His raven-black hair was streaked with random grey, but his face still had the strange bright innocence of a child, though he might have been forty, or sixty. The skin stretched thin over his broad Asiatic cheekbones, his colour was high and hectic, and his eyes were as darting and bright and malicious as a mink's. He had no facial hair nor shadow of it anywhere. Even for a Hun he was as smooth-cheeked and innocent as a boy. He wore his hair up in a topknot after the fashion of the people, but tied with a scrap of bright flowery silk like a woman. He wore a string decorated with little animal skulls round his neck, and bangles and bracelets, also like a woman. He tipped his head to left and to right as he talked, mocking both himself and the man he addressed. His clothes were bright and tattered, and his ripped goatskin shirt, loosely laced, was decorated across his chest and right around the back with coarsely drawn little black stick-men.

When he threw his cloak off and danced, spinning on the spot, his nostrils filled with sweet hemp smoke, his eyes rolling back in his head and his arms held wide, the stick-men whirled round and blurred together, and it was as if there was no distinction between one and another but all men merged together, some ascendant and some descendant on the wheel of fortune, but none in the end more than a brief black blur in the white light of eternity.

He addressed King Attila. The king was at his fireside, eating with a handful of his chosen men. Chanat and Orestes sat close by, and also young Yesukai and wily Geukchu.

Little Bird sat uninvited among the men and held his hands together like a Christian at prayer and smiled sweetly at the king.

'Great Tanjou,' he said, 'what an ascent you have made in the world of dreams, who only seven days' since would not have been allowed into camp even to lick out King Ruga's night-bowl!'

Attila eyed the madman over the legbone he was gnawing. 'Welcome back, Little Bird,' he rumbled.

'My lord!' protested Yesukai.

'Holy and untouchable you may be, boy,' growled Chanat, fixing his dark eyes on the little shaman from under his arched black brows, 'but if you—'

'Hark!' squealed Little Bird, staring at Chanat wide-eyed. 'The old bag of bones comes back to life and speaks. I thought you were dead long since, old Chanat.'

Chanat made to seize him by his dancing topknot and drag him away into the darkness, holy man or no, but Attila held out his arm. 'Words, words, words,' he said.

Little Bird looked away from Chanat with a sneer, and then resumed his sickly sweet smile as he gazed at King Attila again. His voice was singsong and ridiculous.

'A wanderer and an exile upon the earth you were, Lord Widow-Maker, and a detested pariah dog amongst men, with your noble brow cruelly marked with the three shameful scars of a traitor. How far and fast you have climbed in the world of dreams! But one can fall as well as rise, for there is no knowing the will of the wicked and wayward gods, and conquests and triumphs in this world of dreams have all the longevity of virginity! Though doubtless Great Tanjou, oh my Attila, Little Prince of Everything and Nothing – doubtless the gods will favour you especially, and you will live for ever and conquer all the world. Of course you will.'

Still Attila did not react.

Little Bird sighed. He sat cross-legged in the dust and wagged his head in vexation. Then he looked up and said in a more normal

37

voice, 'So, Great Tanjou, where have you been? What have you done?'

Attila set down the legbone and wiped his lips. 'Everywhere,' he said. 'And everything.'

Little Bird liked the answer and smiled. 'And why did you not return earlier?'

'You know that. The law of the tribe was against me.'

'Such a lord as yourself,' put in Geukchu smoothly, 'need have no fear of the law.'

'Do not flatter me,' said Attila, not even looking at him, his eyes still fixed on Little Bird. 'I am not superior to all laws. Nor to all lawgivers.'

There was a silence in the night. Little Bird understood his words.

'Besides,' said Attila, 'there were other things for me to do.'

'What things have you done?' asked Little Bird, his voice quieter.

Attila's voice, too, was quiet. 'What things have I not done?'

The fire crackled. The men around him sat expectant, almost fearful, their eyes upon him. Only Orestes looked at the ground, while his king murmured strange and ancient words.

'I have been a king, I have been a slave,
I have been a warrior, madman, fool and knave,
A dewdrop in the grass, an eagle on its nest,
And a thousand thousand heads have lain upon my breast.'

'These are the words of a shaman,' whispered Little Bird.

Attila nodded. 'You were nine years in the wilderness and on the heights of the holy Altai, Little Bird. But I was thirty. And thirty years is a long time.'

Little Bird shifted where he sat.

'Look into my eyes.'

Little Bird turned away.

'Look into my eyes.'

Little Bird looked, and he did not like what he saw. Those eyes yellow and leonine in the firelight. That gaze as blank and pitiless as the sun. He had seen such eyes before. But not in the face of a man.

Little Bird stared at him a moment longer, then, saying not a word more, he vaulted to his feet like a young acrobat and hurried away among the darkening tents.

The other men, too, felt some nameless dread, and made their obeisances and went soon after in silence with heads lowered. All departed except Chanat, who remained at the fireside, and faithful Orestes, lying back upon the ground with eyelids closed.

Attila gazed long into the fire, and the fire danced in his eyes.

After some time Orestes spoke. Turning to Chanat he said, 'Friend, tell me about Little Bird.'

Chanat thought for a long time, then said, 'I remember the story of Little Bird from when I was still a young man. It is a story that has never left me.' He pulled up some grass, stripped off the seeds and held them in his palm and considered them, before he leaned forwards and blew them from his hand. 'When he was a young man ...' He watched the grass seeds fall into the fire and die.

Attila sat cross-legged on the other side of the fire, staring into the embers, hands upturned on his knees, as brooding and silent as a stone god.

'When he was young he was just as crazy,' said Chanat, 'but not in the way he is now. He was a crazy young boy, with a head full of visions and dreams. Then he met a girl, at a khurim, a feasting meet. She was very beautiful. At first she scorned him utterly.' Chanat smiled. 'How cruel and haughty she was to him! To test his spirit, of course. Like all women she was flattered beyond measure that a man adored her. But she was cruel to him with her tongue, as is the way of the Women of the People. She whipped him and berated him mercilessly. "You puny little man!" she would yell at him in her high girlish voice so that all the camp could hear and laugh. "I despise you and the very earth you walk on! Your hands are like a girl's, you tremble at the mewing of a lamb, a single raindrop on your nose affrights you. Oh, how I detest you!" Her gift of invective was great, as is the way with women when aroused.'

Orestes laughed silently. His eyes were open now, searching among the stars.

'But Little Bird's gift of flattery and charm was greater. Words and songs and poems and extravagant similes flowed from his lips like the waters flow from the heights of the Tavan Bogd, the Five

Kings, in springtime. Bright and sparkling words, a strong current to sweep a young girl away. And so in time she was swept away. Little Bird was without doubt an embarrassment and a catastrophe on the ball field or on the field of the bow. She, Tsengel-Düü her name was, meaning Little Sister of Delight, she would cry out, "Oh, you are an embarrassment and a catastrophe among men, Little Bird! What woman would be foolish enough to have you for a husband? She must needs be deaf and blind and older than a hundred years, your lovely wife who is waiting for you now, you walking disaster of a man!"

'But at night by the firelight he would adore her and compliment her and do it all with a bright gleam in his eye and a bold mirthfulness, rather than that solemn slavish hopeless hangdog yearning which all women find repellent. He flattered her and charmed her, confident as if he knew that in the end he would win her. And so of course he did. They were wed, and soon her belly grew round, and Little Bird's happiness was beyond all bounds and all sense. There was a craziness to it that could have spilled out at any moment into jealousy or worse. But instead …' Chanat pulled up more grass stems. 'Instead, he went into the woods one day. This was in high summer and the People were high to the north on the edge of the forests, hunting roe deer and boar – game was good.

'In the forest it is said he met a raven. The raven sat on a low branch and spoke to Little Bird and greeted him as his brother, and Little Bird asked him what news. The raven said, "The past is done, but much is to come." Little Bird asked him what he meant. And the raven said that he, Little Bird, would kill his beloved with his own right hand. Little Bird stared and stammered, then he ranted and screamed, "Never, never, *never!*" He swore that he would rather see the whole People destroyed and the sun blotted out from the sky than do any harm to his beloved for she was his heart and his life and the fairest in all the plains from the holy mountains to the western sea. He cursed the raven as a fiend sent to torment him. The raven looked at him with his bright black eyes and said that, all the same, Little Bird would kill her. At that Little Bird grew furious beyond all reason, as if a wood demon had taken possession of him, and he drew his knife and struck down the raven with a single blow across the throat. The bird fell to the ground stone dead. Little Bird turned and whirled and threw his head back and yelled defiance up at the blue sky.

'When he had calmed a little he looked back, and there was no raven lying there. Instead, there was his beloved, stretched out on the forest floor with her throat cut.'

The horror and mystery of the story was in the very air around them.

Chanat raised his head. 'Little Bird tried to kill himself three times after that. Each time he failed – something prevented him. He stopped eating but it made no difference. Even today, you will notice, he hardly eats at all. And since then, Little Bird has been crazier or wiser than all other living men. Or perhaps both. Something was taken from him that day when he killed her. But something was given to him, too. Though everything that was precious to him was snatched away by the hand of heaven, in exchange, some vision was vouchsafed.'

Chanat brooded a while, then said softly, 'I would not have the vision that was vouchsafed to Little Bird that day for all the world. I am happy to have the ignorance of a child, and for the ways of the world and the gods to remain hidden from me still.'

He blew the last of the grass halms from his hand and got slowly to his feet. He made to walk away, but looked back one last time and said quietly, 'Respect him, though. He has journeyed far.'

5

THE RAID ON TANAIS

It was mid-afternoon on the following day and Orestes was crossing the camp when a terrible shrieking came from the royal tent.

He drew his sword immediately and burst in, to see two of the younger royal wives in a ferocious argument, face to face, immediately in front of where Attila sat on a stool. They seized each other by the hair and began a vicious catfight. The sound of their shrieks was augmented by the sound of Attila roaring with laughter at the spectacle, sitting back on his stool with folded arms.

Then he caught sight of Orestes and came over, still grinning broadly.

'We have work to do,' he said. He glanced back. 'Besides, one can only watch women fighting for so long.'

Outside he mounted his favourite dusty skewbald, Chagëlghan, and summoned Geukchu to him.

'It is time to build a fitting royal palace.'

Geukchu bowed low. 'An honour that I dream not of, my lord. You shall have the finest shining white tent from here to the Iron River.'

'I shall have the finest royal palace from here to Lake Baikal,' said Attila. 'Built of carved and polished wood, with many rooms for many wives and servants. As for my own throne, let it be of plain and sober build.'

'Wood?' repeated Geukchu.

'Wood.'

'My lord,' said Geukchu, 'the nearest woodlands to our beloved grasslands are a good two days' ride to the north, and the people of the woods are not our brothers.'

'Then take your bows and your swords, and the best wagons for transport. I am leading a raiding party east. We will be no more than a week. The palace will be built upon my return.'

He pulled his horse round and rode away.

'A raiding party?' said Orestes, running after him.

Attila glanced back and growled with irritation, 'Get on a horse, man.' Then he nodded. 'Eastwards, to the Byzantine trading-station at the mouth of the Tanais.'

'But ... it isn't the season for furs.'

'Furs?' he said mockingly. 'It's not furs we need. It's Greeks.'

Minutes later the king rode out of the camp and eastwards into the lawless steppelands with just four men for company: faithful Orestes, young Yesukai, the handsome Aladar, and Csaba, the skinny, far-eyed dreamer. Old Chanat sulked like a boy at not being chosen.

Many thought that he must be crazy to ride off with so little escort and bodyguard, two or three days to the east and into the lands of unknown tribes and nomad bands, now guarding fiercely what pitiful pastures remained at the parched and hungry end of summer. But none dared say it.

They rode well armed, but with supplies for only a day.

The Hun warriors' fingertips were raw with having pulled the bowstring for gruelling hours and days of target practice, under the watchful eye of Orestes, both at standstill and at full gallop; and the soft insides of their left arms were likewise grazed red-raw. But now Attila allowed them to wear leather guards on their left arms, and leather fingerloops, and they fired better each day. The muscles in their arms and chests ached but hardened under the repeated strain of that bowstring and that springing, lethal bow.

They rode south and east until they met the shores of the Maeotis Palus, which is to say the Marsh of the Scythians, which in the barbarian tongue is called the Sea of Azov. It is a haunted place.

The waters were low after the long, hot summer. As they rode in the brackish shallows to cool their horses, they set off flocks of the little dun sandpipers that gathered along the fertile mudflats, gorging on tiny shellfish before their autumn flight far eastwards over the Sea of Ravens and so on to the sunlit lands of India for winter, when all of Scythia would be in the grip of the devils of ice and frost.

'So,' said Orestes at his master's side. 'Greeks.'

Attila said nothing for a long while. Then looking ahead still he said, 'It is not only swords and spears that give us power over the world. It is also facts. So much of what men have invented is but to hide from the facts. Religion is a coverlet to muffle the spiky facts. But the facts of the world were made by God, religion was made by men.'

'And the truth?'

'Aha,' said Attila, turning to Orestes, his eyes dancing. 'The truth. The truth is far otherwise than what men in their dreams and coverlets imagine.'

They rode on.

'Here is a fact,' said Orestes after a while. 'Your brother Bleda is already plotting against you.'

'Of course he is,' said Attila evenly. 'Do you think I am a fool?'

'Heaven forfend, Great Tanjou,' said Orestes with exaggerated obsequiousness.

Attila looked at him askance. 'Forgo the flattery. That's Geukchu's domain.'

Orestes smiled. 'But did you know that Bleda has already sent a messenger with a letter to Constantinople?'

He enjoyed a brief moment of satisfaction. Attila, for once, was taken by surprise.

'My brother ... a letter ... ?'

'To request their help, and their gold, in regaining what is rightfully his, as the elder brother and lawful King of the Huns.'

'My brother!' cried Attila again, and this time he seemed nothing but delighted. He even dropped his reins and clapped his hands with glee. 'He couldn't plot an overthrow in a marmot burrow!' He laughed, he roared. 'Oh, my stupid brother, how you shall entertain us with your plans and plottings!' He actually wiped a tear from his eye with the back of his hand. How good it would be to monitor this unfolding conspiracy. How pleasurable to spy on his brother's manoeuvrings, as clumsy as a camel's in a bazaar. How sweet to savour such knowledge and power. To wait and finally to pounce upon that slow-brained fool, and dismember him for his impertinence and folly.

'Keep me informed,' he said, his laughter at last subsiding. 'Please.'

'Should we not send out to kill the messenger?'

'No,' said Attila. 'Not at all. It's a fine way for the empire to hear of my return.'

'The empire?' said Orestes, quietly and wonderingly, as if he had almost forgotten that word in his thirty years' of wandering.

'The empire,' repeated Attila. As if he had not forgotten the word or the thing behind it. Not one whit. 'Rome.'

They rode hard all day and into dusk, setting camp after dark some miles inland from the mosquitoes and fever of the Marsh. They chewed salt beef and drank weak koumiss and slept on the ground under their horse blankets. Each of them awakened in the dull hours before dawn to roll tighter into his coverings, the damp arising now from the dark earth beneath them to chill their bones with the whispered assurance of the shivering winter to come.

In the pewter dawnlight he had them already roused and mounted and practising their bowshots at stand and at full gallop.

They rode eastwards all that second day in silence. Formed up like a skein of wild geese behind their enigmatic king, seen by the eagles far above their bowed heads as a tiny black v moving slowly over the infinite plain.

Far off they saw the dustcloud of a saiga herd, and a buzzard planed low towards them, swept over their heads near enough for them to see its unblinking amber eyes, and then glided on. They flushed a startled hoopoe from the long feathergrass at their horses' feet, and on a low, close-cropped rise to their left they saw a marmot sitting up on its back legs regarding them, but it vanished into the ground before they could nock an arrow to the bow. They each cursed inwardly at the thought of even a few mouthfuls of its dark, oily meat. They saw no other game. On the third day they came through dry thornbrakes to a brackish inlet of the Marsh, half hidden by sallow and broken alder, and they tethered their horses and waited.

Three nights from home, far out on the great plain. Waiting there by the sluggish, midge-specked water of the inlet for the herds, to come out like knives to hack at vulnerable hocks. But no luck. Not a chance. Shadows of birds. No herd came. And this the third night yet. Out of the night's cliff they hollowed a little cave of firelight. The wind as if in winter had blurred their eyesight. Their eyes like ice deflected the warmth of the fire. Their hearts yawed and flickered feebly like the flames in the downdraft from the shallow swale above, when they saw that their king was gone, alone on the plain. He stood with his head thrown back, his arms outstretched, murmuring words under the moon. Then he was gone altogether. The night was still, the wind dropped. The stars burned. All the world was still. Their heads were heavy, their brains hummed a song of ash. When a trembling deer stepped into the firelight, which they took and killed for God's and their bellies' sake.

They rode through long dry grass as pale as hay all the next day. Towards evening they reached low hills of bitterspar and came up through a shallow valley and crested a green rise, and there in the dusk they could see the distant torchlights of the Greek trading-station of Tanais. Low wooden houses, landing-stages, long logwood wharves, and the great river itself, stretching away limitless in the gloom. A dusty road followed the course of the river northwards, and men walked it or rode small ponies and rackety wagons.

A manmade inlet alongside was clogged with the dark shapes of logs, felled and rolled down far to the north. For the forests of Scythia were limitless, while already the oak woods and chestnut woods, the cypress woods and cedar woods in the mountains of Greece and Cappadocia were growing bare. But such trading-stations as this dealt most profitably of all in rich furs, in the late winter and spring, when pelts were at their thickest: the dark of mink, the russet of sable, marten, beaver. From the mountains to the east came goatcombs of cashmere, straw-pale and greasy to the touch, for the mills of the empire, to be made into the finest robes for the lords and ladies of Byzantium. And from the north, down the great Scythian rivers, came long, shallow-drafted boats with whorled prows, crewed by blue-eyed, bearded northmen, carrying casks of precious Baltic amber.

A little trading-post such as this, on the very edge of the empire, where the last homely lights finally gave way to the endless dark of the barbarian plains, might seem vulnerable to attack. But there had been a generation of peace now, and many of the tribes were foederati, allies or even paid auxiliaries of the Emperor of the East in Constantinople. The little torchlit town lay calmly beside the wide, slow river.

Attila hazed his men backward off the rise until they could just see the road but were themselves hidden.

'Is there no garrison in the town?' whispered Orestes.

Attila's gaze remained fixed on the little outpost of empire below. 'Probably.'

It was almost dark, and some of the men would have been asleep in their saddles were it not for fear of their lord, when from the shadows of the town emerged a longer column. There were perhaps half a dozen mounted men, and then a painted carriage, with a further dozen or so men, women and children on foot behind. From the way they walked, a slow shuffle with shoulders bowed, it was clear that some if not all were manacled. But it was too dark to see clearly. The only colours were the cloudy blue and grey of twilight, the only lights the flickering of torches at the gates of the town and the flash of the troopers' spearheads as they moved like leaves in the wind and caught the first moonlight.

Attila gave no word, no signal. He heeled his horse forward and rode down the slope towards the road. His men, their bellies cold with fear at this attack, held their horses back and waited unseen behind the rise, watching him go, the only sound the swish of his horse's legs through the tall, dry feathergrass.

One of the mounted troopers saw him approaching in the half-light and called a halt, but without alarm. They turned and held their spears ready.

Attila rode forward.

'Halt there!' called one of the troopers, pulling round and riding over to him; evidently their lieutenant. Attila ignored him but made towards the carriage.

At the sound of the lieutenant's command, the drapes of the carriage twitched back and a face peered out. The well-fed city face of a Greek merchant. He almost yelped when, only feet away, he saw a mounted barbarian with knotted hair, wearing only breeches of cross-gartered deerskin, his silhouette in the darkness spiky with weapons.

The barbarian addressed him: 'Linguam loquerisne latinam?'

The merchant, Zosimus by name, stammered that of course he spoke Latin. But he was surprised that ... ?

'Μιροσ μιλατγ Ελ#ηνικα?'

The merchant could hardly believe his ears. A polyglot barbarian, a savage bare to the waist but for his gold earrings and his horrible tattoos of midnight blue, his silver armlets banded tight around biceps as hard as stone. This fierce-eyed creature without knowledge of the law, of letters or any of the other appurtenances of civilised life, addressing him out of the Scythian darkness first in the language of Cicero, then in that of Demosthenes – for all the world as if he had been raised by the finest grammarians and rhetors in the empire, rather than by some bejewelled barbarian woman in a felt tent stinking of leather and sweat and horse-dung fires!

The lieutenant came alongside the barbarian and shook him roughly by the shoulder.

'Back off, Top-Knot,' he growled. 'This column is on imperial business, and it'll be the worse for you if—'

'Μιροσ μιλατγ Ελ#ηνικα?' repeated the barbarian, neither raising his voice nor shifting his gaze from the astonished merchant.

'And Greek, too, naturally,' blurted Zosimus. 'But I fail to see why I should bandy words with a malodorous painted savage such as yourself. Now do as this good man suggests and—'

Attila glanced back over his shoulder at his four companions, now only some twenty or thirty yards away in the dusk. Now he used the language of his people.

'Kill the soldiers,' he called.

And they came galloping over the rise.

He himself did not stir as the arrows flew around him. His horse whinnied and stepped delicately backwards as one of the humming arrows grazed just over its nose, but its rider sat as comfortably as if he were watching a mere game. It was all over in a matter of seconds. One trooper rested gently in his saddle with an arrow through his heart, his head drooping forwards like a flower in autumn. The others toppled sideways or lay dead in the dust beside their horses' hooves. Attila walked his horse among the dead and counted. Then he turned to his men, milling around close by.

'Six men with sixteen arrows,' he said. 'A reasonable performance.'

Then he saw a horse standing trembling with an arrow buried deep in its withers. Its forelegs seemed about to buckle but it gave a great heave of its ribcage, blood frothing from its nostrils, and remained standing.

'Which one of you shot the horse?'

After a moment's hesitation, Yesukai raised his fist.

Attila rode over to the young warrior and put his face very close to his.

'Don't - do - that - again,' he said, his eyes burning.

Yesukai could not speak.

Attila rode back and pulled up before the wounded horse and drew his chekan, his short spike-hatchet. He pushed himself forward on his saddle, swung hard, and buried the long iron spike deep in the horse's forehead, just above the eyes. As the priests would sacrifice the finest horses for a royal burial. He pulled the hatchet free and the horse collapsed and lay dead in the dust.

He gave orders for the other five cavalry horses to be taken, then rode back to the carriage and looked in at the cowering merchant. There were two other men in there with him.

One of them, with a petrified, thin-lipped smile, quavered, 'My lord, I ... I ... These two, they are merchants, but I am a lawyer.'

'A lawyer?' said Attila, staring at him.

'Indeed, yes.' The smile grew sickly. 'With connections in the highest courts in the empire.'

'I hate lawyers.'

A knife appeared in his hand, and he reached from his horse and drew the blade across the lawyer's long, lean throat. The man's head fell forwards instantly upon his sodden chest.

The two merchants were dragged shrieking from the carriage and gagged and trussed up and sat on two of the captured horses, and they turned away westwards for home as the darkness deepened around them. At the last moment, Attila turned back and eyed the dozen or so silent, horror-struck men and women and children in their chains behind the carriage. None of them had moved amid the carnage.

Attila said to them, 'I once knew a boy and a girl who were runaway slaves.' He looked down at each of them in turn. 'The girl was not seven summers, and she died. Her name was Pelagia. A Greek girl. But even she had more fight in her than you.' His horse tossed its head, teeth bared, as if in contemptuous agreement. 'Free yourselves,' he said to them.

And he left them there, their armed guards slain but themselves still manacled, standing with mouths agape on the darkening road.

As they rode west, Aladar came alongside him and said, 'My lord, the lawyer – he was a shaman? One Who Knows?'

'No,' said Attila with a shake of his head. 'Not a lawgiver, a dispenser of wisdom. A law-maker: a petty haggler in courts full of like hagglers. A man who lays chains on other men's souls, who harvests souls for gold. In the Empire of Rome such men are highly regarded, and become orators, senators, politicians.'

'Politicians? Politicians are like kings.'

'No.' He grinned sardonically. 'Politicians are nothing like kings.'

They rode on.

After a while he said, 'In Rome they have laws that forbid the people to ride in a carriage though the town after dark. Any who do so are punished.'

'But surely such contemptible laws are ignored?'

'No, they are obeyed.'

Aladar tried to comprehend this lunacy, then roared with laughter at his failure. 'Why?'

'Because,' said Attila, 'they believe themselves to be free men under the law.'

'The lawyer, he bullied the people that way?'

'No doubt.'

Aladar scowled. 'I would have cut his throat myself.'

After midnight they slept for four hours, and in the cold before dawn they rode on beside the Maeotic Lake.

The soldiers from the garrison at Tanais came after them as the sun rose behind them over the dark lake and the sky glimmered low and white and silver. Attila halted them and swung them round to face east, a tiny skein of wild geese on the wide sands. They watched silently for a while as the brightly armoured troop of imperial cavalrymen galloped towards them. They would be upon them soon.

They beat the two trussed merchants unconscious and hobbled their horses, then kicked their own horses into a gallop. Csaba and Aladar veered left of the oncoming horsemen, while Attila led Yesukai and Orestes right into the shallows, all four keeping moving as they nocked, aimed and loosed their arrows from a distance already lethal.

Attila roared instructions as they rode: 'Hit the front horses!'

Arrows hummed in the bright air and two horses stumbled, one going down in an explosion of sand. Over that sprawl of horse and man, another two troopers tripped and fell. The others came on, twenty or more of them. Two troops from a cavalry ala of eighty or so, in light armour, with long, deadly lances held low. The unarmoured and outnumbered Huns eluded engagement, constantly reforming and then melting aside, galloping furiously beyond the Romans' flanks and firing arrows behind them as they fled, or seemed to flee, then taking the higher ground the troopers had just abandoned. Ceaselessly the thin arrows hissed in the fiery dawnlight and slipped through thin chainmail hauberks and cuirasses and burrowed into chests and stomachs, and burst through again, men toppling ungainly to the ground.

The troopers milled in confusion, most of them stuck with arrows in shoulders or thighs, blood trickling thin and watery over bright steel. Their lieutenant yelled to them to form up and close in with swords drawn, but they had lost all hope of closing with so ghostly a target. Again the barbarian horsemen wheeled down off the ridge into the burning early sun and then back, whooping with joy, turning on the spot almost at full gallop in a slew of sand and stone. Their brute-headed horses were driven back upon their squat, powerful haunches as they turned at a tight gallop, then rose up again and drove forward, straight out of the blinding light from the sun. Everything stinging and hurting and dazzling for the blinded cavalrymen as their assailants came skimming across the lakeshore, flying through the dreamlike shallows, the sluggish waters kicked up into arcs of quicksilver by flashing hooves, spangles of spindrift bright in that luminous morning. The ceaseless swish of arrows curving down through the bright air. The lost soldiers were in disarray, feeling the nooses and nets descending over their heads and shoulders, their horses crippled under them, their forelegs bound by hemp lassoes weighted with leaden hooks cast by these howling invisibles. The air was filled with the flash and dazzle of the mocking sunlight, and whoops of victory and nodding topknots and flying ribbons, wild white-teeth yells and blue tattoos fiercely pulsing. The Roman horses cruelly hobbled and spancelled, kneeling suddenly on the shining mudflats as if in penitence and hopeless supplication, and then the copper-skinned horsemen riding in alongside each baffled cavalryman, knocking aside his sagging lance and despatching him with a single thrust of dagger or spear. Sometimes the wretched cavalryman would raise an arm in a last gesture of defence, at which a Hun sword would slice straight through hardened leather vambrace and forearm both and lop them clean off, then despatch the rider. Men were turning and toppling all around, rolling forward over their horses' lowered heads and dropping softly into the mud, the silvery water of those shining levels stained red by sun and blood, speared horses sighing and sinking into oblivion. The lieutenant was now just a headless trunk on the sand, gouting blood. The last few cavalrymen now seemed to wait like cattle for slaughter, or like a stricken herd of game surrounded by numberless and nameless predators. While the naked warriors laughed and chattered throughout the killing, as if engaged merely in some joyous ritual celebrating the endless wonder and changefulness of creation.

Csaba and Aladar had dismounted and were tramping happily through the shallows, taking scalps. Plain iron helmets lay half drowned in the clouded water, and men curled up or strangely skewed on the mud with their heads sliced asunder, their foreheads fronded with blood, their faces covered and cauled with scarlet, their opened skulls releasing a pearl-grey curd upon the waters. Csaba sang a song of victory. Aladar threw back his head and laughed and held out his right arm weltered with blood to the shoulder. He shook out his fistful of scalps and drops of blood wheeled and arced in the glistening sunlight like some dark molten mineral spewed from the volcanic earth and then fell and dissolved into the waters below as if they had never been.

They left the slain horses and the bodies and the severed limbs lying in the crimson foam at the water's edge and rode on, hallooing with wild triumph. The two Byzantine merchants stirred and groaned, still bound and slung like baggage across the saddles of the captured horses. Csaba had a deep cut across his forehead which had nearly sliced into his eye and was bleeding heavily, but he seemed not to notice. Attila had a bad gash across his upper arm, a flap of skin hanging loose and blood flowing out and down over his forearm. The battle done and their wild victory gallop pulled to a halt, he stopped and tied it closed with a strip from one of the merchant's robes. He ordered Csaba to do the same. Then he looked his men over.

They gazed back at him with something like adoration. Their king. Their undefeated, indefatigable king. Their first blood, first victory. How they longed now for more. For the appetite for victory, as for fame or gold, is inexhaustible. The hunger grows with feeding.

Attila smiled. 'Homeward,' he said.

They spoke not another word all that hard day's riding. But at night, beside the campfire as they ate, he addressed them.

'Some men worship right and wrong, or make good and evil their gods and their goals,' he said. 'I believe in life and death. The question is not "Is it right?" but "Does it make me feel more alive?" This is at the heart of everything! This is the pattern and template by which the gods have made the earth. To be a birthing-bed for life, and yet more life! Even the wheyfaced moralists in their pulpits or the conniving lawyers in their airless courts of law, busy censuring every man around them, do so because it makes them feel more alive. It augments their power over others. And so the herdlike many allow them to do so and believe in them.

'Do not allow them. Only the weak and the slaves allow this. You are your own arbiter and none may judge your deeds but you yourself. Another may no more judge you than the clothes you stand up in. Have you lived? That is the deathbed question.

53

That is the only question. Had you the courage to be yourself, to fulfil your desires? "Vengeance is wrong," say the Christians. "Forgive, forgive," they murmur amid their pale clouds of incense, guilt-stricken, their eyes raised in penitence to heaven, their white hands as soft as candlewax, their bodies bowed in reverence before their god, in their gloomy temples filled with the chants of eunuchs.

'Forgive?' he cried, his voice suddenly harsh. 'What is that to the sweet joy of vengeance? There is life! To wreak bone-crushing vengeance on one's ancient enemies is the sweetest, most life-giving joy. It fills you with sweet laughter, it bathes all the world in a golden light, it makes you glad to be alive. Everything we do should make us glad to be alive, make us rejoice in the life that is given us. Nor should you be anxious that your vengeance and your triumph is the ruined one's defeat. Behold, I give you a mystery. It is his triumph, too. His dark triumph, his apotheosis, the fulfilment of his destiny, to be crushed by a superior, god-ordained might that he could no more oppose than he could oppose the black wings of the storm over the steppes. All men must die; and kings and slaves look brothers in the grave. He can do nothing to save himself from this punishment and this burning, this day of doom, so he goes to his destruction unflinching, a hero, shouting defiance into the face of the storm until the end, until he is cut down like a flower by the scythe, to be sung and hymned evermore for his broken nobility. Nothing so noble as broken nobility.

'I remember my father, Mundzuk.' He nodded and was silent a moment. 'His face is before my face. I remember him – how he was cut down by the treachery of Ruga and the corroded gold of Rome. Was he a lesser man because that foul Ruga cut him down in his prime and his manhood? Was he defeated by this, was his life made null and void and his bloodline ever after a thing of contempt and a laughing stock? It was not! He was glorious in death, and in his broken nobility.

'But is this not a mystery? And is the realisation of this not the most intoxicating liberation of thought and deed? Is it not eternal delight? When this truth breaks through the clouds, it melts all ice of sanctity, and a clean wind blows away all ashen penitence. Why, this could unchain the very shackles of sanity! To know how free we truly are, that there is nothing ... I shall go mad, by the gods, there is a such fire inside me!'

He leaped to his feet and began to pace around, his fists clenched, the muscles in his arms bunched, beating the air in front of him.

'Life gives life. Energy gives energy. If only all men had the courage to be truly alive! Then none would fail, and though there would be death there would be no loss. There would be only heroism, nobility, glory in the world that is, the world of dreams, for this is what the All-Father intended. He gave us life, that we should learn to live. You will not learn to live by bowing your head and your ears before the watery whey-thin words of those pallid preachers in those great stone coffins cold as the grave that they call their sacrosanct churches and place of worship. Those catafalques, those charnel-houses, full of blood-stained statues of gibbeted saints. They would drain away life itself from the world. Energy is eternal delight. Sooner murder an infant in the cradle than nurse unacted desires. Then you will be a beacon to other men and they will truly love you. It is not the whey-faced moralists whom men love. In their secret hearts men hate them and the way they guard their desires and keep censorious watch over the locked and bolted cellars of their dreams. It is those who radiate energy and life, who spread laughter, who enact desire, who break the chains and unbolt the cellars, who take the coarse stuff of the earth and twist it into coloured cloth all the colours under heaven. This is why the stories of the people are of love and battle and death. It is not tales of unacted desires that draw people, but energy, conflict, passion. Here is the fire of life. But the Christians talk only of the water and the bread of life, as insipid and cold as their own souls. I give you the meat and the wine of life! They do not understand, the Christians and the moralists and the paper tyrants in their offices and their courts of law. It must be a weak-spined slave with a backbone of straw who can be bowed or broken by the edicts of paper tyrants. Throw them off! They steal men's very souls.

'The Greeks before Christ understood, and their stories were sad and marvellous, tragical and true. They were a clever people. For a great people harbour the tales even of their own woe, even of the tragedies and desolations of their own people, their own family, their own seed. They nurse their griefs and treasure them in stories, and relay them at night by the campfire to the sorrow of their listeners. And the listeners feel more alive at hearing the sorrowful tale. Here is the mystery: they feel more alive, and they flock to hear yet more, sorrow and heroism, grief and laughter, wreckage and triumph, all commingled and twisted together as in the skein of life itself. And the teller, too, unlocking his word-horde and passing around the dully gleaming coin of his own sorrow, the tragedies that have befallen him from on high or from the world that is, he is magnified and made great and majestic in his superior tales of sorrow, and revered by his listeners as the greater man who has travelled further and endured the more. "Nulla maiestior quam magna maesta," said the ancient Romans in the long-ago days when they still understood. "Nothing is more majestic than a great sorrow.'"

Abruptly his words ceased and he turned and was gone away from them into the darkness of the steppes before they were aware of his going. Gone with his tragical story and with his great sorrow.

6

THE SPIES

When they arrived back at the Hun camp he was all authority and pragmatism again.

He made it clear only now that he had led the raid upon Tanais in order to kidnap the two merchants, so that he could take them back to the camp and force them to teach some chosen men the languages of the empire, and then send those men out into the empire as spies. They were astonished at his brazen confidence.

Such were the beginnings of Attila's spy network, which in time was to stretch across almost all the known world, from the Christian kingdoms of Georgia in the east to the Gaulish shores of the cold Atlantic Ocean. Although his network never rivalled in sheer size and complexity that which reached out from the secretive courts of Constantinople and spread like probing, wavering tentacles into every important meeting-place and household in the empire, nevertheless for a barbarian king to have access to such a fund of information about his enemy was power indeed, and quite beyond the imagination of any other barbarian dreamer in his smoky tent.

Attila ordered the bruised and beaten Byzantine merchants to be efficiently bandaged, fed and watered, and rested, as you would a valued pair of stolen horses. He admired, curtly, the labour and the craftsmanship that had built his magnificent wooden palace in just eight backbreaking days, and he took possession of it at the head of his five wives.

Queen Checa walked alongside him and looped her arm through his as they ascended the steps and entered through the carved wooden doors of the palace. It was against all custom for a wife to walk beside her husband in such a way. But Queen Checa was no customary wife.

The following morning Attila appointed an overseer for the spies he would send out. It was Geukchu. He had his cunning counsellor select twenty men and, to the surprise of many, twenty women of the tribe, and isolated each group in a separate tent on the edge of the camp, where they would be taught to speak, understand and even write Latin and Greek. To the fury of the men, the women performed far better than they did, and seemed to derive pleasure from learning the operations of the strange shapes and squiggles that their reluctant instructor, Zosimus, drew with chalk on slate.

At unannounced times Attila himself visited the tents of the frightened pedagogues, and addressed the pupils sharply in either tongue. For he spoke both perfectly like a Roman, to the mystification and wonder of his people. They replied, stumbling at first, and then with increasing confidence as the weeks wore on.

One day Attila found that Geukchu had brought the two groups together, the men and the women, and ordered them to communicate with each other in the learned tongues. He asked him why.

'In his bitterness,' said Geukchu, 'perhaps one or other of the kidnapped merchants might have been teaching our people wrongly, so that they would be found out when they travelled into the empire. But this way we can be sure they have learned the same and correctly.'

Attila smiled sardonically. 'Wise Geukchu, to suspect every man of being as devious as himself.'

Geukchu brushed aside the backhanded compliment. 'But why, my lord, could you not simply teach our people the two imperial languages yourself, since you speak both so learnedly and fluently?'

Attila eyed the flatterer. 'I have other things to do.'

It was midwinter and the steppes were hidden under six inches of snow now for four long, bitter months. In Scythia, they say, there are really only two seasons, one of fire and one of ice. For mild spring and autumn are both so brief in that land of extremes that they are hardly noticed. The people's black felt tents were laden with snow, and at times showed no more against the endless snowbound plains than stoats in their ermine.

One evening Attila called the twenty men and the twenty women to him in his fine new wooden palace, and gave them each a heavy purse of gold. But he ordered them otherwise to dress plainly. And then he sent them south, in the depths of winter, joking that they would appreciate the sunshine of the Mediterranean lands.

The women and the men went some as husband and wife, or brother and sister, or some in seeming family groups, and the king took care that none should go alone. And he sent them out south and west to the great cities of the empire, some to Sirmium, and some to Constantinople, to Ravenna and Mediolanum and Rome itself, or far to the west, to Treverum and to Narbo, or far south into the heat and dust of Antioch and Alexandria – strange destinations for those horse-people of the steppes! He told them to find work as scribes or servants for wealthy and powerful men, insinuating themselves wherever they might into the households of senators, patricians, landowners, bishops, prefects; and to describe themselves only as 'easterners' if asked about race and homeland. When they had important information, insofar as they could judge, they were to quit their masters at night-time and in secret, and sail home for the steppelands, never trusting a written message to any third party – in fact, never committing anything to paper.

From the distant ports of Massilia and Ravenna, Aquileia, Thessalonika, Alexandria and Antioch they would sail east again, through the Bosphorus and north to the shores of the Euxine Sea, stepping ashore at Tanais or Ophiusa or Chersonesus like the surviving Argonauts at Pagasae, bearing the Golden Fleece. And then upriver and finally by horseback to the camp of the Huns and the palace of Attila himself, where they would give him the treasure of their knowledge and he would bless them and bestow on them goblets and rings of gold beyond their dreams or imaginings.

With mingled fear and excitement, the spies left on their long and arduous journey.

As for the two Byzantine merchants, they had served their purpose. Attila never forgot or forgave their insolence to him on that dark night outside the gates of Tanais. They had learned now but alas, they had learned too late. On the morning of the spies' departure, he ordered Yesukai and Aladar to take them down to the banks of the river. There they were ordered to kneel shivering in the long, frosted sedge, and the two warriors clubbed them to death, the most ignominious death for any man. Their bodies were rolled into the river, where they floated briefly amid the skim ice, the cracked eggs of their empty skulls trailing air bubbles, the grey roe of their brains floating in a greasy slick behind, steaming gently in the dawn in the freezing waters.

All that winter Attila waited, and into spring, when the ice on the river slowly thinned and vanished, smoking under the rising sun, and the snow melted away from the boundless land and the steppes turned as brilliant green under the sun as a kingfisher's wings.

He waited in his solitude and his dreaming. Like the wolf, or the spider. Like the Iron River, the slow and steady and implacable Volga itself, for which, some say, he was named. But no man, I believe, will ever know the true meaning of his name.

In the royal palace, the wooden walls echoed to the sound of not one but two newborn infants, both daughters of the king. And in the tent of the king's concubines, another score or more new lives were made. Attila himself named the boys. The girls were named by their mothers. Such names those proud, flushed women gave them as Aygyzel, meaning Beautiful Moon, and Nesebeda, meaning Everlasting Happiness, and Sevgila, meaning Beloved.

Out on the plains each day, throughout the bitterest winter winds, and then more willingly in springtime, his band of warriors, numbering as yet only a few hundred, galloped and wheeled under command, and learned to stop at an invisible barrier signalled by their commander's call. They learned to fire their arrows at unimaginable speed, and the few bowyers and fletchers left among the people with the art still in their hands and eyes were set to work with a vengeance once more. His band of warriors grew strong, and, more important, confident in their strength. They began to long for battle to try their skills, and the strength of their souls.

One day one of the twenty chosen women returned, and went into the palace. It was many hours before she came out again, and she returned to her patient husband and her children with a pouch bulging with gold rings and a rare smile on her face. After that more came home, all that summer, bringing Attila the information that he wanted, and more.

At last all forty spies had returned, not one having run into danger through his own folly or failed in her mission. Thus he learned what he needed to learn, and daily grew stronger. The people too, the women as much as men, sensed this strange, growing power and energy among them and smiled more fiercely. The women sang their ancient harp-songs again, praising their men curtly for feats of arms, but scorning them lavishly and at length for weakness or doubt.

Their implacable king settled back upon his plain wooden throne in his wooden palace and, smiling, considered. For now it was time. The years pass, he thought, and all things ripen into sweetness. And there is a time, there is a time, to pluck the sweet ripe fruit of Rome. Or rather, to knock it from the tree and trample on it, for it is grown overripe and rotten and is no good to man or beast. And it is time. For I have counsel and strength for war. I shall make my people strong, and a mighty name among the nations. They shall no more be a laughing-stock, nor a footstool under the feet of foreign kings. Do not even the Christians in their holy book say that there is a time for love, and a time for hate, a time for war and a time for peace? Behold, my hand is strong; and I make my lands ready for war. From those sorrowful boyhood years of penal servitude in Rome, he could quote the Romans' scriptures back at them as fluently as the Devil.

He smiled. Now it was a time for war. The gods must, after all, be entertained. Like their creature, man, straining forward in the arena to see the action … the gods, too, must be entertained.

7

THE EMPRESS AND THE GENERAL

This was how things stood, as Attila learned from his spies, in the late summer of the year which by Christian reckoning was called AD 442.

The years after 410 and the Sack of Rome had been bitter years. Yet it seemed to some in those days that at last the world had grown tired of faction and war. How wrong we were. As Plato said, only the dead know nothing of war. The living will never tire of it.

There were six days of sacking and looting, of a kind which surprised the city's emaciated inhabitants in its restraint – King Alaric had given orders that no place of Christian worship should be touched. Then the Gothic armies withdrew from the city and turned south.

Only a few days later Alaric was dead, in mysterious circumstances. There was talk of a plot, of poison, of covert assassination ... But nothing was ever known for certain.

Emperor Honorius' sister, the cold-eyed, brilliant Galla Placidia, married a dull Illyiran general and had two children: a son called Valentinian, born in 419, and a daughter called Honoria, born three years later. Valentinian soon appeared to be as foolish and high-strung as his uncle, Honorius. Honoria was cleverer, playful, sharp-witted, a little charmer. Both children would in time have an untold effect upon their times.

Honorius had no children of his own, and his poor, neglected wife had died young. And then His Divine Majesty began to show more than a purely brotherly affection for his sister.

Emperors' loves run not infrequently to members of their own family: Nero's excessive affection for his mother and Caligula's for his sisters are well known. Even Julius Caesar dreamed once of ravishing his own mother, although the soothsayers calmed his fears by assuring him that this symbolised that he should conquer his Mother Earth. Since the emperor was himself divine, however, perhaps he felt that only a fellow divinity was fit to share his bed. Moreover, so many were constantly plotting to kill him, that maybe the only ones he could trust in his bed were his own flesh and blood. Although, since it was so often his own flesh and blood who were the plotters, this policy of safety-in-incest was perhaps ill-advised.

Galla could have managed a rift with any other. But a rift with her own brother, the emperor, she could neither foresee nor manage.

There was in the court at that time a young cavalry officer of some twenty-five summers, the eldest son of a distinguished master-general of cavalry on the Danube frontier called Gaudentius, now deceased. Tall, straight-limbed, grave and sober beyond his years, the young officer had been promoted with astonishing swiftness from commander of an eighty-strong cavalry ala to legionary tribune to legate. Now, without having committed a single error in the field or, even more importantly, in the courts of power where politics and soldiery so abrasively mixed, and having inflicted a sequence of crushing defeats on tribe after tribe of Rome's borderland enemies, he was raised to the rank of general. He was the youngest general in over two hundred years.

General Aëtius.

Aëtius was praised and respected in all quarters. It was said he would sooner die than break his word. When he gave a promise, it was as unbreakable as the great chain that lay across the harbour of the Golden Horn in Constantinople in time of war.

As handsome as Apollo but as tough as saddlehide, like Caesar he marched and rode and slept just like his men, and they revered him for it. When it hammered with rain or pelted hail in the high Alpine passes in early spring or late autumn, and most generals took to their covered wagons or carriages, General Aëtius bowed his head, pulled up his woollen cloak greased with goosefat, and rode on into the storm, no more protected from the savagery of the elements than his humblest legionary. He rode as hard and as far. He took command in the endless frontier skirmishes with Rome's barbarian neighbours, and he fought alongside his own men in the fury of the battleline, to the disapproval of his fellow generals. Each year he acquired new scars.

A stern and implacable commander, he made it clear to his men that should they ever disobey him, or a single one of them ever break rank and flee before the face of the enemy, he would mete out the ancient punishment of decimation upon the entire legion. That is to say, one in ten men would be taken from the ranks at random, and the rest should club them to death where they stood on the parade ground, so that all should be punished for the cowardice of one. None doubted that he would do as he said. But the time of proof never came. No coward ever served under General Aëtius.

Under his command and his steady blue-eyed gaze, it seemed the army was regaining some of the former strength and spirit that it had not possessed since perhaps the catastrophe of Adrianople, back in 378, when the legions had been cut to pieces by the newly arrived Gothic hordes whom the Romans had recently admitted within their borders as refugees and immigrants. It was a blow from which the Roman war-machine had still not recovered. For years now, the drill had been sloppy, the engagements with the enemy only fitful and inconclusive, and peace with the barbarians had been won more often by gold than grim battle. Even the legionaries' armour grew thinner yearly.

Aëtius saw to it that the imperial armouries were once again well supplied with the finest metals, and visited them, at random and unannounced, to check their work. Any man he found slacking he punished without mercy. He drilled his troops relentlessly, and he pushed them harder and harder into battle with their numberless foes. The army grew in strength and discipline; and as is the way with men of martial bent, grew more fiercely happy with each passing year, sensing in themselves their own growing force and power.

The general was not an unwavering traditionalist in everything, however. When the time came to punish a rebellious town or tribe, he departed from the ancient Roman custom of putting to the sword every man, woman and child of that tribe, every cow and

goat, every cat and dog. 'The ruin of Carthage,' he observed laconic-
ally, 'was before the time of Christ.' Instead he was content simply
to slay all men of an age to bear arms, and sell the rest into slavery.
His mercifulness towards Rome's enemies was renowned.

He was a man of few words, swift actions and deep passions. His
duty was all to Rome.

And yet there was perhaps one woman ...

Although three years his senior, and twice a widow, it was clear
to court observers that Galla was drawn to Aëtius by more than
his martial renown and his calm authority beyond his years. No
scurrilous gossip attached to Galla and the young General, then,
but it was amusing to see how often Galla felt it necessary to call
Aëtius to her private consistory, and how often she demanded his
presence at imperial meetings.

How tedious he found them.

At the announcement of each new imperial decree, the entire
court had to rise to their feet and proclaim, 'We give thanks for this
regulation of Yours!'

Twenty-three times over.

And then, in one voice, 'You have removed the ambiguities of
the imperial constitution!' again repeated twenty-three times.

And then 'Let numerous copies of this code be kept in the provincial government offices!' repeated thirteen times.

Aëtius could barely disguise his contempt for such absurdities.
But he did his duty, as always, and repeated the appointed mantras
with the rest of them.

At dinner parties, too, it was noted, Galla talked and exchanged
witticisms with Aëtius more than was strictly necessary, sometimes
to the neglect of other guests. It surprised none that she should feel
like this towards her general. Many of the women of the court felt
likewise. There was in him a rare combination of integrity, courage,
already slightly battered good looks, effortless nobility, and a certain
underlying melancholy that made him irresistible. It was as if, they
said, he had been born out of his time. He should have been born
in the stern and simple days of the old Republic.

What Aëtius' feelings towards Galla were, none could tell. Like
many men of deep, passionate natures, he concealed his powerful

feelings beneath formality and reserve; only the shallow raise their voices in continual argument and complaint. Aëtius certainly enjoyed Galla's company more than he enjoyed the wearisome rituals of the court – though less than he loved the camp and the battlefield. But it seemed unlikely that he felt any more than that. He could have married Galla and made himself the next emperor with little difficulty. A more ambitious, less principled man would have married Galla anyway, regardless of his feelings. Not Aëtius. He remained deeply loyal to her. But no more.

In time their relationship grew more complex. Whether it would be fair to describe Galla as resenting the general for his high-principled neglect of her as a woman, who can say? Their relationship was always close, but not always happy. Sometimes flirtatious, sometimes fraught and uneasy, sometimes even bitterly antagonistic.

Honorius began to manifest signs of jealousy of the general. On one occasion Aëtius actually had to flee the court of Rome, and leave Italy for the frontier, on hearing substantive rumours that Honorius was plotting his death.

On his return, it was clear that the emperor's attachment to his sister was growing out of hand. All courtiers greeted one another with a kiss on the lips, of course; male and female, young and old, friend or relative. But Honorius' kissing of his sister, morning, afternoon and most of all at night, around the bibulous dining tables, was more than courtesy required. Furthermore, he caressed her in a manner that embarrassed all onlookers. The gossip became scandal, until it was half believed even by those loyal to her. The chronicler Olympiodorus speaks of 'continual sensual caresses and little kisses'. Galla recoiled in disgust and perplexity, and before long there was bitter recrimination between brother and sister.

Some tale-bearers and scandal-mongers whispered that the princess responded readily enough to her brother's amorous advances, and was only infuriated when the scandal leaked out. For my part, though such things are by no means uncommon among ruling families, I do not think Galla was guilty. One thing she was not was a slave to her own desires. She was slave to nothing and no one.

The poor woman, so haughtily controlled in almost every situation which fate had so far thrown at her in her short but turbulent life, seemed quite bewildered as to what to do. This was the Divine

Ruler of the empire, after all. What if he should actually demand, one hot night, flushed with wine and illicit passion … ? It was unthinkable, yet to refuse him would be perilous in the extreme.

There was only one alternative. To leave his presence. To flee, as Aëtius himself had fled before from the unpredictable mad impulses of the emperor, and hope he would forget her in whatever new passion his wavering heart set upon.

So one moonless night, Galla took ship from Ravenna for Constantinople with her three-year-old son, Valentinian, and little Honoria, still a babe in arms. At Spoleto, across the Adriatic, a small party of soldiers joined them. One of them wore the fine scarlet cloak of a general.

'On time as ever, General Aëtius,' Galla observed as he stepped aboard at the head of his men.

He jumped easily down from the gangplank. 'As always, for you, Your Majesty.'

Galla turned away in the dark and smiled.

8

THE NEW ROME

Thus Aëtius and Galla arrived together in the Golden City of Constantinople.

How to describe this majestic metropolis, this city of gleaming towers and golden domes, of august monuments and smooth marble pavements, situated so superbly on the Golden Horn, overlooking the Bosphorus, that very nexus of two continents of Europe and Asia, as if both knelt as tributaries before her haughty feet? After Rome, I loved Constantinople above all other places. In its newness and its relative innocence beside the sunbright Sea of Marmara, I confess that sometimes this New Rome made the Old seem dark, and bloody, and corrupt, stained by the long centuries, and by the dark desires of men.

At this time, Constantinople was a city of a million people, presiding over the finest natural harbour in the world. Founded by Constantine the Great nearly two centuries earlier, on the site of the ancient Greek fishing-port of Byzantium, it was declared the new capital of the Roman Empire and named after the God-Emperor himself. Constantine was never a man for false modesty.

The proud new capital was a city of fantastic wealth and monumental architecture. The richness of its seas was legendary. You had only to throw a net into the water, it was said, and you would haul in a weighty catch. And with its free hospitals, state-employed doctors and teachers, its subsidised entertainments for the masses, elaborate postal services, rates, taxes, customs and excise, street lighting, price-fixing, and its inexhaustible obsession with sport, it was a very modern city indeed.

Three things united the Byzantines above all: the Christian faith, Roman citizenship, and a passion for chariot racing. This last meant that everybody, from the emperor downwards, was either a Blue or a Green, depending on which chariot team they supported. And woe betide anyone bumping into a crowd of rival fans in a dark alley on race-day …

It was also a city of endless theological disputes. Whereas, historically, most mobs have rioted from hunger, injustice or cruel oppression, Byzantine mobs rioted over fine points of Christian theology, or minute changes to the liturgy. In vexation, various emperors involved themselves in these disputes, trying to comprehend the complexities and suggesting new doctrines which might unite the bitterly opposing factions. 'Aphthartodocetism' was one such doctrine, proposed by old Theodosius the Great, but it failed to catch on. The Christians remained just as factious and turbulent as the chariot teams.

Had it not been only a few years earlier, in the Year of Grace 415, that the brilliant Hypatia was butchered in the streets of Alexandria by a mob of savage Christians, urged on by Bishop Cyril himself? Hypatia was one of the most brilliant women of her age, an astronomer, poet, physician, and philosopher. But a pagan. She had never accepted the deity of the Jewish carpenter, and could outwit and defeat any who argued against her, with the scintillating brilliance and deftness of a Cretan blade. At last the Christians grew sick of her clever, articulate, erudite scepticism – and perhaps her intellectual superiority, her high-minded passion, the purer fire that burned within her, her ardour for the truth, and her faith in things other than the primitive mystery cults of Palestine. Her unshakeable sweet reasonableness must certainly have enraged these devotees of their own blazing irrationality. So they set upon her in the street, and beat her to death. Then, still unsatisfied, these professors of the religion of brotherly love scraped the flesh from her bones with oyster shells, and heaped the remains of bleeding meat in the gutter for the dogs to eat as they had once devoured the flesh of the wicked Jezebel, according to their own blood-stained Scriptures.

Even the theologians complained there was too much theology around. That great doctor of the Eastern Church, St Gregory of Nazianzus, said despairingly that you couldn't even buy a loaf of bread in Constantinople without becoming embroiled in a theological disputation with the baker regarding the true relationship between the Father and the Son. Likewise, he continued, 'The money-changer will talk about the Begotten and the Unbegotten instead of giving you your money, and if you want a bath, the bath-keeper assures you that the Son surely proceeds from nothing.' Poor Gregory was made unwilling patriarch of the city by old Emperor Theodosius, but he lasted only a year before he fled back to his native village and became a hermit.

In the streets between the crowded red-tiled houses, arguing about theology you would hear a Babel of different voices: Greek and Syrian, Latin and Hebrew, Persian and Armenian. There were even a few Goths serving in the imperial armies by this time; but with their long ungainly limbs and horrid ruddy faces, their coarse blond hair and cold blue eyes, they were widely despised as racial inferiors.

The rich rode in carriages under fringed canopies, drawn by pairs of milk-white mules. Camel caravans crowded the market-places, having come from Persia, India, or along the silk route from China. (Although in time this trade would drop off markedly when an enterprising merchant smuggled some silkworm eggs out of Soghdiana, and Byzantine silk production began.) Grain came via Alexandria from the plentiful granaries of Egypt, while timber, furs and barbaric amber jewellery came south out of the steppes of Scythia and the forests of Germany.

In the city's Forum stood a gigantic statue of Apollo topped with the head of Constantine, on a column of red porphyry. Out of the Forum led the high street of Constantinople, the Mese, running a full three miles to the Golden Gate in the great wall of the city. The Mese was where the noble lords and ladies of Byzantium came to do their shopping, at the most lavish jewellers and perfumers, in cool marble arcades piled high with fabulously expensive bolts of coloured silk, or at the little stalls of artisan leatherworkers, where they liked to buy the softest belts and the most delicate purses made from the hides of aborted kid-goats. For it is well known that the rich always have exquisite taste in such things.

Everywhere there was bustle and wealth and plenty.

Unless, of course, you were poor.

The most wretched and destitute inhabitants of the city survived in foul-smelling alleys where kites picked over the piles of rubbish and rats bit their children at night. The true nature of the Son mattered little to them, and jewellery and silks were very far from them.

Galla arrived on a day when the city was still in a warm hubbub of self-congratulatory triumph, after the defeat of the ever-threatening Persian armies to the east, and the subsequent marriage of young Emperor Theodosius II to his beautiful bride.

Theodosius was Galla's nephew, and she was fond of him. He was at this time in his early twenties: gentle, scholarly, a good horseman, and in other fields no more than mildly incompetent. But he had some capable generals, and the mighty Sassanid dynasty of Persia had only recently found that the Eastern Roman legions were still more than a match for them.

It was Theodosius' fearsome, pious, grimly virginal older sister, Pulcheria, who exerted the most influence in the Byzantine court.

Rumour flourishes in courts and palaces as nowhere else. It was said that, despite her loudly advertised virginity, Pulcheria seemed to spend rather a lot of time closeted with her favourite saints and holy men in her private chambers. But most of these rumours arose among the Nestorian faction – her theological enemies, for reasons too tiresome to go into – and can be dismissed like the rumours of Galla's incest with her brother.

It was in the winter of 414 that the twelve-year old Theodosius had succeeded to the throne of the Eastern Empire. Pulcheria, then barely fifteen years of age, was declared official guardian of her brother and invested with the title of 'Augusta', an empty honour, so it was thought. But from that moment the adolescent girl began to rule, and she effectively held the reins of power over the teeming, hugely wealthy Eastern Empire for the next thirty-six years.

Her brother, as he grew in years and wisdom, was no fool, as I have said: no Honorius. Scholarly, gentle and humane, he had a love of handwriting in a variety of beautiful and elaborate scripts, so that he became nicknamed 'Theodosius Kalligraphos'. All the Eastern emperors had nicknames in this way. Another had had the misfortune to be nicknamed 'Constantine Copronymos', on account of his having unfortuitously shat in the font when he was being baptised as an infant.

Under Pulcheria's unsmiling influence, the Imperial Palace had grown into a virtual nunnery. All males were scrupulously excluded from the female quarters; and in an elaborate and lengthy ritual in the Church of the Holy Wisdom, amid much chanting and incense, she and her sisters, Arcadia and Marina, dedicated their virginity to God. Inscribed tablets of gold and gems were offered up before the altar, as kind of celestial promissory notes. Within hours the vulgar streetraders and hucksters in the Agora were chuckling at the news, saying that this was not much of an offering, since none but God would want their virginity. It was sad but true: the emperor's sisters, with their long, cold faces, and their flat fronts apparently uninterrupted by anything resembling breasts, were not exactly the adornments of their age.

Disapproving of all indulgences of the flesh as she did, Pulcheria could hardly be filled with joy when a certain new girl came dancing and laughing into this gloomy, curtained court: the adornment of her age, beyond a doubt. She who was to be empress. Even her name was beautiful: Athenaïs. Her laughter, her brilliant eyes, her wit and smiles, her glossy black hair tumbling in waves about her shoulders. The arch of her brows, the curve of her slender neck, those eyes like black honey, meeting yours beneath those raven lashes. The sway of her hips as she sashayed away from you, having just silenced you with some teasing barb, murmured from those full carmine lips.

Athenaïs: the most beautiful girl I ever saw.

9

THE STORY OF ATHENAÏS

More than beautiful, though. It takes more than mere beauty not only to capture a man's heart, but to hold it. And Athenaïs was much more than merely beautiful.

She first came to the imperial court in the conduct of a lawsuit: ardent, passionately indignant at a miscarriage of justice, brilliantly articulate, magnificently scornful of those she felt trying to cheat her of her due inheritance. And still a girl of eighteen.

She was born the daughter of a prominent and brilliant philosophy professor in Athens, by the name of Leontius. In him, it was said, there burned brightly something of the pure, clear light that had illuminated Athens so many centuries ago, in the days when the Lyceum and the Academy still hummed with life and excitement. On the death of Leontius, a will was discovered which left everything to his two older sons and not a penny to his daughter, whom he loved above all else in this world. At first Athenaïs tried to reason with her brothers, but they laughed her to scorn. They had always resented the greater love that their father had had for her. And so she came to the highest court in the Eastern Empire: the Court of the Imperial Justice itself, in Constantinople, and presented herself before it, unaccompanied by a single advocate or lawyer.

'I could not afford one,' she said with simple dignity, standing before the open-mouthed court lawyers in her simple white stola gathered round the waist by a slim leather belt. 'So I shall argue my case myself.'

It was true. Her aunt, Leontius' aged sister, had scraped together a small purseful of silver coins: just enough to buy her passage from the Piraeus to the Golden Horn, and no more.

The will was read out again before the court. After dividing all his estate equally between his two sons, Leontius left only a laconic coda to his daughter: 'To Athenaïs, I leave not a penny. She will have good luck enough elsewhere.'

Athenaïs flinched when she heard her father's cruel words read out. Then, composing herself, she began to argue her case.

After a short while, someone was sent to fetch Theodosius himself. The scholarly-minded emperor would enjoy a strange spectacle such as this.

To the astonishment of the assembled legates and priests, counsellors and praetors, this young slip of a girl supported her case with the fluency of the most experienced, smooth-tongued old law-hound in the basilica. She understood precisely the venerable four divisions of Roman law: *lex*, *ius*, *mos* and *fas*. She quoted freely and word-perfectly from the ancient authorities: from the most obscure imperial decretals, from the entire canon of the *ius civile*, which she appeared to have at her fingertips; from the *Orations* of Cicero, and the *Institutes* of Quintilian; from the *Digesta* of Ulpian, and the *Quaestiones* of Papinian; from dusty and half-forgotten pandects, from shadowy and unfrequented corners of the *responsa iurisprudentium*. Even from Demosthenes' 'Against Boeotus', with a learned and scintillating digression on why the arguments of that great Athenian orator still held true, even if Greek law were an utterly separate thing from Roman.

'For laws, like men, are born to die,' she said. 'But justice is immortal.'

Whether it was the spellbinding softness and clarity of her voice or the luminous beauty of her person or her astonishing erudition that silenced the assembled greybeards and venerables, it was impossible to say. Perhaps the implausible combination of all three. But silenced they were. Some of them there on those hard stone benches had already begun to ponder how easy it might be to take this penniless provincial girl for a wife. While others began to curse inwardly that this was a commitment they had already made to another, long ago, and that the commitment still lived.

It was unheard of for a girl to have been taught in the same way as a boy. But Leontius himself had taught her; unorthodox in his views on child-rearing, as in the wording of his will.

The slim Athenian girl quoted even from the Holy Book of the Christians, although she was not baptised into the True Church and her upbringing had been wholly pagan. She cited the example of the daughters of Zelopehad, from the book of Numbers: 'And the Lord spake unto Moses, saying, "The daughters of Zelopehad speak right: thou shalt surely give them a possession of an inheritance among their father's brethren; and thou shalt cause the inheritance of their father to pass unto them."' A citation from their own Holy Scriptures so learned and so obscure that it had more than one priest amongst that assembly of great minds scrambling from his bench to find a Bible to consult.

Eventually her argument was finished, and she stood silently awaiting judgement.

If the court found against her, she would be turned out onto the streets without a penny. A beautiful girl like that – it was clear how she would have to make her way in the world. Some of the greybeards on their benches even began to delve surreptitiously beneath their robes and into their purses, to see how many solidi they had on them. Why, they could hurry after her and make her a kindly offer even on the steps of the court ...

At last, after muffled discussion with his private circle of juris-consults, Theodosius rose to give his verdict.

He cleared his throat and looked steadily down at the girl. 'I find the will of Leontius just,' he said.

Those there commented that, even as he spoke the words, he seemed to grow in stature and gravity. It was as if in those few short minutes in court, in the presence of Athenaïs, he had suddenly grown up into a man of strength and character. Which was true: he had grown up, because for the first time in his life he had fallen in love.

'Leontius, your wise and far-sighted father, was correct,' went on the emperor. 'You have no need of any legacy. You will prosper quite well on your own.'

Athenaïs' eyes flamed with dark anger but she said nothing.

'You will depart from our court as penniless as you arrived,' said Theodosius, seeming to add more cruelty to the verdict. His courtiers heard his words and looked to the girl. Her expression was a powerful mix of resolution and despair.

Unspeaking, she turned to go.

'However,' Theodosius called after her, and his voice was gentler now, 'if you will consent to be my wife, you will find your present poverty of less concern.'

She halted, her back turned to the emperor against all etiquette, her head still bowed.

The silence in the court could have been snapped in two.

Then she turned to face him.

Any other girl in her situation would have consented immediately, would have fallen at the emperor's feet and wept with humble gratitude. But Athenaïs was not any other girl.

She looked the young emperor in the face, once again breaching all rules of court etiquette. She saw before her, for the first time, not an abstract symbol of power and majesty, more gilded icon than man of flesh and blood, robed in the legendary Tyrian purple and the dazzling gold of a living god. She saw a young, fresh-faced, rather lanky boy, with gentle features and myopic eyes, but eyes nevertheless full of intelligence, humour and longing. Perhaps she also saw in him some of the melancholy and loneliness that always accompany emperors and kings.

She thought in a flash that this was a man she could grow to love.

'I'll consider it,' she said.

And without another word, or a single copper coin in her purse, she turned and swept out of the court.

She wandered the streets of Constantinople as if in a dream.

All this ... all this could be hers ... Empress of half the Roman World. What power and wealth she would have. What good she could do. But she would have to forswear all pagan philosophy, a thousand years of the finest thought and striving of the Greeks, and submit to being baptised into that Asiatic mystery religion of miracles and blood and human sacrifice which the rulers of the empire now professed.

What would her father say? Her father had been wiser, perhaps, than even he knew.

She stood at the heart of the city, that crowded square of the

Augusteion bounded by those four monumental buildings which seemed to represent the soul of humanity in all its nobility and squalor: from the most lofty, spiritual and orderly, to the darkest and most chthonic forces in the hearts of men. Along one side, the great complex of the Mega Palation, the Imperial Palace and its courts, which she had just left. Along another, the grave Senate House. Along the third, the fine old Church of Hagia Sophia, the Holy Wisdom. And along the fourth, the Hippodrome, the arena for the chariot races between those bitter rivals, the Blues and the Greens. Almost daily the poor of the city crowded inside to watch their teams gallop furiously amid the dust and sometimes the carnage of snapped axletrees and flying chariots, broken men and screaming horses; or erupted into scuffles and fights after the contest was won, cornering some poor isolated supporter from the opposite team in a dank, shadowy alley and slicing off an admonitory ear, a nose, a finger ...

She looked up at the four great buildings and they seemed to revolve around her. Then she shook herself and left the square and began to wander westwards up the Mese, which runs like a gleaming marble artery through the city, and is one of the wonders of the world. She passed through the marvellous marble-paved oval Forum of Constantine, with its towering hundred-foot column of porphyry in the centre, transported by ship from Egypt, from Heliopolis, the City of the Sun. (Oh, I can see it all now before me, as real and sunlit as ever: I, Priscus, knew it well; and never, never, never will I set eyes upon that beloved city again.) The plinth on which the column stood contained the hatchet with which Noah built the Ark, the baskets and the remains of the loaves with which Christ had fed the multitude; and, out of respect for the more ancient ways, the figure of Athene brought from Troy to the Old Rome by Aeneas himself. On the summit of the column, far away in the upper air where only birds and angels flew, gazing out over the rooftops of the city, stood another figure. The body was that of Apollo, carved by Phidias, but the head, surrounded by a halo representing the rays of the sun, was that of Emperor Constantine himself, Ruler of all the Earth under Heaven.

Here half the citizenry of the city was gathered, so it seemed. A vast, milling throng of whores and hucksters, fishwives, fig-sellers, knife-grinders, songbird-vendors, pickpockets, con men and worse. The gangs of child pickpockets were the worst, all bright, gleaming eyes and deft little fingers, like felonious dormice looking to store away a secret hoard against the winter to come.

In one corner a coarse-voiced man was reading aloud to an entranced crowd of illiterate listeners from that scandalous daily news-sheet, *The Acts of the Roman People.* They cheered raucously when he announced that today was the birthday of one of the minor members of the imperial family, and they listened agog as he read from the list headed 'Crimes, Punishments, Weddings, Divorces, Deaths, Portents and Abominations'. They were moved to tears at news of the recent death of the Blessed St Thecla, over in Asia, in the wilderness beyond Nicopolis. She had been thrown to savage beasts by a wicked and idolatrous emperor back in the time of the persecutions, but her virginal followers had cast flowers into the arena to calm them. Then she was thrown into a lake of savage seals, but they had all been killed by miraculous lightning. She had baptised herself in a ditch, and later lived for over a hundred and fifty years in a cave, eating nothing but juniper berries. Many sick, lame and blind had come to her there, and she had healed them all. Now she had passed away into a better world. The crowd crossed themselves reverently and prayed that St Thecla would remember them in heaven.

They were captivated by the story of a crow which recently lived in the marketplace beside the Church of St James the Apostle. Apparently the crow had spoken perfect Latin, to general amazement, and attracted sightseers from far and wide. But it had, alas, been bludgeoned to death by an irate shoe-seller for continually defecating on his stall. The other traders in the marketplace had given the shoe-seller a sound drubbing, and paid for the crow to have a lavish funeral.

Such is the arrant nonsense that delights the unlettered multitude. They gasped with horror or cackled with loud gusts of halitotic laughter: the urban masses in all their ghastliness.

In another corner a religious madman stood on an upturned wooden crate, addressing a small but devoted audience. Athenaïs stopped to listen, and learned that this man had had revealed to him the secret Book of Elchasai the Prophet. He had met the Son of God in the desert, who was ninety-six miles high with footprints four miles long, and was accompanied by his Holy Sister of similar dimensions. He recommended the use of dust and toads' blood to treat skin diseases, and forty days of consecutive baptism to cure consumption.

Athenaïs thought back to Athens the Beautiful, Pindar's violet-clouded citadel, and she saw it being eclipsed and replaced by these great, swarming, fanatical cities of the east; the religion of Athens, the religion of reason and public argument, obscured by strange cults and devotions, hidden mysteries; private ecstasies in small, dark chapels filled with incense and gloom.

She walked on through the neighbouring Forum of Theodosius; by the Amastrium, and the immense Aqueduct of Valens, and the Church of the Holy Apostles. After some time she left the Mese and plunged into the darker alleys of the city, heading north, past a scruffy little colonnade grandly called the Portico of the Lentil Dealers, and then an even scruffier called the Portico of the Scribes and Booksellers. Here they sold salacious tales of the lowest type called novels, that most wretched and plebeian of all literary forms over which no muse presides, and which shall never know respectability. She glanced briefly at their grubby covers, vulgarly bound into pages rather than traditional and elegant scrolls. One grimy, ink-stained and impoverished-looking bookseller tried to sell her *The True and Astounding Adventures of the Whore Lubricia, Throughout Every Land and Also in the Underworld*, but she looked away and hurried on.

From thence she made her way down Rim of the Jar Lane, then left into Three Birds Alley, quickly along the Street of Doubtful Fortune and past the drunks and wolf-whistlers at the Sign of the Melancholy Elephant. She declined their offer of a cup of wine and stopped instead to refresh herself briefly at the Fountain of the Four Fishes, wondering as she did so what terrible curses all the little gold curse-plates might bear, nailed face-down to the bottom of the fountain so that only the spirits might read them. There was a lot of graffiti round the side of the fountain, much of it of a lewd nature, but she was unable to prevent herself from reading some of it: 'Amaryllis is a slut ... Silvius sucks cock ... I had the barmaid at the Melancholy Elephant.'

She went on eastwards until she came to the Golden Horn, and looked out over the great ships riding at anchor there, the salt-faded reds and blues of their furled sails, the gulls wheeling, the smaller lighters bringing grain and textiles and amphorae to the docks along the shore, and the ever-obscene cries of the dockers as they worked. Then she wound back again westwards, and rested a while, leaning against a wall, slipping one tired and dusty foot from her sandal and rubbing it between her fingers.

A man rested his hand on her shoulder, leaned close to her ear, and muttered with vinous breath, 'I'd give you a plump roast quail for it, love, or even a brace of 'em, so I would.'

She slipped her sandal back on and stood straight, brushing his hand from her shoulder as she would a bluebottle. She looked down and saw a crooked, bleary-eyed, unshaven creature grinning up at her.

'A quail?' she repeated in bewilderment.

'Or a brace, so I would, now I see you from the front up straight and proud and all lovely like that.' A runnel of spittle appeared over his stubbly chin. 'You could be like my fresh young wifey for an hour. Just back in my cookshop over the street.' He jerked his head and the spittle flew into the air. She pressed herself against the wall. 'Just in the back there,' he said; 'the wife's down the market.' His legs appeared to be trembling with expectation, and his voice grew strange in timbre. His hands were agitated beneath his tunic 'Bend you forwards over me breadoven, so I would, hitch your skirts up, run my hands through your lovely raven hair ...'

She felt that she was about to be sick.

Abruptly, the man turned and raised his hands against the attack of a skinny old woman with a stick, who was filling the air with the foulest language imaginable. Athenaïs put her hands over her ears, but still heard both the male and female pudibunda freely adverted to.

The man swore as foully at the old woman in return, but under the thwacks of her stick he began to retreat, and finally broke and ran back to the greasy darkness of his cookshop over the street.

The woman set her stick on the ground and leaned over it, bent almost double, gasping for breath after her exertions.

Athenaïs stared at her uncertainly.

At last the woman creaked upright again and regarded the girl with her one good eye; the other was milky white.

'Where's your guardian, girl?' she demanded crossly. Her voice was hoarse and her breath wheezy. 'You can't just wander around round here on your own, you know. About as safe as a lamb in a wood full of wolves you are here.'

'I ... I'm alone,' said Athenaïs.

'You're a young fool,' said the woman. She fumbled in her ancient woollen wraps and pulled out a breadroll. 'Yours for a copper.'

Athenaïs shook her head. 'I haven't got any money.'

The woman looked at her more closely. 'What's your story?'

'I can't say.'

'Hm. Nice rich husband you had, till he come home late one night and finds you in bed with one his Armenian slaveboys lying between your open thighs, showing his bottom to the moon.'

'Certainly not!' said Athenaïs indignantly. 'It's none of your business, anyway.'

'Hm,' said the old woman. She tore the breadroll in two and pushed an entire half into her wrinkled mouth, where she began to chew it as best she could with her one remaining incisor. 'You look wore out,' she mumbled through the mouthful.

Athenaïs looked down. 'A little.'

The old woman considered, and then thrust the other half of the breadroll into the girls's hand. 'Here you are, dearie.' She cackled. 'Never thought I'd be the one people'd come to for charity!'

Athenaïs looked the old woman over, from the filthy woollen cap covering her wispy white hair, down to her cracked and curled-up feet.

'Go on,' she urged. 'You have to eat.'

So Athenaïs took the breadroll and ate it slowly. It tasted surprisingly good.

'The baker down there, he gives me a loaf or so every morning, God bless him.'

The girl nodded and swallowed. When she had finished she said, 'Do you live hereabouts?'

The old woman grinned, showing her single mustard-coloured tooth. She pointed across the street under the arches, where there was a neat little bundle wrapped in a brown woollen blanket. 'My house,' she said, beaming.

Athenaïs smiled. 'Thank you for the bread.'

'Not at all, dearie.'

As she walked away the old woman called after her, 'You want to make for the Metanoia, my girl. The House of Repentance is the only place for you now.'

She walked in the city all afternoon. She was thirsty, but another from among the nameless poor, a blind and legless beggar who sat beside the Fountain of Saint Irenaeus, lent her his old chipped drinking-pot to drink from.

Then she went into the dark cavern of the Church of St Stephanos, and saw amid the flickering candlelight the famous icon of Theotokos Pammakaristos, the All-Joyous Mother of God. She had the distant, serene face of one far removed from the squalor and troubles of the city and the world. The gold, worm-eaten frame from which she looked out was covered in the red lipstick kisses of the city's whores who came here every day out of love for her. They revered her as their own, talking softly with her as their gentle all-seeing mother in heaven, kneeling for hours in the aromatic dark with their red lips and their bruised eyes, the sweat and odour of their last client still upon them.

She was sitting outside on the steps of the church, considering the fickleness of fortune and longing for some ripe, juicy grapes, when a gilded carriage, drawn by a single white mule caparisoned in crimson, stopped at the bottom of the steps. The door was opened by one of the six statuesque, fashionably Nubian slaves who accompanied the carriage on foot, dressed in immaculate white tunics, and a great lady of the city stepped out. The kind of lady who keeps numberless 'whisperers' in her grand townhouse, which is to say those little naked slaveboys kept by rich ladies for amusement, to bring them almonds and candied fruits and whisper compliments and sweet nothings in their pearl-ringed ears.

This lady wore a magnificent cloak of midnight-blue silk, stiffly brocaded with pearls and golden thread, illustrating the miraculous life and martyr's death of one of her favourite saints, Polycarp, Bishop of Smyrna. He was shown in three separate embroidered panels, bound to a stake, slain with a sword, and then finally burned.

It was a remarkable piece of work. Furthermore this great lady had at home many more such embroidered cloaks, each one carrying illustrations of a different favourite saint and, ideally, martyr. On the whole she preferred her saints to be martyrs as well, because the embroidered illustrations of their deaths in pearls and gold were so much more elaborate and striking. Her favourite of all, perhaps, was her cloak in bright spring green, showing the dramatic martyrdom of dear St Ignatius of Antioch, thrown to the lions in the Colosseum in the reign of Emperor Trajan. She always looked forward to his feast-day, 17 October, when the cloak could correctly be worn without spiritual pride or impropriety. Furthermore, on her fingers she wore an assortment of massive gold rings, set with precious stones or decorated with cloisonné enamel. Within one of them, inside a tiny locket, was curled a single lock of John the Baptist's flaxen hair.

She was a very great and holy lady indeed.

No sooner had she begun to ascend the steps of the church which she herself had so generously endowed, the hem of her cloak raised up from the dusty ground by two of her slaves, when a street-girl stepped in front of her, as bold as you please.

The great lady arched her delicate pencilled eyebrows.

Athenaïs held her hand out, and drew breath to speak, but got no further.

The great lady looked her up and down in one swift movement, and then turned haughtily away.

Athenaïs stepped in front of her again and looked her straight in the eye.

The great lady was outraged. 'Out of my way, you hussy! And how you dare you look at me so!'

Athenaïs smiled softly. 'The day will come soon when you will not dare to look at me.'

The great lady turned to one of her attendants, astonished. 'Why, the girl's mad! Or drunk, more probably. Move her out of my way.'

'Remember me,' said Athenaïs, speaking softly still, even as one of the handsome attendants took her firmly by her arm and pulled her aside. 'Look me in the face, and remember me.'

The great lady, despite herself, looked at the impertinent jade, who was pretty in a sluttish, plebeian sort of way, and found to her intense irritation that, even during the most moving and rapturous moments of the ensuing high mass in the Church of St Stephanos, she was still able to picture the girl's face quite clearly.

It was growing dark when Athenaïs came back to the great square of the Imperial Palace, and saw the lamps burning in the tall windows, and felt the air growing cool. She wrapped her arms round herself, sat in the corner of an alley and brooded. She could not go begging at that grandiose door. Not yet. Not yet, though this city was a wood full of wolves.

It was after the great cathedral bells had tolled midnight, and few were left in the streets but whores and thieves and *vigiles*, the watchmen of the city, who crouched round their braziers, wrapped in their cloaks, with their long, sharpened staves, themselves as wretched and often as drunk as the scoundrels in the streets they were policing. It was not a good place for a solitary girl.

Finally she asked one of the watchmen about a house called the Metanoia. After an obscene invitation to her, to which she did not deign to reply, he grudgingly pointed the way. She walked for a few minutes and came to the door of a low building beside a chapel in a side street. She knocked timidly on the wooden door. After some time a panel was drawn back and a woman's face appeared.

She didn't need to say a word.

Almost immediately the door was opened and she stepped inside.

She spent seven days there. Among the prostitutes of the House of Metanoia, which is to say Repentance, cared for wordlessly and with infinite kindness by the nuns of that place, themselves often high-born daughters of noblemen who would not spare the dowry to find their daughters a husband.

She ate and slept and chattered among those prostitutes, young and old, haggard, withdrawn or laughing still, despite the foulness and the outrageous injustice of their short lives hitherto. Pocked with sores, scarred with drunken knife-cuts, some still bruised from the last client they had had before they finally revolted and fled to this place for sanctuary. She told a simple story of herself. The other

84

women also told their stories soon enough, unburdening themselves in stumbling sentences, and her eyes grew round with horror.

She learned a lot in those seven days.

It was in the twilight of the following Sunday when she presented herself at the great doors of the Imperial Palace again. A beautiful, unknown girl in a plain white stola.

How many ranks of household servants, eunuchs and chamberlains she had to pass through, saying to each one, 'The emperor himself is expecting me'; how much scorn, incredulous laughter, impatience, indifference. It was many hours before she was admitted into a vestibule and told to wait.

Very soon, a man stepped into the room, closed the door behind him and looked across at her. A young man, eager, kindly, with much to learn still.

He was tongue-tied, so she went to him.

'You knew I would return,' she said with mock resentfulness. 'What choice did I have?'

'I,' he said, 'I …' Hesitantly he took her hand in his. 'No, but I hoped you would.'

The elderly, arthritic but still zealous Bishop Atticus was instructed to teach the young pagan girl the rudiments of Christianity in time for her baptism and subsequent marriage. The bishop was shocked to find that the girl – clever, articulate, and as pretty as one of those she-demons who so tormented St Anthony in the Theban desert – already knew the rudiments of Christianity, and a lot more besides. He was shocked because it was evident that the girl, having previously heard and understood the Gospel preached with perfect clarity and doctrinal orthodoxy, had nevertheless, on consideration, rejected it as untrue. As if still blissfully unaware of her own wretched sinfulness, and her urgent need to be washed clean in the blood of the Lamb who was slain!

Atticus had been commanded not to pry too closely. So he ran through the essential doctrines of the True Church once more, with brief but ferocious digressions on the ghastly and damnable creeds of the Arians, the Monophysites, the Hieroconodulians and other hell-destined heretics, until he was satisfied that the girl, expressionless and without any obvious spiritual ardour, was able to recount them herself with reasonable fluency.

She was baptised in the private chapel of the palace, where she was given the new name of Eudoxia: rather more Christian a name than the distinctly pagan Athenaïs. One of the ladies-in-waiting was overheard to say after the baptism that it seemed a shame, as Athenaïs had been such a pretty name. At which the emperor's grim-faced sister Pulcheria shot the foolish woman such a look as might wither a cedar of Lebanon.

The woman left the imperial household the following day.

Eudoxia accepted everything with smiling sweetness and serenity. But in private, it was whispered, the emperor still called her Athenaïs.

They were married on the seventh day of June, in the Year of Grace 421, in the great rectangular basilica of the Church of Hagia Sophia, by Patriarch Epiphanius.

They travelled there in a lavishly carved and gilded coach, drawn by four white horses through the streets of Constantinople. Heralds and trumpeters acclaimed the procession, while the people surged through the streets, strewing herbs and flowers in their path, casting wreaths over every statue and garlanding every doorway they passed with myrtle, rosemary, ivy and box, in the ceremony of 'crowning the town'.

Theodosius wore a robe of cloth of gold, purple shoes, and an emerald sash. Athenaïs wore a stiff dalmatic stitched with precious stones. Indian pearls shone in her dark hair. Descending from the imperial coach, they made their solemn and stately way up the aisle of the church, gleaming with candlelight, the air filled with the sonorous chants of 'Kyrie eleison'.

Among the congregation were Athenaïs' humble family: the kindly old aunt who had paid for her journey to Constantinople; and, to the astonishment of many, her two elder brothers, who had so hard-heartedly dealt with her in the matter of their father's will. Now they sat near the back of the church, disbelieving, watching their sister marry the emperor himself. Shamefaced and bright-eyed in the gloom of that great church, filled with remorse and regret, and acknowledging in their hearts at last that, after all, their sister was a better person and a sweeter soul than they would ever be.

From that day forth, they were devoted to her. And not merely because she was the empress.

Amid the solemn priests and the deacons, the incense and chanting, and throughout the blessed sacrament and symbolic marital ritual of the blood in a silver spoon, the empress's two brothers were as joyful in their hearts as any there. She had conquered them, as she would conquer so many in the years to come, by goodness rather than strength.

It is a sorrowfully rare stratagem.

The imperial couple stood before the altar and Patriarch Epiphanius with his bejewelled fingers and his long scented hair. The patriarch turned to the purple cloaks and diadems laid out ready on velvet cushions. He blessed the cloaks before they were taken up by the attendant *vestitores* and fastened about the imperial pair with golden brooches.

The Patriarch placed the diadems on their heads, saying, 'In the name of the Father and of the Son and of the Holy Ghost.'

The congregation chanted, 'Holy, holy, holy, glory to God in the highest, and peace to his people on earth!'

The emperor and empress turned and walked down the aisle, passing rows of all the noblest and wealthiest citizens of Constantinople. One among their number was a very holy and noble lady who wore a cloak of such elaborate embroidery, illustrating the lurid tortures and deaths of those two blessed brothers, Primus and Felician, saints and martyrs, that other women around her had tutted that she looked as if she was trying to outshine the bride herself. But in truth there was no great danger of that, for the holy and noble lady was by no means so attractive in her features as she liked to believe.

As the newly married couple passed by, the empress seemed to slow a little, and gaze very keenly into the face of the noble lady, and smile. Such was the lady's rapture at being thus acknowledged by the empress herself, that she gave a little scream, and clasped a hanky to her mouth, and succumbed to a fit of the vapours, and had to be quickly carried out of a side door into the street and splashed with holy water.

After the ceremony they returned to the palace where, flanked by armed guards and eunuchs, they entered the secret passage and ascended the spiral staircase to emerge into the Kathisma, the grandiose imperial box on the north side of the Hippodrome. Theodosius made the sign of the cross over his loyal subjects, and a hundred thousand people roared, 'Long live the emperor! God bless the empress!'

There followed a great wedding feast in the palace, with the imperial pair seated together on a high dais. Princess Pulcheria had been reduced to a lower seating order. She ate very little, drank nothing, and scowled throughout. When a slavegirl bumped her, she pinched the girl's arm viciously.

And then came the hymeneal hymn. One of the most admired court poets of Rome had been specially shipped over for the occasion. His name was Claudian Claudianus, an Alexandrian by birth. He was getting on in years, but his inspiration was in no way faltering, and his poems remained as lengthy and ornate as ever. Several guests had to be excused during the recitation of the hymn, which lasted almost an hour, and surprisingly failed to return to the table.

I shall quote only the delicate closing lines of the hymn, after Claudian had delightfully pictured the new empress's virginal modesty being overcome during the wedding night ahead.

> Then when your lips and limbs have found their rest,
> Untied soul to soul, ye both shall sleep,
> And Morpheus' train shall still your throbbing breath.
> When rosy-fingered dawn shall find you lying
> Entangled in the coverlets, arm in arm,
> The couch shall still be warm with princely wooing,
> New stains ennobling sheets of Tyrian dye.'

When he at last finished and mopped his perspiring brow, the applause was tremendous.

In the days immediately following the marriage of the emperor and his beautiful new empress, a beggarwoman in a side street near the north end of the Mese found that some crazy fool with more money than sense had hidden a bag of solid gold pieces in the brown woollen blanket on the pavement where she slept. She waited a few days in case anyone should come back to collect their money with menaces, but none did. She concluded that God had chosen to wait until her seventh decade before bestowing His blessings upon her, and that His Ways were mysterious and wonderful, and that the money was hers. It would enable her to rent a little apartment above the shop of her friend the baker, and live in comfort for the rest of her days.

Likewise, a blind and legless beggar who sat all day and shivered all night beside the Fountain of Saint Irenaeus, as he sat there one evening, pulling his thin cloak round his skinny shoulders as best he could and praying that the chill wind out of Asia would drop, felt his hand taken by another, a slim, soft hand.

He jerked in blind astonishment. The hand held him gently but firmly.

'Who are you?' he whispered hoarsely, his eyes searching the darkness before him as if he might yet see. 'The Magdalene? The Mother of God?'

He was lifted up into a carriage and driven through the streets, and he knew that the girl or angel or even the Mother of God herself was sitting next to him, but she would say nothing. They passed through some gates into a courtyard, the sound of the carriage-wheels clattering on the cobbles and echoing off the surrounding walls. He was taken and washed, and his sores were bathed in oil and bandaged, and he was laid to sleep in a little narrow chamber, with warm woollen blankets to keep him from the cold.

The following day a fellow who gruffly said he was called Braccus and worked here at this paupers' hospital carried the beggar out into a sunny garden sheltered by high walls from the wind off the nearby sea. The old man was set down in some sort of arbour, and he sat there all day and on into evening in happy wonder, until the night air was filled with the sweet fragrance of jasmine.

10

THE JOURNEY TO JERUSALEM

I, too, knew her. For at about this time, as well as continuing to
serve as chief clerk in the office of the Count of the Sacred Largesse
(the title is more impressive than the office, I assure you), I was
raised to the rank of clerk-in-Consistory. This meant that I took
records of all the proceedings in the Imperial Council Chamber.
After some years of diligent service here, it was not unknown for
some of the senior senators, or even the emperor himself, to turn to
me on a point of order, or to ask if there was a precedent for such
and such an imperial decision or decree. In time, in fact, it began
to feel as if I was not so much a mere clerk as a valued counsellor.
For this reason I was often despatched to the court of the Western
Empire in Ravenna or Mediolanum or Rome, and so had intimate
acquaintance with all the operations of the time.

And I, too, fell under the spell of the new, girlish empress. What
man could not?

Once, I recall, she encountered me scurrying along a marble corridor of the palace in Constantinople, uncharacteristically late for
that morning's session in Consistory, owing to my having had to
spend a longer time than usual at stool. Indeed, I was still writing
a hurried mental note to myself to eat more lentils in future, when
the empress stopped and smiled at me, and all thought of stools
and lentils fled. I slowed my pace, and she asked me in the sweetest,
softest voice to come and take a letter for her.

'Your Sacred Highness,' I began to babble, 'I fain would do as
you command, but I, I ...'

But one fatal glance into those huge dark eyes, and I was lost for ever. Knowing that I would earn a terrible scolding for my absence from Consistory that morning, I nevertheless followed her meekly back to her private chambers to take a letter, imagining the words flowing honeylike from her sweet lips to my pen. My heart pounded within me. The woman was a witch, a spellbinder, of the most enchanting kind. A dream-weaver, weaving dreams from which you never wanted to awaken.

Of course she knew it. Her mouth twitched with amusement at my stammering, hopeless, infatuated obedience to her every whim. She could have ordered me to stand on the high window ledge of the chamber and throw myself to the ground three floors below, and I would have obeyed. But naturally she would not. Proud she may have been; vain of her beauty, certainly – what woman would not be? But cruel? No. In a cruel world, and a cruel and fickle court, Athenaïs was never cruel. She loved all humanity with a generous, spontaneous outpouring of affection.

She began to speak.

My pen quivered, and I began to write.

When I ran to make my humblest apologies for my absence later that morning to the court chamberlain, a tall, unsmiling eunuch called Nicephorus, he merely waved me away with his long-fingered hand, festooned with signet rings.

'The empress has already made your pardons for you,' he said. 'You were required elsewhere this morning.'

No one else would have troubled thus to save a humble court clerk from a tongue lashing. But that was Athenaïs: loved as much for her kindness of heart as for her beauty.

They are rare companions in a woman.

I doted on her. Sometimes to the sly ridicule of my fellow scribes and clerks, I adored her.

This then was the palace and its inhabitants on the eve of the arrival of Galla, Aëtius and her small retinue, only months after the imperial wedding. It was a moonless night when they arrived at that great fortified compound with its mighty walls of red Egyptian granite, and its interior lavishly decorated with porphyry from Ptolemais in Palestine, Attic marble, rich damask hangings from Damascus, ivory and sandalwood from India, silken brocades and porcelain from China. A dream-palace where even the chamber-pots were made of purest silver.

The fugitives from the West were treated with great kindness upon their arrival – Galla Placidia and Theodosius were, after all, aunt and nephew: she the daughter and he the grandson of Emperor Theodosius the Great. And perhaps the pure Pulcheria admired Galla the more when she found that the reason for her precipitate flight from Italy had been to preserve herself from the unchaste advances of a man.

They were given some of the finest suites in the Imperial Palace, overlooking that bright sunlit sea, so different and so far away from the marshes and the gloom of Ravenna, and they were lavished with gifts of gold, and precious gems, and fine robes. All these things Galla rejoiced in. Aëtius was perhaps less impressed, but he said nothing. He had been to Constantinople before. He knew the city of old.

At dusk the following day a firm knock came on my door.

I was engaged in some tedious but necessary work for the Count of the Sacred Largesse – adding up columns of figures, in other words. I couldn't help wishing there were a symbol … It seems madness to say so, but I couldn't help wishing there were a symbol for nothing, as well as for all the numerals denoting somethings. A special number signifying no number. Idly I even drew a round 'O' in the margin of my paper, to signify emptiness, absence. Surely it would make adding up easier in some ways? But I scribbled it out again. It was a foolish notion, and would only earn me ridicule; and I suffered enough ridicule as it was from my fellow clerks, owing to my great devotion to the Empress.

'Enter,' I said, not looking round.

The door opened, and someone stood behind me. Still I did not look, but then the power of his presence was overwhelming, and I glanced back.

It was him. My pupil. My dear, my much-missed, grave-eyed, tall, lean pupil. A general, at twenty-five!

Before I knew what I was doing I had scrambled to my feet and embraced him. It was contrary to all court etiquette, of course, for a mere slave-born pedagogue even to approach a nobleman unbidden, or address words to him first, let alone to embrace him. But Aëtius and I had always been more to each other than mere slave-teacher and master-pupil. He embraced me fondly in return, his blue eyes shining with affection, and perhaps amused remembrance of our long hours of learning together which he had so openly detested.

We stood back and regarded each other.

It was good to have him back in the court, for however short a while. His very presence, so still and strong, was a calmative, in a world which seemed increasingly beset by winds of violent change from without, and unhealthy miasmas of weakness and madness from within. News from Ravenna of Emperor Honorius was not good. Aëtius stood through it all, this lean, hard young man, steady-eyed, unflinching, like a pillar of granite in a hailstorm.

'So,' he said, his hands on my shoulders, looking down at me. 'You work here in Constantinople now?'

I nodded. 'After my years of pedagogy had finished, and I had seen my most brilliant though idle pupil off into the wide world – you remember faithfully all your lessons in logic, I trust? And the three categories: demonstrative, persuasive, and sophistic?'

'Only in your late twenties yourself,' said Aëtius, clapping me on the arm, 'and talking like an aged pedant already.'

'Already talking like an aged pedant,' I corrected him. 'It is vulgar to end a sentence with an adverb.'

He smiled. 'What little logic I ever learned is long forgotten. Besides,' he added, the smile fading, 'the wide world you saw me off into but rarely conforms to its laws.'

I looked away, out of the window and across the shimmering Golden Horn. Gulls wheeled low in the twilight beyond the bars.

'After you had gone off to the frontier to learn soldiering, I was despatched from the court of Honorius to come east. It is peaceful here.' I looked back at him. 'But what of yourself? I have no other great news, but what of you? What news?'

'I hear that the emperor has married,' murmured Aëtius. 'News enough, I would have thought.'

'Ah, yes,' I said. 'Athenaïs.'

'You speak of her as a man speaks of his beloved.'

'Ssshh!' I hissed, alarmed. 'Do not even whisper such things!'

93

He laughed. I glared. Fine for him to fear nothing, but we slave-born pedagogues have a great deal to fear in an imperial court.

'So,' he said, 'this Athenaïs – Eudoxia, we should say, I think – she is very beautiful?'

'Hmph.' I still glared. 'You can decide for yourself when you meet her. She returns from the Summer Palace at Hieron in two days' time.'

'What other news?'

I shrugged. 'No other news. You know better than that. Humble scribes such as myself do not have news. Whereas generals ...'

'You wish to hear my news?'

I nodded. 'Of course.'

He considered, then sighed, pulled over a splintery stool from the shadows and sat down. After long rumination he began. 'During my last season on the Danube station, at Viminacium—'

'Wait, wait!' I cried, hurriedly sharpening my goosequill as best I could.

'You're writing all this down?' he said.

'Every word,' I said. 'For the day when ...'

He raised his eyebrows. 'The Annals of Priscus of Panium?'

I nodded sheepishly. 'It won't be Tacitus, I know. But—'

He laid his powerful hand on my arm, and said, 'Do not be so sure. We live in interesting times.'

Our eyes met. We both understood the bleak irony in his words.

I rested my hands on the brim of my writing lectern, dipped my quill, and waited.

'Well,' he began. 'News from the Danube station.'

It was a daily delight to me to see my dear pupil, Aëtius, in his red general's robes, attending the interminable meetings and sessions of statutes in the imperial Consistory with great forbearance for a man of action such as himself. 'With attainments beyond his years, and a steadiness of character beyond his attainments', as St Gregory of Nazianzus said.

He served as dutifully in Consistory as on the battlefield. The frontier was quiet for now; there were no major campaigns to be fought and, besides, the summer campaigning season was almost at an end. So he took his place obediently in the great semicircle of the court, with Theodosius enthroned at the centre, and his senators, counsellors, generals and bishops ranged round the sides. Beyond this heart of the imperial administration, the palace teemed with eunuchs, slaves, ladies' maids, ridiculous ceremonials, titles, grandiose honours. My own immediate master at this time, the Count of the Sacred Largesse, held one of the simpler offices of state.

Two days after the arrival of the little group from Ravenna, the empress returned from a week beside the cool fountains in the gardens of the Summer Palace at Hieron, which she loved. It stands on a wind-cooled promontory where the straits meet the Euxine Sea, and is especially grateful at the dry, rank end of the season, when even the voices of the cicadas sound hoarse and choke with dust.

And I was there; I, Priscus. I was there, present as a humble and unremarked court scribe, when their haunted, bewildered eyes first met. In the Triclinium of the Nineteen Couches. Aëtius and Athenaïs, both so confident and self-assured beyond their years, though in wholly different ways. There I saw all confidence and self-assurance flee from them.

'The Princess Galla Placidia, and Master-General Aëtius of the Western Legions,' announced the chamberlain.

They stepped into the room, first Galla, then Aëtius. Galla and Theodosius smiled politely at each other, then the emperor stepped forward and they kissed.

Aëtius seemed strangely frozen to the spot.

Athenaïs likewise.

For then she knew what true love was. Her whole being seemed to lurch towards him and she thought with instant desperation: This is the man I love and will always love. Oh, what have I done?

I saw how they avoided each other all that winter. How for them even to see the other was the sweetest, acutest pain imaginable. They barely spoke a word to each other. When a diplomatic mission to the court of the Sassanid kingdom of Persia departed, Aëtius went with them, to the surprise of some. He spent the winter out east.

Athenaïs seemed sometimes strangely distracted for a young bride; and at other times she boasted too loudly and too publicly, to some embarrassment, about the marvellousness of her husband. Women who boast excessively of their husbands are rarely the most faithful. But in her case people put it down to natural warmth and generosity of spirit.

In the spring it was announced that the empress would be going on a pilgrimage to Jerusalem.

'And,' Theodosius announced, 'though the route through our empire is perfectly safe, she will be accompanied by the First Cohort of the Imperial Guard, under the command of General Aëtius.'

The emperor had a high regard for the young general, and proudly felt that only the finest military escort would do for his beloved wife.

It was the best and worst thing that could have happened. To spend time together – on the orders of her own husband! It could only add to the pain. And yet perhaps they secretly wanted the pain. Does the human heart want to feel happiness, or does it merely want to feel much, greatly, intensely? No matter what the emotion?

I went with them, and I saw all and wrote nothing. But now in these last days, when only I am left of all that brave and beautiful company ... now the truth may be told.

The empress's party stepped abroad the royal barge, which rode at anchor on a mild sea in the Harbour of Phospherion. They traversed the narrow straits of the Bosphorus, and made landfall upon the Asian shore amid crowds of cheering people waving branches of olive and myrtle. There they dined with the urbane governor of the golden city of Chrysopolis. Some already commented that the empress and the general must despise each other, for they barely looked at each other, let alone exchanged a civil word. When forced to be in close company, at dinner for instance, they kept their eyes and their voices lowered as if in obscure shame.

They processed east and traversed the province of Bithynia to Nicomedia. The empress rode in a fine four-wheeled carriage. Aëtius and the guard rode far ahead.

The empress travelled next to Hierapolis, to bathe her lovely limbs in the health-giving hot sulphur springs. From thence she visited the Asian Mount Olympus and its monasteries, and held long and learned talk with the monks there, which left them aston- ished, humbled, and some of the younger and more hot-blooded, adoring of their new empress to the point of idolatry. She was likewise welcomed and fêted in Smyrna, and Sardis, and Ephesus, and all the great cities of the Ionian coast, and south to Pamphylia in the shadow of the Taurus mountains, and so on to Seleucia, and Tarsus, the home of the evangelical tentmaker.

So this ostensible pleasure jaunt fulfilled its secret political purpose of cementing the love of the people, the Church, and the political and senatorial classes across the Levant for the young emperor and his beautiful bride, and making the radiant imperial presence known and respected far beyond the walls of Constantinople.

After several weeks of travelling they came to the teeming city of Antioch, 'the third city of the empire', a bewildering hubbub of Cretans, Syrians, Jews, Greeks, Persians, Armenians. It was also called 'Antioch the Beautiful'; its famed marble streets had been laid down by Herod the Great, and it was the place where the term '*christianoi*', 'Christians', was first used. Athenaïs loved it on sight. She visited the sanctuary of Apollo, where Mark Antony and Cleopatra had been married, now half destroyed by her zealous co-religionists. And she insisted on an afternoon trip out of the heat and dust of the city, and beyond the miles of shanty-towns that stretched over the surrounding hillsides, to see for herself the notorious Grove of Daphne, where hundreds of prostitutes still plied their trade 'in honour of the goddess'.

At a dinner she gave a magnificent extempore speech upon the glories of Antioch's magnificent past, and quoted from the *Odyssey*, 'ὑμετέρης γενεῆς τε καὶ αἵματος εὔχομαι εἶναι.'

'I claim proud kinship with your race and blood.' It always goes down well when a visiting foreign dignitary claims to be of the same descent as his audience.

The next day they rode out of the city southwards, heading for the magnificent temple of Baalbek; but on the empress's orders they turned east and headed out into the desert, following the crowds who streamed over the hills in their hundreds to visit the product of a religion very different from that which built proud Baalbek: the celebrated ascetic St Simeon Stylites on his pillar, out near Telanessa. There, in the shimmering Syrian desert, Athenaïs and Aëtius and their entourage saw with their own eyes the famous saint, sitting atop his pillar seventy feet into the sky, where he had already sat for ten years, and would sit another twenty yet. The crowds of devotees sat round the foot of the pillar, gazing up in wonder at the saint's holiness, and collecting the lice that fell from his filthy, emaciated body to the ground. These they tucked away among their own robes as precious relics, calling them 'the pearls of God'.

Neither Athenaïs nor Aëtius collected any pearls.

In the years to come, many came to imitate Simeon. News spread of his great act of penance, his self-hatred made manifest, his self-abasement raised high, the odour of him spreading out across the valley. As far away as the Ardennes forest in Gaul, a Lombard deacon tried to emulate his example until his rather more pragmatic bishop told him not to be so foolish.

Near Simeon sat another pillar-dweller, Daniel Stylites. Daniel had started on a rather small pillar, but a wealthy benefactor had paid for a magnificent double-column to be erected for him. He had managed to cross to it from his first pillar, by way of a make-shift bridge of planks, so that he never had to sully his feet with the dust of the world. And there he sat, and prayed, and excreted, and praised the Lord.

When they came to the magnificent temple of Baalbek it was evening, and the deserted temple stood proud and pagan in the late rose-light that stretched across the desert. They wondered at the cedar-roofed Portico of Caracalla, the magnificent mosaics in the marble floors, the bas relief of Jupiter Heliopolitan, and above all, at the breathtaking temple of Jupiter, its columns of a size unrivalled anywhere in the world: some eighty feet in height and eighteen feet in girth. They never shall be rivalled, I think, in all the days and works of man. One of the foundation stones of the temple weighed over a thousand tons. Already the knowledge of how to cut and move such titanic blocks is vanishing from the earth. Never shall we see such majesty again.

They saw, too, the temple of Venus, goddess of love and beauty, now a basilica dedicated to St Barbara, virgin and martyr. It was whispered in the neighbouring town that the ancient rites still took place around the temple complex, to the anger of the Christian authorities but with the secret cognisance of more secular powers;

and that these silent stones yet witnessed the nature worship of the old gods, ancient even compared to the Olympians who overcame them: Astarte, and Atargatis, and Baal himself, who glared out darkly over his devotees two thousand years before Christ walked on earth.

Eusebius wrote only a century ago that men and women still came here to 'clasp together' before the altar in honour of the goddess. Husbands and fathers allowed their wives and daughters to sell themselves publicly to passers-by and worshippers, in honour of their mysterious goddess of love, and some men even took a lewd pleasure in seeing their womenfolk thus made harlots. All night they sang, and drank, and danced, accompanied by the sound of barbarous drums and flutes. Baalbek was never a place with a naturally Christian soul.

It was a place of sacrificial blood as well as sacred love. Can one exist without the other? There was no gentleness in the ancient religion. Blood was riotously shed upon these stones. 'Anath, the sister of Baal, waded up to her knees, up to her neck in human blood,' say the ancient texts. 'Human hands lay at her feet, they flew about her like locusts. She tied human heads around her neck, and hands upon her belt. She washed her hands in the streams of human blood that flowed about her knees ...'

At Baalbek, it seems, gods are mortal. They are born, and worshipped; they flourish, and have mighty temples built to them. Later, when men and women cease to believe in them, they wither and die, and a new generation of mortal gods takes their place. In time, too, even Christ will die for ever from the earth.

None of the imperial party spoke their secret thoughts at Baalbek. But they lingered there a long time.

Finally Jerusalem, the Holy City of Zion. This place, too, Athenaïs greatly loved, and she lingered here for longer that might seem appropriate. For her husband awaited her in Constantinople, and it was high time she was back in his bed. Her highest duty now was to give him sons. An empress had no other reason to live than this.

It was the last night in Jerusalem, before they were due to descend from that holy mountain to the coast, to Caesarea, and take ship for home. The empress was walking on the lonely terrace of the modest palace where they were residing, overlooking the valley of Gehenna, the valley of Sheol, where the ancient Hebrews had tumbled the bodies of their dead into the smoking abyss below and burned them. From beyond the place of Hell came the gentle breezes from the garden of Gethsemane upon the Mount of Olives.

Another figure stepped out from the shadows of the palace onto the terrace to take the night air before retiring. The two of them almost collided. They stepped back and stared with the same wide-eyed astonishment as when they had first set eyes upon each other, three long months before. Their eyes were wide and bright and innocent under the eastern moon. And then like sleepwalkers they moved towards each other again in the soft velvet night. From the olivegroves across the valley came the harsh warning call of a bird, and the moon was golden in the late summer sky over the Valley of Sheol, where the air was hazed with the chaff beaten from the late summer wheat in the surrounding country, and misty with smoke from the chaff heaped up for the burning.

They said nothing. And with consummate awkwardness, like two adolescents—

It is impossible to say who kissed whom. Their lips met. They both fought not to give in to this desire, or rather this need, to touch the other. Both were proud. But both were defeated.

After they had kissed they drew back and looked at each other for a long time. They said nothing. Minutes passed. Neither of them moved. Neither of them could move.

The next day at dawn they left the city for the long journey down to the coast. They rode far apart, heads bowed and silent, like two people recently bereaved.

Galla knew. Galla saw it, with her gimlet eyes, the moment they returned.

Marriage and hardship had perhaps softened Galla's heart. Motherhood certainly had. She responded to others' weakness with pity more than with scorn as heretofore. She saw this living agony before her eyes: Athenaïs and Aëtius unwillingly yet so willingly, so longingly, in each other's company, constrained by the cruelty of circumstance and the stiff rituals and formalities of the court. Her reaction was that of a woman who is herself a little in love with a man who loves another: a sad smile, and silence.

Perhaps also she recognised already that she and Aëtius had something in common, that would endure all their lives: they each loved another, and neither of them would ever in this world possess that other.

Between Galla and Athenaïs, where you might have expected rancour, cattiness, or worse, there was none. Between Pulcheria and Galla, there was as much warmth as that life-sworn virgin, the emperor's thin-lipped sister could ever muster for a fellow creature of flesh and blood. Pulcheria's feelings toward Athenaïs were, inevitably, seething jealousy and resentment, disguised as pious reserve. (Prudes are driven by jealousy, not morality. Those who can, do. Those who can't, preach.) But as for cool, green-eyed Galla, perhaps she saw that Athenaïs' feelings for Aëtius mirrored her own. Perhaps she saw also that the poor girl, married so young and with so much love in her to give, to one whom she was fond of but would never come truly to love, would find only unhappiness in her life. Perhaps. Whatever the reason, she never treated the young empress, so different from herself in temperament, with anything but kindness.

And then on the twenty-sixth day of August 423, a messenger came with shocking news from Rome. Emperor Honorius had died of dropsy, and a usurper, Johannes, had raised legions in Illyria and declared himself the new Emperor of the West.

Aëtius seemed relieved to be getting away at last. 'The enemies of Rome are not growing any fewer,' he observed dryly. 'There is fighting to be done.'

11

THE BARBARY COAST IN FLAMES

The shops of Constantinople were shut for seven days, in a demonstration of public grief for Honorius. The new emperor, Theodosius, even ordered the horse-races to be cancelled, which nearly caused a riot.

Thus at last Galla returned to Rome, together with Aëtius, and her son was made emperor at the age of four.

From an early age, Valentinian displayed every sign of taking after his uncle rather than his father: a lamentable inheritance. He was slothful, greedy, childish, petulant and cruel. Galla herself, it was poisonously gossiped, had deliberately made her son stupid with feeble education and enervating superstition. Though Christian in name, Valentinian was obsessed with the darkest arts of magic and divination.

To blame these failings on the teachings of his mother was sheer ill-informed malice: Galla's faith in the Christian God was real, and sober. Not for her the hoarse gabblings of haruspices amid the splashes and flecks of a dying pigeon's blood, and all the other tawdry trappings of a moribund paganism. In an age when loud professions of religious zeal were everywhere, and true, divinely inspired loving-kindness almost nowhere – that is to say, an age much like any other – Galla, for all her ruthlessness and pride, devoted herself all her life to the officially sanctioned religion of the empire.

Besides, those sly gossips were ignoring one salient fact: Valentinian was quite stupid and corrupt enough to discover the joys of witchcraft for himself.

Nevertheless, as the only obvious heir to the western throne, the crafty-eyed little boy was solemnly crowned with the diadem and the imperial purple; and his mother became effectively ruler in the West.

For some years after that, the Empire knew an uneasy, unaccustomed peace, except for one stunning loss, which seemed to happen overnight, and to resist every attempt at recapture: the grainfields of North Africa were taken by the Vandals.

Suddenly, in the blazing June of 429, the Barbary Coast was in flames. The Vandal raiders were a Germanic horse-people of the steppes, lately settled in southern Spain but with an appetite for conquest and destruction unabated. In a single generation, so it seemed, they had mastered the arts of both shipbuilding and sailing from their native Spanish subjects. From their kingdom of Vandalusia, or 'Andalusia', as the Berbers called it, they had crossed the narrow straits, overrun the province of Mauretania, and fallen upon the precious grainfields of Numidia and Libya with fire and sword.

Rome was taken utterly by surprise. None but Aëtius seemed aware of how disastrous this was. It is said that when he heard the news he sat down, ashen-faced, gripping his left wrist in his right hand, and did not speak for half a day.

The imperial court, the wealthy senatorial classes and the chattering crowds of Rome carried blithely on, as if unaware of the vast, blood-dark cloud slowly seeping across their sky from the far horizon.

The following year the Vandal armies set out eastwards across the Mahgreb, bent on 'conquest to the gates of the rising sun'. City after city fell to their fury. On clear nights, it was said, you could see the African shore lit up as if with mighty beacon fires all along the coast from Tingis to Leptis Magna.

The summer of 432 saw them besieging the city of Hippo Regius. In the third month of that terrible siege, when starving people killed each other over a rat, one of the great voices of the Church, St Augustine of Hippo, closed his eyes upon the ruins of a world which he had so desired and feared. He died on the twenty-eighth day of August, aged seventy-five. A few weeks later Hippo was taken and burned almost to a shell. But Augustine's writings and his personal library were by some miracle saved: two hundred and thirty-two books, plus treatises and commentaries, epistles and homilies, and those immortal works the *Confessions* and *The City of God*.

The years passed, the Vandal conquerors made North Africa their own, and the young and hesitant Emperor Valentinian hesitated. Aëtius argued for reconquest by land and sea, vigorously at first, and then furiously. When Galla Placidia concurred with the general and urged her son in the same direction, the weak and paranoid adolescent rebelled against them, called them 'bossy', refused point blank to do anything about Africa, and sent Aëtius into exile.

Not for the last time, Aëtius took refuge at the court of the Visigoths in Tolosa. Valentinian, meanwhile, sued for dishonourable peace with Genseric, the wrathful, debauched king of the Vandals, who had once been a hostage prince in the court of Rome, with his younger brother Beric; the latter had long since died in an 'accident'.

Genseric was fierce and blood-thirsty, delighting always in spectacles of the utmost cruelty and depravity. He especially liked to see women forced to couple with animals, in supposed tableaux of ancient myths: a wild bull, representing Zeus, mated with a naked slave-girl, representing Europa, tied down over a cartwheel. Perhaps Genseric believed that, by showing his appreciation for such entertainments, he was demonstrating his affinity with the elevated culture of the classical world. He spoke little, was short in stature, and he struggled to sleep with women in the normal way. When he did so, it was with hatred.

To the dismay of many, the Vandal kingdom of North Africa under the rule of the monstrous Genseric became an established fact. Rome's resources shrank still further.

Indeed, the streets of Rome were filled with more and more threadbare and starving refugees from the Vandal fury in North Africa, and tiny wooden boats bobbed across the Mediterranean from the Numidian or Mauretanian shore to make landfall in Italy. More and more desperate, hungry mouths, and less and less grain to go round. But still the people lived blithely, and did not want to see that the blood-dark cloud now nearly filled the sky.

12

THE PRINCESS AND THE SLAVE-GIRL

The years passed, and Valentinian's sister, Honoria, grew into young womanhood. No sooner had she reached that turbulent age, not sixteen summers old, than she betrayed her true character, and the name 'Honoria' showed itself absurdly unsuitable for this inveterate lover of pleasure. 'Oh, incongruous name!' one monkish chronicler has written. 'For never was there a female so shameless in her carnal appetites as the Princess Honoria!'

It is not for a humble scribe like myself to have opinions one way or another about the girl's behaviour, but many other chroniclers have felt differently, describing her as 'a she-daemon of sensuality', 'a succubus who inflamed men's flesh and scoured their souls', and even 'the Great Scarlet Whore whose appearance marked the End of the World'. The more censorious have written that they could not possibly commit to writing the horrifying stories they heard about her lusts and depravities, before going on to do so in extensive and unblushing detail. Whatever the truth about the princess, as a responsible historian I must record what I have heard about her without demur.

Honoria was born three years after her brother, in 422, the daughter of the gloomy Flavius Constantius and his chaste and upright wife the Princess Galla Placidia, so that in the year 437 she was just 15. She appeared to have only three interests in life: beautifying her body; attracting attention to herself, from both men and women; and sensual pleasure. No greater difference between mother and daughter could be imagined, so that palace wits said that surely Princess Galla must have borne her daughter not by the noble if taciturn Flavius, but rather following a visitation from one of the insatiable and lecherous gods of the pagan pantheon. Perhaps Zeus had visited Galla in the likeness of a shower of gold, as he did Danaë; or a swan, as he did Leda. For the daughter of Galla, like the daughter of Leda, Helen of Troy, would prove irresistible to men, both because of her beauty and because of her evident lustfulness. And she would set off a train of events as calamitous and tragic as that caused by Helen, providing a similar feast of entertainment for the sardonically laughing gods above. For the sorrowful tale of Troy is known to those high gods as the Wrath of Achilles, but humanity remembers it as the Death of Hector.

If not Father Zeus, perhaps it was the great god Pan, or some ithyphallic satyr in his train, who fathered Honoria upon the chaste and haughty Galla as she slept in her icy composure and self-restraint. Certainly the disparity between mother and daughter was great, and often remarked.

Beauty alone in a woman is not enough to reduce men to love-struck foolishness. Such a woman must also make it clear, by the fluttering of her eyelashes, and by the glittering steadiness with which she returns a man's gaze, with the dark kohl-rimmed drowning-pools of her eyes, and by the pretty pouting of her carmine lips, and by the gentle touch of her fingertips upon his arm, and by bending forward to retrieve, shall we say, her napkin from the floor, giving him a heady glimpse of her sweet and fruitlike breasts with their erect and roseate nipples – such a woman conquers men, as I say, both by her beauty and by her explicit sensuality. For which reason, as St Augustine has warned us, 'women are the greatest snare that the devil has set for men'; and as the Bible itself reminds us, 'All wickedness is but little to the wickedness of a woman.'

All these tricks and harlotries Princess Honoria understood very well from her earliest years; and no sooner had she begun to show the first outward signs of womanhood, if palace gossip is to be believed, than she was demanding sexual pleasure from her slaves. No Agrippina, no Messalina, was ever so debauched as she. And in the morally dubious palace of Ravenna, with its slaves numbering some twenty thousand, each one bound to do the bidding of master or mistress, there was no scarcity of potential servants for her lust.

More shocking still was the princess's indifference to whether

her companion in the pleasures of the flesh were male or female; for, like Sappho of Lesbos, whose works are largely lost to posterity, Decency be thanked, she took her pleasures where she found them: her love being not only towards men but, with rather too much generosity, towards all humanity.

It was said that one person was particularly responsible for the first awakening in Princess Honoria of her desire for pleasure. One day a new slave-girl came into her private chambers from the slave-markets of Alexandria. Her name was Sosostris, which means simply 'Sister' in the old Egyptian, and is a typical term of affection for a slave. Other slave-names, signifying even more than mere affection, and reminding the bearer of the name that they existed to pleasure their owners on demand, included Desire, Kiss, Pleasure, Beloved, and even Sexy. Sosostris herself might well have borne any of these alternative names, as it turned out, such was her hot temperament. 'Sister' was a more ambiguous term, perhaps; but many was the slave-master who took perverse pleasure in calling his 'sister' to his bed at night.

Sosostris was some eighteen or nineteen years of age, an Egyptian, slim and dark-skinned and very beautiful. Now, you know of the reputation of the Egyptians, both men and women; for in ancient times, before the coming of Christ, the utmost lubricity was common in Egypt, and women went not only bare-legged but even bare-breasted throughout the day. At evening they sat at table with their husbands and their husbands' friends, boldly conversing as if they were men's intellectual equals! Their full round breasts were on proud and wanton display, the allure of their dusky nipples even augmented by subtle applications of cosmetics and rouge!

But I digress.

Regarding Sosostris and Princess Honoria, I heard it from another scribe in the court of Ravenna, who heard it from the Egyptian herself, whom he later took to his own bed, deriving much lewd and revolting pleasure from hearing her recount her youthful adventures in the arms of men and women alike; such are the corruptions of the times. And although it is true that Rumour is never so speedy on her feet, nor so wholly unreliable, as when she hastens to report in the market-place on matters which belong in the bedroom, I feel that there may be some lamentable truth in the scenes that were laid before my shocked imagination by the luridly detailed description of this shameless scribe. They are scenes that I have turned over and over in my mind many times since, in my pure desire to know whether they could be true or not; so that it is now almost as if I witnessed such appalling scenes for myself.

It was Princess Honoria's habit to take a bath in the evening as well as the morning, and thereafter to lie sleepily upon her couch and have her slaves anoint and massage her with warm oil perfumed with the petals of roses. Soon it was noticed that this task was reserved exclusively for Sosostris, while the other slaves were dismissed from the royal presence. Furthermore, by day, the looks and glances exchanged by the princess and the slave-girl seemed to betoken more than the merely affectionate relations that might obtain between a mistress and a loyal slave. It was as though their looks communicated some illicit and secretive passion, only augmented by their subtle smiles exchanged in public, as they silently remembered together the pleasures of the night before, and anticipated the pleasures of the night ahead. Sometimes, it was said, cries were heard coming from the Princess Honoria's private chambers after dark, which sounded very strange to the ears of those who had always assumed that such cries in a woman could only be provoked by the presence and the dutiful attentions of a husband.

Indeed, if Rumour is to be believed, the worst fears of the palace were well founded. For on her very first night in Honoria's service Sosostris began to administer those seductive oils to her mistress, murmuring gently that she had great skill in this art. The other slave-girls helped the young princess from her bath, wrapped her in soft cloths, carried her over to her wide, cushioned couch, laid her down on her stomach and carefully dried her.

Then the Egyptian took her bowl of perfumed unguents, and poured them into the hollow of Honoria's back, and with her slim and delicate brown hands she began to rub and knead the oils into the princess's shoulders and neck, her back and flanks. To looks of some surprise from the other slave-girls, she began to run her hands beneath the soft white cloths that covered the princess's modesty, and also to massage her smooth white buttocks.

After a few moments, the cloths slipped aside altogether and fell silently to the floor, leaving the princess naked and exposed, but she seemed to mind not a whit. And then, to the great astonishment of the attendant slave-girls, who not being Egyptian would never have dreamed of taking such a liberty with the royal person, Sosostris took up the bowl again and poured a thin golden trickle down between the princess's thighs, which were still at this point held tightly and chastely together. And the impudent Egyptian, a knowing smile playing upon her lips, actually sat down beside her mistress on the couch, rather than kneeling subserviently beside it, as was the usual custom. She was wearing a long white tunic, loosely belted about the waist with a red sash. Now, to make it easier to sit on the royal couch, albeit uninvited, she shamelessly drew up her dress almost to her knees, baring her long, smooth legs for all the world to see, and exhibiting her fine leather sandals, saucily high-laced in the brazen manner of a common harlot of the Suburra.

She leaned over her mistress closely so as to press more of her weight upon her hands, but as she did so her own ripe breasts beneath the white linen tunic brushed lightly against the princess's back with a shocking intimacy, and the princess stirred beneath that touch, making no move to reprimand it. Then the impudent slave began to run her fingertips teasingly up and down the smooth and glistening crevice from the princess's buttocks down to knees and back again, but teasingly, as if she were engaged not in work at all, but in pure play.

Then, before the shocked eyes of the other slave-girls, Sosostris actually eased those young white thighs apart. Leaning down, she unloosed her tresses and shook them free, and began to sweep her long black hair up and down between her mistress's thighs, and up over her buttocks and her back and then down again. Sosostris's hair was of that magnificent Egyptian hue, blue-black in intensity, long and perfectly straight and reaching almost to her waist. Now she used it not as mere decoration but as an implement of seduction. Under her wicked ministrations, Princess Honoria gave a soft moan and, almost despite herself, it seemed, raised her buttocks a little and arched her slender back. When she settled herself again upon the silken cushions beneath her, it just so happened that her thighs were no longer quite together, but just a little apart, as if with lewd invitation. The Egyptian girl smiled a smile of quiet triumph, and dipped her fingertips into the bowl of perfumed oil again.

At this point it is said, though I would fain not believe it, Honoria turned her head slightly, and murmured to the rest of the slave-girls that they were dismissed, at which they all retired from the chamber. But, women being slaves to concupiscence as well as to insatiable curiosity and gossip, they did not retire completely, but concealed themselves in a neighbouring antechamber, pretending to close the doors, before opening them again silently and peeking out between the drawn curtains at the Egyptian slave-girl's treatment of their mistress.

It seemed Sosostris was no innocent as to this, either, for after a few moments she glanced towards where the other slave-girls were concealed, and looked saucily at them, even though she could barely have seen them there in the shadows. And she arched her eyebrows and smiled at them, as if she knew very well that they were there and watching, and even enjoyed the knowledge that her pleasuring of the princess was being watched.

Now she ... But here I must break off, for decency's sake. There is more to tell, much more; but let not such scandalous lewdness stain the pages of my humble chronicle. Other writers of a lower type may write of the loves of Princess Honoria as they choose, and make a grubby penny thereby. Let that not be my fate, O Muse!

For there is no way to tell all that I know of the Princess Honoria and remain within the bounds of decency. Many a time after that, the secretly watching slave-girls stood long into the night, and heard many more sighs and moans, and witnessed many more outrageous lecheries performed between girl and girl, which would have shamed the most shameless quayside whore of Corinth. Yet how to tell more without offending beyond recall the modesty of my readers?

How to tell of how those two wanton hussies, one a royal princess and one a mere slave, spent that whole night devising new depravities, and attaining thereby new and hitherto undreamed-of summits of pleasure? How to tell of the night when they half dressed each other again, but only to augment the delight they took in each other's semi-nakedness, which is always more lewd than pure and unadorned nakedness, as any whore knows? How to describe the slave-girl seating her mistress upon the couch, and lacing the giggling princess into her own high-laced red leather sandals, and clasping a slim gold chain round her slim girlish waist, and applying fresh lipstick to her already swollen and cherry lips, and dark kohl round her eyes, until the hitherto innocent girl, in appearance now as well as in conduct, looked like the most fatal succubus of every chaste man's dreams? And how the Egyptian slave-girl ...

But no, *horresco referens*, I shudder to relate. No more I say, for shame. It would be grievously wrong to detail further acts of such wickedness.

Now my lamp burns low, and the hills of Italy beyond my window are fallen silent for the night, but for the lonely cry of the lych-owl. There I must break off. At my age it is not good to work so late, as I shall exhaust myself. The silent *scriptorium* is growing chilly, and yet I feel a strange and over-rapid beating of my heart, as if from great exertion, and a heated perturbation within myself. Suffice it to say that Princess Honoria, as I have painted, was most shamelessly given up to pleasures of the flesh, to which she gave her exclusive attention; and that these pleasures were equally derived from, and slavishly bestowed upon, both men and women, with all the indifference that is the true mark of the inveterately promiscuous and enflamed temperament. But it would be wrong to dwell further on the princess's private and lamentable practices.

And so to bed; and the Lord keep me from lewd and unchaste thoughts.

13

THE DOOM OF ROME

The following morning: and to return to Honoria.

After the awakening of her lower nature, and while she still enjoyed the vile attentions of Sosostris to the full, it was only a matter of time before this incorrigible nymphomaniac surrendered more dangerously to the charms of a man. His name was Eugenius, and he was her chamberlain. In the midst of the tedious limitations and formalities of the royal court, the princess yielded to the impulse of her nature and threw herself into his arms, more out of a longing for experience and adventure, perhaps, than from any real love for him. Her guilt and shame were betrayed soon enough by pregnancy, made even more obvious by her slim form.

Her mother, reserved and correct in all things, was angered and shamed beyond telling. She had the poor girl instantly confined to one of the darkest, dimmest chambers of the Imperial Palace behind a locked door, and put on a starvation diet such as you might impose on the most disgusting criminal the night before his execution. Honoria's brother, meanwhile, ever vengeful, suspicious, and still without children of his own, plotted an even worse punishment.

One twilight evening, an old crone scuttled into the palace and was led to that darkened chamber. There, to cries of the utmost distress, she performed her horrible craft with abortifacient herbs: tansy and mugwort, asafoetida, called 'devil's dung' from its foul smell, and infusions of boiled pennyroyal. Once these ancient and unhallowed emmenagogues had begun to take effect, and the poor girl's innards felt as if they were being crushed in a giant fist, the old crone had the girl held down and splayed, while she peered and delved and dragged with specula and long, hooked needles. Finally she pulled forth the swollen purple remnants of a three-month old foetus, which she tied up in filthy linen rags and tossed into a pail by her side. Mopping up the copious blood and tissue, she said by way of consoling the girl that the creature would not have lived anyway, for its spine was badly deformed.

Honoria lay in silence for more than a week, her mind moving through blank despair to grief, to bitterness, recrimination, and thoughts of blackest revenge. Even confined as she was, she managed to establish communication with others in the palace and beyond, in return for the promise of rich future rewards. Her plot was no less than to have her idiot brother murdered, and Eugenius, her slave-born lover, placed on the throne in his stead. It is hard to know whether to laugh at her audacity, or pity her naivety in thinking that an empire can be so easily overturned.

The plot was discovered, and she narrowly escaped with her life. Valentinian, in hysterical rage, wanted her killed instantly, and swore he would do it himself, 'with a brooch-pin if necessary'. Galla restrained him, and persuaded him that his troublesome sister would be better sent into exile far away. The chamberlain Eugenius, needless to say, was put to death in the slowest and most horrible way, with prolonged and multiple tortures applied especially to those manly parts which had caused such disgrace to the imperial family. But let us not dwell. Some punishments may be just, but not edifying.

A few hours later, in the middle of the night, there was a knock at the door of Princess Honoria's prison chamber. Her silence was taken as consent. The heavy door was unbolted from the outside, and a large silver platter covered with a cloth of crimson velvet was set beside the girl's couch where she lay. Too young and innocent still to suspect what she should have suspected, she leaned down and drew off the cloth and saw what was there. Her screams of horror were heard through half the palace.

Eventually the princess, broken of spirit and blank of face, was taken from her prison-chamber and led to the women's quarters, where she was dressed and coiffed as plainly as a nun, and sent under guard down to the port of Ostia. Thence she took ship for

Constantinople. And once there, she was kept a virtual prisoner in barred chambers, in a high tower of Theodosius' imperial palace, under the grim supervision of the chaste and unsmiling Pulcheria. Honoria was the only non-virgin among a bevy of dreary chanting virgins.

It was to be twelve long years before the world heard of her again. But when it did – when her extraordinary plan, long hatched in the bitterness of her heart at last came to vengeful fruition – the world itself was shaken to its roots. Ultimately, indeed, the Western Empire was destroyed as much by the vengeance of Honoria as by anything. Never underestimate the power of a beautiful woman, who is prepared to use her beauty in the pursuit of power. As Helen was the doom of Troy – so Honoria was the doom of Rome.

More recently, a secret messenger from the Huns had come to the court of Constantinople from one Bleda, who called himself the rightful King of the Huns. He brought strange news: fat, gold-greedy old King Ruga had been murdered on his throne by a mysterious newcomer from out of the wilderness, Attila, a lost son of the royal house now grown to manhood. Theodosius heard the message and was troubled, and sent the news on to Galla Placidia in Ravenna, for she knew more of the Huns than he did. They were a coarse, half-animal people who had lived peacefully and almost forgotten somewhere beyond the Pannonian borders for more than a generation. But Theodosius was troubled, nevertheless, and felt he had some vague memory of this new name among them. He had heard stories, when a child ...

In Ravenna, Galla received the message personally. Her expression was one that her son had never seen before, and it surprised him.

'What is it?' he said. 'Mother? What is it?'

She looked ashen grey, shocked, angered, and afraid all at once. At first she could barely answer, shaking her head in disbelief. At last she said, 'The Huns have a new king.'

'Those malodorous, slitty-eyed horsemen? Well? What of it?' Valentinian sneered. 'They wear fur jackets stitched from the skins of fieldmice, I heard!'

'They do not wear the skins of fieldmice,' said Galla in a curious, flat tone. 'They wear hardened-leather body armour. Sometimes the skins of wolves, which their boys kill at the age of twelve as an initiation rite, out in the wild, armed with only a single spear.'

'Why are you telling me this?' said Valentinian. He sat back and crossed his arms.

She appeared to ignore him, looking far away, somewhere.

Valentinian felt a spasm of anger with his mother – a not infrequent sensation. She was so … superior. How did she know all this? Who was actually emperor, anyway?

'They are the most dangerous of all the barbarian peoples,' she said.

'They've been living happily on our borders now for three decades without a murmur!' cried Valentinian. 'Probably a useful barrier between us and a whole lot worse out there in Scythia. The Huns are not our enemies.'

'They are now,' said Galla.

Attila sat back and considered all that his spies had told him, stroking his wispy grey beard, his eyes glittering with amusement and quicksilver intelligence. Then he laughed, a short, abrupt bark of a laugh.

How many weaknesses! How many faultlines in Rome's impregnable-seeming carapace!

Galla was still alive, and the power behind the throne in the West. That cold, green-eyed monster, the torment and torture of his boyhood years: she had hunted him across Italy like vermin, and would have killed him like a rat. But now he would return, that little rat-boy whom she would have exterminated. That little nuisance. He would return and she would quake to look him in the eye. His eye, which had seen such things … He would return at the head of an army of warriors as numberless as the stars. The enervated legions of Rome would barely stand and fight against them.

She would see her world brought down in flames. The green vineyards of the Moselle, the wheatfields of Gaul, the sun-warmed olive groves of Toscana, all trampled into dust. The villas of the rich in Campania left scorched and blackened ruins in their wake. The proud palaces and temples of Rome itself, the solemn courts of law, the churches and cathedrals of the Christians, all dragged down and razed to the earth, the common clay earth, their mother, whom the Christians so haughtily despised. All of Galla's beloved empire trampled into ruins by the horses of the Huns.

Let her know. Let her know. It is sweet to know that she still lives, that cold, green-eyed woman. Oh, how sweet to know that she still lives. And that she will live on to see her fate come to pass and her empire fall.

On top of that, her daughter was a slut! He jerked back his head and laughed again. Her son was Western Emperor, and as much of a fool as his uncle before him. In the East, Theodosius was no match for his grandfather, Theodosius the Great. He preferred calligraphy to battle.

How many armies? The Western Army could still command a hundred and eighty regiments in the field, and the Eastern a further hundred and fifty. And the man who commanded them was no fool.

His smile faded.

Aëtius. Almost unconsciously Attila had tried to avoid thinking of him. He didn't want this name on the mental list of his enemies. The others he would bring down and devour with pleasure, as a lion does an antelope. But Aëtius … A man worth killing. A man worth sparing.

'His family?' snapped Attila at his gathering of spies. He turned to a woman who had returned straight from Ravenna.

She looked blank.

'Aëtius,' he rasped. 'The general.'

She shook her head. 'He has never married.'

Attila looked puzzled.

'They say,' said the woman, 'that he still loves Athenaïs, the empress.'

'What has that to do with it? Doesn't he want sons?'

She shook her head. She did not understand, either.

Attila sat back and brooded. The honourable lover. The honourable soldier. The last of the Romans worthy of his respect. His boyhood friend. His greatest enemy. His shadow, his nemesis.

'Where is he now?'

'In the court of the Visigoths. The Court of King Theodoric, at Tolosa. He has offended Emperor Valentinian again by his plain speaking.'

Attila smiled thinly. 'I fear Valentinian will suffer still greater offence before long. And then he will have need of his Aëtius.'

But he understood Aëtius' exile.

Such a man could not but be viewed with suspicion and sullen resentment by the craven Emperor Valentinian. Generals such as Aëtius invariably eyed the purple for themselves: so it was commonly held. Therefore it was with wearisome frequency that news was brought to Aëtius in his campaign tent: there was a plot against him, and he must flee to save his life. Sometimes the news came, so it was rumoured, from Galla Placidia herself. He would go into exile, to the court of the Franks or the Burgundians or the Visigoths, against whom he had fought all his life. Those huge, brawny, red-faced Germanic warriors always welcomed him like a brother, pressing foaming goblets of ale into his hand and urging him to stay with them for good, to ride against Rome and take it for himself. And he would sup his ale and thank them for their hospitality and say no more. When they laughed at him, he merely smiled. And when word came that the imperial court had forgiven him for whatever imaginary crime he had committed, he would mount his horse, bid his magnanimous hosts farewell, ride back south unescorted, and take up command of the Western Army again without a word of reproach.

Such was the man the blue-eyed youth had become. How clearly Attila remembered him, standing solemnly there in the waist-high feathergrass of the steppes, the day he first set eyes on him. The tall, proud, clean-limbed boy, who spent his earliest years in the alien camp of the Huns, as Attila spent his in Rome. When they rode out together across the Scythian plains on those long summer days, all life and all the world lay bright and sunlit before them.

Attila gruffly dismissed his spies from his presence, and passed his hand over his eyes, unfocused, deep in memories.

They had ridden out together one day, he and Aëtius and their two slaveboys, just the four of them together, and killed that monstrous boar, and dragged it all the way back to camp! And now he learned that Aëtius, too, had spent much of his manhood life in exile from his own beloved people.

All humour had gone from his eyes, all sardonic merriment at the absurdity of the world. Surely there was a meaning and a pattern to it after all; and the dramatist of the world was a tragedian.

A sadness like an old man's filled his eyes.

That straight-limbed Roman boy, who had stepped forward with his hand on his swordhilt when Ruga struck Attila across the face, who would have drawn his sword in Attila's defence. The two of them had lain all night on a wagonbed out on the plain for punishment, bound and tied, laughing, shivering, shouting off the jackals ...

Oh, Aëtius.

O you gods. You gods.

Part II

THE BINDING OF THE TRIBES

1

THE SWORD OF SAVASH AND
THE TRIBUTE KINGS

The news spread like a plains fire from the Danube to the shores of the Aral Sea: the Sword of Savash had been found!

Savash was the Hun god of war, and it was told in legend that whoever found his sword should wield power over all the earth.

The tale of its discovery was strange.

A shepherd was out on the plains when he saw that one of his animals had cut its foot. He followed the trail of blood back through the grass and a beautiful sword half-buried in the ground. Fine scrollwork, a sinuous, tapering blade, the like of which he had never seen before. Superstitiously he took it back to Attila, and the king seized his opportunity. Raising the sword above his head, he declared that the Sword of Savash had been found.

One man alone among the crowds did not cheer but stared, and then his usual impassive features took on a look of shock. It was Orestes the Greek. He alone among all those cheering people saw that the sword the king held aloft was none other than the sword given to the boy Attila, by a Roman general called Stilicho.

An act of grossest cynicism? The duping of his own people by their cunning, unprincipled king? Dazzling them with a magical 'sword of the gods', really forged in some imperial armoury in Italy, in the heartland of their enemies?

But no. It was not so simple. The shock on Orestes' face gradually settled into acceptance again.

Attila often liked to murmur the mysterious rhyme, 'Whether we fall by ambition, blood or lust, /Like diamonds we are cut with our own dust.'

Orestes understood his blood-brother of old well enough by now.

Attila proclaimed himself King of all the Huns from the Danube to the Wall of China. He received Indian pearls and eastern silks and Baltic furs in tribute. At night he stood and addressed his people in the midst of their feasting, and told them that their empire would soon cover the whole world; and they believed in him.

A great altar of wood was built, as high as the king's palace. Many animals were slain, and the altar was sprinkled with the blood and fat of sheep and cattle and horses.

In the days that followed, upon hearing the news that spread eastwards over the vast plains of Scythia, many came to visit and pay their respects: petty princelings, rulers over tiny, scattered bands of White Huns from the shores of the Caspian, bow-legged chieftains of the Hepthalite Huns from beside the Aral Sea. From even further east came others who hardly looked like Huns at all, and dressed, you would say, more like bandits than kings. They came on their tough little horses from the lush green grasslands in the shadows of the Tien Shan mountains, and bowed to King Attila, and then they stood again and hugged him as a long-lost friend. He received the same fond greetings from those desert Huns who came from south of the Holy Altai, and the unspeakable deserts of the Takla Makan.

His people's hearts grew large to see how widely loved and known their king was among all the wide-wandering Hun peoples, and they began to guess where he had ridden in exile, and what sufferings he must have endured and what feats he must have performed to have won the hearts of so many. Like a hero from the mythology of the people. Like Tarkan himself, when he performed his Seven Labours to win the hand of the Tanjou of Baikal's beautiful daughter, whose beauty had petrified every other suitor into a pillar of sandstone.

Attila received them all gracefully, and showed them the magical sword, which, kneeling, they kissed in silence and awe. Yet more impressive was the demeanour of the man who held the sword. Those hard tribal leaders of the plains and the mountains and the deserts knew well enough that any charlatan could wave a pretty sword aloft and claim it was the Sword of Savash. But here was no charlatan. Here was a man who radiated such power that it thrilled through their bones as they stood before him, like some wild contagion. This was the half-legendary son of Mundzuk, sent far eastwards into exile long ago. They had heard the tale. And now here he stood, king in his own right, possessing an aura of kingship which made the lesser princelings stand proud with fear and devotion. So the camp of King Attila grew.

White Huns and Yellow Huns, riven with feuding and enmity by ancient tradition, gathered among the tents of the People of Attila, and at his urging, his careful persuasion, or sometimes his fiery oratory, they began to see themselves as one mighty people, united by blood, language and the worship of their ancestors, the heroic Sons of Astur.

The gathering of the scattered tribes turned into a full-scale festival of the people, and went on for days, and then weeks. From dawn to dusk there were games and celebrations, and all evening there was feasting and drinking among the tents of the Huns. In the hot summer night in the shadows there were new liaisons formed between the sons of Attila and the daughters of the princelings, and vice versa. And in the morning many a young maiden's cheeks (though maiden no more) were flushed, and her eyes were cast down in shame, mingled with remembered pleasure; and many a young man's eyes kept wandering from the game in hand to a girl sitting meekly on the sidelines, and many a ball was fumbled, to the huge scorn and mockery of his fellow players.

Attila took several fresh young wives himself from among the visiting tribute peoples, and they said that they were running out of different names for all his children. It was thought they numbered over two hundred, but no one was quite sure. He presided over it all with unshakeable serenity and iron will. To some of his closest followers, to Chanat and to Candac, it seemed as if the whole camp of the Huns was turning into chaos – and at the end of summer, too. Soon they would have to move to their winter pastures, but the people and their horses and herds were so many that any new pastures would be quickly exhausted. The people of Ruga had numbered no more than three or four thousand in all, with as many horses and sheep again. Now they were ten times that number, and the surrounding steppelands were already grazed bare.

The king's advisers were filled with foreboding at quarrels breaking out over pastureland, quarrels turning into blood-feuds and full-scale internecine war. Little Bird, true to form, sang bloody little songs and rhymes to a half-broken lyre to that end.

But Attila's smiling serenity never faltered, as if all this celebratory chaos were merely part of a wider plan whose lineaments lay hidden in his breast. Already his followers seemed to trust him. Even Chanat, spitting in the dust and muttering that no good would come of it, knew in his heart that his king saw further than he – further than any man he had ever known.

'We are too many,' he grumbled. He and his king and a few of the chosen men were standing on a small mound looking out over the sprawling camp. 'There is not enough pasture for us all. We are too many.'

'On the contrary,' said Attila. He smiled. 'We are too few.'

He summoned the heads of the different clans to him and they stood round the mound expectantly. It was time for them to bid him farewell and return to their homelands, but Attila had other plans.

'Those among you who must move to fresh pastures may do so. But they will return to our camp in the spring. This is good pasture when the snows have melted.' He pointed up at the moon, still a sliver in the early-morning sky. 'When that moon has waxed and waned twelve times and no more, I will return.'

He told them nothing else.

His brother Bleda he bade govern wisely in his absence. Bleda grunted and nodded.

He made up a body of a hundred men. He selected his eight chosen men, and also his two eldest sons, Dengizek and Ellak, who looked as pleased as puppies. The other ninety Orestes picked from the ranks. Attila had the ten leaders start drilling their own war-bands as he had drilled them. He ordered his sons to choose two hundred of the best horses from the corral. Each man would have one horse to ride and one pack-horse, carrying weapons, arrows, tents, provisions. He ordered the women to get busy.

For three days they worked tirelessly. The men hunted marmot out on the steppes and brought them in piles to the women round the campfires. The women worked expertly with their sharp little knives, chattering and laughing incessantly but falling silent any time a man came within earshot. The man would hesitate and waver and then walk away uneasily. What did women talk about all day? The women exchanged secretive smiles.

They flayed the marmot flesh from the skin and smoked it strung out high above the fires. They hung the hides likewise in the dry sun, strung up in gaunt leather shapes like decapitated bats. They drew mare's milk, rich and creamy and frothing, and poured it into huge sacks of stiff leather. They simmered goats' milk and poured it into fine cloth bags hanging from wooden posts. The clear yellow whey ran freely down into leather pails at the foot of the posts for making yogkhurt for tomorrow, and with the remaining white curd they made aarul, dried curd cheese that would keep for many weeks out on the steppes.

They inspected the meat store and dismissed the lean black meat with scornful cries of 'Khar makh!' choosing instead the large white cudgels of mutton fat barely streaked with shards of meat, such as are loved by the nomad peoples of all harsh lands, to keep their menfolk alive upon the freezing plains they must ride and through the bitter days and nights they must endure.

The last evening before they left, some of the clan elders sat cross-leggged on the ground round their dung fires, wrapped in their patched old horse-blankets, and shook their heads and mumbled that he was crazy, this one. This was no season to be riding out on some fool's errand, the Sword of Savash in his hand or no. The frost-giants and the ice-giants were stalking southwards from the legendary northlands where there dwelt monstrous white bears taller than the tallest firs. Those terrible giants of ice and frost were covering miles with each stride, freezing the earth beneath huge feet as they came. The People should be fleeing southwards before them, making for the winter pastures. This was no season to be riding out on a war party.

But this one, they said, was no ordinary man. The fire of war burned in his eyes the long year round.

There was little ceremony to mark their going. In the night shamans slaughtered a chosen lamb and cut it open. They took a handful of bloodfilled intestine, a shive of heart, a shin bone and a gobbet of fat and threw them spitting onto the fire for the gods.

Little Bird was near, a clay pipe in his hand and hemp smoke issuing from his nostrils, his flamed eyes shining bloodily in the firelight.

The omens were good. They went to the king's palace to tell him, but he wasn't interested.

He spent the last night alone in the palace with Queen Checa.

Some said they heard them arguing in the night. Some said they heard the shrill, fierce voice of Queen Checa saying she had not borne his weight on her, and then borne the pangs of childbirth for him nine months later, and given suck from her own breast for two more years, for him now to ride off with her beloved young sons on some wild quest and lose them! Those who heard her voice marvelled at how well it carried. How sustained and forceful was the voice of Queen Checa! They listened for the deeper, slower voice of their king, or perhaps for the sound of lashes and blows. But none came.

At dawn Attila emerged and gave one last order. His sons Dengizek and Ellak would not go, after all. The two boys hung their heads in deep gloom, standing outside the royal palace. Then Queen Checa herself appeared between her sons, smaller than they, in her long quilted gown, her hair scraped neatly back. She looked out over the assembled troop and nodded and smiled her firm smile. Her eyes met those of her husband and he turned away.

He ordered the horses into line and rode at the head with his guard of chosen men. Wives rushed out to dab milk on the foreheads of the warriors' horses for luck, and some wept. Others told them to bring back many scalps. Children ran about laughing excitedly, waving sheaves of grass or little wooden rattles, or throwing long blades of feathergrass like spears.

They left in light autumn rain.

After only half a mile or so, Little Bird came galloping up alongside the king. 'So, you ride out without your two fine sons today?'

Attila grunted and said nothing.

'What is it they say in Rome? As I recall, a jest Orestes told me of. Some jest among those powerful, white-haired senators. "Rome rules the world. We rule Rome. And our wives rule us!"' Little Bird pondered earnestly. 'Do you think this is truly the case in Rome, Great Tanjou, my totipotent lord and master? In fact, might it not be the case in all countries and kingdoms of the world?'

Attila said nothing for a while. Then he told Little Bird to get back to the camp with the other women. Little Bird laughed, wheeled his horse round and vanished back over the plain.

When they had gone it was as though the spirit had departed, the hearth-fire gone out in the camp.

Before long it was as the elders had feared. The summer fat of the land was ended, the livestock grew thin and lean, the wind blew colder daily, and then disease broke out: dry scab, mange, glanders killing the asses and the horses and threatening to spread to the people. The cattle reeled at the water courses from mad staggers. Even the sheep and the goats, toughest of all animals, were badged and patched with infestations of lice, their raucous calls reduced to dry, malnourished croaks, drinking in deadly liver fluke at the edge of the fouled autumn streams. There was great dread among the tents that not only would quarrels break out, but so also would the terrible *tarvag takal*, the plague of buboes, which comes, it is said, from eating sick marmot and kills even the strongest man or woman in days.

A man from another clan was killed by one of Attila's men in some argument over a woman, and a full-scale blood-feud was only narrowly avoided with lavish gifts of horses, fine rugs and gold. Slowly the other clans, who had come in such high hopes to worship the Sword of Savash, began to drift away desultorily east and south.

'Remember to return after twelve moons, as your master, Attila Tanjou, bade you!' called Little Bird after the retreating wagons. 'Little Bird himself waits humbly for the master!'

Little Bird took refuge from the disconsolate tribe among the children, whom he loved. They sat around him cross-legged, tiny children with their perfectly round Hun faces and rosy cheeks and wide eyes, while he spun them such tales – of mountains that fought each other by spewing burning molten rock and huge boulders out of their mouths; of mammoths that tunnelled underground as fast as horses gallop, and so caused earthquakes in the world of men.

Then he stopped abruptly, and leaned over sideways in his extraordinary way, touched his ear to the ground, and opened his eyes wide with astonishment. The children's eyes grew wider still.

Little Bird said that he could hear ants fighting, two whole miles away. He sat up. 'Over there,' he pointed, 'on the other side of that hillock. Can't you hear? It is a terrible fight. They are fighting bitterly over who should be king of the hillock. By nightfall many of the bravest ants will be dead.'

The clever children laughed at this nonsense, while the foolish and gullible children looked sad and anxious for the ants. Though perhaps the sad and anxious children were not so foolish after all. Those who think, laugh. Those who feel, weep.

Little Bird told them another story to console them, about a family of mice with whom he was on friendly terms, who were great travellers. They sailed on the Sea of Ravens in seashells, and travelled over the snowbound wastes in winter on little sleds made from blades of grass.

When the children had finally curled up and fallen asleep beside the campfire, Little Bird sighed and took himself away and sat high on his favourite sandy bluff, looking out on the dark sea of grass, and sang:

'When hunger bites us daily and the wind blows from the north,
And the saiga in their autumn coats go by,
And only sickness stays with us,
Then Little Bird the Wise
Sits apart and talks with his only friend, the sky.'

The next morning Little Bird was seen trembling by a dead dung-fire in the early dawn, and one of the women asked him if he was sick.

'Nightmares, nightmare upon nightmare,' said Little Bird, staring fixedly into the powdery ashes of the dead fire. 'Dreaming of snakes again. Snakes coiled about my throat and about my head. About my heart.' He closed his eyes and his voice dropped to a whisper. 'They will be the death of me.'

2

RIDING EAST: MEMORIES OF CHINA

The hundred men with Attila at their head rode eastwards for seventeen days and seventeen nights, crossing the Iron River well north of its marshes and its hundred mouths and passing by the vast flat salt-sown shore north of the Sea of Ravens. Then they turned south.

Already the grasslands were beginning to fail and fade beneath their horses' hooves, and the short golden season of autumn was rushing past, fleeing before the oncoming winter. Deer fled before them like ghostly ancestors, and there were the light tracks of wolves in the sand among the dying grasses. Sometimes they came upon haunting reminders of where tents had previously stood: pale yellow rings in the grass, among windblown middens and scatterings of the bleached white bones of animals. Tattered nomad bands of nameless peoples, perhaps their distant kinsmen, perhaps their enemies, who had vanished into the endless eastern steppes, with no more substance left to them than the shadow rings of their tents in the withered grass.

They came down into a shallow canyon in late afternoon, passing great strewn boulders copper-coloured in the setting sun, filed down a narrow stony path and saw reeds and stunted trees below; the air was cooler and smelt of streams. In a silent valley already out of the sun they passed through a cool green curtain of willows and watered their horses and rested.

The next morning they climbed up out of the canyon on the farther side, through a thin copse of orange pine, the ground strewn with fragile needles and the air full of resin, and they rode on.

At noon their leader called a halt near a high cairn of tumbled stones. The men let their reins drop and their shoulders sank and they sagged in their saddles, and the horses leaned and tugged at the thin grass at their feet. Attila swung his leg over his horse's head, jumped to the ground, walked over to the high cairn and climbed it, as graceful and easy as a child. He pulled off his battered felt *kalpak*, scooped his fingers through his dark shaggy hair streaked iron grey, his mouth set hard in that characteristic, sardonic, world-mocking smile, and gazed out to the far horizon. As far as the eye could see the wind shimmered softly through the sunfaded grass, which billowed like a feather-grey ocean, and beneath his feet it soughed through the little caverns and passageways among the cairn of rocks. To the south, as he squinted into the brightness, the grass looked yellow, and the horizon was blurred with dust where the steppeland finally ebbed away to desert. Far to the north and east, maybe a tint of green, the rich dark green where the silent pine forests started. But maybe not. No man can see as far as he thinks he can, not even a king.

He turned to jump down, and there from the direction they had come rode a single horseman. He remained on the cairn and watched and waited. The warriors followed his gaze. The lone horseman shimmered and came on.

After many minutes the figure grew in size, and then they could hear the swish of the horse's legs through the grass and see the horseman's tattooed face. Finally he stood before them.

'So,' said Attila, jumping down from the cairn. 'Little Bird. The world's madman.'

'It is I,' confirmed Little Bird grandly, giving a little bow of his head. 'Life was dull in the camp. There was a danger I might have lived for ever and grown as old and useless as old Chanat.'

Attila grinned and remounted and gave the order for them to ride on.

Little Bird came alongside him. 'Besides,' he added, 'there was a woman.'

Attila glanced sideways and raised an eyebrow.

'At first it was sweet to lie between her thighs. But soon she became to me a deep pain in the fundament both morning and evening, as if I were passing stools the size and shape of wagon-spokes.'

'A hazard of the amorous temperament,' said Attila gravely.

'But war will bring relief,' said Little Bird.

At dusk in the fading light one of the pack-horses stumbled in a marmot hole. The men instantly drew their knives, their mouths already savouring fresh horsemeat roasted on a slow fire, but Attila forbade them. Little Bird went over to the animal, which stood patient and shivering with pain, fresh dung lying pungent between its hindlegs, a foreleg crooked and resting on the rim of its hoof. The shaman spoke in its ear and stroked his hennaed hand over the horse's fetlock. He murmured over and over words that none who heard understood.

In the morning the horse was healed.

They crossed a desolate plain where the heavy grey sky over their heads suddenly came alive with the cries of wild geese. The cries startled and then comforted them with the sense of living creatures in company with them in this wilderness. The geese passed on and their cries faded away and the air grew silent around again and the men slumped down a little in their cloaks and bowed their heads and rode on. The sky overhead was a darkening grey, a beaten iron shield, but along the horizon was a seam of silver light that seemed to seep in from an enchanted world beyond, as if they rode under a giant lid, claustrophobic, shut off from grace. Their fear grew continually, and their courage grew to meet it. All of them were quite prepared to die, and half expected it, this far from home and they so few in number. But they would go down fighting.

And then, standing alone and many days from its herd and from its native woodland; for no reason that they could discern, they saw an auroch: a massive white bull, one of the wild cattle that roamed freely in the birchwoods far to the north. The mountainous white beast stood like a statue, like a creature from heraldry, amid a pile of broken rocks, with an arrow buried deep in its withers. Again here was good meat for the taking, but the men knew that the uncanny creature was somehow removed from them and forbidden. They squinted and saw that the arrow was of no shape they recognised.

It would not be long now.

Chanat trotted nearer to the wounded animal, which turned and lowered its massive head towards him. He reined in at a safe distance, his right hand resting lightly on the shaft of the spear slung at his side. A full-grown auroch, wounded or not, could disembowel a horse with one swipe of its long, curved horns.

He turned sideways and squinted at the animal a little longer, then rode back.

'Kutrigur Huns,' he said. 'The Budun-Boru.'

Attila looked sharply at him. 'So far west?'

Chanat shuddered a little, as if shaking himself free of some infestation. 'All the tribes are moving west, and have been for two generations. They say that the heart of the world and the high plains will never see rain again.'

Attila brooded.

'Who is this arrow-master amongst us?' sneered Little Bird. 'And what does this rank old goat know of the arrows of the fearsome Budun-Boru?'

Chanat turned on him furiously. 'You will know of the arrows of the Budun-Boru yourself soon enough, when they are stuck in your shivering hide and you are yelping like a spitted puppy!'

Little Bird laughed and rode out of Chanat's range. 'There is truth in the arrow's sting, old Chanat, as much as in the song of a beautiful girl!'

Chanat growled wordlessly at the capering fool.

Attila ignored them both, looking at the unearthly animal across the plain.

On its broken cairn, taking its last stand dying and motionless, no blood staining its fine white pelt, the auroch stood bellowing with rage at the cold plains stretching endlessly away on every side, and then raised its great heavy head and bellowed at cold Heaven itself. Heaven echoed back its roar of pain and nothing changed.

Attila shook his head and said softly, 'Leave it. It is its destiny.' He flicked his reins and kicked his horse forward again. 'It is not any more in nature.'

After the injured horse and the auroch, there was the eagle: a triad of animals or animal spirits both for good omen and for admonition. Do not despair, the spirits seemed to say: the horse was healed. Do not presume: the bull was not healed. And thirdly there came a spirit for ever untouched and unharmed, unattainable in his perfection in the tormented world of men.

The hail came out of nowhere, drumming the plains around them into invisibility. They rode on into it, but then a hailstone the size of a child's fist smashed and broke over the muzzle of Orestes' horse and slithered away in shards of ice to the ground. The horse shook its head and reared belatedly, teeth bared, screaming with pain and indignation. They dismounted and pulled their horses close and took shelter in that pitiful lee as best they could. The din of the hailstorm forbade speech.

A few minutes later the roiling angry clouds passed on and then vanished altogether to the east, and the sky returned blue and clean again. They rode on over the now sunlit plain scattered for miles with bright droplets clinging to the broken grass-stems. Reaching down from heaven to the horizon hung the multicoloured Bow of Tengri, the god of the sky. Away to the west they could see curling snakes of mist steaming off the sunbaked pan, and for many miles as they rode, cloudy and opaque hailstones nestled in the roots of the long grass and crunched under the hooves of their horses, and then brightened and melted in their wake like passing pearls.

The sun burned down on them again and their greased woollen cloaks and their horses steamed with a rich woolly stink, and beyond that the air was filled with the sweet scent of damp, beaten grass and their hearts lightened.

Attila suddenly seized his bow, nocked an arrow and fired it high into the blue sky overhead. Only then, looking up, did his men see the great deep golden shape of an eagle passing over them, and they flinched with horror at the blasphemy of what he had done. But of course the arrow curved and passed harmlessly in the air far below the eagle's flight, many weary lengths short of killing a god. The eagle flew on unheeding, its amber eyes set on other distant things, on mountain ranges they would never live to see.

Their crazed king pushed himself up and twisted in his saddle to look back at the eagle, face full into the sun and aglow in that blazing light, his golden earrings dancing in reflection, his head back, laughing, teeth white and wolfish. He threw his arms wide and looked over his men.

'The people who are born on a smoking shield!' he cried. 'The people who shoot arrows in search of the gods!'

And Astur his father passed away westwards, impervious and indestructible.

At evening they stopped and hobbled the horses. Attila set out watchmen with arrows already fitted to their bows, and they lit dung fires and cooked. The smoke rose in a slow column into the windless night. A lonesome wolf howled in a neighbouring valley, its howl like the voice of the desolate landscape itself. Two whooper swans passed overhead in the twilight, the soft beating of their wings heard over the crackle of the dung fires and the call of the lonely wolf the only sounds in that vast country.

Some of them thought good to make a low windbreak of saddles and horse-blankets, and then to heap up more saddles and blankets into a makeshift throne for their king to sit on at the fireside, a thing that they had never done before. But he chided them and kicked the saddles and blankets angrily away. He scuffed the dusty ground quite flat again with the soles of his battered deerksin boots, and sat crosslegged on the ground in the dust along with the rest of them. He drew his sheath knife, leaned forward and cut a strip of meat from the sizzling haunch on the iron spit.

Geukchu sat close as they ate, which was unusual as he was a man who liked to eat alone, wary, like a dog. When he had finished chewing he took a swig of koumiss and shucked his teeth and passed the flask on and said softly, 'We are being followed.'

Attila nodded. 'By outriders only. It is not the main force yet.'

'How do you know?'

The king took a long draught of koumiss and smiled into the firelight. 'If the main force were near, we would know it by now.' He looked around at his chosen men, each of them with their eyes on him. Orestes sat a little way away whittling a stick, apparently not listening. But he always looked that way. He heard every word.

'Keep your men prepared but do not panic them. In the imaginations of their hearts the Budun-Boru are demons and spirits, evil, beyond explanation, no more to be defeated that a river in full spate may be stopped with arrows – the People of the Wolf, who change into wolves in their very flesh and bone and devour their fellow men by moonlight. But they are men of mortal flesh like any other. Indeed, they are our distant kin, and they worship

Astur, too, and bid each other "Sain bainu" when they meet, and "Bayartai" when they depart. And if you prick them, they bleed.' He signalled for the flask of koumiss to come round again. 'I know. I have had dealings with them before.'

'A shaman: one who knows,' said a little singsong voice nearby. It was Little Bird, tangential as ever. He even revolved around the outside of the seated circle in some self-moved and eccentric planetary orbit as he taunted. 'What a lot you know, my lord Widow-Maker!'

'And what a lot you have to learn, my little singsong fool.'

Little Bird tripped into the circle and took his place beside Chanat. He beamed up adoringly at the old warrior. Chanat scowled down at him. The other men laughed.

'But,' said Little Bird, leaning back and staring up at the still stars, 'the shadowlands ruled by Tengri, Lord of the Sun, and by Itugen, Lady of the Moon, are debatable lands. And the way to the spirits is littered with the souls of fallen shamans.' He looked at Attila. 'It is a bitter calling.'

There was no sound but the crackling of the fire for a while.

Then Attila stirred and said, 'For a long while, I did not know this: I did not know the will of the gods.'

Little Bird said, 'He who presumes to know the will or the design of the gods knows less than nothing.'

Attila regarded him and continued, 'For long I puzzled in my heart over the destiny of our people and over our treatment at the hands of the spirits; how Astur turned us out into the wilderness to be a homeless people and the scorn of all men, despised and travel-weary, dust-blown and starving. There is a people who live in the empire of Rome called the Jews, and they, too, have no home.' He fell silent a while.

'But now I see. We shall gather all the clans and all the tribes of the wide-wandering Hun people, all who answer our call, and all others who will serve under our banners. All our kindred amongst the White Huns of the west, and the Hepthalite Huns from beside the Aral Sea, and even the Budun-Boru, the Kutrigur Huns, whom we have so feared for generations. Perhaps yet others who do not speak our language or worship our gods, but who in their valour or despair will answer our call.'

'I once knew two brothers called Valour and Despair,' said Little Bird. 'Twins they were.'

Attila ignored him. 'Whoever will answer our call will ride with us against the Western Empire. We shall be such an army as the world has never seen, our horsemen as numberless as the sands of the Takla Makan. We shall ride west, and we will destroy Rome and raze it to the ground and every vestige of it that stands. Not one stone shall rest upon another, for they have hated and despised and insulted our people from the beginning. Finally, when our own empire stretches from that far grey sea they call the Atlantic, which is the western border of Rome, eastwards across all of Asia to the very shadow of the Great Wall – then we will turn on our most ancient enemy of all. Our immemorial enemy, generations before the name of Rome was heard of among the Huns. The empire of China.'

The word hung in the air like a curse. Little Bird hissed at it and looked away, wincing. The other men barely dared look at each other. The cursed word. The word never to be spoken. Their nemesis in ancient times. 'The empire to the east', they customarily called it, if they referred to it at all. Never 'China'. That word hurt their eardrums, soured their palates, ached in their skulls even as they heard it. A word under a curse. The rune of ancient catastrophe.

'Our power then will be very great,' he said. 'China will fall, and the whole world be ours.'

The men tried to take in his words, to digest his vision. Chanat said afterwards that he felt as if he was trying to swallow a whole cow.

An empire of the Huns, encompassing the whole world from the ruins of Rome to the ruins of China. It was beyond imagination.

Attila talked to them of their past and of their future, their god-given destiny. He conjured in their imaginations images of once-great Hun cities laid waste by the armies of China in ancient times. For once they were kings, he said, and lived in majestic cities, within a wide northern loop of the Yellow River, in a rich and well-watered land called the Ordos.

'I dispute this,' growled a low old voice.

It was Chanat.

The others drew in breath at his insolence, but Attila smiled and listened. His fondness for the fearless old warrior was very great and he gave Chanat free rein.

'I dispute this talk of cities,' said Chanat. 'We were born on horseback. You know the myths of our people.'

Attila inclined his head. 'Perhaps, perhaps not,' he said. 'But that China is our ancient enemy you would not dispute.'

Chanat pondered, stroking his long grey moustaches, then shook his head and said gruffly, 'That I would not dispute.'

At this Little Bird took from his cloak a strange, battered instrument with a single string. He plucked at it softly and changed the note by bending the wooden frame of the instrument one way or another, from a low drone note to higher, more insistent and mournful tones. And he recited one of the ancient lays of the people from that time, in his hypnotic and haunting voice which was not quite singing and not quite speaking, this little riddle of a shaman who was not quite man and not quite child, not quite mad and not quite sane, and who sat backwards on his horse as often as forwards.

He sang of a great king, Tumen, who gave his eldest son, Motun, to a neighbouring tribe as a hostage, and favoured his second son as his heir. Then, wanting Motun dead, Tumen attacked this neighbouring tribe, but Motun escaped and returned home. Tumen greeted with him with false smiles and feasting, plotting in his wicked heart all the while to kill his own son. But the son was plotting in his turn to kill his own father, and his plan was dark indeed: he would make all his men as guilty of regicide as he, so none could rebel.

First he drilled his men cruelly. 'Shoot whatever I shoot,' he cried, 'and death to any who hesitates!'

Then he went hunting. Every animal he shot, his men shot too. Saiga were stuck like porcupines, wild boar lay dead like giant hedgehogs. Then he raised the stakes. He turned his bow on his own favourite horse, one of the Heavenly Horses. Some men hesitated and he promptly had them executed. Then Prince Motun turned his bow on his favourite wife – again, some men did as he did, and some hesitated. Again, he had those weak ones killed. Finally he turned his bow on his father's most treasured horse. More arrows; none wavered.

Then on a hunting expedition he rode behind his father and nocked an arrow to his bow and shot him in the back. His father reeled in his saddle, agonised, astonished. The rest of Motun's men, so drilled in obedience now that they did not hesitate, did likewise. In an instant King Tumen lay dead on the ground, his body so stuck with arrows that there was no room for one more.

Motun had the remains of his father burned and scattered to the four winds, taking only his flensed skull as a drinking goblet. He became a great king, and conquered and united many tribes. Such were the beginnings of the Hun kingdom in the northern bend of the Yellow River, in the land known as the Ordos.

Little Bird laid down his instrument. 'Many kingdoms have been born out of feuding families,' he said. 'I have even heard it related that Rome was born when a warrior, Romulus, slew his brother Remus.' The little shaman looked at Attila and smiled.

'But the kingdom of Motun did not endure,' said Attila. He scowled into the firelight. 'Though he ruled over thirty walled cities throughout Mongolia and Xinkiang, and our people, the Khunu in the ancient tongue, were equal in pride and glory to the empire of China, and though Motun ruled at his capital, called Noyan Uul, with a rod of iron, upon the Mountain of the Lord, nevertheless they were despised by China. Although the Khunu meant only 'the People' to them, to the Chinese it sounded like Xioung Nu, which means 'the wicked slaves' in the language of China, and they flung this insult in their faces.

'War broke out between them, and the Chinese brought down fierce warriors from Manchuria, and there were many years of war, and treachery undid them. In the end the thirty majestic cities were laid waste, and the proud towers and palaces of Noyan Uul were burned to the ground, and the few Khunu who had not gone to their deaths in battle were sent broken and starving out into the wilderness. Many are the peoples who have been 'abolished' by empires like China. They drifted westwards into the void of Central Asia and were lost for ever.'

He nodded slowly, still gazing into the fire. 'And there we Khunu became a mythical, insubstantial people of the wastes, impoverished bands of wilderness wanderers, tent dwellers, cannibals, so it was said, preying upon settlers' children like vagabond dogs.

Scavengers in sandblown rags and tatters, the offspring of witches and demons of the wind. Well, let them believe it, if it serves to chill their bones.

'They were our fathers.'

So Attila spoke, so the Hun mythology went, and who was to say that it was not the truth? He knew from his boyhood the tale of how the father of Rome, pious Aeneas, defeated by an ancient enemy, fled westwards from crumbling Troy, carrying old Anchises on his broad shoulders. Were not the parallels and echoes uncanny? You heard in those echoes the laughter of the gods.

Then there was Emperor Titus, who destroyed the temple of Jerusalem and drove the Jews out into the world to be a nationless and accursed tribe of wanderers for ever. Just so, like the Trojans or the Jews, the Huns' forefathers had fled westwards from their crumbling cities, whose very names were now lost in the desert sands, but for towering and majestic Noyan Uul. And as the Greeks were the doom of the Trojans, and the Romans the doom of the Jews, so the Chinese were the doom of the wandering Huns. But it is hard to be a wanderer, and a nomad's life is much bitterness and wordless endurance.

Once there was a tribe that appeared in the empire of Rome: the Ampsivarii, they were called, and they were nomads. Tacitus tells the entire story of that nation in two curt, typical sentences. 'In their protracted wanderings, the exiles were treated first as guests, then as beggars, then as enemies. Finally their fighting-men were exterminated and the young and old distributed as booty.' Of the Ampsivarii, we know not a jot more.

It was almost the same story with the Jews. Trajan considered exterminating that entire troublesome and bellicose tribe, stiff-necked and superior and proud in their own conceit as the 'Chosen People'. But surely it would be madness to think you could exterminate a whole people? Then remember the Ampsivarii, now forgotten, along with their language, their customs, their gods. Or remember the Nasamones of the Libyan shore. No, you do not remember them, nor does History herself. They have vanished as if they never were. For once they rebelled against paying taxes to Domitian, and that cruel emperor promptly ordered them exterminated, man, woman and child. When it was done he declared simply, 'I have stopped the Nasamones existing' – as if he were a god! Which, of course, he was: a divine Caesar. So perhaps Trajan could have done the same to those irritating Jews after all. But now the recognised god of the world is a Jewish carpenter, and consubstantial with his heavenly father.

What twists and turns the Muse of History takes, and how the laughter of the gods echoes over our bowed heads.

3

THE FATE OF THE MERCHANTS
FROM PERSIA

In the morning in the first grey light before they rode out, he put them, as always, through lengthy drills and practices with horse and bow, galloping and wheeling in tight formation at his every command. Each troop of ten had its own recognised signal and moved independently. The hundred horsemen could split and gallop, reform and turn in the dust, appearing far greater in number than they really were. Their skill with the bow was already terrifying, their speed breathtaking, and their strength and endurance on that long journey unbreakable.

Likewise, each troop began to take on the character of its commander. The warriors under Yesukai were flamboyant and reckless, as were those under Csaba the Poet and handsome Aladar. They would do well in some wild headlong charge that would terrify the enemy with its fearlessness, and they would all die howling and happy. Those under the three burly brothers Juchi, Bela and Noyan were staunch and dogged, and would make a strong centre. Those under old Chanat were steady and wily, those under Candac similar. They would wait patiently on the wings until the order was given, and then swiftly cut into the flanks of the enemy, without noise or fuss, but with ruthless force and despatch, like the horns of a bull. Those under Geukchu might ride roundabout for miles, might ford some supposedly unfordable river way upstream with artful bladders made from goathides, floating over unseen in an evening mist, and fall on an enemy camp by night, cutting throats before their victims even awoke.

Tough as they were, each day they grew tougher, their minds as

well as their muscles hardening like the plains under the unrelent-
ing sun.

They rode in the louring, stone-coloured light of dawn, past
huge grey boulders nestled in the grass, stained with lichen like
melted coins. They passed a dead yak, grass growing tall from the
eyesockets, flaps of sunbaked hide hanging from the vast bleached
ribcage stranded like an upturned boat hurled far inland by unimaginable storms. Then the sun broke through the clouds on
the eastern horizon, as if from a burning abyss glimpsed through
fathomless deeps.

This was the great Asian steppeland, not hostile or scornful of
the tiny, transient scrabblings of humanity, like the mountains with
their ferocious blizzards, or the destroying, storm-riven sea. It was
filled only with a vast, desolate, silent indifference. In springtime,
leave a spear thrust in the ground overnight and the next day you
couldn't find it, the new grass had grown so high. The Plains of
Külündü: the Plains of Plenty.

So numerous were the antelope and the smaller, lighter cousins of
the forest bison that they covered the plains in a carpet of a million
chestnut hides. In summer they would come to the banks of a river
and drink it dry. Those were the days, the years of God's plenty. The
city dwellers and the farmers would swallow up everything free that
moves on the face of the earth, thought the warriors, gazing out
over those sacred plains with a rapture that was kin to heartbreak
– joyful heartbreak, because they loved so much and what they
loved must pass. All things fall and cease, and nothing passes so
quickly as a happy man's life.

They hunted saiga across the limitless steppes, the vast herds of
those strange trumpet-muzzled antelope which trotted faster than
a man could run, and ran forty or fifty miles in an hour. Their
heads held low, they snuffed up the freezing or the hot and dusty
steppeland air equally through their long and tuberous noses.

As they rode along a low rise, one single antelope stood out from
the herd, eyeing them. It had seen their cloaks fluttering out behind
them in the wind and twitched its nose, snuffing the air strongly.
Its large brown eyes looked curious but unafraid, and then it sprang
forward and veered suddenly into the herd. The great herd and
the small band of warriors broke into a gallop simultaneously, the

horses swooping down off the rise and flying over the autumnal lion-coloured plains.

Naturally Attila had long before sent a few men, Geukchu's troop, the long way round to lie in ambush for the panicked herd. Now they veered out from the hide of the long grass, whooping with glee, came alongside the vast panic-stricken herd and began to kill. The saiga ran faster than their horses but the hunters came in close and leaned from their saddles, their legs brushed and bumped by the fleeing animals, and fired down directly into their necks and withers. The arrows flew deep and entered their hearts. Saiga tumbled dead in the dust, front legs sprawling and snapping under their own dead weight, others skittering into them from behind, sometimes leaping free and rejoining the herd's whirlwind flight, but sometimes tripping and cartwheeling at full gallop into the air, then crashing into the dust to lie stunned, trampled by their fellows or else quickly despatched by the horsemen.

The horsemen suffered, too, in that mad crush, but every moment of suffering was to them part of the glorious game. Their hearts were full and pumping so furiously that nothing hurt them, and they vied with each other in acts of aimless valour. One adolescent warrior, naked to the waist, the handle of his *chekan*, his spiked hatchet, clutched between his bared teeth, leaped from his horse and fell lengthways upon the back of a fullgrown male antelope. As he fell seized the antelope's horns, beautiful, amber-coloured, lyre-shaped horns with deep rings, as he boasted later by the fireside, 'so easy to hold on to'. Then the boy flung himself to one side and wrestled the bellowing saiga to the ground, though he stripped the skin and flesh from both an arm and a leg in doing so. He scrabbled out from under it, took the chekan from between his teeth, and swung the long curved spike into the saiga's skull. He came up out of the dust grinning from ear to ear, with the antelope sagging at his feet like a weighted sack, and held its head up by a sinuous horn, laughing with victorious joy. Desert dust, streaked with his own blood and the antelope's pungent urine, coated his right side from shoulder to shin where the stricken beast had dragged him for a while over the excoriating earth as he clung on to its furious bucking head.

Other warriors finished up similarly coated in dust and blood, or with fresh tattoos of bruises from the hard ground or from flying hooves. Teeth glinting whitely through split lips, roaring with laughter and wild delight, they dismounted and patrolled on foot, killing any wounded saiga with their long knives, as they would wounded enemies on a battlefield. The herd had long since vanished in a great cloud of russet dust that drifted across the horizon. The rest of the war party joined them and there was back-slapping and mockery in equal measure. How few they had killed! What paltry leavings! Why had they taken only the oldest and foulest of the herd? Women hunted better!

They took the choicest cuts and made camp back on the far side of the rise, facing east to be ready to greet the sun in the morning, and dined on raw liver still warm, and broke open the knuckle-bones to suck the soft marrow. They smoked more meat over the fire and gave thanks as the sweet savour rose with the smoke up to the drifting stars. They slept easy and well, dreaming of the saiga herd moving on southward over the plains for the winter, their buff coats whitening in accordance with the coming snows. When they rode on the next day after sun-up, both their panniers and their bellies were bulging.

There was a camel train of traders from Bokhara, bearded, dark-eyed, their faces closely wrapped and hidden. They rode near where the grasslands gave way to scrub and then desert, thinking they would be safer there from encounters with nomad warriors. One of them looked back as he rode; he called out and they stopped. They looked where he was pointing, and each prayed to Ahura Mazda and waited. The savages came galloping across the level grassland towards them and then reined in. Their leader rode close and inspected them. He had blue tattoos on his cheeks and the traces of three thin scars on his wide, sun-bronzed forehead, and his eyes were narrow and cruel. He smiled at them.

The traders were tall men. Their camels were the usual mangy, two-humped creatures but their horses were very fine, with harnesses decorated with charms of turquoise and smoky silver alloys. The leader of the savages asked them what news, and the traders told him, trembling, wondering what method of death he would choose for them. Crucifixion? Impaling?

But the leader waved his hand regally over them, as if he were a king, and bade them good day. He turned back to his company of bandits and they rode on east. The traders looked after them astonished. Then they looked heavenwards and gave thanks to the astonishing and unpredictable ways of Ahura Mazda and rode on west.

'They will never make Bokhara alive,' said Attila, turning in his saddle and looking after them. 'This is no country for traders or merchantmen. The fools.'

They rode across scrubland and desert, 'wild Chorasmia', to the Greeks, and a day later came to remote oilfields where black pitch soaked through the barren sands to the surface, some of the tarpits smoking perpetually. The horses stood and eyed the lakes of oil with suspicion.

Sometimes this pitch ignited of its own accord and burned for days or even years, as Herodotus says it does in the deserts of Parthia. The Persians call it *rhadinake*, and even that clever, sly and untrustworthy people find no use for this black and unctuous pollution. It kills the crops, poisons the air, is death to both man and beast, and it burns without extinction, tall amber flames bursting sheer out of the ground, seen in the starlit nighttime for many miles around. But in daylight it was a very different sight: a black, smoky and hellish place, death to everything that lives and breathes.

Nevertheless, Attila saw some use for it, and without further explanation, had four of his men dismount and gather large leather panniers full of the black ooze, to their disgruntlement.

He urged his men on into that unhallowed place, which lay in perpetual twilight even though the midday sun shone on all the world around. The sun burned only weakly through the pall of dense smoke, the horses lowered their heads and half-closed their eyes and their nostrils. The air was dark and choking, the light sulphurous and smoky. The stench of seeping or burning oil was foul, and there was not a sound but for the soft footfalls of their horses in the sand. There were demons here. At any instant a warrior might feel his horse sinking beneath him, the hushed, leaden air rent briefly with the beast's screams. Man and horse would fall into a lake of pitch, sinking down and down into everlasting darkness, limbs outstretched, mouths open and gasping silently in the blackness, warrior still mounted on his drowning horse, the two of them united in hellish bond, falling for ever to the centre of the dead and midnight world.

Soon after this monstrosity of nature they came across a monstrosity of men. It was the merchants from Bokhara, laid out for them across their path as if for welcome. They must have been captured many miles to the west and brought here. Games were being played. Their evil kin, the Kutrigur Huns, were taunting them, with an eye for the theatrical.

Some of the merchants still groaned alive on their stakes. Chanat dismounted, drew his knife and brought an end to their suffering. He wiped the blade clean on one of their blue silk robes and remounted, looking disgusted. Impaling was a rare punishment among the People, reserved for the most grievous of crimes such as the ravishing of a royal wife or daughter, base treachery or the dishonouring of a burial-ground. But the Kutrigur impaled for recreation, for reasons of humour. They were jackals among men, and, like all cruel men, cowardly as well as cruel. The People of the Wolf.

Chanat leaned from his horse and spat. 'Death take them.'

'Men do as they do,' said Attila. 'It is not the gods who prevent them.'

The line of impaled merchants led them deeper into the uncertain light of the oilsmoke, their horses whinnying in fear, their lungs smarting. At times they thought they saw dark shadows moving through the fog around them, behind them, but they said nothing, not wanting to strengthen their fears with words. They killed some more who hung in the fog dying their foul slow deaths. The Kutrigur had impaled them with great craftsmanship, sharpening the staves to a fine point first and greasing them with animal fat. Then they would have taken their time to ease the point of the stave into each naked captive crouched in the sand, so as not to kill him, the point entering slowly over some time, gently pushing aside the internal organs, the liver and spleen, intestines and stomach and lungs as it progressed. Then the tormentors would cut a deep slice at the shoulder so that the greased stake could slide out again, and they would bind their captive's feet to the stake and his arms behind him likewise so that he would not slide down, and then they would set it upright in the ground, and there the impaled wretch would hang for two or three days before his longed-for death.

A little further on they came to stouter stakes bearing the severed heads of the merchants' camels, the ragged red flaps of their necks hanging down and dripping. The Kutrigur despised camels. The horses they had taken, and the plunder.

When they emerged from that smoky twilight valley and rode over scrubland, some of them broke into a mad gallop to shake off their uncleanness and disgust. Then, abruptly, they reined in and looked up.

On a low ridge of dusty chaparral to the north-east two Kutrigur tribesmen were sitting their ponies, spears held above their heads in defiance. Then they turned their ponies and vanished down the far side of the ridge.

Attila kicked his horse into an instant, furious gallop after them, scornful apparently of death or worse, and reared to a halt on the crest of the ridge and looked beyond. His men came up behind him, and surveyed the shallow valley that lay before them. The two horsemen had vanished over a farther ridge. Below, a huge ring-camp was burned into the dying grass. The Kutrigur Huns were gone.

A few miles further on they came upon further scenes of horror. A stunted thorn in a dry gully, a few last withered berries, deep red as ox-blood. Impaled on the long black thorns, were human hands, raggedly severed at the wrist. They stopped and stared, almost unable to comprehend this new atrocity. Eventually Attila spurred forward and examined the hands. Marmoreal white, unreal, a ragged ribbon of blood and skin around each wrist, they were small hands. Nearby, another thornbush was draped with intestines in grey and glistening coils.

'They are afraid of us,' said Chanat, trying to discern some good. 'They are trying to frighten us off, as if they do not wish to fight us.'

'They are not afraid of us,' said Attila. 'They are testing us to see whether we are afraid of them.'

He gave the signal and they rode on. Most now rode with bows and a few arrows clutched ready in their fists. They had felt a fierce joy when hunting the saiga, and a burning pride in being alive throughout this journey, even in the harshest landscapes. But now they were hunting men, and where men are, there is also the light of good and the shadow of evil, and their hearts were grave and solemn and dutiful.

4

THE VILLAGE

The desert night is always cold, but now the desert days grew cold as well. The wax and wane of one more moon, and the days would be at their shortest, the nights long and cold, hospitable only to witchcraft and the demons of the night.

There was grey gravel desert, and then some dying greenery by the shores of a steel-grey lake. It would be snowing up in the Tien Shan mountains and on the peaks of the Tavan Bogd, the Five Kings. But here, after brief autumn rains and occasional hail, it was dry and forlorn and cold.

The Kutrigur had left other signs for them: dropped feathers, tufts of horsehair caught on thorns, a spatter of blood on a pale-grey rock, like unnatural rust-red lichen, haunting and inexplicable. A deer lay recently slain beside the trail, part butchered but left with fresh meat on its shoulders, a little ragged from the beaks of birds but substantial nevertheless.

'Looks good to me,' said young Yesukai.

Attila shook his head. 'Our kinsmen in their black cloaks do not leave gifts for their enemies. Eat that and you'll soon be as dead as the deer.'

'Ah.' Yesukai nodded, and they rode on.

They rode over desolate saltflats, setting off clouds of little pied birds pecking for shellfish. Stark and solitary greygreen thistles grew out of the crusted earth. Afar off, over the plains, they saw a single round white tent, a nomad ger, flaring like Greek fire against the dark sky. And so onward, eastward ever eastward, drawn deeper into the wasteland as some strong disillusioned men are drawn into self-destruction. They had long since forded the Amu Darya, the Oxus, and the Syr Darya, the Jaxartes, and passed through the low green Hills of Ulutau, and by Lake Tenghiz, and seen the snow-white Tien Shan rise to the south, and passed by the vast still waters of iron-grey Lake Balkhash where monsters lived. In those marshy plains their horses swishing through the long sodden grass set the plovers calling over the wetlands, and startled the coots in the reedbeds; they heard the heron's harsh cry and saw its tufted head among the tufted grassheads. The sun went down in fire through the reeds where they camped, bars of molten copper on the river.

They were weakening with hunger, but each day they came upon those hungrier than they. They rode into the Desert Kingdom, over lifeless saltpans, and into the Kyzyl Kum, the Red Sands, a blistering sandscape spiked with lonely stands of coarse sandyellow grass. They saw occasional oases, gravel deserts, watercourses, herds of haggard horses. The riders bowed their heads in their hoods and remembered that drought is always the nomad's greatest enemy. Why did they ride east into this world of desert and drought? So that they could increase their numbers, and then turn west for the green pastures and gentle woodlands of Europe. Let that day come soon.

In the furrows of the sand and its dunes carved by the hot wind, the sorrowing men read prophecies of long sleeps and sudden awakenings. The sand blinded their pawing horses, which whinnied mournfully, red sand thick in their manes and in their long eye-lashes. Beneath the sands hereabouts, they said, lived a bloodworm that spat acid; headless, eyeless, lurking underground, a thing of horror.

They rode over a high, stony plateau, and in a wide hollow beside a dying lake four bony cows stood disconsolate with withered udders on the hard, cracked shores of sunbaked mud. Some bareboned villagers were sluicing grey water into a trough for a huddle of flyblown sheep with long, scrawny necks, the wool shedding in hanks from their heads and necks from disease. Some of the younger warriors prepared to take the sheep for meat, anyhow, putting arrows to their bows, but Attila stayed their hands.

The people stood and stared, the young naked, the old toothless, the children caked in mud, flies at their eyes and noses, passively awaiting some event from heaven over which they had not even the power of prayer. Their eyes followed these horsemen from another world but blankly and unblinking, as if they could not see them at all.

After being asked about the Kutrigur Huns, which questions they greeted with sullen silence, one or two of them began to speak brokenly, interrupting each other. Their language was strange but Attila understood it well enough.

They said they had been raided many times by the horsemen in black. Their winter stores had been dragged off, their best livestock slain. Some of those evil riders had tipped slain livestock down their wells. Why did they do this? They were not their enemies. Why such cruelty, even to strangers? Surely there was no justice under the sun.

An old woman came forward from amongst the wretched villagers, leaning heavily on a stout stick, her face cracked and fissured by sun and wind like the cracked mud by the lakeshore. She addressed Attila angrily, fearlessly, as if in argument with him already.

'For years we have been at the mercy of that people,' she said. 'Where they camp now, east, down by the river, we are forbidden to take water. Only this bitter lake is ours now, as if the gods made the river for them alone.' She thumped her stick in the dust. 'Did the gods do so?'

'They did not,' Attila said. 'The rivers were made by the gods for all men alike and without distinction. Every land was made for the nomad riders of the world. The Western Lands were not made by the gods to be an empire for Rome, yet they shut out the poor of Asia from their green pastures and gentle woods and guard them as jealously as misers in their caves. The forests of Europe, the plains and the great rivers of Scythia, the mountains of Asia – they were all made alike without fence or demarcation for all men alike and without distinction.' He spoke over his shoulder for his followers as well. 'Remember this when you come into your kingdom, when you look on the great walls and towers and the numberless armies of Rome and your hearts freeze within you.'

One or two of the younger warriors laughed nervously at his words. One or two.

'But that is not the worst,' said the old woman, shaking her stick and setting it in the dust again. She would not let this nomad king go until she had spoken. She demanded he listen to her. 'There is the tribute we must pay them, every eighth day. We must take a carcase that we have hunted, in weight not less than a man, or else we must take one of our own sheep or cows. Every eight days.' She thrust her hand out, palm open and empty. 'What have we left? Four cows, some broken-winded oxen, a huddle of goats, some sheep – aye, and some blowfly with 'em. How can we continue to pay this tribute and not end by paying with our lives? The winter is coming. Already our children and infants sicken with hunger. But they do not care, those people, the Budun-Boru. They are devils – devils born of devils.'

Attila considered, then gave orders for two of the packhorses to be unladen, and he distributed amongst the poor villagers *aarul*, some fat hunks of mutton on the bone and some goat meat. They stood and looked up silently, as if pleading for they knew not what, exhausted, their eyes as dry as dust.

He gave the order for his men to turn about and they rode round the north side of the wretched lake and onward.

As they rode away Chanat said, his voice bitter, 'They will have to break camp and move.'

'The world is wide,' said Attila. 'All the tribes are on the move.'

'And the great tribes trample the little as they ride.'

Attila nodded. 'They will bump into the defences of the empire, as the Goths did before them, and starve and die there in their vast, ragged camps on the banks of the Danube, looking across into the promised land of Europe.'

They glanced back one last time. In the eye of a reddening sandstorm from the south-west, the tattered villagers stood looking after them with hopeless longing, too weak to move, hands clutching the smaller withered hands of their offspring standing by their sides, sheltering from the coming sandstorm in their parents' shadows. Emaciated children naked but for coverings of fine dust, the sun going down on them, the shadows lengthening. And then they would be lost to sight over the rim of the earth as if they had never been.

'The world is as it is,' said Attila. 'And it will not be made otherwise.'

'And yet ...' said Chanat.

Attila wrenched at his reins. Even Chagëlghan seemed to hesitate, looking back pitifully into the sandstorm in some sudden and unequine access of remorse.

'We did not ride out to be nursemaids to the wretched of the earth,' growled Attila. 'Those are not our people.'

'But we could shelter from the storm among them,' said Chanat. 'And perhaps tomorrow ...'

'Chanat,' said Attila with a sigh. He bowed his head so low that his chin rested on his chest. 'Your kingly nobility and magnanimity make my bowels ache.'

'Chanat is as he is,' said the old warrior, grinning delightedly, 'and he will not be made otherwise.' He pulled his horse round once more and rode back into the coming storm.

Little Bird lingered nearby. 'My lord Widow-Maker is growing a heart!' he sang in his piping, childlike voice above the rising wind. 'But have a care, my lord, have a care! The larger and softer your heart, the easier the target for your enemies' arrows.'

They took shelter in the lee of the village huts with their cloaks wrapped round their faces and their heads dropped low to keep out the scouring red sands. But Attila and Chanat and Orestes were pulled into one tattered hut by the old woman with the stick. She shooed them into the darkness of her hut, latched the door and threw some fresh faggots on the fire in the centre of the hut. They sat around it cross-legged in the smoky gloom, listened to the howling wind, and drank the fermented ewe's milk – she called it *arak* – that she passed around in a cracked bowl.

As the fire crackled into life again, they saw she was very old. She still seemed sprightly, though, and her bright little eyes, hard and enamelled like a snake's, still twinkled in her wrinkled visage. Her cheeks were furrowed and crisscrossed crazily with deep wrinkles, like land ploughed in darkness by a lunatic. But when she pulled her shawl back off her head they saw she still braided her long white hair with a few coloured braids like a vain young girl, and they smiled.

Attila passed the bowl to her courteously.

'So,' he said, 'the Kutrigur, the raiders. How many are they?'

She took a long drink and smacked her lips, which were thin and withered with age and the desert wind. She smiled. Then she took another, set the bowl down and wiped her lips with the corner of her shawl.

'How many?' she said. She held her arms wide. 'Many.'

He knew what that meant. It meant there was no word in her language for such a great number.

'For each of us,' he pressed her, 'how many of them?'

She picked up the bowl again, emptied it, and ordered Orestes to fill it up from the leather pitcher in the corner. Orestes looked at Attila. Attila looked amused. Orestes did as he was ordered.

'How many for each of you?' she said. 'Enough.' She cackled. 'Ten of them for each of you.'

'A thousand.'

'Perhaps twenty.'

Attila looked at Chanat. 'Perhaps two thousand, she says.'

Chanat grimaced. 'My lord, we cannot—'

Attila smiled faintly. 'We stay, as you desired, brave Chanat. But do not be anxious. Thorns make strong allies.'

Chanat frowned.

Attila said to her, 'When do they return? The raiders?'

She shook her head. 'It is ours to go to them. In two days' they are due another tribute.' She spat into the fire with impressive force, and the fire sizzled and cowered under her bitterness.

'Two days,' said Attila. 'Then tomorrow we will go and find a carcase for them.'

The old woman looked puzzled.

Attila laughed.

The next day was still after the storm, the high tableland parched and sandblasted, looking like the coat of a mangy wild dog and more desolate than ever. Attila took four of his men, Orestes and Chanat, Yesukai and Geukchu, and they rode slowly eastwards towards the low country and the river where the Kutrigur were camped. It was very cold.

They came down off the high stony plateau onto a flat plain of grey grass dotted with stone cairns like the petrified stumps of trees of some long-vanished forest. The bitter wind keened among the cairns and the rose-grey light of dawn was no more than a chill ribbon of sky on the far horizon. They rode trailing long shadows that flickered and danced upon the grass, and they moved uneasily among the cairns, the memorial *ovoos* of nameless nomadic people, decorated and hung with coloured plaits of wool, scapulae of sheep and skulls of birds, rocks with strange patterns etched into them, whorls and ridges and curlicues, as if the shapes of ancient seashells were trapped within them.

Then there arose on their right hand sharp mountains of dark-grey shale, with late yellow and purple bindweed and vetch still clinging to life in the sunwarmed crannies. High on the slopes of the mountains they saw a file of Bactrian camels crossing from left to right, ruminating on cud as they went. The horsemen stopped and watched the creatures, their big soft feet noiseless on the flat stone, their aristocratic melancholy, their threadbare nobility, enduring here on nothing amid the wind and the stones.

They crossed the desolate grassland and filed down a narrow gully with ominous high shale walls dark and shiny with water, and then out into a wide, shallow valley and there was the river and there by its edge was the largest camp they had ever seen.

They waited until near dusk, when the winter sun was almost touching the dark rim of the world and its blood-red light ran along the horizon. They silenced their horses with gags of thick rope tied round their muzzles and knotted inside their mouths; the horses bucked their heads and flared their nostrils angrily but in merciful silence. Then they trotted them askance and veered round near the camp under the shelter of a low rise scoured up out of the valley floor by the river in some ancient, boiling flood.

They dismounted and crawled to the top of the rise.

The camp was some three or four hundred paces off, and must have numbered a thousand tents or more. The wind had dropped, and they could hear distant cries and the whinnying of horses. There were men walking among the tents, flickering campfires, children running to and fro, women cooking or nursing. Some women were bringing water back from the river, in huge pitchers on yokes across their shoulders. Stands of spears at the corners of the camp had black leather bucklers hanging from them. Beyond, in the gloom, was a corral of many thousands of horses.

A single star shone above, a single wandering planet almost

ahead, over the vast camp. Mercury on his silent course. A flurry of muted black and white shapes downriver was some lapwings taking to the air over the darkening mudflats.

And then another flurry of wings nearby. Yesukai had crawled into a covey of partridges and they had finally taken to the air, as reluctant to leave their warm nests as a hare its form. Their wings whirred in the dark air as they glided away along the ridge to safety. But not before eager Yesukai had nocked an arrow to his bow, rolled over on his back and, still rolling, loosed the arrow at a flying bird. Orestes hissed angrily but too late at the young warrior. Yesukai had learned his bowcraft well and his arrow struck home. The dying partridge tumbled out of the sky, its bright white throat and underwings catching brilliantly the last of the failing sunlight in the west.

Yesukai grinned.

Orestes looked down at the camp.

Attila was already watching.

In the dusk, on the nearside of a camp, a single warrior was looking towards them.

They couldn't see his face at this distance, but he was burly in build and dressed in black or dark colours. He walked a few yards in their direction, uncertainly, narrowing his eyes. He had heard the partridges take to the air, and turned in time to see one of them fall, flashing out of the sky. He stopped a little way out of the camp, stared a while, then turned and went back.

Orestes sighed and bowed his head, cradling it in his hands.

Attila kept watching.

The warrior passed out of sight behind a wide low tent, and re-emerged a few moments later leading a horse.

Attila looked at Orestes.

Orestes looked at Attila.

Both men looked at Yesukai.

'You have eel-shit for brains,' said Orestes.

'What?' said Yesukai, startled. 'What?' And he started scrambling up the slope to see what they could see.

'*Stay – down*,' said Attila over his shoulder, in such a tone that Yesukai stayed down.

Attila turned back.

The warrior had mounted and was trotting purposefully towards them. As he came nearer they saw that he wore black leather breeches and boots, and a black leather jerkin loosely knotted, which showed his thick, powerful arms. He held a spear low in his right hand, the reins taut in his left. His long, straight hair was raven-black against the last of the sun, and his broad high-cheekboned face cleanshaven but for a thin moustache that hung down long and finely combed. His eyes were fixed on the rise where they lay.

Attila scrambled back.

'Mount up,' he ordered. 'Here comes our offering.'

The instant the warrior crested the rise, he was hit from both sides by whirling ropes. There was a danger the nooses would knock each other askew, but Attila and Orestes threw them with split-second timing, one and then the other, so that the two nooses settled over his head and round his throat in close succession before he could cry out. They spurred their horses apart so that the leader ropes tautened round the high pommels of their wooden saddles, and the warrior's neck was half cut through. At the same instant Chanat put an arrow into the horse's heart and it collapsed, its mouth open, but dead before it could bellow out its pain. It hit the grass and tumbled away down the slope, the Kutrigur warrior pulled free and dangling with his feet barely touching the ground, still caught round his neck by the tight ropes. Yesukai rode in and drove his spearpoint into the warrior's heart but it was not necessary.

While the rest of them removed the nooses from the dead man's neck and loaded his hefty corpse across one of their horses, Attila dismounted and crawled back up through the grass to inspect the camp.

Nothing stirred. He continued to watch for some while. Still nothing stirred.

He vaulted back onto Chagëlghan and they cantered away, the slain warrior tied tight across the rump of Orestes' peacable horse, his eyes still open, his head lolling weighty and half loose from his neck, leaking black, bruised blood.

5

THE BUDUN-BORU:
THE PEOPLE OF THE WOLF

It was dark and there was no moon; they rode by starlight only, their faint star-shadows gliding over the still grass and there was only darkness and shadow under heaven. But upon their return, far into the night, there was great bustle, and the now gleeful villagers sang them back into the village by torchlight, the children dancing with delight leaning forward to spit on the Wolf-Man, reaching up little dirty hands to slap and pinch his senseless corpse. Women threw their heads back and ululated improvised paeans to the noble conquerors, and even the ancient priestess performed a few victory jigs round her stick in the dust.

'A little early yet,' murmured Chanat.

They unloaded the corpse, bound it tight to a long stake and wrapped it in heavy hopsack so it would not be eaten by the rats. They raised the stake and lodged it stretching between the roofs of two huts so that the village dogs could not come and tear at it.

'How do you know that others will not come and tear at us in our turn, while we sleep?' said Chanat.

Attila shook his head. 'We were not followed. The Kutrigur will attack us precisely when I want them to – and in disarray.'

Chanat gazed steadily at his lord. He knew his lord was telling the truth, though he did not know how.

They slept.

The next day the villagers feasted them. It was the most pitiful feast they had ever known. They chewed and swallowed slowly, and exchanged looks and their expressions were much moved. They ate strips of nameless meat so dry they thought it would crack their teeth, and sour arak, and morsels of *aarul* cheese they had brought themselves, and they heartily pronounced it the finest meal they had ever eaten. The villagers beamed with pride.

Later the old woman, the priestess, took a sheepish adolescent boy by the hand and led him three times round a campfire whilst murmuring inaudible incantations. At each revolution of the fire she tossed a handful of grain into the flames, and the sound of her voice rose a little and then subsided again.

In the evening when they sat by the fireside Attila asked her what the ceremony was for. 'For a wife?'

'A wife! Is a wife such good luck?' She rocked backward and cackled. 'Maybe. Maybe to bring him a wife, to bring him good luck of any kind – rain on a dry day, a newborn calf, anything, any favour that the gods let drop from heaven.' She eyed them slyly. 'Perhaps you are the good luck he will have. Perhaps his good luck is to see the destruction of our enemies.'

'Tell us what you know of your enemies. Tell us about the Kutrigur Huns, the Budun-Boru.'

The old priestess stirred the fire with a thin stick, prodding stray embers back into the centre.

'By their names you shall know them,' she said. 'They have such names as Red Craw and Black Ven, Snakeskin and Sky-in-Tatters, Pebbletooth, Half-Ear, Bloody Midnight and Hawk-in-the-Rain. These are not the names of human beings. These are the names of demons out of hell.'

Attila jerked his head towards the dead warrior bound to his high stake. 'Demons are not so easily killed as that.'

The old woman licked her lips and grinned slyly. 'Perhaps you, too, are demons, but stronger demons than they.'

She gazed back into the firelight. Her smile faded. She said again that the Kutrigurs were not human beings, they were demons in the shapes of men.

'Let me tell you about that people.' She spat into the fire. 'About that people, and about my own dying people.'

There was a long silence while the old woman called her story back to memory. When she spoke her voice was low and had great authority.

'We believed that we were the whole human race, my people.

159

There were no others. In the time before time, when Naga, the Great Mother, first lay with Ot-Utsir, the Cause of the Years, and bore us out of her womb, her children. When we first encountered others, crossing the great sand sea, we believed they were animals, not like us. Now we know we were wrong. But about the Kutrigurs we were not wrong. They are still not human beings. The Great Mother, on the day she made that tribe, dropped her clay in a bed of evil flowers: nightshade and ivy … bracken to a horse. That is what the Kutrigurs are made of. Poison runs in their veins, snakes nest in their hair. Their nails are claws. They are the neglected offspring, the evil children, of Naga and Ot-Utsir, and it delights them to be so. For evil is like a potent drink. When you first drink it, you are sickened. But after a while you desire more, your appetite for it waxes, and you need more, and then more …

'We ourselves, we the tribe of Human Beings, are afflicted now with the curse of the Kutrigurs. The Great Mother has visited us in anger and we do not know how or why.

'There was a girl—' The old priestess stopped.

She was breathing rapidly – they could see her thin chest moving – and her face was bowed very low. Her fists were clenched tight upon her knees. They waited for her. She raised her face a little and went on.

'In the days when we were still a great people, when we had more horses in our corrals than we could count, there was a girl, a beautiful girl.' She swallowed. 'She was like a bird, a sunbird, and her husband was like an eagle. She … One day she rode out onto the plains with her son, her little red-cheeked son. The boy had seen two summers, two winters. Choro, he was called, for he would have been a great leader. He was too small then even to put his plump little arms right around his mother's waist.' She laughed a sudden, grief-stricken laugh.

They waited.

'Her little boy. He held on to his mother as best he could with his pudgy fists. She took him out onto the spring plains to see the antelope. He loved to watch the animals – all children do. Her husband had said, "Take care. Take care of our son, for he is our firstborn and our only child." And she had laughed and said she would take care. She had no fear, she threw back her lovely head and laughed. She was a sunbird.

'They saw many antelope, and the girl took her slender bow, for she was a skilled archer, and she shot a hare and also a partridge for hearth and home. On their return they saw a lone deer, but the girl did not slay it, though she might have done. She was a sunbird.'

There was another long silence.

'As the girl rode away for home she thought she heard something whistle in the air, and she was afraid. She rode harder, faster, driving her heels into the belly of her pony. But something was wrong. Some horror had come upon her. It was the whistle of an arrow that she had heard. Even as she fled like the wind across the steppes for home, another arrow whistled and struck with a smack.' The prestess smacked her tongue up into the roof of her mouth, and the sound made the warriors flinch. 'The girl felt a pain in her back, but the pain in her heart was greater, a horror in her heart. She called out to her son as she rode but he made no reply. She reached back with one hand, reins bunched tight in the other, and felt for him, and he was lolling back like one dead. The arrow had passed straight through the body of the infant, killing him instantly, and passed on into the girl's own flesh. Not deeply, though deep enough. But it was not her own wound that wounded her to her heart.

'She reined in her horse with a cry that echoed across the steppes like a howling wind, and she endured the unimaginable horror of reaching back and grasping that arrow in her fist, and wrenching it back by the flight out of her own body, and holding on to the dead body of her son as she almost fell from the horse, a wound in her back near her spine. Her dress was sticky with her own blood and the mingled blood of her son, as once their blood was mingled in her womb. Then in life, now in death.'

The weatherbeaten warriors who sat around her sat in silence, and some of their grim faces were furrowed with bright tears.

'She lifted the dead body of her son to the ground, broke the head off the arrow and pulled the shaft from his body, and she kissed his face – quite without expression he was, he had died so young. She should have closed his eyes but she could not bring herself to do so. She passed her hand over his face, over his eyes, and looked into them, and they were wide open but there was nothing there any more. The light had gone out of them. She held him to her breast and wept.

'When she looked up, horsemen were gathered around her. They dragged the dead infant from her and they put a few more arrows into him to make sure, though there was no need. And they threw her to the ground, wounded as she was, and each of them used her as he inclined. Afterwards they hitched up their breeches and spat on her and laughed and took her horse and rode away.

'Such, great warriors, are the ways of the Budun-Boru, the People of the Wolf.'

The fire burned low. The night air was still and cold.

'They are the demons that you say they are,' said Chanat at last.

'They had none to oppose them. They still have not, perhaps.'

'The girl,' said Attila. 'Did she live?'

The old woman smiled a bitter smile. 'Oh yes, she lived. She lay out on the ground a day and a night, and then she rose and found her son's tiny body cold in the long grass and she bound it in cloth and carrying it in her arms she walked all the way back to the camp of her people. And she thought her heart would break.

'But when she came into the camp of her people, and her strong husband came running to her, her eagle, her lion, his dark eyes flashing, his white teeth shining and his black hair flowing, so glad to see her again, and he saw with his own eyes the bundle that she carried in her arms in its bloodstained cloths.

'Then her heart did break.'

She looked up at her listeners, and as one man they looked away, unable to bear her gaze.

'It has not mended from that day to this.'

Their hearts were heavy. In their ears hummed a song of ash.

'The man,' said Attila at last, his voice very low. 'Her husband.'

'He never spoke to her again. He never forgave her. The next day he rode out alone against his enemies, against all pleading. She never saw him again after that day.'

The old woman bowed her head and there was a long silence. At last she shifted and turned, still crosslegged on the dirt floor of the hut. She reached back and pulled aside her cloak and shawl, unknotted her robe and pulled it apart. There in the dying fire-light, beside her bony spine, they saw the puckered outline of an old arrow wound, and they understood. She pulled her coverings round her once more and turned back to them.

She signalled for the bowl of arak, drank deep from the bowl and set it down again. Her eyes were watery in the orange light.

'Surely grief is great in this world,' she said at last. 'And I am not so old as you might think. Old age knocks on some doors sooner than others.'

The warriors took deep draughts of arak. They had nothing to say, nothing to offer. She had travelled far, much farther than they might ever travel.

'And yet are we to rail at the gods, to blame them?' she resumed, her voice stronger again. 'For they made the Kutrigurs as they are, and we cannot know why. There are other tribes as terrible, in the eastern deserts, in the forests to the north. Our eyes are shut to their ways. So should we blame the gods for making us out of the suffering clay and setting us upon the suffering earth, knowing what our destinies will bring each of us? Are we to wail like children and be forever hating and resenting the gods as a foolish child does its parents? Are we to be forever cursing and bewailing our destinies like children? For does not a mother bring forth her child in a welter of blood, both of them weeping, and she knowing full well what grief and suffering and finally what death her child will have to endure? She is, as it were, bestowing these things upon her child as she bears it. And yet do we say wrong when we say that that mother loves her child? Would die for it, if she could?' She nodded and smiled an inexpressible smile. 'Oh yes. There are few mothers on earth who would not die for their children. Such is the way of a mother.' She nodded again.

'There was an old woman who taught me much when I was young, a priestess in her turn, who walked and talked often with Mother Naga. One day we walked out and we came to a young hare pinioned by a younger eagle, which had stooped on it and caught it and now stared at it as if stupid, not yet knowing how to kill. The first hare it had ever caught, perhaps. And so the hare had not been killed cleanly, as a full-grown eagle would do, but was in agony, stuck to the earth by the eagle's claws, and it screamed. It screamed. And I, still a child then, with never a crack in my heart, I turned to the old woman whom I loved, and asked why the Great

Mother did not come and save the poor hare. How could Naga let the hare suffer so? She turned to me and touched my head, and in that moment, in my childish way, perhaps I thought that this old woman was Naga herself. And she said, her voice so soft and gentle as I can hear it even now, she said that the Great Mother was not in some far distant heaven watching over all. She was no cold Queen of Heaven, no lofty princess, no artful, conspiring Cause of the Years. She was here, now. She was with us, suffering. She was in the hare. She was in the hare's scream.'

The old woman nodded. 'I believe it is so.'

The warriors drank and pondered and then slept.

6

THE TRIBUTE, IN WEIGHT
NOT LESS THAN A MAN

Attila was up for the dawn as it broke over the earth.

He stretched his arms and his chest and grinned into the rising sun. It was a good day for fighting.

By that first light he rode round and inspected the village and the wide rocky plateau on which it stood. The attack would come soon.

Orestes was soon at his side. 'So they have not tracked us yet?'

Attila looked out towards the slate horizon. 'Or they have not yet chosen to. Do they even know about us?'

'If they had followed us immediately and attacked us in the night?'

'It would have been glorious.' He turned to his Greek blood-brother and laughed. 'We would have been massacred to a man, of course. But it would have been glorious!'

Orestes turned away, shaking his head.

'But it did not happen. I knew it would not. They will attack when I am ready for them. Not before.' He looked away across the plateau again.

'Get the men up,' he called after Orestes. 'And the rest of the village.'

He ordered the villagers to take their few oxen down to the valley and rope up thorn scrub and drag it back to the village. He ordered the children out onto the plateau to gather rocks and stones, as big as they could carry, 'and no smaller than your own heads', which he had them drop round the perimeter of the village in a great circle. The rocks lay scattered in the dust, only inches high.

'A powerful defence, my master,' said Little Bird, nodding his topknot solemnly, 'if they attack on mice.'

'Go and gather thorns,' said Attila.

'I?' Little Bird's voice was high-pitched with indignation. He touched his fingertips delicately to his chest and gave a sarcastic, incredulous little bow. 'I? Am I a mere shrub-gathering peasant like these dung-bespattered yokels?'

Attila drew his bullhide lasso and advanced on him.

Little Bird went to gather thorns.

Attila had them drag the thorns within the circle of the rocks, and bind them all together with strong ropes in a smaller inner circle, except for one narrow section which he had them rope together separately, to be dragged in and out of its gap like a thorn gateway. He demanded more thorns, stacked wider, higher. They brought more, and then he wanted more. They had to travel further down the valley each time, grumbling, hands and wrists bleeding from long thin scratches, vulnerable with their thin, exhausted, slow-moving oxen, eyeing the far horizon as they returned to see when a line of black clad horsemen would appear up over the rim of the world and their deaths would be assured.

Next he addressed the tired villagers. 'I take it you have spades? Hoes?'

The people nodded dumbly.

'Bring them.'

Attila's men looked at each other doubtfully. Spades and hoes won no wars. They were wielded by mere farmers, drudges of the earth. No nomad ever wielded a spade. Farming was good for the Goths. But not for Huns.

Attila ordered them from their horses and into line and pointed them towards the heap of crude farmers' tools.

'Noble warriors,' he said, 'it is high time you leaned how to dig a hole.'

Finally, when they had dug to the point of exhaustion, there was one more task. He had his men unload some mysterious bundles wrapped in canvas that each carried slung from his packhorse. The villagers saw that each packhorse had carried all this way three long, fire-hardened staves, cut from the northern forests. This was a tree-less country and the sight of so much wood astonished them. But it was not for burning.

He had the children bring pitchers of water from the acrid lake and pour it out to soften the cracked and adamantine earth. When the ground had softened sufficiently, he showed them himself, wielding a long iron-headed mallet, and with a flurry of mighty blows, how it was just possible to drive each stake into the ground at a cruel angle. He had them set the stakes in a circle inside the thorn brake.

'Inside, my lord?' queried his men, puzzled.

'Inside,' he said. 'The stakes are not for burning, but the thorn brake will burn only too well.' He looked away. 'Sooner or later.'

They did not understand him but, grumbling, they did all that he said. This madman, muttered the villagers amongst themselves, had already slain one of the warriors of the Kutrigur, as if to annoy them. You might as well annoy a hornet's nest, or a herd of buffalo, run at them defenceless and naked, waving your arms and hallooing. What hope was there in that? What sense? He had slain a Kutrigur and then returned here for refuge. In their joy they had held a night-time feast, but now in the cold daylight they began to wonder again, and to doubt. He was a madman, with that sardonic smile, that harsh laugh. He loved adversity. Like a shaman who talks backwards, rides backwards on his horse, weeps when other men laugh, laughs when other men weep.

Yet something made them trust his grim-faced madness nevertheless.

He also had the villagers drive what livestock they could into the centre of the thorn brake, and store what fresh water they could in whatever containers they could. And he had them dismantle the wooden walls of one hut and take the wooden slats into the thorn circle and set them up again in the shape of a rough wooden tent, large enough for the villagers, all fifty or sixty of them, to crawl into on their hands and knees, tight-packed as salted fish in a barrel. A crude armour against enemy arrows, but it would suffice.

At last it was done and he nodded with some satisfaction. The thorn brake now stood as high as a man, sometimes higher.

'Yesukai,' he called.

The eager young warrior rode over.

He nodded at the thorn brake. 'Jump it.'

Yesukai patted his horse's neck and hesitated. 'My lord, it is too high. And the staves …'

'Then take it at a gallop.'

'But I cannot gallop over those rocks.'

Attila nodded and smiled. 'Quite.'

After a meagre breakfast the next day, Attila took Geukchu and Candac aside and spoke to them quietly. Then he sent them off with their twenty men, and the entire troop of one hundred packhorses, and all but twenty of the warhorses. At this even his most loyal warriors looked dismayed and bitter. Not only must they dig holes in the earth, like ignoble farmers, but now, it seemed, they must fight on foot, their beloved horses taken from them. They watched for a long time as Geukchu and Candac and his men hazed the horses far out across the plateau towards the south, and finally over the horizon and were lost to sight.

Attila kept his own, of course. He mounted his beloved, ugly, tireless skewbald, Chagëlghan, and his closest men mounted likewise. He and Orestes rode out ahead, with Chanat and Yesukai behind them carrying the slain Kutrigur warrior, still bound to the long stake, slung between their horses.

'We will be back before noon,' he called to his men and the anxious villagers. 'So will the Budun-Boru!' And he laughed.

They rode across the grasslands and through the ominous high shale gully and then out onto the plain, heading for the river. They did not halt, though the other three warriors felt their stomachs churning, their hands sweaty on their reins and bows, their scalps and their upper lips beading with sweat, their hearts hot and strained in their chests. Surely they would die now, today. But they had thought so before, under his command, and they still lived.

They walked their horses slowly and steadily across the plain towards the river and the vast encampments of black tents smoking sullenly in the still early-morning air. Both men and horses could smell more men and horses, dung smoke, the presence of the tribe. They crested the last rise, the last possible place of refuge and cover, where Yesukai had startled the partidges into the air. Then onward and downward to the edge of the camp, feeling as exposed as infants. They tried not to grip their bows too hard.

A crude ceremonial way led down the slope to the camp. They skirted it and rode around. The way was lined with stakes, and on each stake was impaled a human head. Kites and crows were feeding on them. Everywhere there were totems of witchcraft, crucified birds nailed to crosses, figurines of feather and fur, eyes hollowed out from wooden masks, mouths agape and crying out in silent horror. Chanat eyed the totems and sucked in his breath through clenched teeth. Such evil would not wash away for generations.

The Kutrigur set out no watchmen, such was their power and reputation. The four horsemen were almost in the camp before anyone noticed. And then one or two men moved silently across their path, reaching for their spears, looking more puzzled than anything else. One or two called out angrily, Who were they? How dare they ride into their camp uninvited? One nocked an arrow to his bow but Attila turned and looked at him and shook his head and the bewildered warrior let his bow drop.

At the heart of the camp was a wide, dusty circle, and the greatest tent of all with a high central tentpole cut from a single larch. They stopped and waited, and soon enough a man stepped out of the great tent, still wrapping a richly embroidered blanket around his shoulders. He stood tall again and looked at the four horsemen. He had a nose flattened by a terrible blow, heavily hooded eyes, and a face pockmarked by some old disease. His face was without expression, as befits a chieftain.

'Who are you that dare invade my domain?'

'We come from the village,' said Attila, jerking his thumb back towards the high plateau to the west.

'You lie,' said the chieftain. His brow darkened. 'We have tracked you for many days from the west. You know it well. Why have you come to that village now? Why do you stop there? What is your purpose? Tell me, before you die.'

For a time the strange bandit king returned no answer. And then at last he said, 'My answer would not be within your understanding.'

A ripple of disbelief at such insolence went through the gathering warriors.

The Kutrigur chief looked around. Most of his men were mounted now, bows in hand.

Attila, too, glanced around. The circle about them was not yet complete. He spoke again. 'We bring you our offering, our tribute. A fine carcase.' He smiled grimly. 'In weight not less than a man, as you have stipulated.'

Turning his horse, he grasped the hopsack that lay draped over the slain warrior and snatched it off.

A gasp of disbelief ran around the circle. In that moment, before the disbelief had transmuted into fury and vengeance, Attila kicked his horse into a violent gallop. The other three did likewise, Chanat and Yesukai letting the stake with its burden of bloated corpse fall to the ground in ignominy.

The four were already galloping among the black tents before any of the Kutrigur warriors had overcome their astonishment and marshalled their anger enough to act with sense. And then they were in pursuit.

Attila dragged spears from the ground as he rode and pulled down tents into adjacent campfires. His men did likewise, leaving a trail of scattered wreckage behind them. They galloped through the tents as a hare runs through the grass beneath the jaws of a predator, zigzagging furiously to left and right, never allowing their pursuers to follow a neat, straight line. The air was filled with dust and enraged cries and the thunderous galloping of dozens—of hundreds of flying hooves, and the arrows began to whistle. The four crouched low in their saddles and no arrows found their target. It was as Attila had thought: the Kutrigur were numerous and cruel, but not greatly skilled. It was a relief to know, as another arrow whistled and smacked wide into the side of a tent as he passed. A woman ran out of it, screeching like an angry fowl, and their pursuers were slowed further by a mother's fist shaken angrily in the faces of their horses, their path strewn with fiery obscenities.

Finally they were free of the camp and galloping across the grassy plains to the narrow gully and the high plateau, the pitiful protection of the village and the thorn brake. There was now no ducking and weaving, but a gallop as straight as an arrow's flight for home, their pursuers not two or three hundred yards behind. Occasional arrows zinged around them but nothing slowed their mad gallop, and nothing could speed it, either. Their squat, fearless horses were at full stretch, with their thick, muscular necks outstretched into the wind, their lips drawn back over their teeth, their legs moving in so fast a flurry through the dusty air that they could not be seen or reckoned. The Kutrigurs came on, but the gap could not be closed.

The four horsemen galloped into the gully and up the narrow slope, between the high dank sides, the drumming of their horses' hooves and their own wild shouts and cries echoing off the walls and about their maddened ears, and they began to whoop and holler with glee. As he galloped, Orestes fitted an arrow to his bow and, almost as if for recreation, or in a spirit of pure inquiry perhaps, curious as to whether it could be done, he half turned in his saddle, pulled the powerful bowstring back to his chest, and bent low to sight it. When the first of their pursuers appeared at the end of the gully, jostling clumsily with each other to come first through the narrow gap in bellowing pursuit, he let fly the arrow and the sound of it thumping into a warrior's chest reached his ears even as he galloped away.

The narrow defile rang with the cries of the dead man's comrades as he toppled from his horse and fell in their path, his wrist tangled in the reins. His horse reared out of control and the others barged into it, and heeled their horses over its rider's prostrate form in their insatiate fury to get at his killers. The sounds of screaming horses and jostling men squeezed into so narrow a gap echoed off the high walls, as four raiders rode onwards.

Suddenly Chanat's horse tripped among the grey rocks scattered treacherously over the high plateau, lying concealed among the grey grasses as they fled amongst the *ovoo*s where the wind soughed and sighed and the funerary pennants fluttered. His flying horse stumbled and buckled forward, the sound of its breaking cannonbones echoed in the clear air. As it fell it revolved, it seemed, in a perfect circle over and over, its rider flung far clear into the grass and landing on his back with a thump. The other three were already a hundred – two hundred – yards off when they realised. They jerked up their reins and stopped and wheeled.

It couldn't be done.

Chanat raised himself painfully from the grass where he lay on his elbows and shook his head clear.

The Kutrigurs were at full, crazy gallop, not four or five hundred yards away, a little uphill. Chanat lay almost halfway between them and his king, who would get to him only moments before the enemy.

It couldn't be done. Chanat would die.

If they came back for him they would all die.

It couldn't be done. It would be madness.

Chanat got unsteadily to his feet, rubbed the heels of his hands in his eyes and looked down the grassy slope at the horde of approaching horseman. His three comrades saw him tense and he stood very still. Then he turned his back on his approaching enemies and looked up the slope towards his old comrades. He raised his right hand and he was steady now, all shock and unsteadiness gone. He threw back his grizzled old head and the copper torc strained tight around his strong, muscular neck and the sun flashed on his broad copper-skinned brow and he smiled. Then in one swift movement he turned away from them, drew his sword and held it two-handed above his head, roaring his last defiance at his enemies and death and all the world.

The Kutrigurs howled down upon him.

It couldn't be done.

Attila, Orestes and Yesukai drove their heels into their horses' flanks and pounded back down the slope to meet them. Three against a thousand.

Arrows should have rained down upon them now, but the Kutrigurs were coarse and unskilled warriors, as they had seen, and could barely gallop and shoot at the same time. The horde held their spears low and leaned forwards eagerly in their saddles and came on.

The three skidded to a halt beside Chanat and Yesukai leaned down, off his saddle and seized him round his chest, under his arms, and with a terrific heave pulled him up. The old warrior kicked out in rage and Yesukai's horse almost toppled sideways under the double load, fighting furiously against the pull of the earth. Attila and Orestes drew their horses round and glanced back. Only a few horses' lengths between them now. The very air was deafened with cries. Some of the lead warriors were at last nocking arrows to their bows, others drawing swords, pushing themselves up high in their saddles to land the final fatal blows.

The two fired off a bunch of arrows as they turned and galloped away uphill. The Kutrigurs were almost on their horses' tails. It was impossible that Yesukai should escape them, his horse burdened with Chanat as well. But they must try. They could not be defeated here now, not with all the world still left to conquer.

Attila slashed out and cut the warrior across the chest. He had almost pulled alongside them, his sword arm raised. He tumbled into the dust at blinding speed, his riderless horse continuing to gallop alongside them with its tongue lolling from its foaming mouth. The Kutrigurs' horses were not so hardened as theirs. But still, it was impossible that they should survive this. They were almost surrounded. More Kutrigurs were surrounding them, some of them smiling. They would take their time. Some cantered easily uphill and still kept pace with their own exhausted mounts at desperate gallop. They would be taken alive. They would be kept alive for many days. They would be half flayed with great skill by the Kutrigur women, then bound and laid across anthills out on the steppes, to be devoured by a million tiny mouths over several days.

Yesukai's strength and pride knew no bounds. Chanat sat behind him now, and they both fought, from horseback, slashing to left and right. The Kutrigurs mocked and veered and laughed. None seemed to carry lassos. But soon they would be brought down. It was a game to them. Soon they would end it.

Suddenly, with bewildering speed Kutrigurs started to fall back and go down. The air was torn with horses' high screams and filled with belches of dust. Meaty thumps, and then, above those sounds, the whistle of arrowshafts in the air. Ahead of them, the doomed four saw a line of horsemen sitting their still and patient horses atop the rise, firing arrow after patient arrow, motionless otherwise, their aim sure and steady, finding a target every time in a pursuant warrior's chest.

In the camp Little Bird had grown hysterical, talking of snakes again, and Csaba had ordered the troops of Juchi, Bela and Noyan, the three rocklike brothers, the sons of Akal, to ride out on the few horses remaining in the thorn corral. It was their steady troop of men, a line of unmoved thirty, who now fired their arrows undaunted into the approaching horde.

173

The four on their three horses galloped into them with their hearts aflame with pride in their people and their fearless comrades. The line parted magically before them and they rode on through. The land levelled out across the flat plateau and away in the distance they could see the village with its meagre thorn brake. The three brothers and their men behind them continued to fire with murderous accuracy, quite expressionless, their horses still and steady beneath them, and the Kutrigurs, reeling in ferocious confusion before this onslaught, slowed their horses and stopped. Men cried out and toppled, horses jostled, the slope was already strewn with their own dead. They howled in fury.

And then they began to fall back.

The brothers and their men waited until the Kutrigurs were in full retreat, then turned and cantered back to the village after their king.

The four and then the thirty slowed their horses and walked them carefully over the strewn rocks. The thorn gate was dragged open and they rode in through the narrow gap between the last of the staves, now set bone hard in the dry cold ground, and the gate was pulled shut behind them. They fell still gasping from their horses, bowed down, doubled up, reins still in their hands, laughing. The horses foaming with sweat, saliva drooling from their lips, leg muscles trembling, but never panicking, never sagging with despair. Not for them the rolling eyes and flicking ears of highstrung berber steeds with their prancing gait and glossy beauty. The horses of the Huns endured.

The men were gasping and laughing, all except for Chanat, who stood a little apart, scowling bitterly.

Yesukai lay stretched out in the dirt on his back. 'The gods rode with us today,' he gasped. 'By my horse's arse they did.'

Attila fought for breath, too, as one of the village women used a wet rag to clean the blood that ran from his left shoulder.

'They did,' he muttered. He looked over at Chanat. 'Did they not, Chanat?'

Chanat harrumphed.

The men laughed.

'And you, sons of Akal. "Akal's trident", we should call you. You did well.'

The three taciturn brothers looked as pleased as they ever did.

'Right.' He clapped his hands together. 'The tribe will be here soon. And this time they will not be turned back so easily.' He looked up and scanned the low hills away to the south. 'Geukchu and Candac and their men ... ?'

'We have not seen them, my lord, since they rode out this morning.'

'With the horses,' added another.

He nodded. 'Good. Then to your stations.'

7

A FEW YARDS OF GREY DESERT

Attila, Chanat and Orestes sat their horses behind the thorn brake, looking out.

Across from them lay the straggling ruins of the once prosperous village. They had herded what livestock they could into the thorn corral, and the silent villagers sat with them. The rest of the livestock remained outside and would soon be slain by their attackers.

'When I was a boy,' said Chanat softly, 'I dreamed often of a glorious death on some bright battlefield.'

The other two looked at him curiously. Chanat was not a man much given to reminiscence.

'My brothers and I,' said Chanat. 'Four brothers I had, and I have buried them all. We played at being warriors, out on the steppes the livelong summer day. And we all dreamed likewise. As a man, I outgrew such foolish dreams. But now in old age – though the battlefield looks hardly as bright and heroic as it did in my boyhood dreams – those boyhood dreams of a battle-death come again.'

Attila said gently, 'Our boyhoods made us all.'

Bare under heaven lay the sorrowful village of that dying people. Not a spot of shade, not a tree. The flat salt desert only, and the wretched dying lake. The occasional passing herds too far and fleet for them. Their best hunters all long gone, hunted into extinction themselves by greater, crueller hunters. The cold winter to come and then a little grass in the hollows, perhaps. An existence pitiable, threadbare, a people clinging to their own lives by a thread, to the skin of the parched earth like fleas clinging to a dog's hide. To be brushed away indifferently at any moment and indifferently by a greater power, into oblivion, into empty air.

'A small thing it is we fight for,' muttered Chanat. 'A few yards of grey desert.'

'We fought for a smaller thing this morning,' said Attila. 'A single life.'

'You were fools.'

Attila laughed. 'Your gratitude embarrasses me, Chanat.'

The old warrior coughed and spat.

'I knew you'd resist,' said Attila. 'I actually had my hand on the butt of my lariat, ready to knock you cold.'

Chanat eyed him.

'You're such an old mule, you would have started arguing – in the very shadow of our enemies.'

Chanat grunted. 'It's possible.'

'And then we would all have been killed.'

'As I said, you were fools.'

Orestes said in his quiet voice, his hands clasped, his clear blue eyes still fixed straight ahead across the empty plateau, 'Do you never do anything foolish yourself, wise Chanat?'

'Only when a woman's involved,' growled the old warrior. And he stalked away to the other side of the corral.

Attila and Orestes exchanged smiles.

They shared a flask of water and wiped their mouths.

The cold blue sky above them. A stillness. All the world waiting. Only the goatbells sounded in the oppressive silence as the animals moved and grazed among the scrub, happily oblivious. Death was coming.

'This reminds me of many times before,' said Attila. 'This waiting.' His forehead was beaded with sweat.

Orestes nodded. A runnel of sweat ran down his own forehead and over his nose, despite the coolness of the day. You never conquer the fear before a battle. He swiped the sweat away with the back of his hand.

'The time we fought on foot on the green plains of Manchuria,' murmured Attila, 'because our horses were sick, do you remember? And the time we fought the forest kings, who wore wreaths of leaves for armour?'

Orestes smiled his faint smile. 'And when we stood at arms beside the Yellow River, and you fought with a spade because your sword was broken.' He shook his head. 'So much fighting we have done together, have we not? And now it is come to this: a flyblown village beside a dying lake, in a land not yet given a name.'

Attila brooded. Then he said, 'There was a time in Italy, when I was still a boy and a hostage with the Romans, when we came under attack from Romans. They wanted me dead.' His lips curled as he said these words.

'But other Romans saved you.'

'There was one good Roman. A young officer.'

'There are good Romans, then?'

'One or two.'

'And the boy in your uncle's camp? Aëtius?'

Attila said nothing.

They drank again.

'Before I came to you,' said Attila, 'you and your sister, in your Apennine cave and then in that haunted valley.'

'I have not forgotten.'

'Nor I.' His voice was soft and low.

'Four will fight for the end of the world,
One with an empire,
One with a sword,
Two will be saved and one will be heard,
One with a son
And one with a word.'

There was silence, and then Orestes said, 'There is much that we do not understand.'

'There is much that we will never understand,' said Attila. 'But war is a great teacher.' He touched his hand to the hilt of his sword, his beautiful inlaid sword which had been given him by a Roman general, and which he had shown to his people as the Sword of Savash. They had believed. Did he himself believe? Who can say? Who can say what a man like Attila truly believed?

He nodded towards the far horizon.

Orestes looked, and it seemed to him that the horizon itself was astir. As if it were smouldering, and the smoke was dust. He wiped the sweat from his face again.

'An ordinary raiding party would number only a few dozen,' mused Orestes. 'That is no few dozen. That is no ordinary raiding party.'

'Two thousand will come. They want revenge. And we want them all to come.'

Orestes let out a long, hissing sigh. 'You're crazy. With all due respect and that, my lord. But you are madder than a monkey's tail.'

Attila said nothing for a while, his flint gaze set on that distant, smoking horizon. His eyes narrowed, his earrings flashed in the sunlight. He said softly, not turning, 'With respect, old comrade, we want them all to come, so that their camp will be left unguarded.'

And then the People of the Wolf came howling in.

They came howling in with an animal music which grew louder and more terrifying as they approached at full gallop. Yowling and yikkering, whooping and screaming, they came riding out of the dust across the plateau. They erupted in a thunder of hooves and drums, spears held aloft, arrows already notched to bowstrings.

The old priestess had underestimated when she had said that there were a thousand of them, maybe two.

Many wore next to nothing, and what they wore was purely decorative, for they had taken time to dress themselves for the killing. Their womenfolk had decorated their warriors further, with great care and pride, and sent them off into battle with much dancing and ululation, bidding them come back covered in the blood of their enemies or else their own. 'Let no man come back to us unbloodied!' the women sang.

Now they rode down upon this insolent little band of nameless and unknown enemies. They were decorated with scars and weals of paint, with dots and lines scratched out at needlepoint by their women, ink poured drop by delicate drop into the oozing cuts. Dressed in feathers and furs, their reins were hung with the severed heads of their enemies or any other they had happened upon, knotted by their own hair. They rode bedizened with offcuts of Chinese silk and the bloodied vestments of slain priests and the incongruous floating muslin veils of maidens, from ransacked cities, now similarly bloodied and soiled and wrapped round thick wrists or powerful biceps as spoils of war and emblems of victory. Bracelets of hares' feet and capes of buffalo hide were tied at their throats. Wolfskins and wolf pelts being of great totemic power, the highest warriors among them wore headdresses of wolves' heads, jaws set perpetually agape, and necklaces of severed wolves' ears. Others wore fur kalpaks stuck with the dyed antlers of deer, and long tresses of captured women's hair tied vainly into their own.

Their faces were tattooed and gaudily painted with white and ochre and red, cheeks and foreheads patterned crimson with fearsome devices drawn with knifepoints dipped in the blood of beetles crushed in mortars by their women. Upon their broad hairless chests were etched grinning suns and moons and blue faces with writhing snakes for hair, and upon their dusty backs were bloody handprints slapped by their fellows. Their horses' flanks were decorated with birds and fish and bright yellow ochre chevrons and reddish handprints, some printed from real hands severed from the bodies of their groaning vanquished.

Some wore the dark blue turban-cloths of slaughtered Persians artlessly wrapped round their heads or throats, some wore rawhide helmets stuck with the horns of bulls or saiga, embossed with strange designs of occult power. They clutched bunches of arrows in their fists, and clenched more between their filed and sharpened teeth, for some of them were cannibals. And some had coloured their lips and around their mouths a brilliant carmine red, to that end as if to suggest to their enemies that there were others lying dead already, as if their mouths were still laced with blood from the last massacre, where they fallen on the slain and drunk wildly.

Thus they came howling, and from behind their pitiful thorn brake Attila and his men saw that some among the enemy rode perversely naked but for bangles and bracelets straining round their thick wrists, spurring their horses onward with sparkling anklets of costly looted jewellery, like murderous mounted whores. Some wore nothing but leather belts round their waists, circled with hatchets and daggers and scalps tied thereto by the bloodcrusted fronds of their own hair. Further scalps and heads festooned these, and they clutched evil curved picks and lariats of crude nettle-rope, their very flesh stuck with shards of broken glass, bright beads, jewels. Some were already in a state of excitement, panting and with eyes half closed as they approached another slaughterous climax.

And Attila's men behind the thorn brake knew how they would die if they were captured alive, in what foul manner, and how slowly.

Such was the legion of thousands that came howling down upon them that day, their appearance and noise abominable, drumming up clouds of dust through which they erupted terrible and demoniac. And behind them came many of their women and older children, readying themselves with little knives and daggers for the final despatches to be made upon the groaning battlefield after the fury of battle was done.

Among them came also the witch Enkhtuya.

Attila's little army looked out aghast at this monstrous horde and tried to assure themselves that they had faced worse in the past and triumphed – though just for the moment they could not recall when. They steeled themselves as best they could and trusted to their king.

Orestes glanced sidelong and saw Attila with his bow gripped in his left hand, his face raised, that old sardonic grin flickering about him even now; that laughter in the face of death, as if to lose like this were no loss but, against such absurd and impossible odds, in this nameless wasteland, with a final shout of laughter for your last gasp, a kind of despairing victory.

Orestes shook his head. 'Lose the smile, in Hades' name,' he growled. 'You're making me nervous.'

'I was just thinking,' said Attila with equanimity, his smile growing broader by the second.

'Thinking what?'

'I was just thinking: imagine how the legions of Rome will react to a sight such as this, to this legion of howling horribles. They have faced many enemies, but they have never faced anything like the Kutrigur Huns in full rampage.'

Orestes shook his head. 'First things first,' he said. He plucked up his first arrow from the ranks of them stuck in the earth at his feet, and nocked it to the string.

'Not until I give the order.'

'Yes, my lord,' muttered the Greek with a certain sarcasm.

Attila nodded towards the horror rushing on them in fury and dust. 'Observe.'

The Kutrigur had galloped easily over the featureless plateau beaten flat by the years and the wind and even the pitiless sun. The miserable huddle of their foes stood behind their contemptible thorn brake, less than a hundred in number, peering out over the rim like marmots peering out of a burrow. There was laughter amid the howling, and some of the warriors bit their lips bloody in their excitement.

'Now,' said Attila.

The front rank of the Kutrigur horses had come galloping among the rocks strewn on the hard, unforgiving earth, lying almost camouflaged in the pale desert dust. One, a single horse, took a tumble, and the rest slowed and reeled upward and began to step carefully. Their enraged riders beat them with lariats, belts and whips, but the horses could no more gallop through this slew of rocks than a camel can gallop over sand dunes. Warriors coming up behind drove their horses onward in an unabated gallop into the stalled front rank and they began to cram powerlessly together.

Attila raised his right arm. His eighty men watched him, not their enemy.

He waited. Then he saw one warrior strike out at one of his fellows, who veered sideways and almost fell from his horse. He slammed into a third warrior, whose horse bucked with indignation and then came down painfully on a rock, its rear leg hobbling.

Attila dropped his arm. 'Now!' he roared.

The eighty bowmen were gathered round only one side of the thorn brake. The Kutrigurs in their red rage and incompetence had not even encircled them, but packed together in one jostling, milling band.

'They have no experience of attacking a fortified position,' said Orestes.

Attila nodded. 'Not even one as pitifully fortified as ours.'

The arrows came at their appointed rate upon them, each bowman firing a dozen a minute, arcing high into the eternal blue sky and then falling down through the air and down through helms and hauberks and cuirasses of oxleather, through brain and flesh and bone. They fell like rain. A thousand arrows fell upon the Kutrigurs in the first minute, by which time hundreds were wounded and at least a hundred dead. Horses reared and rampaged, biting each other in their agony and madness.

At last, from somewhere behind the ranks of the chaotic beleaguered horsemen, came a voice of authority. Somewhere the old, grim-faced chieftain, with his pockmarked cheeks and nose battered flat, was giving his orders. The flanks of the jostling horsemen began to move out, and the warriors to separate. Those on the left flank began to gallop after all. Gaps appeared between them. Arrows began to fall from the sky and hit the dust. More and more failed to find their target. The horsemen scattered further apart, found their space. And then all began to gallop. They thinned out and moved, faster and faster. Not towards the thorn brake, over the treacherous slew of rocks, but round it. They set up a warcry and moved as fast as dust-demons round the brake, and the eighty men's arrows missed their whirling targets more and more. Then the Kutrigurs began to nock arrows to their own bows and fire back. Their discipline was poor and their marksmanship little better, as had already been divined by testing. But so many, firing so prolifically ... Their arrows began to tell.

Attila nodded grimly. He had expected as much.

He ordered his men to keep low and keep firing.

Through the pell-mell and melée of dust and galloping hooves, they glimpsed further Kutrigur warriors lassoing the last of the livestock, the droop-eared goats and the skinny-ribbed cattle, and dragging them to the ground and killing them. They set torches and burning brands to the huddled huts of the village and flames roared into the sky.

The villagers huddled in the centre of the thorn brake in their tent of leaning wooden slats and clutched each other in terror and silence. The old priestess's lips worked furiously with incantation, though none could hear her words over the sound of the furious battle, the cries of men and the screams of horses, and the endless thump of arrows into the thin wooden slats over their heads.

The galloping Kutrigurs also began to drop arrows down onto the livestock inside the thorn brake, and the few horses that remained. The villagers watched the horses' agony in an agony of their own. There was no shelter for them, nothing they could do. Now they understood why Attila had given the order for most of the animals to be driven off earlier, to some place of safety, some green and innocent valley beyond the horizon, far beyond the reach of men and their falling arrows.

Two of Attila's warriors fell back with arrows in their chests, for while the thorn brake was a good horse barrier it was a poor barrier to arrows. But it was all they had, all they could muster. Now the galloping Kutrigurs began to learn, and instead of arcing their arrows into the air, fired them directly into the thorns. A few picked their way determinedly among the rocks and assembled at the perimeter of the thorn brake but they were easily brought down by arrows or long spear-thrusts. Others went crashing into the ditch dug by the Attila's grumbling warriors – it was roughly but effectively covered by stretches of canvas strewn with sand – and were similarly finished. But the ground had been too hard, and the time too little, to make of the ditch a proper defence. It was enough to break the legs and bring down the riders of a few front-running horses, but no more. Attila had inspected it earlier and muttered, 'Not up to Roman standards, but it'll have to do.'

Now he ordered his men to drop to the ground. Just at that moment, Yesukai reeled and spun round, clutching his upper arm and bellowing in anger: there was an arrow straight through his arm. Chanat leaped to his feet again and ran to him, in obedience to no order but to look to Yesukai.

The warriors lay flat on the ground and fired as best they could through the thorns, but now the difference in numbers was taking its toll. One of Attila's men suddenly reared up – he had an arrow straight in the top of his head. He half turned, then his eyes rolled upwards to the whites and he fell dead in the dust.

Many Kutrigurs lay dead beyond the thorn brake, but many more came on, vaulting over the corpses of their comrades as they rode. The defenders' bow arms, though as hard as steel, began to tire. Each draw of the string was like pulling yourself up by one hand from an overhead branch. Each warrior had fired a hundred times or more. There were arrows remaining in store, but the archers themselves were only flesh and blood. And the Kutrigurs, like jackals, scented blood and injury and came closer.

Some slowed their horses and still tried to trot through the field of rocks but were quickly shot down. Others, however, did something no Hun warrior ever did willingly, and it came as a surprise. They dismounted, dropped to the ground and began to make their way across the mere hundred yards or so to the thorn brake on their stomachs. Hatchets, daggers, clubs and short stabbing-spears clutched between their teeth, they crawled zigzag on their elbows and knees like an army of lizards. They clung flat to the ground among the strewn rocks and were hard to hit. Attila's men rolled low and fired out at them but the target was small and too often their hard-drawn arrows only clattered off the shielding rocks or skittered over the dusty earth and ceased.

Some got close enough to lash out with long lassos, with ropes hooked and barbed, and managed to drag sections of thorn brake clear and came crawling through. The sharpened staves within might stop warriors on horseback but they could not stop men on foot or crawling on reptilian bellies. Then they stood and came running in, naked and howling, weapons held above their heads. It became as desperate a face-to-face battle, on foot, as Attila had foreseen.

'Aladar's men!' he roared out across the circle. 'To my left! Hold that gap!'

The men rushed to attack the Kutrigurs breaking through, and all was chaos and dust.

Seeing that the battle was reaching its endpoint, old Chanat cast aside his offensive weapon, his bow, the weapon of hope among the Huns, and instead drew his old sword, its dulled edge nicked and serrated by six decades of unforgiving blows. Attila glanced across and saw the old warrior standing proud and looking out over the thorn brake and stiffening himself against the coming onslaught. And the king turned aside and for a moment could look no more, not at Chanat, not at anything.

Then he drew his sword likewise and waited.

A naked savage came at Chanat, jabbing at him with a short stabbing-spear. Chanat swept his sword low. The savage stepped backwards, yikkering like a monkey, his spear held out low in defence, and Chanat stepped towards him, raising his arm for a second right-handed swipe. At the last instant he turned easily on the ball of his right foot, spun in a swift semi-circle and stabbed backwards from this new and unexpected angle, close in to his enemy's exposed left side. The old warrior stood straight, pulled his sword free of the dead man's ribs, and turned to fight again without looking back at him once.

And there was Orestes, fighting two at once. Chanat tripped one of them, knocked him to the ground and cut his head off. The Greek fought as silently as a cat, and perhaps with the same pleasure.

Chanat was injured now. He fought on, his neck wound bleeding afresh with each mighty stroke he gave, longing for rest. But there would be no rest on this battlefield before the grave. 'Then let it be,' he growled. Another Kutrigur turned and fled, and one of Aladar's men put an arrow in his back and he came down.

Chanat approached his king, covered in dust and blood, his neck slick with blood, his leather jerkin ripped almost from his broad chest.

'Geukchu and Candac,' he said gruffly, jerking his head. 'You sent them away with the horses. And for reinforcements?'

'Of a kind,' said Attila.

'Then where are they? If they come not very soon they come too late. And we have need of their fresh strength.'

'It is not fresh strength that they bring,' said Attila. 'On the contrary. They are coming back with old weakness.'

Chanat scowled and muttered bitterly that this was no time for riddles and runes: 'Riddles win no battles.' His king only raised an eyebrow, then turned to drive his sword deep into the ribcage of a Kutrigur who had vaulted the loosened brake, slipped between the staves and came running at him with teeth bared like a wolverine.

Behind the crawling Kutrigurs, the mounted horsemen heard another order go out from their cunning old chieftain – no man remained chieftain of the Kutrigurs for long without the keenest and cruellest cunning. Then some passed burning brands along their lines, and others broke away and collected arrows from a flatbed wagon; women passed them out, smiling and chirruping. These arrows had shafts tightly wrapped in resinous reeds, the kind that do not freeze or die beside the marshes, however icy the weather. Some were also dipped in oil from the desert oilbeds, and once lit from a burning brand would not be extinguished until they had burned out. The Kutrigurs lit these fire-arrows from handheld torches, smoking flambeaux held aloft and fluttering like victorious pennants, or else lit them from the blazing huts of the village itself. Leisurely taking careful aim, they began to fire them down upon the thorn brake. Instantly the dry thorn brake was ablaze and burning merrily.

Flames exploded before Orestes' and Attila's faces and both men fell back in an instant, Orestes staggering a little.

It was as Attila had foreseen. Once the thorn brake had been fired, their best line of defence was its momentary flames, and then the staves. The brake would soon fall apart, lying a tattered and black smoking ruin, and the Kutrigurs would be through on foot. And then this little band of warriors and adventurers, so far from home, would be slain with ease, no matter how valiantly they fought.

Arrows still flew. Another warrior, one of Aladar's men bearing the brunt of the attack where the thorn brake had given away, fell back and went walking slowly across the compound towards the centre where the terrified villagers crouched. He cradled the flight of white feathers that nestled up into his stomach, walking slowly, carefully, nursing the feathers as if they were a baby bird. Another arrow, two more, struck him as if randomly, insolently in the back as he walked before he fell and lay dead.

Among the villagers huddled under their wooden slats, the sound of weeping was heard.

The first horses had stumbled and fallen into the ditch outside the thorn brake, their hooves dabbling at the empty air, their lips drawn back over their long teeth, whinnying. They had scrabbled desperately to clamber up the crumbling sides of the cruel, half-concealed barrier before the thorn brake that now towered above them, and there they and their riders had been shot at close range. But now the ditch was half filled by the dead and dying, and the thorn brake was aflame and falling into ruins.

Now mounted warriors came up close and fearlessly to the brake, just the other side of the choked ditch, and lashed at its last remnants with their long lariats, catching the thorns and dragging them away. The ditch filled with horses and men, footsoldiers taking axes to the fire-blackened staves and splintering them into pieces, and the finest of the Kutrigur cavalry riding in, still fresh for battle.

'Aladar!' yelled Attila desperately. 'Get your men over here. Hold this gap whatever happens!'

Aladar and his men sprinted across the circle and did more than hold the gap. Aladar fell on the lariat ropes with his dagger and cut them, and his men fell to their knees in the very shadows of their enemies' rearing horses and fired arrows straight up into the horsemen. One Kutrigur half slipped from his stumbling horse, but regained his feet. He drew his long, curved sword and faced Aladar. Aladar ran at him sidelong and with a single backhanded swipe of his sword took off the top of the man's skull, which spun away through the air like a bone dinner-plate. The man stood stock still, his eyes wide, astonished. His brains oozed over the top of his opened skull like grey porridge bubbling over the rim of a cauldron. Aladar spun on his heel and cut back across the man's stomach, opening his belly. The doomed man remained alive long enough to see his own seal-grey guts slip to the ground before him, like a mass of writhing eels. Then he fell dead upon them.

Nearby, Yesukai passed his hand over his face and his chest heaved, and fresh, bright blood seeped from under his arm. The arrow had penetrated further than it seemed.

Orestes pulled further back from the collapsing furnace of the thorn brake and looked at Attila, the whites of his eyes shining in his soot-blackened face. He said nothing. What was there to say? They had fought their way through war-torn Italy together when they were yet boys, evading Goths and Romans alike. They had buried a third child, Orestes' own flesh and blood, his beloved little sister Pelagia, and had walked on unbeaten. They had escaped a Roman legionary city and crossed the Danube under fire. Since then they had fought across Scythia, and as far as the wide, sandy shores of the Yellow River and across the emerald green grasslands of Manchuria. At other times in their long brotherhood they had fought across the parched plains of Transoxiana, and in the mountains and the precipitous passes of Khurasan, against the might of the Sassanid Kings. And they had fought in strange and unholy battles amid the ruins of the Kushan Empire, and sometimes they had fought for Indian princes and at other times they had fought against Indian kings, and they fought for both gold and glory. And now it had come to this, in a land, as Orestes said, not yet named. They had faced poor odds before, but none so terrible as this. The day was at last against them.

Attila knew what Orestes' thoughts were, and the thoughts of all his failing men. He turned and strode among them, his sword whirling and flashing over his head, his stride that of a conqueror. He proclaimed to them in a voice that carried even above the din of battle that this was not how it would end. This was not his destiny, to end here, nor was it theirs. Their destiny was still to ride against Rome and to destroy it, and then to ride against China. For all the world was theirs. He said that he had heard word of it from Astur the All-Father, and it would not end here, and not now. And though each and every warrior knew well in his heart that this was exactly where it ended, and that their time was come and they would go down fighting amidst this blaze of thorns, under the arrows and blades of the Kutrigurs, nevertheless, at the same time, somehow they still believed in him.

He shouted a brief command and instantly his weary but well-drilled men did as he ordered. They abandoned the broken line of brake and staves and moved backwards. Now, to huddle together in a desperate last stand about the wooden tent of slats would apparently have been the best sense, but there they would have made a good, single target for the Kutrigurs' murderous arrows. Instead Attila's order was that each gather into his own small troop of ten, or however many of that ten remained alive, and fight as a mobile unit.

It was a cunning stroke. The Kutrigurs were unable to fire their arrows into the mass because there was no mass, and they might well hit their own. As they came riding in, yelling and whooping over the smoking ruins of the thorn brake, they were obliged to attack each small unit separately. And as they attacked one, they themselves were savagely attacked on the flank or rear by another. It was a military tactic of small extent but great effect. The strength and swordsmanship of Attila's men, and their fanatical comradeship towards both each other and their visionary king took a terrible toll, and the bodies of Kutrigurs piled up at many times the rate of their own. Though none but one man there knew it, the tiny units of Attila's men were fighting like miniature Roman legions; and against the milling, bewildered, clumsily close-packed cavalry of the Kutrigurs, they were proving just as unbreakable.

Smoke and dust filled the air, and cries more like those of animals than of men. A weariness descended over the fighting crowd, slaughterous drudgery of stab and despatch, stab and despatch. How much longer could they go on? It would be weariness that killed them, not the valour or strength of their enemies. It is almost always thus for a warrior. It is tiredness that kills.

Attila and Orestes and his closest men fought back to back near the eastern edge of the circle, trying to draw in towards the centre. But their attackers kept coming. They couldn't move, couldn't reposition. It was all they could do to stay alive.

Attila cried a warning, and Orestes turned and saw a Kutrigur almost upon him, a tall, lean fellow with his long hair scooped upwards and cemented with white clay, his face splashed and printed with fresh blood, his beribboned spear raised. Orestes held his longsword out horizontally and made as if to sweep it sidelong into the warrior's belly. The warrior pulled up, lowered his spear and held it out two-handed and vertical in an artless blocking stance. Thus he could break his attacker's stroke and then swiftly turn his spear, even if the shaft was broken, and drive it into his side. But Orestes had his adversary just as he wanted him. He was making one of his favourite moves, in his usual, expressionless silence, as if practising swordplay with a friend.

The moment the warrior's spear tilted downward into the defensive, Orestes changed his stroke and in a single fluid movement he swept his sword-blade up over the warrior's head, switched the position of his hands on the hilt even as the sword flashed through the air, and then brought it back down, left-handed and with punishing force, across the back of his adversary's legs, slicing through his hamstrings, his muscles, and halfway through the bone.

He drew the sword free and straightened up and held it right-handed once more. The bewildered warrior's legs buckled as if the muscle had been stripped out of them entire at that lethal stroke, and he sank to his knees in a pool of his own spreading blood, still not understanding what had happened, what had gone wrong. He would never understand. But the gods had given the nod that day, and granted death his request. For death makes the request regarding every man, each and every day. And the day dawns when the gods give the nod to death for each and every man.

Orestes drove his sword into the man's torso and pulled it free again. He planted his foot in the small of his back and booted his lifeless body into the burning thorn brake.

It had been more like an execution than an even fight.

But they were losing. No matter how ferociously they fought, how bravely and with what murderous skill, it was certain that they should lose. A dozen of them lay dead already; two or three times that number bore scarlet wounds. Their weariness almost overwhelmed them even as they fought on, unyielding. Their enemies were numberless: for every howling savage they killed, two more took his place. And the day wore on.

Attila still strode among his men, marshalling them, ducking random spear-thrusts, impatiently swirling and cutting a man almost in half at the waist when he came at him, snarling, as the king was trying to order his men to turn their other side. He roared to them and then they took heart from it and fought more bitterly yet. But they were losing.

The sun was going down at last on that short cold winter day, and still they fought, warriors becoming no more than unreal, flame-rimmed silhouettes against the sunset, puppets of the gods in lethal shadowplay. There was a nightmare beauty to the field of blood: the sky of fiery orange, warriors groaning and buckling, falling back into their comrades' arms and dying there, warriors crying out curt battle laments before leaping into the fray once more to take what lives they could before being cut down and sent below in their turn.

High above, against the enflamed sky, a skein of wild geese passed over, black shadows likewise against the setting sun, and some warriors stopped amidst the carnage and looked up at them and could think of nothing, no words to express what they felt when they saw those silent blackwinged forms pass overhead distant and serene heading west into the flaming dying sun.

Three things happened in quick succession. Chanat groaned, turned away from the line of battle and took shelter amid the handful of his fellow warriors. Attila, before his own men's horror-struck eyes, dropped his head and clutched his chest. Then he dropped his sword as well, and reeled a little, and as he reeled, they saw that he had been hit by a black-feathered arrow. It was no minor wound to be battle-dressed, patched and forgotten. The arrowhead was sunk in between his ribs, though not on the heart side, in dense chest-muscle. Attila broke the shaft off and threw it away, closed his leather jerkin over the wound, knotted it and stood upright again.

Almost at the same moment, there came a weird far-off sound, muffled and eerie in the dust-choked air. The fighting slowed, became hesitant, dreamlike. One Kutrigur stopped in mid-swipe and half turned. He could have been killed in that instant, but the sound came again, and his adversary – it was Yesukai, drenched in blood down one side from shoulder to thigh – stopped likewise and looked blindly into the east.

A third time the sound came, an unaccountably mournful sound which rumbled though the air and the ground itself. The Kutrigurs ceased fighting altogether, and at their rear their old chieftain turned and stopped still. It was as if some unseen god had given the order that battle should cease. The field fell still and waited.

8

THE CAPTURED, THE WOUNDED
AND THE DAMNED

The dust drifted and passed away. Low fires still crackled and burned from the huts of the village, but the thorn brake itself was gone, no more now than a charcoal perimeter to the fighting, like the boundary marker to some complex and murderous game.

The air cleared. The sky above was a deepening velvet blue stuck with a lone golden planet.

The Kutrigurs and their enemies looked the same way and saw that a distant fire rent the horizon. It was not a great fire, but great enough to be seen, to the east, some five miles off, where the Kutrigurs' camp lay. Against the deep-blue sky, black smoke rose high into the cooling air, like smoke from a furnace, like black smoke from the accursed oilfields of the wild Chorasmian shore, blotting out even the distant purity of the single glow hung like a lantern in heaven.

Attila's last ally. Black fire.

Up a low rise, perhaps half a mile away, came shuffling a sorrowful line of people. Not an army of noble warriors come to his aid in the hour of need, in recompense for some act of heroic comradeship long ago. Their rescuers were, as he said, marked not for their strength but for their weakness: ancients with bound and skeletal hands, women roped together with hemp ropes of their own making, children draggled and nervous. As many as a hundred of them, perhaps more, terrified, held at spearpoint.

The deep moan of the horn came again, and it was Geukchu who blew it. He and Candac and their troop of twenty men now also showed on the skyline to the east in the growing darkness, mounted, flanking their prisoners, roped and shackled and dejected. The horn that was sounded was an immense crescent of ivory, yellow and cracked with age. It was the Kutrigur priests' sacred horn, dug from the ground generations ago, the hollowed-out tusk of some ancient animal whose bones had appeared out of the ochre dust in some crumbling cliff of limestone and whose offspring, it seemed, no longer walked the earth at all.

The Kutrigurs stared long and hard at the sight of their own people in chains. The old chieftain's eyes were not strong, not in the failing light. But many among his warriors strained and thought they could see their aged fathers and mothers among the wretched captives, or their sisters still too young to come to battle with their little curved knives, their wives nursing their infants, the infants wrapped in their mothers' arms, or the toddlers holding their mothers' hands. Ruthlessly roped together at wrist and ankle, while the twenty mounted warriors who flanked them held their spears levelled and unwavering towards their captives' chests and throats. They had the prisoners tightly circled in perfect, disciplined formation, and any who tried to break ranks and run would have been instantly skewered. Their baleful guardians sat their horses still and silent, like those who will do just as they promise to do. A mere twenty! But more than enough for the purpose.

Curse them. Curse these intruders who had outwitted them, outflanked them even in the heat of battle, sent out a secret detachment behind their backs, and fallen on their own defenceless camp as the men were away fighting.

Some of the younger and more impulsive Kutrigurs ground their teeth and whirled back towards their enemy for one final merciless assault, and the instant they did so their leader responded in kind. That fierce fighter with his blue tattoos and ragged topknot, whom they had picked out long ago but could not get near, or getting near, could not get away again alive. As the weary made to attack again, to ride in and finish these wretched brigands and insolent trespassers in their domain, that tattooed leader raised his sword in his right hand. At the same instant, as if in mirror image, as if there were no time or distance between them, the leader of the twenty horsemen on the hill raised his spear and prepared to drive it into the body of the nearest rope-bound captive. The captive, a thin girl in her teens, pulled away and cowered.

The chieftain of the Kutrigurs saw it all, and roared to his men to be still. The girl was his daughter.

An impasse settled upon them all.

The sour-faced old chieftain looked long towards the rise where so many of his own people stood in ropes and chains. He thought of the great camp beside the river that they had left that morning in such hot blood; it now, he doubted not, lay in fire-blackened ruins. His livestock must have been slain, his best horses taken and driven off, and the rest stuck with arrows and dying with thirst, mouths agape, lying on their swollen sides kicking their legs in slow agony by the winding river's edge. For a moment the blood ran hot again through his thin old veins and he thought they should ride on and finish their enemies regardless, letting their old and their young go as sacrifice.

A sacrifice willingly made for the death of our hated enemies, he brooded. Our infants? There are more where they came from. But you, our enemies? He turned back and regarded the exhausted, bloodied men behind their pathetic ranks of staves. You dogs of cowardice and treachery, you vicious rats of men. The chance to destroy you may come but once.

But it would be no good. His men would turn on him in their fury and grief, and he would be finished as a chieftain and killed.

He must find some good in this. He must act the chieftain in this dark hour, or his men would be like wolves to a stag and rend him.

Slowly he walked his horse towards the battle line. He carried no weapon, only his wooden staff. His men parted before him. He stopped before the wreckage of the thorn brake. His warriors all fell back. The enemy leader had remounted his horse to meet him. His right side was drenched and dark, but he sat still and straight and did not waver. His horse was a grubby little skewbald with a fierce eye. It was a fighter's horse. But the old chieftain knew that by now. He knew that these few dozen men were fighters such as he had never encountered before – God's curse on them.

The two leaders faced each other.

'So,' said the chieftain, 'you attack our women and slaughter our children. You put our suckling infants to the sword. This is how you fight, how you win your battles.'

'Your eyes grow dim, old man,' said Attila. 'Look again. Those may be your ways. They are not ours. Your women and your children still live, unlike many hundreds of your finest warriors.'

'You spawn of a—'

'I am a merciful man,' said Attila. 'What shall I signal my warriors to do? To kill all your women and your children in your sight? They will all be slain before you can gallop that far to stop them. It will be the work of a few heartbeats to slay them all. My men are fast workers.' He smiled. 'But they have no wish to kill the defenceless and weak. They are merciful as I am merciful. Let us parley.'

'You are a devil.'

Attila shook his head. 'You cannot parley with heated blood. Perhaps you need to rest after the exertions of battle, old man, and then we can parley. But remember your women and children on the hill yonder; as shall we. Until you are ready to talk truce, we shall take care of them.' And he smiled again his wolfish white-toothed smile, folded his powerful forearms across his chest and tossed his head back high.

'I need no rest,' growled the chieftain. His face was dark with anger. He fixed his glowering eyes upon the stranger's yellow eyes and said, 'What is your name?'

It was a sign of weakness among all the steppe peoples to surrender your own name first; an admission of weakness. But Attila was ever scornful of such customs, as if he well knew where true strength and weakness lay.

'I am called Attila,' he said, 'son of Mundzuk.'

The chieftain narrowed his eyes. He had heard this name before. He had heard great things of this name. Even further east, among the mountains, there had been a bandit king . . .

'And your name?'

The old chieftain steadied his restless horse beneath him. 'I am called Kizil-Bogaz,' he said, 'Red Craw. Chief of all the Kutrigur Huns.'

'All?' repeated Attila mockingly. 'All that remain. Look around you. You cannot defeat us. Already half your men lie dead, stuck with arrows like hedgehogs. Already the desert rats and flies devour them. Look out over your dead army. Will you see the other half slain likewise, and your own power blown away like a dead thorn in a gust of desert wind? Look over my men. I have a hundred men, no more, no less. How many lie dead?'

'How many?' The old chieftain knew the answer well enough. He had neither need nor desire to look again. He knew the evil arithmetic of this battle. This overbearing bandit king had lost no more than a handful. But as for his own people – another such battle and they would be finished. They had never known such attrition. This morning he had ridden out with two thousand warriors at his back. Now, littering the stony ground, and piled up in stained heaps within that fatal circle, as many as five hundred lay dead. As many again had fallen back and lay in the gathering gloom, tending arrow wounds, sword cuts, broken limbs, as best they could. There was no camp to retreat to, no felt tents to rest in. No women with beakers of cool water and gentle hands. Even their tents lay mangled and burned to ruins. God curse this yellow-eyed laughing bandit king.

'How many of yours lie dead?' repeated the old chief bitterly. 'Not enough.'

'Your army was numerous but weak,' said Attila. 'Join with me and I will make you strong.' He nodded. 'Join us.'

Red Craw stared at him. 'You have slain fathers, sons, brothers on this field. The Budun-Boru do not easily forgive.'

'Then we can decide it in single combat,' said Attila. 'You and I.'

Red Craw eyed him, with the wound still wet in his side, but sitting as still and hard as stone. Clearly the wound was not a serious one. He looked away.

'Your ancients and women and your infants are not the only reward you will have from joining with us.'

Red Craw looked back, curious despite himself. 'Speak.'

'We ride west. Against the empire of Rome.'

Red Craw frowned. 'What is Rome?'

'A great empire. You will ride with us. We are brothers. We will ride together against Rome, an empire as great as China.'

Red Craw smiled for the first time, though there was little mirth in it. 'There is no empire as great as China.'

'There is one as rich, but not as strong: the Empire of Rome.'

Red Craw brooded. What reason had he to believe this murderous, treacherous upstart? Except that he knew from some men's eyes you saw the truth burn like a lantern in a window. Curse him.

'Besides,' said Attila, laying his left hand flat over the right side of his chest. 'I need a healer. Many of my men, too, and even more of yours.'

'You have burned our tents. There is nowhere to go.'

'Very well,' said Attila. 'We have parleyed enough.' He looked towards the horizon and raised his sword. The lead horsemen on the rise, barely distinguishable now in the gloom, raised his spear likewise. The line of shackled people swayed before it like corn before the wind.

'Wait,' said Red Craw.

He looked down at his dusty, bloody hands on the pommel of his wooden saddle. He sighed. Then he pulled his horse round, and rode back slowly to his men.

Attila waited.

He and his men hardly understood what happened next. Red Craw spoke briefly to his captains, and then he dismounted before them, which was unusual. They could not hear the words spoken between them. Red Craw suddenly sank to his knees before them, as if asking their forgiveness for the botched battle against so small an enemy. Then he fell away to one side, and they saw with horror that he was only a headless trunk. His head rolled in the dust before him. The warrior facing him still had a short curved sword in his hand. He had sliced clean through Red Craw's neck.

The warrior straightened again. He had many feathers stuck in his clay-whitened hair, and he was much younger than Red Craw. No more than forty, perhaps younger. His chest was broad and thickly muscled and he looked as strong as a bull. He sheathed his sword again without cleaning the blood off, and heeled his horse over.

'My name is Sky-in-Tatters,' he said without preamble, 'chief of the Kutrigur Huns. We accept your offer. You are our brothers. You fight well. We will ride with you.'

He was squatly built and very strong but his voice was hoarse and strangely high-pitched. His eyes were small and suspicious, and had none of Red Craw's brooding intelligence. He would not be a good chief.

Attila nodded. 'Welcome,' he said.

The two tribes burned their dead. Eight of Attila's men lay dead. Most of the living carried a wound of some sort or other.

Yesukai, eager young Yesukai, always wanting to be the first in everything … He was the first now, too: the first among Attila's captains to go the way of all flesh, though the youngest. It is often so in war.

The arrow that had pierced his upper arm had gone further and also pierced his chest. The blood that coated him from shoulder to thigh, as he fought on regardless throughout that bitter day, was his own blood. He had given it up carelessly, as if his life were a thing of no moment.

He lay dying against one of the blackened staves and Chanat cradled his head. He would drink no water. He spoke very quietly with his eyes half closed, and each time the blood bubbled from his lips Chanat wiped it away again as tenderly as a mother wiping milk from her baby's lips. Aladar, Attila and Orestes stood nearby in the gloom. In turn, according to custom, they and all the captains knelt before Yesukai and asked his forgiveness for any wrongs they might have done him in life. In reply, to each of them, young Yesukai smiled his boyish smile and murmured, 'No wrong, no wrong,' and reached out and laid his other, unbloodied hand on their foreheads in blessing. Each of them got to his feet again with tears blurring his sight. For they had been like brothers on the long ride and in the long fight.

'My women,' murmured Yesukai. 'My youngest, Kamar. She was very dear to me.' His head dropped and they thought he was gone. But then he said, 'My heart is sorry for Kamar.' His eyes were closed, his words almost inaudible. Attila knelt near him to hear. 'And my children, my sons and my daughters. Care for them.'

'As the sons and daughters of a king,' said Attila.

Chanat wiped the young man's mouth one last time, and then there was no more blood.

It was night when they burned his body on a great pyre of dry scrub, along with the bodies of the eight other men who had died that day. The funeral pyre was only one of many such pyres that covered the dark battlefield: the Kutrigurs were also burning their fallen. Little beacons in the vast and silent landscape, under the midnight blue vault of heaven. Among the beacons, firelit creatures moving as slow as ghosts, heads bowed low, and then stopping and groaning, and falling to their knees beside headless trunks and broken bodies, and weeping unconsolably. Mothers and wives, sisters and aged fathers from among the Kutrigurs, come seeking among the living and finding only the dead. Children and toddlers standing around, grubby-faced, barely understanding.

As the centre of his pyre, Yesukai's body was seen amid the flames, his ribcage bare of flesh and ablaze and falling apart in white ash. The sparks flew upwards and were lost among the stars, and they sang his soul to heaven. Their lament was for themselves, after the custom, and the noble friend and comrade they had lost.

'He has fallen, he has fled from us, noble Yesukai,
Yesukai of the laughing eyes, Yesukai of the brave heart and the
  high soul,
Kings are not, captains are not, who fought and died like Yesukai,
An eagle among men, a leopard, he has left his people poor;
Let the vultures cry among the Tien Shan, let the winds tell it
  over the Plains of Plenty,
Let the rains fall year long on the green grasslands in mourning
  for Yesukai!
The sword is cast away, the bow is broken, the weapons of war are
  perished,
Comfort is not, consolation is not,
For our noble friend, our Yesukai, is fled from us,
And we are left alone.'

At last the funeral pyres burned down low and they mounted their horses again and moved slowly away east.

The chief of the Kutrigurs, their uncertain allies, called out to them in the darkness, 'Where are you riding?'

Attila regarded him. At last he nodded and said quietly, almost with tenderness, 'Come.'

After half an hour's ride through the desolate night, towards the river, with the women and children and the ancients of the Kutrigurs, restored to them and now unroped and unshackled, trudging along in the rearguard, they emerged onto the lush floodplain of the great river. They sat their horses and waited for the Kutrigurs to draw up alongside them on the rise.

Sky-in-Tatters came alongside Attila and gasped.

Ahead of them burned the remnants of a huge fire, some way from the camp of black felt tents. It was an artificial fire, made of brushwood drenched with pailfuls of the foul black oil that Attila had made his men collect in the desert. Now they understood: another of Attila's tricks. The black smoke that the Kutrigurs had seen on the skyline, and assumed was their camp going up in flames …

The camp still lay by the river's edge, as ever, under a soft and benevolent moon. The horses' were breathing and peaceful in the corrals, the tents deserted and unharmed.

Sky-in-Tatters tore his gaze away from the sight of the untouched camp and gazed with grudging admiration at this yellow-eyed bandit king, Attila, son of Mundzuk.

'You fought like lions today, and sent many a warrior of my people to his grave. But our old and our young, our women and our virgins, and even the tents and the corralled horses of our camp, you left untouched.'

'It is our usual way.'

Sky-In-Tatters grunted. 'You are not the biggest fools I have ever met.'

Attila smiled.

Finally Sky-In-Tatters pushed himself up in the saddle, raised his spear and shouted a declaration to his ranks of exhausted and bewildered men.

'From this day onward,' he cried, 'there is neither Black Hun nor Kutrigur Hun! There are only the Huns. And it is as we have heard. We shall be a great nation on the earth!'

The fifteen hundred horsemen, despite exhaustion and injury and a longing for sleep rather keener, at this moment, than any longing for conquest or empire, responded with a mighty shout which was heard for many miles over the treeless steppes, and set even the golden jackals in their lairs shivering with fear.

9

GOOD MEDICINE, BAD MEDICINE

Sky-in-Tatters took possession of Red Craw's tall tent at once, and indicated that Attila should take his rest there, too. Seeing that he was wounded, he offered him a couch and sent out for a medicine woman.

The bandit king lay down gratefully on a sheepskin.

'We are the same people, you and I,' said Sky-in-Tatters. Attila said nothing. 'We are kings among men. And our men are no more desert Huns or steppe Huns, or, to the east, the Huns of the mountains. We Huns shall be one people, and we shall be the terror of the earth.' He passed Attila a beaker of koumiss and gulped another down.

'The villagers you fought so hard to defend,' he went on, 'those slaves. Why did you fight for them?'

Attila laid back his head and closed his eyes.

Sky-in-Tatters went on, 'We know of your people, Uldin's people of old, and how you forged west. We thought you had vanished over the rim of the earth, dared its uttermost bounds, and paid the price.' He nodded grimly. 'How wrong we were, and what a price we paid today.'

There was a movement at the tent door and Sky-in-Tatters stood. 'Your medicine woman. I shall leave you.'

The woman knelt at Attila's side, saying not a word, keeping her face bowed low. She very carefully unlaced his leather jerkin and pulled the sodden material gently off his chest. Her heart sank. The arrowhead was buried deep. No blood bubbled on his lips, so the arrow had not pierced his lung, but it was perilously close. He would have to be strong.

'Push,' he grunted. 'Right through.'

She reached for a long, thin steel bar. She would have to be strong, too.

It was many minutes later that she was finally able to sew up the garish exit wound with horsehair and a fine needle, and poultice both entry and exit wounds with boiled herbs, and bind his chest with fine white linen bandages.

How strong he would have to be.

Suddenly an iron grip on her slender wrist made her cry out in shock and pain.

He raised himself. 'Do not try to poison me as you pretend to heal me, woman. You will not succeed. I will live, despite your poisons. And I will kill you.'

She did not doubt him.

Poison or no, the king grew steadily weaker. The arrow had gone deep, and pushing it free had caused much agony, much loss of blood. Perhaps there was infection. It did not yet stink in the way that said the gods had marked a man for death, even though the arrow itself was long gone. But he was fighting. His face was pale, and then he was racked by fever. They fed the fever as best they could, piling thick sheepskins over him until his face was blood-lessly pale and drenched in sweat, like ice melting in the sun. They made him drink only the freshest, sweetest water straight from the river, taken upstream each morning at dawn.

Still the fever raged, and at times he ranted: mysterious and terrible words, verses that sounded like prophecies of the apocalypse. He muttered and raved about a king of terror, and the fall of burning cities, of a great lion, an eagle, and a rough-haired slouching beast who would yet come into his kingdom and exact vengeance for twelve long centuries of sin. The woman mopped his brow and made him drink and pitied him his nightmares.

Little Bird came to visit him. His king could barely see him.

'There is poison,' he murmured, 'but it came not from the woman's hand.' He choked a little and spat. 'Where were you in the battle? I had forgotten you.'

'Where was I?' said Little Bird. 'Surviving. That's where I was.'

Attila almost managed a smile. He looked sidelong at Little Bird and saw an old man, sad-eyed and weary. He forgot how old the shaman was, he always seemed so ageless. But not now.

He held his hand out and Little Bird took it, like a son taking the hand of his father on his deathbed. The thick, snaking, ropy veins were fallen flat and gone, as if there was no blood left in him. Nevertheless, when Little Bird spoke, his voice remained sprightly and careless, such were the contradictions of his heart.

He said he had learned that Sky-in-Tatters was in fact one of the sons of the old chief, Red Craw.

'The eldest?'

Little Bird shook his head. 'But the eldest to live.' His eyes glittered. 'He is not the only great chief to have killed his father. I heard a rumour of it.'

'Peace, Little Bird,' croaked the dying king. He was like a very old man. Little Bird could not cease from his cruel barbs and pointed jests, for it was in his nature and in the nature of his wisdom to speak thus, yet even as he joked he bowed his head and wiped the tears from his cheeks to see his Father brought low like this, laid at death's door on a bloodstained sheepskin bier, breathing painful rasping breaths, his chest arched, his ribcage straining, his lungs, his veins, his unbreakable iron body filling up with poison and decay. Soon death's door would open and dust-grey hands would reach out and take him, and the door would close and he would be gone for ever. Then Little Bird himself would have no more reason to live than if the sun itself were suddenly snuffed out like a candle in the sky. For he would never live to see another king like this, and all his days would be lived in shadow.

Clouds rolled overhead. The circle of sunlight on the floor of the tent was eclipsed and darkened.

Orestes sat with him all day and all night, too, and hardly seemed to sleep. Sometimes Attila cried out, choking, and coughed up matter from his infected lungs.

Orestes roared at anyone else present to get out of the tent. Then he wept, 'My brother,' and cradled his king's head. Attila's breathing was laboured and terrible to hear, and his face green and liverish.

One visitor would not be frightened off, however. She came marching through the camp with her stick and a single pitcher of water, ignoring every cry and question. It was the old priestess from the village.

'How did you know he was sick?' asked Orestes.

'In a dream,' she said a little crossly. 'How do you think? Now, out of my way.'

She spoke to the king in a low voice, and then she drew off his bandages and used the water to wash his wounds.

She nodded at the pitcher she had brought. 'From the lake,' she said. 'There's no pleasure in drinking it, but it salves all wounds, drives away all infections of the flesh.' She grinned her one-toothed grin. 'God alone knows what he put in it!'

Orestes sniffed the water cautiously. 'Salts,' he murmured. 'Saline compounds, incarnatives ...'

The priestess looked at him askance. 'Long words won't help your lord now. Pass me those wrappings.'

The wounds seemed to heal faster under the old priestess's ministrations, but the fever remained and the king grew weaker. The infection was inside him now. The old woman stayed with him – Orestes permitted it – and prayed over him tirelessly, day and night.

Now, there was among the Kutrigur Huns the witch Enkhtuya, a sorceress, a seer, and a handler of snakes.

Orestes and Little Bird were sitting with their dying king one evening. The fire in the centre of the tent burned low. There was a commotion at the tent door and then there she stood within, smiling at them, her dark skin shining in the firelight.

When Little Bird set eyes on her, his reaction was that of a madman. He hissed and wailed, and leaped to his feet, sending his little three-legged stool flying. He screamed and capered and stopped and stared and then screamed and capered again. He yelled at her to 'Get out! *Get out!*' But Enkhtuya only stood and smiled the more.

Little Bird ran back and tore wildly at Attila's arm and screamed that she must be turned out, she must be killed, her eyes were set with iron like a snake's and her innards were nothing but a twisted nest of snakes. 'Listen to me, not her, listen to me!' he screamed, his mouth almost at the king's ear. 'She will not heal you! She heals only to harm! Turn her out, I say, or the Snake of Anashti will devour you and all your people!'

Attila groaned. 'Get the witch out of my sight.'

'Yet the time will come, and soon,' said Enkhtuya in her strange voice, high and whining like a stinging insect. She clawed the air as she was removed. 'The time will come,' she said, 'and you will listen.'

And it was as Enkhtuya said. Twice more she appeared in the king's tent, and each time the king was nearer death. On the third day he did not order her to leave. Little Bird went berserk.

Orestes was on his feet and pulled the shaman back, locking his arms behind him. Little Bird tried to kick his shins, but Orestes raised him painfully by his own twisted arms and then dropped him to the dusty floor.

'Peace, fool,' he growled. 'Give your master some peace.'

But Little Bird would not be silenced. He lay there babbling with anger and fear, curled up on the ground like an unborn child, lying on his side with his knees clutched up to his chest. Orestes gave him a kicking, until the little shaman leaped to his feet, dashed across the tent, fell to his knees and scrambled out through the tent flap.

Orestes looked again at the newcomer. He had glimpsed her previously, far off, walking among the tents, and wondered who she might be. Even Attila turned his head, sallow, thin, beaded with sweat.

She was an extraordinary figure, very tall – taller than most of the men in her tribe – and very thin. Her tawny hair, dyed that colour, perhaps, was twisted up and resined and knotted on top of her narrow head, making her look even taller. Her cheekbones were as sharp as those of a corpse, her lips very thin. Her age was indeterminate. She was very dark in complexion, and her skin was like honey, not the sweet, pale honey of Hymettus, but the darkest chestnut honey, gleaming and shining in the firelight. But her eyes were a pale, piercing blue, as blue as ice in slanting winter light. Everything about her was uncanny, wrong, and Orestes himself was uncertain of her. His deep, silent scrutiny of men and their hearts over the years had taught him much, and forewarned him now that this was no ordinary visitor.

Impossible to say even what race she was, with that dark, gleaming skin and those pale-blue northern eyes. And though she was a woman there was no gentleness or hint of maternal kindness in that flat and bony breast. All practitioners of the occult arts know the uncanny power of that which cannot be defined. They practise their craft and cast their spells at crossroads, which are neither one road nor another, and at midnight, the witching hour, which is neither one day nor another. In Enkhtuya, who seemed to incarnate this shadow and uncertainty in her very self, neither quite dark nor fair, woman nor man, this power seemed magnified a hundredfold.

Round her throat she wore a twisted snakeskin, and round her skeletal wrists and arms she wore further snakeskins twisted into torcs. The scales of the sloughed skins stuck to her own skin here and there and gleamed dully, and in uncertain light or in the soft light of the fires at night among the tents it looked almost as if her own skin were as scaly as that of her beloved snakes. She carried two live snakes in a little leather pouch around her waist, fearfully venomous. Sometimes she took them out and toyed with them, stroking their curling bodies, nuzzling them against her sunken cheeks and purring like a child with a kitten. They would stare at her with their unblinking obsidian eyes and flicker their grey tongues, and none came near Enkhtuya while she had those snakes in her hand. Perhaps they never bit her. But some said that they bit her often enough, for you can no more train a snake not to bite than a dog not to bark, and that it was only that Enkhtuya was under the protection of the moon goddess, and impervious to their venom.

Others were not impervious, however: not the prisoners whom the Kutrigurs sometimes tied to stakes at the edge of the camp, and not the wounded and dying still groaning on the field of battle. Through the smoke and in the dusk, Enkhtuya could often be seen like some angel from death's dominion, carrying her beloved snakes. Kneeling like a gentle nurse beside the wounded and dying, holding her snakes out as if they were little ministers of healing. Squeezing them just behind their heads to make them angry, she would kneel by a wounded warrior of an alien tribe, and hold the snake to his lips as if she were some demonic shadow of a medicine woman kneeling at the side of a sick man to give him a cup of water. Her eyes shone with delight as she watched the snake coming closer and closer to the dying man, the man scrabbling powerlessly in the dirt, perhaps the stump of a severed arm waggling as he sought purchase in the dust to crawl away from this nightmare apparition. At last she would put the snake directly on to him, and smile as it sank its fangs into his lips, his cheeks, his eyes ...

Enkhtuya was indeed a sorceress, and she knew well how to harm as well as heal.

Now she knelt by the side of another dying man. She said not a word, for she knew as well as any monarch that silence is power. But Orestes said to her, 'I am watching you.'

She turned and gazed on him full with her ice-blue eyes, and even Orestes felt something shiver in his soul. Then she nodded. She understood him. She worked carefully.

She produced a small pot containing a foul and choking mix of honey, salt, mutton fat and the juices of certain steppeland flowers, and she forced this noxious paste into Attila's mouth. Soon he choked, and kept choking.

'*I am watching you,*' repeated Orestes.

She worked on.

As the dying king choked still on the foul paste, she lowered her head and put her ear to his chest. She moved her head a little and listened again. Finally she listened longest in his right side, near the original arrow wound: a long, rattling, gruelling râle.

She sat straight again, slipped her hand inside her robe and pulled out a long, lean knife. She leaned close to the barely conscious king and seemed to sniff, like an animal. Then she neatly sliced open his bandages, positioned the tip of the knife between his ribs, near the old arrow wound, and drove it into the lung. The king arched and gasped, and there was a whistle of air.

She looked up at Orestes from under her black brows.

'If it runs pale, he lives,' she said. 'If it runs thick and yellow, he dies.'

'Is that the extent of your sorceress's powers?' retorted Orestes savagely.

She ignored him, and slowly drew the knife from the deep, narrow wound. Pus bubbled out after it.

Orestes' shoulders sank and he bowed his head.

It ran as clear as water from a spring.

She soaked up the pus with an absorbent linen cloth. She let it run again, and cleaned it again. Finally she made a little plug with a further roll of linen and sealed the wound.

She stood abruptly and walked out of the tent, saying as she went that she would return tomorrow.

Orestes slept where he sat, his head resting at the foot of his master's bed.

She was as good as her word. Each day at morning and evening she performed the same gruesome operation, and each day the pus ran a little less. By the third day, the king's fever had broken. His breathing was careful and laboured with his good lung, but the other was healing fast.

Enkhtuya made poultices and plasters of mullein and clover leaves, boiled hulwort, horehound, flax seed moistened with the juice of houndsberry and woad. Attila coughed violently for a couple more days. But on the seventh day after Enkhtuya had come to him, he was up and on his feet when Orestes entered the tent.

'You need rest!' he exclaimed.

Attila turned on him, snatching down his sword from where it hung on a tentpost, drawing it from its scabbard and swinging it at Orestes all in one swift, easy movement. Orestes ducked only just in time to avoid serious injury.

He stood straight again. 'Christ in heaven!'

Attila sheathed his sword and grinned.

10

HUSBANDS AND WIVES

At first there was discontent and opposition among his own men at the thought of joining with the Kutrigur Huns.

'Imagine what terror we will strike into the hearts of our enemies now!' said Geukchu. 'With such great numbers! My lord, what strength in unity we shall have!' But it was impossible to tell if Geukchu was sincere.

'Let us hope,' chirruped Little Bird, his meaning both sarcastic and insincere and sincere all at once, as always. 'Let us hope that we do not pass by a clear lake on our journey. Our reflection would surely kill us with terror! And let us hope, also, that our pleasant amity with our Kutrigur kinsmen lasts. Civil war is always so messy and—'

'Peace, fool,' Attila cut him off. 'We march under one banner.'

'And one king?'

'There can be only one king.' Attila glared at Little Bird. 'And another thing. I will not have you throwing your barbs at the chieftain, Sky-in-Tatters.' Little Bird's eyes glittered with malicious expectation at the thought of taunting that ox-like fool, but Attila narrowed his eyes and pointed his forefinger at him. 'Understand. You can throw your barbs at me all you like, I care not. Words are just words. But men like Sky-in-Tatters do not take kindly to such humiliation. Words frighten them. And you will not break up this fragile alliance of our two tribes with your mischief.'

Chanat sat cross-legged in the dust. He did not look up, his long shaggy greying hair half-concealing his face. He spoke quietly but clearly.

'My lord, the Kutrigurs are not our people. Their ways are not our ways. Their customs …' He turned aside and spat into the dust, and they all knew to which customs he was referring. 'Their customs are not our customs.'

'Nor are the customs of …' Little Bird shivered and could not say her name. 'Nor are the customs of the witch my customs.'

'She saved my life.'

'Yet she smells of death.'

Attila stroked his thin beard and ignored Little Bird, but he looked steadily at Chanat with glittering eyes, every fibre tensed like steel.

'You are telling me,' he said very softly, 'that I am mistaken?'

Chanat looked up and returned his king's gaze. 'I am. My lord, I beg you, let us return another way and leave these people. They are not our kin, they are not our people, and I fear that their customs and their dark name will follow us to the ends of the earth. Shake them off as a dog shakes off its fleas.'

The atmosphere was tense with opposition. Any moment the king could have flared out in fury. The silence was exhausting.

At last Attila gave his judgement: 'The Kutrigur Huns, our kinsmen, stay with us.'

There was a moment's silence, then Chanat drove his knife-blade into the dust, got to his feet and walked away into the darkness.

Beside a campfire he saw the witch, Enkhtuya, cooking a gobbet of meat on a stick. It looked like a heart.

Enkhtuya did not come back to Attila. His dressings were changed again by the woman who had ministered to him that first day. She was gentle, and she breathed on her cupped hands to warm them before she unwrapped his dressings. She was not so young, but her hands were still soft.

'You have a husband?'

She kept her head down low and did not meet his eyes. 'He was killed. Not in the battle,' she added hurriedly. 'Last winter.'

'Hm.'

When she had finished, he ran his hand under the hem of her deerskin dress and caressed the back of her thigh.

She looked away with her head bowed low. But she did not move.

211

Later, as she left the tent, she dared to look back at him and murmur, 'You are feeling better, my lord?'

He turned and growled after her and she fled.

Already, what had been an uneasy truce between enemies was growing into something else. Though it had seemed impossible that men who had seen their brothers, father and sons slain by these arrogant intruders should end serving shoulder to shoulder with them in battle, now it began to seem that it might come to pass. A unity might be forged. The Kutrigurs loved war and conquest more than they loved hatred and revenge. Though cruel and barbarous in their customs, they were not without a rude nobility.

Attila talked for long hours with Sky-in-Tatters. Him, too, he found more amenable than at first. The bull-necked chieftain had no cunning, and no insight into men's hearts, but he was strong, simple and candid, and Attila began to warm to him.

Out on the wintry plains, in a dusting of snow, he began to observe and then to lead the Kutrigurs in field exercises.

Sky-in-Tatters would remain chief of the Kutrigurs, of course. In matters of tribal law and punishment, in the arranging and approving of marriages, in the burial of the dead, he would remain supreme authority among his people. But in matters of warfare, he gave way, acknowledging the newcomer's superiority. And he who rules in war rules in everything.

Attila's men numbered ninety-one, of the chosen band of one hundred who had originally set out. Many of the wounded Kutrigurs had died groaning in their tents, bewailed by women dishevelled and cloaked in ashes. But many more had mended. The number of their combined men-at-arms still stood at over two thousand, their horses at four times that number. Their ambition was limitless as the sky.

And so by the common mingling of the two tribes, by the growth of ordinary comradeship, by the Hun nations' inveterate delight in war, greed for gold and longing for plunder from that great, fabled, tottering empire to the west that was called Rome, as well as by the gentler powers of courtship and marriage, the Black and the Kutrigur Huns were hammered into a unity.

There would be jewels heaped up in gleaming piles, and dark-eyed slavegirls, and horses, the finest horses, from Araby, from the Barbary Coast, the equal of the Horses of Heaven.

At this, even Sky-in-Tatters objected. 'There are no horses like the Horses of Heaven,' he said. 'Even the Emperor of China longs to be the owner of the Horses of Heaven.'

'The horses of Araby are their equal,' said Attila.

'You lie.'

'I do not lie.'

Again Sky-in-Tatters saw the lantern-light of truth in those unflinching yellow eyes, and was forced to admit grudging defeat. 'I should like to see these horses of Araby.'

To his own men, Attila said that they might take widows for wives, or any old women – that is to say, any women older than thirty summers. He had done as much himself. The woman he had taken was a widow, and at twenty-eight certainly approaching old age. But they were to take or pursue no virgins. His men looked disgruntled, but did as he commanded.

'My lord,' said old Chanat afterwards in private. 'The women of the Kutrigurs. If we must take them to wife, as you command . . .'

Attila turned and regarded him quizzically.

'First impressions are not good.' Chanat whittled a stick.

'Not so good,' agreed his king.

'It is long since I have looked on a woman. Usually such length of time alone in one's tent is enough to lower one's standards.'

'Broaden one's interests,' said Attila.

'You speak like a Persian.'

A woman passed among the tents some way off, carrying water.

'Look at that one,' said Attila, nodding. 'What about her?'

Chanat screwed up his eyes, and then his whole face, as if he was sucking a lemon. 'She must be nearly forty summers.'

'Older women,' said Attila, 'have more experience, more appetite, and much more gratitude.'

Chanat grunted.

The next day Chanat came to his king again.

'The breasts are not good,' he said, 'a pair of horsechestnut leaves in autumn. But the other things you said are compensation.'

'My heart soars like a hawk for you, Chanat,' said Attila.

He was sitting crosslegged at the fireside with Orestes in

213

companionable silence when he heard a familiar tread behind him. He held up his hand.

'Chanat, if it is to tell me more about your marital problems, I'm not interested.'

'On the contrary, my lord.'

Attila twisted round and saw that the old warrior was grinning from ear to ear.

'And I have no greater wish to hear about your marital triumphs, either.'

'I have discovered,' went on Chanat unabashed, 'that my new woman's husband was the man we killed on the first day, on the rise, when Yesukai, rest him, set the partridges off into the air.'

'I remember. So why are you grinning like a monkey? You have to tie her hand and foot before you can sleep at night, in case she cuts your throat while you snore?'

'On the contrary,' cried Chanat, laughing. 'She detested him with all her ferocious heart!' He came over and stood near, talking as rapidly and excitedly as a young man bragging to his fellows. 'She hated him. It was good that this man died. He was a brute to her, he beat her for pleasure. He had a long seasoned cane that he kept specially for the purpose. He laughed. It amused him to count her bruises each morning, to set her foolish tasks, only to see her drudge and droil. We should have killed him with sticks.'

Attila grunted.

'And you know why he was so angry a man?' Chanat put his hand to his groin, crooked his little finger and waggled it absurdly. 'Like a marmot!' he cried. 'Like a gnat!' Attila regarded him with curiosity. Chanat was almost choking with laughter. He recovered himself a little and wiped the tears of mirth from his eyes. 'You know, of course, that all men so cursed by the ill-humour of the gods are petty-minded and irritable, bad-tempered, spiteful and vain.'

'And naturally, none of these qualities applies to you, friend Chanat.'

'Of course not!' he roared, holding his sinewy forearm bolt upright before his face by way of illustration. 'And as for my woman, not only does her new man not beat her for amusement, but she is only too happy to see his long seasoned cane, I can tell you! She is a very happy woman! There is nothing she will not do for me!' With another roar of laughter he turned and strode out of the tent.

They looked after him.

'This new wife,' murmured Orestes. 'She may be old, but her attentions are making him like a young man again.'

'It is what the Chinese call the mixing of yin and yang,' said Attila. 'Remember our conversations with our captive monk beside the Yellow River? Chanat's ch'i is again in full flow.'

Orestes shuddered. Attila grinned.

Orestes reached into his robe and pulled out a small carved ornament. 'Talking of the Chinese,' he said, and handed it to Attila.

The king examined it closely. It was a bronze clasp for a nobleman's robe. 'Where did you find it?'

'Not I,' said Orestes. 'Geukchu – eyes like a hawk. Out on the plains, in the grass. Not far from the Dzungarian gap.'

'So far north,' Attila mused. 'Plunder?'

'It's possible. But it's also possible the armies of the Northern Wei are on the march.'

It was midwinter, and the steppes stretched away on every side boundless and bare, dusted white with snow. Three months ago they had said goodbye to their women and to their tiny, wide-eyed children and set out from their camp. It seemed to some of the men that it was many years ago. It had been late autumn then, and their going at that drear time of year had astonished many of the elders. Since then it had grown much colder. But Attila said the shortest day of the year was now past. Soon it would be Tsagaan Sar, the new year, and soon after that spring. They laughed bitterly. Spring came slowly up this way, and never soon enough.

Sometimes the north wind blew out of the heart of Scythia, and then even the strongest men sat in the tents with the women and jostled for a place by the fireside. In the corrals, horses died on their feet, fell to the hard ground in a cloud of ice. But sometimes a southerly breeze blew, and then it was almost warm enough for the snow to melt, and for the great slow-moving ice floes coming downriver from the north to thaw and melt in midstream. Then the men strolled around bare-armed and basked in the thin sunshine, the younger naked to the waist, grinning and joking how balmy it was, their coppery skin showing a distinct and curious blue-grey undertone.

Attila went to Sky-in-Tatters on such a balmy day. 'It is time we broke camp and went east.'

The chief looked at him in astonishment. 'It is midwinter,' he said.

'Time does not stand still,' said Attila. 'Nor should we.'

'What is your hurry?'

Attila grimaced. 'There is the whole world left to conquer.'

'You want to ride against this empire of Rome? In winter?'

He shook his head. 'It will take more than our two thousand to ride against Rome, however drilled they are. We ride east. There are more allies there who will join us. And among the mountains of the Altun Shan, there is a remote kingdom, ruled by a syphilitic god-king. His people are numerous, his warriors are idle but strong. There are still others. Many will join us. We must not linger.'

Sky-in-Tatters folded his thick arms across his chest and stuck out his jaw. 'It is not possible,' he said, 'to ride into the mountains in winter.'

'What does not kill us makes us stronger.'

'I have spoken in judgement,' said Sky-in-Tatters. 'We ride out in spring. The day of the first windflower, and not before.'

They rode out three days later, Sky-in-Tatters rueful and silent. This yellow-eyed bandit king's powers of persuasion were very great.

Before they went east, Attila broke away from the huge, lumbering train of oxen and wagons and numberless horses, and rode alone back to the high plateau. He found the villagers huddled under mere awnings amid the blackened ruins of their huts. He sought out the old priestess. She emerged and offered him bread and salt. He declined.

'We ride east,' he said.

'In winter? That is folly.'

He sighed. 'I have had this argument before.'

She pulled a face. Other villagers gathered curiously around.

'The river is yours. It is restored to you.'

The people stared at him in astonishment, and then at each other. Then they began to babble and laugh, and they moved forward to embrace their saviour's legs, his horse's neck, anything. He heeled Chagëlghan gently backwards and bowed.

'The river is yours, as it always was,' he said. 'Your gods be thanked.'

The old priestess was regarding him curiously.

'You can even eat fish again,' said Attila, 'if you must.'

She almost managed a smile. 'You do not like fish?'

'As lovers do the dawn, madam.' He grinned and yawed his horse furiously round and several villagers leaped aside to avoid him. 'As lovers do the dawn!' He bunched the reins tight in his fists and his biceps bulged and he drove his heels into his horse's flanks and roared a grating 'Yah!' and Chagëlghan gathered himself upon his thick, squat haunches, reared and surged forward. In a flurry of dust and powdery snow, horse and rider vanished across the desolate plateau.

The villagers rushed about like excited ants. By nightfall they would be restored to their beloved riverside. They would pick up driftwood there, coming down from the northern forests, and soon build themselves new huts. Then they would drink and feast and praise their gods and their Mother Naga as never before. Only one figure stood still among the commotion. The old priestess hunched over her knobbly stick, gazing out eastwards over the plateau, her thin lips moving as if in prayer.

Many among both the Black and the Kutrigur Huns looked back on that winter ride into the east as they might on an uncertain dream. Always at their head, face bowed to the snow and the blizzards of daggers and ice, rode that single, solitary, implacable figure, hunched over in a black bearskin, refusing to countenance any other way.

How many of them died on that trail of ice and snow, it was hard to say. Enough men buried their women by the wayside, enough women buried their children as well as they could beneath cairns of ice, to have caused an angry rebellion. But there was none. The yellow-eyed bandit king had spoken, and it was as if a far higher authority had spoken, an authority no man could gainsay.

They rode over frozen rocklands and stones, and through the cruel Dzungarian gap, a fifty-mile corridor of brutal wind that they called the buran, howling between the holy Altai Mountains and the towering Tien Shan, the Mountains of Heaven. As they passed by Attila made a sign of sacred respect towards the High Altai, as if he knew them for a second home. He had been there long, it was said, in his time. But what gods, what shamans, what occult rites he had seen or known in those distant mountains, no man can say.

In summer those mountains were a land of green and plenty, crocuses breaking from the brown earth as the days warmed, and pistachio and walnut forests growing on the southern slopes. But they passed by on the northern side, and in winter, and there was no warmth or respite for them.

Hunting was sparse and the animals were lean. At times they caught great bustard on the grasslands ringed by the mountains, which ringed them about and watched like cold, indifferent heavenly spectators over the vast, treeless plain. Occasionally their outriders glimpsed ibex, corsac fox, even the rare and magical sight of the snow leopard pacing slow and silent over the drifts upon the lower slopes. Camped by frozen rivers, where they had to smash the ice with picks to reach water, they were joined after dark by other animals drawn to the river: wild dogs, grunting brown bears, the last fleet-footed, high-strung Asian cheetahs.

The cold and leaden skies were patrolled by black vultures and imperial eagles, watching them in their turn. They buried their dead deep.

11

THE COLUMN OF THE NORTHERN WEI

They had been out upon the vast plain ringed by those towering mountains for seven days, and with their wagons and oxen and the arduous river crossings they were doing only ten miles a day, perhaps a little more. It was clear cold day, with a little powdery snow underfoot, the air crisp, a sickle of moon high in the cold blue sky.

At the head of the great trundling column, Geukchu of the hawk-eyes slowed his horse almost to a standstill and stared. Attila raised his hand and the column stopped.

They waited. There was nothing. Geukchu continued to stare eastwards. Impatient young Aladar came galloping up.

'My eyes are half the age of yours, Geukchu!' he cried. 'And I see nothing.'

Geukchu ignored him. Time passed. Chagëlghan harrumphed and tossed his big ugly head. Attila pulled him up.

Geukchu said, 'There. Like a drift of smoke on the horizon. There is another column approaching us.'

Attila stared, too. Nothing. 'It is the wind,' he said, 'stirring up the snow.'

Geukchu shook his head. 'No wind blows so steady. It is a column.'

Orestes spoke, though none had noticed him come up behind them; even his horse trod lightly. 'It is a column.'

Some time later, Attila said, 'It is a Chinese column, a column of the Northern Wei.' He looked round at his men and his eyes gleamed and danced. 'Good practice.'

He gave low orders to Aladar and Geukchu and they pulled their horses back and began to supervise the men. The women and children were led further back and left undefended among the wagons.

Attila and Orestes sat side by side.

'Just like old times,' murmured the bare-headed Greek.

'The emperors of the Northern Wei were Toba people once, a steppe people.'

Orestes nodded. 'And now look,' he said. 'How quickly Chinese silk and civilization weaken them.' He added sardonically, 'Syphilization.'

The Chinese general rode under an embroidered yellow palanquin, reclining upon one elbow. Then one of his horsemen came riding to him, and he was suddenly sitting very upright indeed.

The two armies drew up opposite each other. A mile or more still lay between them. The numbers of the Northern Wei were perhaps four or five thousand, every one a trained man-at-arms.

Attila had long since broken all his warriors into divisions under his chosen captains, mingling Black Hun and Kutrigur together and setting them competing against each other, striving to outdo each other in valour on the field. Like proud regiments, like the Roman legions themselves, quite dissolving any former ties they may have had to each other or to their people, and fixing all their loyalty upon their own band and their captain. On his far left wing, Aladar rode at the head not of a pitiful little troop of ten, but of more than three hundred bristling mounted warriors. They were the youngest and most hot-blooded, their horses the fastest, all bunched and rippling haunches, deep chests enclosing mighty hearts and lungs. Aladar's warriors were the finest of them all, and they knew it. They knotted black pennants behind their spearheads and crimson bands round their upper arms.

The three brothers, Juchi, Bela and Noyan, commanded some eight hundred in the centre, on the heavier horses, and skilled with the lance. Csaba with his fleet three hundred occupied the right flank, where there was more space between the column and the first low foothills of the mountains to the south. Behind were the troops of Chanat, and of Geukchu and Candac, bows readied and arrows to the string.

Attila sat at the forefront of his army, Orestes a little behind him to his right, and Sky-in-Tatters to his left.

He held his men steady and motionless as the main ranks of Chinese cavalry began to walk and then trot towards them, red banners gradually taking shape and billowing out behind them as they moved faster and faster over the frost-hard grass. The watching Huns would always remember this moment as one of great beauty as well as terror. Neither the Kutrigurs nor the Black Huns had ever faced such a massed professional army in the open field before. Attila himself only smiled into the sun, as if all the training and drilling, grouping and regrouping, had been in preparation for this, and the day were already won.

For to empire-dreamers and lovers of war, there can be no sight more beautiful in the morning sunlight than ranks of mounted warriors, their pennants fluttering from the spearhafts in the breeze, the silvery winter light glancing from bronze helms and damascened scabbards and rippling chain-mail hauberks, horses champing and tossing their heads, manes flying. The immemorial cult of war to which men of heroic blood have been devoted since they first looked out unblinking on the world and understood that life was vain but death could make it glorious; and that war was the supreme rite of Death, the oldest and the greatest god of all.

Attila raised his hand and dropped it in one swift and easy movement, supremely confident. The whole battle was conducted this way, as if against a gang of insolent boys rather than a five thousand-strong column of the Northern Wei. The arrows did their work, falling accurate and lethal into the close-packed ranks of armoured warriors, their armour merely useless weight against that stinging rain. Men reeled and fell and the snow cushioned their falling, as it muffled their cries and the cries of their horses. Indeed, the whole brief battle was muffled in near silence, an eerie and unreal encounter upon that desolate snowbound plain, ringed about by the white and watching mountains. Red banners trembled and tottered and fell and lay stretched and motionless against the white snow. Iron arrowheads burst armour casings and bone lappings alike, and sprays of blood dotted the powdered snow as red as bryony berries in that slow midwinter massacre.

As the Chinese attack slowed and jostled and struggled to

maintain formation, the heart of Attila's army did the strangest thing. It melted away. The Chinese armoured knights now came on again with a vengeance, spurring their horses forward into a gallop, only to find that the ranks of barbarian horsemen they galloped against were no longer there. But the barbarian arrows kept coming. The heart of Attila's army had turned and fled, it seemed. But as they galloped away, as fast as the Chinese pursued them, they continued to fire volley after volley of arrows back into the massed ranks of the oncoming enemy. The volleys were perfectly judged, and fell murderously time after time, like clouds of black hawks stooping on their prey. The Chinese pursuers trying to fire after the retreating Huns in their turn, found that their arrows fell relentlessly short. It was like trying to pursue a ghost, but a ghost armed with weapons of iron.

Meanwhile, Attila had ordered the horns of his army to separate from the main body – another outrageous deviation from the Chinese rule-book of war which left them baffled. An outnumbered army in the open field, under attack, must always stick together and keep formation. Unity is its only hope. But not this evanescent army with its deadly arrows. The wings commanded by Aladar and Csaba moved outwards like the horns of the buffalo, Aladar to the left and Csaba to the right, howling a war-song, racing out over the snow-dusted grass and arcing round on their wild ride, cantering far beyond the exposed flanks of the Chinese army and then moving up from a canter into a full-tilt and furious gallop, slicing back like scythes into the enemy's undefended sides.

Until the very moment of their attack, Attila dared to have his own retreating archers continue to drop volley after volley of arrows onto the stricken ranks of the Chinese. Only when Aladar and Csaba came with a hundred yards, fifty, did he finally give the signal for the murderous rain to stop. And not one of his own galloping men was hit. The warriors of Aladar and Csaba slammed into the flanks of the Northern Wei, swords whirling in the bright air, and began to roll them up into one single mound of the dead.

Attila called a halt to his main body of men and turned them round again and settled them. Immediately behind him, the eight hundred warriors of Juchi, Bela and Noyan, the solid heart of his little army, were as frustrated as their champing horses at this waiting, longing to move forward into the attack. But there was nothing for them to do. The six hundred warriors who comprised the two scything wings were handling it all on their own, and there was nothing for the rest but to watch. Even Sky-in-Tatters looked on in disbelief and laughed. This was what Huns could do at their best, drilled and lethal. It was almost too easy.

The warcries of the Hun cavalry carried across the snow, and the spectacle of their mad courage, their shocking contempt for death, panicked the Chinese and they lurched back and into each other pell-mell. Any formation or room to manoeuvre was gone now, and everything was confusion and entanglement and steady slaughter.

Finally Attila gave the order, and the rest of his army surged forward to finish the work. There were units of footsoldiers behind the mêlée of dying Chinese cavalry, and they needed mopping up. None of them had even been engaged in the battle, although sturdy drawn-up footsoldiers could often be the best defence against a wild mounted attack.

Attila lay almost flat upon his horse's outstretched neck, his sword held out forwards like a lance, and its long sinuous tip went straight into the open crimson mouth of a Chinese knight in mid-cry, ripping out again sideways through his jaw, Chagëlghan barely slowing his charge all the while.

Geukchu and Candac had taken their troops round to surround the Chinese rearguard and prevent any escape, and to finish off the bewildered, milling footsoldiers. A secondary order had been to take at least two senior Chinese officers alive. It was a while before Geukchu could find any. Eventually he lassoed one, a squat Chinese captain with grey moustaches, and dragged him away from the battlefield, bellowing, as he would have dragged an unruly steer from the herd. He stood with his sword to the man's neck, and the man turned with the cruel hemp rope tight around his bound arms, and watched grim-faced as his comrades struggled even to draw their swords in the press, and were cut down in wave after wave, like summer grass before the reaper.

The horses reared and screamed, throwing their riders and trampling them underfoot, panicked and horrified, as horses are, to see that they had trampled other living creatures to death. Horses slammed sideways into each other, and men were trapped between horses, dragged from their fine-tooled leather saddles, squeezed lifeless between sweating flanks, falling to their knees and crawling, abjectly searching for dropped weapons, stumbling over fallen comrades, slithering on slicks of blood coating the cold hard earth. Others crawling free, hoping to flee away from the horror over the plain, were brought down by a single thrust from a lance, or a single straight-flying arrow, fired on the turn from horseback with negligent ease.

Huns were already dismounting and walking on foot, to make the final despatch easier.

A young Wei soldier, a boy of fifteen, lay unable to move in the snow, his legs numb, looking out sidelong across the plain, his left cheek freezing. His sad brown eyes saw not this plain of death but his father's house. The hearth-fire, the cedarwood rice-chest, the small carved figures of the ancestors in their niche. Outside, the duckpond, and his mother throwing grain to the ducks. The longnecked white ducks stretching forwards eagerly. He felt someone standing close behind him, and his fingers crawled forwards in the snow as if for grasp, but still he only saw his village with its rising woodsmoke, his home. Little children clapping. His sisters, his brothers. His mother flapping her white apron. The dog with his long tongue out, laughing. The goldfinch in his cage of willow twigs, and the green shadows of spring under the willows.

The boy's head was lifted off the ground and dropped back, and his big brown eyes, still open wide and looking out across the snow-white plain, were lifeless and saw nothing more. Aladar had taken his scalp.

Hiding under the collapsed palanquin at the very heart of the slaughter, the rich yellow watered silk now speckled and streaked here and there with red, they found a Wei monk on all fours.

Attila reached down and dragged the silk canopy off him, rolled it up roughly and tossed it to Sky-in-Tatters. 'First loot,' he said.

Then he stooped down to the half-concussed monk and shook him hard.

'Xioung Nu,' murmured the monk, sitting back on his haunches and looking up at Attila with fluttering eyelids. 'Xioung Nu.'

'Hunnu,' said Attila. 'Your ancient enemy.' But the monk did not understand this harsh, barbaric language, spoken from the back of the throat. He looked up expectantly at the other fearsome Hun warriors standing around him. They were sweat-stained and some even blood-stained, with long black moustaches, and strands of their long black unkempt hair still plastered across their grimy cheeks. Their reddened swords were still in their hands. He said a prayer in his heart.

Then he reached inside his orange robe and pulled out a little ivory plaque of carved openwork and prayed to it. He prayed to the Lord Buddha, and spoke in his language of the Buddha Sakyamuni, and traced his fingers over the Buddha sitting peacefully beneath the śala trees with his disciples. He touched his fingertips softly to the ivory figures.

Attila took the little ivory plaque from the monk, who watched him anxiously. He touched his filthy, broken fingernails to those delicately carven faces. He ran his stubby, battle-scarred fingers over those serene figures beneath their ancient trees.

'Buddha,' he said softly.

'Buddha,' said the monk, nodding with great eagerness. 'Buddha Sakyamuni.'

Attila squatted down beside the monk, and the monk pointed to each of the Buddha's disciples in turn. 'Manjusri,' he said. And 'Samatabhadra,' and 'Mahakasyapa,' as if those names so dear to him and so alien to his captors were talismans of power that might save his life even in the midst of this nightmare. At each name the Hun chieftain nodded thoughtfully, and the monk began to look more and more hopeful. 'Buddha,' he said again, his eyes pleading.

Attila remained squatting, looking at the delicate ivory plaque and stroking his thin grey beard. Then he shook his head. 'I do not know this god.' He smiled at the monk, a little regretfully, drew his dagger from its sheath on his broad leather belt, took hold of the monk by his sparse topknot and cut his throat. He stood up and sent the little ivory plaque spinning through the air to Chanat.

'Might make a good knife-handle,' he said.

In the cold white light, there was Enkhtuya passing over the battlefield with her snakes, a tall gaunt figure moving silently among the dying and the dead.

225

Sky-in-Tatters looked on, still disbelieving. Already his men were calling it the Battle of Forty Breaths, it was over so quickly. Some four or five thousand Chinese warriors had lost their lives on this battlefield in the space of an hour. Among the Huns, fewer than fifty were dead. He turned to Attila, his eyes shining. 'Let us ride on. Nothing can stop us now. They fell before us like men already slain. Now all the riches of China lie before us – gold and pearls, silks and ivory, and tiny barefoot girls with high-arched brows.'

Attila slapped him on the shoulder. 'Comrade,' he said, 'this was an easy battle but it would take more than our two thousand to destroy China.' He looked up. 'Or Rome. Our power may be great, but our time is not. Rome first.' He nodded. 'Then we will come back for China.'

Geukchu drove over the captured Chinese officer at spearpoint. Csaba brought him a head in a soggy sack, the head of the general who only half an hour before had lain under his palanquin, enjoying his ambling, well-protected tour of the emperor's northern borders.

Attila loosed the rope from round the man's burly chest and arms, and handed him the sack. 'You alone are free to go. But you will take this to the emperor and tell him that the Xioung Nu will yet return.' He added, 'The bad slaves,' and spat.

The officer looked him in the eye, nodded, and took the sack. Attila signalled for him to be given a horse, and the officer mounted, tied the sack to the pommel of his saddle. He rode away east, shrank to a wavering black figure on the vast snowbound plain and was gone.

They burned the Chinese dead like dogs, and the few of their own men they had lost that morning with appropriate honours and lamentations. The Kutrigur women and children walked among the dead and expertly stripped them of any valuables left on them. They gathered as many arrows as they could, both Hun and Chinese, and three wagonloads of swords and helmets and spears. Only the heavy, unwieldy rectangular infantry shields of the Chinese footsoldiers were useless to these horse-warriors, but they loaded them up anyway for barter or scrap. Some of the Hun warriors now wore battered hauberks and jerkins of lamellar armour, but most continued to disdain such cumbersome apparel, continuing to believe in the virtues of hardened but lightweight leather. The women dismembered other bits of armour and wore the bright little plates of bronze as earrings, or threaded them on strings for necklaces. The children hoarded little bags of bright plates eagerly, and the boys fought for them and the girls played elaborate games for them.

It was mid-afternoon before they left the battlefield. They rode for a while and then stopped to eat. Some of the children cheekily bartered weapons for food.

Then they turned south and left the battle plain, and ascended into the foothills of the mountains called the Qilian Shan. They camped for the night in a cold valley, and by midnight fog had settled in the hollows and chilled their hobbled horses to the bone, more so even than the distant, muffled howling of the wolves. But at the fireside in their tents, reliving the glorious day and the Battle of Forty Breaths in glittering detail, the warriors' hearts still burned within them.

12

THE MOUNTAINS

The next day the fog slowly lifted in the low sunlight forking in from the east between the mountains, and they saw how great those mountains were. These people of the steppes had never seen anything like them, although they were among the legends of the People. The summits of the mountains were lost in the still further summits of white air, towering cloud-capped palaces of sun-white clouds. It seemed a blasphemy almost to breathe in the sight of them.

There were valleys where the sun rested and stayed and the snow fled in that false spring. Forks of sunlight raked the yellow grass, and then there was some game, and they would gallop off in a mad hunt, yelling and hallooing, their crazed winter quest briefly forgotten. At night they gorged on half-cooked antelope meat and fell asleep with stomachs groaning with pleasure and pain.

There were a few villages, their livestock brought into their own huts for the winter. The villagers gaped at the approach of the two thousand horsemen, the four- or five-thousand-strong tribe of people on the move. But the passers-by took nothing, looted nothing. Many of them looked gaunt and hungry, but they did no plunder. Near one village, a grubby little girl standing high on a grey precipice of rocks with a herd of droop-eared goats saw them pass by in the valley below, and in the half an hour it took them all to pass not a single other villager set eyes on them. In the evening the girl told her mother and father that she had seen an army that afternoon, more than she could count, armed with bows and arrows and spears and very frightening. Her parents told her not to tell tall stories. She insisted that it was true, and her parents sent her to bed without any supper.

In the morning the father went down to the valley to check his snares and saw the numberless hoofprints at the upper end of the valley where the army had drawn together into the pass, and he stood and reeled and stared. Then he took the hare he had caught, climbed back up to the village and ordered his wife to give the little girl an extra egg for breakfast. He felt he needed an extra egg himself. And he wondered what sort of an army passes by without commandeering all the grain and meat and livestock in a village.

They ascended into a silent and alien world of barbed white peaks and pine forests as dark as pitch, as dark as the oil that bubbles out of the Chorasmian desert sand. There were glaciers that hung like robes of purest mother-of-pearl from haughty mountaintops, and snowcliffs that tottered above them as they wound their way along precipitous paths, the wind blowing gusts of snowdust off the cliffs and into their streaming eyes. Their horses stumbled blindly, the sweat on their necks and bellies freezing into crystals of ice.

They rounded the frozen lower slopes of a vast mountain blazing a luminous fiery red above them in the dying sun, a single crystal of ice a mile high. A terrible abyss lay to their right that none dared look into. They kept their heads down and eyes ahead like blinkered horses, frightened of what lay alongside. And then one of the wagons tilted and gave a low groan and slid freely sideways across the icy path pulling the two drafthorses with it. The animals spread their shaggy hooves wide, surprised, unafraid, not understanding. They continued to slide, and the heavy wagon laden with Chinese infantry shields slid over the side of the path, tilted a little and then fell away into the noiseless abyss below. The horses likewise. The people tiptoed forward and peered over the edge of the precipice. They saw the wagon falling silently into the abyss, its wheels slowly turning, and the horses pawing at the empty air, making no sound, the bright red and gold Chinese shields falling through the air around them in a glittering cloud. Not a sound to accompany their falling, not a moan. Only the wind sighing up from the darkening abyss, and silence among the people as they waited for some sound of the fall, and no sound, not a sound from the abyss, only returning silence and the soft wind everlasting.

The wagons and the packhorses and many of the very young and the very old could go no further. Attila divided his forces, and sent all the women and children and the old men and the remaining wagons back down from the mountains under the escort of Juchi and Bela and Noyan and their troop of eight hundred men. The three brothers scowled bitterly at being left behind, but they said nothing. Attila gave them instructions where to make camp. The twelve hundred mounted warriors rode on.

They saw two buzzards, high in the blue sky, tip and tilt and steady again against the wind, a pair of them working the valley, their high and faraway mew as filled with longing as a gull's. These were the only living creatures they saw for three days. There was no snow and no wind and the air was clear and the skies at night were dazzling with stars. But anyone foolish enough to stay outside and gaze admiringly heavenwards soon lost his ears and fingers.

It was so cold that the little flagons of Chinese wine they had plundered turned to viscous syrup. You could have eaten it like honey, except it would freeze your tongue. They descended again to the treeline, but it was no warmer, and even as they rode, living trees at the edge of the forest exploded with a crack like a giant's bullwhip, and one horse reared in fright and came down and broke its leg. Their bones broke like brittle ice in this cold. Rocks cracked apart likewise, and when they chopped logs for firewood the wood gave off blue sparks like iron. Their exhaled breath fell to the ground in a whispering shower of crystals. They felt both wonder and terror at how the strange the world was.

It was madness to ride on like this, in this punishing cold. Already some men were now riding two to a horse because they had lost so many of the animals, and some of those men had lost fingers. But it was harder to go back than to go on. Ahead, so said their implacable leader at the head of the column, lay a mountain kingdom that would soon be theirs for the taking.

They came off the mountains and over a gravel plateau riven with dirty grey ice and low ridges and kames of sand and loess, where long ago, when the world was warmer and the gods kinder, some lost river had sloughed its way over the plain and moved rocks the size of funeral mounds. Or perhaps it was a river of ice. Perhaps it would have taken a frozen river of ice to move such boulders. The warriors looked and wondered and shivered. But in their dreams they saw the plain as it once might have been: only delicate skim ice on the midnight-blue river, birds calling, a bittern clinging to the reeds, and a breeze in the farther grass, creatures moving and alive and beautiful.

But this was now the bleakest of terrain, dour and lifeless, and the spirits of the warriors were at their lowest. The cold grey plateau was unforgiving, the wind cut like a knife through bearskin and wolfskin cloaks, through their long, tight-belted quilted coats, and through the hides of the horses. The horses' chests laboured and they breathed with difficulty, their poor hides stretched taut over their skinny ribs. No grass grew here. It was hard to imagine that grass had ever grown in such a desolate world. And there was little fodder, and what was left was going fast, and two thousand horses in winter can die as easily as flies if they are not fed.

That night, when they camped in the bitter cold, their tent doors turned to the south where a watery sun shone by day and mocked their hopes, Attila's chosen men and Sky-in-Tatters and some of the chief men of the Kutrigur Huns came to him in his modest tent and said that the warriors were losing faith. They could not go on like this.

The king said nothing. Instead Little Bird appeared unbidden nearby and began to sing. His old cracked lute sounded gentle, and his voice was soft and low. He sang of how, in the older days, a blue wolf and a fallow deer came from across the grey seas, in the innocent dawn of the world, and on the slopes of Burkhan Khaldun, the holy mountain, at the head of the running Onon river, they coupled and the fallow deer soon bore a human child. Tengri, the Lord of the Sun, and Itugen, the Lady of the Moon, shone down together at the moment of his birth, and were like two lamps of equal and miraculous brightness in the sky. The child born under sun and moon was Astur, the All-Father, by whom man and woman were made.

It was the oldest story of the People, and in the bitter night on the comfortless plateau, the chiefs and captains forgot their complaints, drew close to the fire and listened with half-closed eyes.

The god-child Astur, laughing with glee and squeezing the little figures out from wet clay, made Batacaqican the first magician, and Tarkan the Mighty, and also Manas, the great hero. He gave Manas a horse fit for a hero, with legs of bronze and hooves the size of a burned-out campfire. The horse had eyes like a raven's, his muscles rippled like a river, he fed on cornflowers and pasqueflowers and windflowers and only the sweetest spring grass. After Manas died fighting in the great war against the frost-giants, his horse took his wife, Kanikei, and their baby son, Semetai, and galloped all night through the starlit sky to bring them to the Plains of Plenty. And there Semetai grew up to be the wisest of all the kings of the People.

Little Bird fell silent, and the chiefs and captain nodded and their heads drooped and they slept.

The next day they rode on, climbing up from the bitter gravel plain with its scouring wind and into the mountains again. It was another day's ride, and late afternoon with the sun razing in low from the west, when they felt their bones growing warmer. The plateau felt far behind them, and these mountains somehow caught the heat more, as well as being sheltered from the north. They came up over a ridge and there before them was a wide, shallow valley some half a mile across, green with winter grass. The horses pulled away from even the strongest riders and grazed it down to its yellow roots.

They camped there for the night.

As darkness fell, Attila went to Sky-in-Tatters and roused him. The chief grumbled bitterly, but the implacable king said there was something he wanted to show him. Sky-in-Tatters wrapped himself in his cloak and stumbled outside and saw that the other chosen men were all mounted up and ready. He got onto his horse and they rode away north across the grassy plain, leaving the camp far behind.

They rode for nearly an hour and rose up on the other side of the shallow valley, climbing over low green, snow-flecked hills. The horses were tired and they rode slowly. Finally they were climbing up stony paths over bare mountainsides, and could look back on the valley behind them dotted with campfires. Above them the sky was studded with silver and the bright coin of the moon, and there was no wind. You could almost say it was mild.

At last Attila climbed up a ridge and stopped, and the chosen men and the Kutrigur chieftain came up alongside. Sky-in-Tatters gasped. He was still in his tent, dreaming. This could not be.

Below them the mountains fell away again, and down there, under the great canopy of the night, lay another valley vast and ringed by mountains and hidden from the world. In the silverblue moonlight he could see it distinctly. The broad valley stretched east to west, perhaps as much as twenty miles long, and down it ran a bright silver river. But the most astonishing thing was the wall of mountains opposite them, some five miles distant. For the wall, almost sheer and bathed in moonlight, was also studded with stars, red and orange stars, like fires. Screwing up his eyes, it seemed to Sky-in-Tatters that he could make out ...

'This cannot be,' he said.

Attila turned to him and his teeth shone white in the moonlight. 'The Valley of Oroncha, the kingdom of the god-king, Tokuz-Ok, Nine Arrows.' His teeth showed even more. 'A more martial name than he deserves.'

Sky-in-Tatters gaped. 'How do you know this? You have not been here before. It is not possible.'

Attila did not answer. Instead he said, 'I also know that the kingdom of Tokuz-Ok is a great kingdom. The Oronchan people are many. You know how farmers breed. Look at this valley by daylight tomorrow and you will see a lush, well-watered valley full of orchards, grainfields, meadows and pastureland. His people are many, many thousand. His army is numerous.'

'Army?' snorted a grizzled voice behind. 'An army of farmers? Ruled by their wives, and with hoes and pitchforks for weapons?'

It was, inevitably, Chanat.

'An army of as many as twenty thousand men,' said Attila. 'It is possible. And the mountainside that you see opposite, dotted with fires, which you do not believe? That is their city. It clings to the mountainside like a raven's nest, and is as safe. It is warmed all day by the sun, and never feels the north wind. The whole valley catches the sun likewise, and the mountains are its windbreak. No invading army could ever take that city. They would have to be mounted on eagles.'

Sky-in-Tatters felt a surge of excitement, despite himself. An

233

army of farmers, but an army of twenty thousand! There was no limit to their power if they commanded such an army. This bandit king, this Attila – the power in him, the intelligence as sharp as a knife, the certainty of success. Sky-in-Tatters could taste victory on his tongue like honey.

'How can we conquer this kingdom?'

Attila was already pulling his horse round and heading home. 'Where strength will not,' came his voice out of the darkness, 'guile will serve.'

13

THE MOUNTAIN KINGDOM OF
THE SYPHILITIC GOD-KING

At dawn Attila rode into the kingdom of the god-king alone.

He rode unarmed and slow. He came down from the mountains and then over the grassy slopes flecked with snow, and the rising sun cut in from the east low over the mountaintops and warmed the valley as he had said.

The green hillsides levelled out and he rode through orchards and meadowlands, and past small clusters of thatched huts with bee skeps on the broad shelves of thatched bee sheds in their bare winter gardens. People stopped and stared at him but no one challenged him. The country was running with silver streams, and water wheels clacked beside cressbeds. This peaceful, settled existence reminded him of long ago, and Italy. How could people live in one valley all their lives, as if in scorn of the rest of the world God made?

There were many people in the fields already, and others rose from their pallets to see the foreign horseman in his long quilted coat and strange pointed hat. There were farmers yoking their oxen up, and housewives in their yards, throwing woodash out onto their winter vegetables and rebuilding the smoored fire that had smouldered all night in the hearth. Children herded geese down to the streams, and old men wrapped in blankets sat on doorsteps with rheumy eyes, drinking hot chai from clay bowls. People were everywhere, clustered thickly, thousands of them; like corn ripe for harvesting.

After a slow walk through the rich farmland, the mountains ahead began to tower up, dark and forbidding, and he emerged onto a bare road that led to a great gate. The gate was open, and the road twisted and ran up the side of the ascending cliff to another. From here upwards, built clinging to the sides of the mountain and linked only by the most precipitous paths, were the palaces of noblemen, the temples of priests, the monasteries of monks and, above them all, the palace of the god-king himself.

The peacefulness of the mountainside city amused him. Monks with shaven heads, in rust-red robes, stopped and bowed, then scampered away before him. Women carrying heavy baskets on their heads stopped and gawped, then looked away and hurried on. Only at the top of the road at another broad gateway flanked by grey stone towers did two guards step forward, block his way with their long pikes and demand to know his business. This was clearly not a city accustomed to war.

He stopped, and looked at them, and Chagëlghan signalled his contempt for the hard manmade stones beneath his hooves by lifting his tail and manuring them liberally.

'I seek an audience with the king,' said Attila.

The men objected, politely and at length.

'I had a dream of nine arrows,' said Attila, 'and then a tenth arrow, which flew and broke all the other nine.'

The men stammered and stared at each other, and one ran to talk to his lieutenant. The lieutenant peered out of a little booth, then sent the guard running up the steep hill to another authority. And so, by slow and bureaucratic degrees, this strange yellow-eyed nomad savage was admitted higher up into the city, past magnificent carved and painted temples releasing incense and the tinkling of tiny bells into the still morning air. At last, with deepest respect, they asked him to dismount, and ushered him through a small postern gateway of ornate stonework.

Within was a covered terrace, looking out southwards over the valley. The view was magnificent. Attila turned his back on it, leaned against the balustrade and crossed his arms and waited. Who ruled over this view? Who possessed it?

'A dream you say? Well, well,' said a voice, high-pitched and excitable. Through a doorway at the opposite end of the terrace stepped a large robed figure. His round face was beaming and sottish, his nose half eaten away at the nostrils. He wore a bizarre piece of headgear, a crown of beaten gold which radiated out in horizontal spokes from around his skull. Stepping through the door he had knocked it askew and now he paused to straighten it. 'Well, well,' he said again.

Behind the syphilitic god-king came a character of a different stamp, a short, squat, burly, white-haired general of some sixty years, unarmed but in a full coat of mail. His nose was blunt, severally broken, but undevoured by plague or disease. His long white moustache was carefully combed and his eyes were bright and unyielding. He stood just within the doorway and kept his eyes on the visitor.

The god-king lifted the hem of his robe, exposing small feet encased in bejewelled kidskin slippers, and took little steps over to the visitor. He smiled. His few remaining teeth were not good: grey shards collapsing drunkenly into each other. His lips were painted vermilion, and from the fat, elongated lobes of his ears hung heavy gold rings. As befitted a god-king, his robe was the colour of the sun, except under the armpits where it was a little dark and greasy. His stomach was a wobbling mound when he moved, and his head, crowned with the gold crown of the sun, was a bald dome with rolls of fat round its base. He stopped a few paces from the silent visitor in his long grubby coat and looked over the terrace, making an odd hissing sound. Beneath them was a wider terrace where numerous pubescent concubines with crippled feet sat around prettifying themselves and awaiting his command.

Attila did not look or stir.

The god-king hesitated and beamed at him again. The heavenly father of his people, and the earthly father of inbred dozens.He had already forgotten about the dream. He was uncertain why this visitor was here.

'Come!' he commanded, and beckoned him over to the back of the terrace. Here a colonnade of stone pillars gave way to a row of doorways leading off into darkened chambers, hollowed out of the very rock itself.

Attila stepped into the gloom after the god-king, and heard the tough old general close behind.

'Bayan-Kasgar!' called the god-king from inside the gloomy chamber. 'Bring us more light!'

Attila and the god-king waited patiently, standing opposite each other in the gloom. Attila could feel the little knife nestling coldly against the skin of his belly. The old general was gone. The chamber was very still. The god-king smiled at him fixedly, then wiped a little tear of pus from his nose with the back of his ringed hand. He did not deserve to survive. The whole kingdom did not deserve to survive.

'Bayan-Kasgar,' repeated Attila. 'Beautiful Wolf. Wolf-like, maybe, but … beautiful?'

The god-king stared uneasily at the stranger. What an odd thing to say. He wondered if he ought to call more guards. How was he supposed to know what to do? Where was his chamberlain? Why was he on his own now? He felt very annoyed. To mask his annoyance he burst into a peel of high-pitched giggles. The stranger laughed along with him, and took a step towards him.

Then dear Bayan-Kasgar returned at the head of a troop of guards carrying tall, elaborate bronze candelabra which they set on the ground. Attila realised the size of the chamber for the first time, a vast lumber-room of accumulated stuff as appeals to sedentary emperors everywhere. Like that ardent collector in Rome. Stuff. God-kings always accumulated stuff, to weigh them down. Perhaps to give them the comforting illusion of a gravity and substance that they could never in their mere selves possess. The kings of settled people who had never learned, or had wilfully forgotten, that the more you have, the less you are.

He nodded admiringly, and the god-king giggled again and began to show him round his collection.

In the dim candlelight Attila expressed his heartfelt admiration for the god-king's outlandish treasury. His tortoiseshell boxes of musk and ginseng root from neighbouring tribal overlords; his tall vases full of the brightly coloured feathers of vanished birds; his cedarwood chest of gold nuggets from Bei Kem. The god-king stooped wheezily over the chest, picked up one of the rough nuggets between pudgy forefinger and thumb and put it to his mouth. He turned back to Attila, grinning idiotically, sucking the nugget like a child sucking a plum. After he had sucked it a while to his satisfaction, he drew it from his mouth, smacked his lips and handed it, looped with saliva, to the visitor. Attila shook his head in polite demurral. The god-king looked momentarily sulky, and dropped it back in the chest. But he soon cheered up again when he showed off to the visitor his suits of Chinese armour, and his long swords in decorated scabbards. Attila's hand settled on one of the sword-hilts and then released it. Bayan-Kasgar stood not far away to his right. His troop of guards looked on from the doorway.

'In my stables down in the valley I have a thousand white camels, and two thousand white horses,' said the god-king, speaking very rapidly and excitedly. Attila said he should like to see these white horses, perhaps even to ride them, but the god-king rattled on, oblivious.

He had three hundred wives and two thousand concubines, and also some boys, and one of them was black from head to foot, can you imagine that? Except for the palms of his hands and the soles of his feet, and his pinky pinky tongue! And every new moon he, Tokuz-Ok, Lord of All the World under Heaven, created fire out of nothing, in the temple of Itugen, behind a little curtain. After he had blessed a bare stone, he came back out and two monks went in. A little later they emerged again and they carried the stone burning brightly with magical fire that he had created. It was a monthly miracle. Like a lady's ...

'Itugen,' repeated Attila. 'The Lady of the Moon.'

'And of the earth,' said the god-king, trying to sound solemn. 'It is she who blesses our crops and lades our orchards in summer.'

He returned to his treasures, wondering secretly what marvellous new treasure this visitor might have brought in tribute for him. He showed the visitor a ten-pound lump of amber from the shores of the frozen sea, and bags of pearls from Indian rajas, and at the back of the chamber, leaning against the bare rock wall, a pair of walrus tusks. Beyond that in the darkness was a little arched doorway that led into yet another chamber. The candelabra were brought in, and the god-king went on to show the visitor a chest full of gently rotting furs, of fabulously rare white beaver, and blue sable, and black panther. That great fur was more of a faded grey now, and motheaten, and as the god-king pawed at it, it gave off weight-less tufts which rose and spiralled and fell noiselessly through the soporific candelit air.

The god-king also showed him manuscripts in scrolls in red and gold lettering, which he said had fluttered down from heaven like birds, and stone tablets from the west from ancient vanished kingdoms with carved angular script, and then in another chamber a menagerie of stuffed animals, including a sloth, a boa constrictor, and a tiger with obsidian eyes.

Attila admired them all with great sincerity, and the god-king led him back out onto the terrace. He looked out over his little kingdom and beamed.

'So,' he said, 'what tribute have you brought me, stranger?'

'My men,' said Attila, 'will bring you a fitting tribute.'

The god-king turned to Attila and his big pasty face seemed to pale a little. 'Your ... men?'

Attila said nothing. He merely nodded towards the distant mountains overlooking the valley from the south. The god-king turned and his knees trembled and his throat went very dry. All along the mountaintops to the south, little black figures bristled against the brightening sky. Hundreds of them. Thousands ... The god-king made an odd little squeaking noise in his throat.

Bayan-Kasgar stepped up. 'What is this?' he rasped. 'I will have you—'

Attila looked round at him curiously. 'The tribute is on its way,' he said. 'It will take many men to carry it here.'

The old general began to speak angrily again, but Tokuz-Ok ordered him to be silent. The god-king could not be disobeyed. Bayan-Kasgar stepped back, and look down at the stone terrace floor, fuming silently. He must send out the order to his divisions to arm at once.

'It must be a mighty tribute,' said the god-king.

'Sackloads and sackloads,' said Attila. 'Wagonloads.'

The god-king clapped his hands together and looked heavenwards, then without a word of farewell he tripped away across the terrace, through the door at the end and was gone.

The troop followed him. Bayan-Kasgar raised his head and stared at the visitor one more time. Then he turned on his heel and marched out after them.

As he reached the archway, he felt a powerful forearm clamp round his neck and he was dragged backwards, his heels scraping over the stone. He was hauled into the nearest chamber and flung up against the wall with that forearm still around his neck like a vice, half-throttling him. There was also a cold knife-blade at his throat for good measure. He tried to speak but could not. This was no dreamer of dreams who knew how to fight like this. Bayan-Kasgar cursed him in his heart.

The nomad savage leaned close to the old general and whispered in his ear, 'He is no king.' Then he released him.

Bayan-Kasgar turned, rubbing his neck, and stared at the savage, who held his knife out low towards him. One hasty move, he knew, and he would be bleeding to death on the stones. But soon the troop would return. Any moment now.

'He is no king,' hissed the savage again. 'Nine Arrows! One arrow will break him. He is no king, and he is certainly no god. You know that you despise him.'

'He is the seventeenth son of the son of heaven,' rasped the general. But there was a fatal uncertainty in his voice, something both hesitant and ironic. Attila smiled to hear it. The general went on doggedly, 'You cannot destroy the city, no matter how many men you command up there on the mountaintops.'

'We cannot destroy the city, but we can lay waste the land, the whole Valley of Oroncha, and you will starve. You know this is true.'

Bayan-Kasgar said nothing.

'One arrow,' Attila said again. He stepped close and in a flash the knife-blade was at the general's throat again. He moved like a snake, this one. He spoke very rapidly but the general heard and remembered every word. 'You will kill him. You will make yourself emperor. You will join with us and ride out with us and we will conquer all who stand against us and I will give you a great empire. You will return to this valley wondering that you waited so long. You and your sons will be the mightiest of emperors of this country.

'You worship Itugen, the Lady of the Moon, and Astur, and you remember the deeds of Manas. You were Huns once.'

'We came from the southern deserts, long ago,' said the general vaguely. 'We warred with China.'

'And you shall again. Join with us.'

'We are farmers now.'

'I will make warriors of your farmers yet.'

Bayan-Kasgar looked doubtful. 'We are a settled people. How

blessed this valley is, see for yourself. We cannot abandon it.'

Attila grew impatient. 'Your women and children and your old men can farm it till you return. Any clod can turn a clod. Raise your divisions and ride with me. You will return. It will not be long. A year, two years of campaigning, and you will return a great conqueror. Your name will live for ever. This trash' – he gestured contemptuously about – 'you will use to stoke your fires, or you will melt it down into coin stamped with your likeness. You will inherit not a valley but an empire.' His eyes burned. Bayan-Kasgar could feel the heat of those eyes on his very skin.

'I have no sons,' he murmured. 'My wife is dead.'

'Take another.'

'The law forbids it. Only the emperor can take more than one wife.'

Attila did not deign to reply to this absurdity. Instead he stepped back and slashed his knife in two lightning diagonals before the old general's eyes, as if bewitching him and blessing him in a single sign.

'Kill him,' he said. 'Then come to me.'

With another movement of snakelike swiftness he was at the door, looking back, holding up his forefinger as one final prompt to regicide. Then he was gone.

The troop of guards reappeared a few moments later, peering into the gloom of the chamber, blind as bats.

Attila rode down from the mountainside city unmolested. He bade farewell to the women washing at the stream, to the children netting for minnows in the back pools. And, farther off, to the manaschi in his cloak of blue-black velvet and gold embroideries, standing beneath the bare-branched peach trees in the orchard, chanting the endless lays.

14

BAYAN-KASGAR

The Huns waited two more days, growing impatient. On the dawn of the second day, they had a visitor, though not the one they wanted.

When they rose in the morning, on the edge of the camp they saw a bold little man with darting eyes, sitting in a donkey cart with his wife and two children, surrounded and indeed quite hemmed in by sacks of barley loaves, apples, cheeses, crude clay pots and flagons. It was one of the locals, who had heard of their presence and seized the opportunity for some trade. A couple of the Kutrigurs went over to cut the family's throats and take their supplies. Orestes saw what was about to happen and cantered over and hailed them off, so impressed was he by the fellow's irrepressible mercantilism, not to mention his insane courage.

'Friends, yes?' the little grocer called over to them, nodding eagerly. 'I bring you good things.' He rubbed his belly.

'Farmers,' harrumphed Chanat, reining in his horse close to Orestes, 'come to sell us food. Merchants.' He hawked and spat lavishly. 'Coin-hoarders, spade-wielders, earth under their nails. House-dwellers with brats in the sacks, middens in their midst and shit on their doorstep, counting out their—'

Orestes could not help laughing at this tremendous and poetical diatribe. Then he went over to the farmer in his donkey cart and paid him in coins of Chinese silver for his wares.

'Bread?' Chanat sneered at him as he came back. 'Bread? A man who eats bread is made of bread – and crumbles like bread, too.'

Orestes munched cheerfully. 'Delicious,' he mumbled. 'Reminds me of my boyhood.' Chanat's scowl made him laugh so much that he sprayed the old warrior in detested crumbs.

The farmer and his family were driven over to Attila. The farmer dismounted warily from the cart and bowed low before the king.

Attila bade him stand straight. 'You are bold.'

'Bold makes gold,' chirruped the little man sententiously. 'Prudent stays poor.' He turned and rummaged in his donkey cart. His wife sighed, found what he was looking for and handed it to him. He passed it on to the nomad king. It was revolting, sugary sticky stuff, apricots or something. Attila thanked him and passed the pot on to Orestes.

'Fruit from the forest,' said the farmer. 'Very dangerous to collect.'

'How so?'

'Bears live in the forest.'

'And other tribes?'

'The Chinchin!' exclaimed the little man.

Attila waited patiently.

The Chinchin, he said, were a people only two feet tall and covered with thick dark hair all over. Their knees did not bend and they progressed by little leaps, their legs held together. 'Like this,' said the grocer, and demonstrated the gait of the Chinchin himself.

'We hunt them by leaving out dishes of sweet fruits, such as this' – he pointed to the one he had given Attila – 'or else we leave out dishes of wine for them among the trees. They become intoxicated with the wine, merrily crying, "Chinchin! Chinchin!" and then they fall asleep and we put them in bags and bring them home to cook. Their flesh is very good.' He rubbed his belly and nodded vigorously and smiled.

'You have actually seen these fabulous people yourself?'

'Oh yes,' the man assured him.

'And eaten them?'

'Oh yes. Delicious!' But he sounded more hesitant now. His wife looked away.

Attila took a slow step towards him. 'You have hunted and eaten them yourself?'

'Well ...' said the Oronchan gourmet. He sighed. 'Well, no.

I have not. No. Not myself. But it is among the legends of the people. I do not doubt it.' He looked at the nomad king anxiously. 'Surely you do not doubt it?'

Attila did not reply. Instead he thanked the visitor for his gift, and gave him safe passage through the camp to sell his wares.

Once the merchant was gone, Attila looked sideways at Orestes. 'We will not recruit the Chinchin into our army, I think.'

Orestes shook his head. 'Best not.'

On the third day, Bayan-Kasgar rode into the camp alone and sought audience with Attila in his tent.

They sat on low stools. The general planted his fists on his knees.

'So,' said Attila. 'I take it one arrow was sufficient.'

The general grunted and said, 'Rhubarb leaves.'

Attila looked questioning.

'A plant we eat – parts of it. None of it is to my taste, in truth, but the leaves are poisonous: a powerful laxative. Fatal in quantity.'

'Hm. It must have been a messy death.'

'Fitting,' grunted the general. 'He was a swine.'

A scintilla of humour passed between them. They clasped hands, and laid their other hands on each others' arms and swore fealty unto death.

Thus the Huns of Attila, already united with the Kutrigur Huns, were further united with the people of the valley of Oroncha, and their emperor, Bayan-Kasgar, Beautiful Wolf.

Attila said he would prefer to call him Beyaz-Kasgar, or White Wolf. He told the old general that he had many virtues; but beauty, alas, was not among them. Bayan-Kasgar acknowledged the truth of this ruefully, but said that a man's name was not a thing that could be lightly changed.

When Attila grew to know him better and they had shared a bowl or two of koumiss, the nomad king called him Ravent-Yaprak, which is to say, Rhubarb Leaf. But only Attila dared to call him that. The general might be into his seventh decade but his temper was that of a young bull.

He brought with him more warriors than they could number, some mounted on the slain god-king's herd of two thousand

245

prancing white horses, in whom the blood of the Horses of Heaven clearly ran. Many more rode horses of a more common but sturdy breed, skewbalds and piebalds and dusty bays and stocky little greys. A horde of farmers, suddenly taken with the spirit of adventure, wanted to learn again the ancient arts of their fathers with arrow and bow, shield and flashing sword. Young men not yet married, and more eager to fight than marry. And older men, husbands and fathers, bidding bitter wives and tearful children farewell at the cottage gate, and riding away torn between guilt and excitement. Before long the excitement triumphed, and any remaining guilt was irritably dismissed or forgotten amid the headlong rush of galloping horses and the wide and limitless freedom of the plains.

The union of the Black and the Kutrigur Huns had been forged in bloody battle. But the union of their conjoined forces and the people of the valley was effected only by guile, threat and shrewd judgement of men, and with the loss of only a single and unlamented life.

Attila led them north in the bitter early months of the new year, and they were reunited with the rest of the Kutrigur people, the women and children, and with Juchi and Bela and Noyan and their eight hundred horsemen. They rode for two famished but strangely exhilarated weeks until they found pasture in a great depression in the midst of the desert where moisture collected and green grass grew all the year round. The yellow-eyed nomad king had known it was there, none knew how. Other nomads were camped there already when the great army hove in view, but they did not linger, and soon many thousands of horses were grazing the grass to its roots.

Soon other bands of nomads came to join them, having heard fantastical tales of a mighty army of Asiatic peoples, and a great quest, and a commander and king who shone with the favour of heaven, against whom no man or empire could stand. Some bands numbered no more than a dozen, some several hundred, and the spring grass struggled to grow fast enough to feed the horses' many thousands of mouths. Horses and weapons and goods were amicably traded, marriages were made, and even the hardiest warriors grumbled in their tents at night at the din of all the wailing newborns in the night. And so, by fame and alliance, courtship and copulation, the numbers of the people grew and grew.

Each people formed its own regiment, but learned its discipline and took its orders from Attila and his chosen men. When not drilling they played the furious, competitive games of the steppe peoples. Picking up tiny gold rings from the grass at full gallop, or lunatic wrestling matches between two men each mounted and galloping side by side. Trying to steal kisses, and more intimate forfeits, from young maidens who rode armed with long whips with which they lashed their pursuers mercilessly. The lashing they gave with their tongues was even worse.

Then it was time to break camp for the last time, and begin the long journey west, for the first signs of spring were appearing everywhere and the horses and livestock could forage as they went. Early clover and vetch, sainfoin, corn spurrey and slender oatgrass coloured the warming plains.

'To Rome!' cried Attila, raising his sword high. 'Even to the shores of the Atlantic!' His numberless thousands of warriors gave a great shout, most having no clue what 'Atlantic' meant but liking the grandeur of the word.

Little Bird, sitting his pony close to the king, did not shout with them but only gave a heretical sigh amidst all this martial rejoicing. 'All the same, I would have liked to have seen China, my father,' he said. 'Before I died.'

'You will see China,' said Attila, wrenching at his reins. His voice was fierce, but Little Bird's voice was soft and melancholy.

'Only in dreams,' he said. 'In a dream, I climbed to the top of a high hill from where I could see all of China.' He spoke now in his sing-song rhythmical lilt, as if reciting a poem. 'The hanging gardens of the emperor's summer palace, the jade streams singing, the glimmering bird-girls in their leaves of silk and gold.'

He stopped and smiled at Attila.

Attila said nothing in reply to Little Bird's haunting words, so rich and strange, of such sad omen.

The shaman's eyes were silver pools, quite inscrutable.

'Ah, but China is vast,
You will never see it all.
The mountains are high, the emperor is far away.
The emperor is forever far away.'

15

HOMECOMING

The great army looped northwards and towards the time when the days grew as long as the nights, they met the edge of the northern forests where the spring grasses were lush and green, and followed their path westward that way. There remained patches of shrinking snow in the shady hollows, but in such threshold places, between forest and steppe, as between land and sea, there is always good hunting.

At times, with the sun setting low in their eyes, it seemed as if autumn had returned in all its majesty, the branches of the trees burning gold in the dying blaze. And at times the jaws of winter snapped at them still, and sharp flurries of wolf-weather returned. The king was always urging them on into the night, the children exhausted, asleep in the wagons. Sometimes they looped northwards to find fords across the great rivers of that country, riding through the midnight forest, snow aslant, wolves tracing them, shadows through the firs, the most mournful howls echoing across the starlit sky. Beyond the wolves, other figures moved through the forest, watching them, pushing through the towering pines as a man walks through grass: vast, nameless beings more powerful than any wolf that ever lived.

But spring came on steadily, and each day they drew further west out of the iron jaws of central Scythia, and towards the rich pastures beside the Euxine Sea. They rode through long, damp grass beside the forest's edge with dewladen bittercress brushing their horse's hocks. They came through the country of gentle, brown-eyed woodland people, who used jawbones of pike to tattoo their bodies with numberless waves and spirals. They lived in bark-covered tepees, said Little Bird the Wise, though only the children believed him. The adults scoffed and laughed to hear the mad little shaman talk of woodland people who ate moss, and in winter rode through the snow on reindeer with bridle and saddle. Still farther north there were people who hunted seals with obsidian-tipped spears, and roofed their huts of ice with the ribs of whales.

At the riversides the Huns stopped to water their horses among the broadleaved poplars. This was a land so mild and gentle and filled with birdsong that it seemed to them like some great king's private hunting park. They sometimes glimpsed the people of the woodlands, who had long since glimpsed them through the trees: a horde of hellish horsemen, armed to the teeth, eyes as restless as those of hungry wolves. The woodland people had watched them approach for a while with big, mournful eyes, hidden in their bird-skin capes, and had slipped quietly away, taking to their coracles and their leaf-shaped canoes and vanishing northwards into the safety of the deep and endless forest.

There were the pale green shoots of wild onions, the aroma of wild thyme beneath their horses' hooves. A stream of snowmelt so young that it flowed in a streambed merely of flattened green grass, padded and silent, the world so bright and young, as if new made by the All-Father's unseen hands in the night. There are no words for expressing the joy of spring after such winter bitterness as is felt by all nomads and wanderers. Not for them the safety of stone houses. Not for them steaming hypocausts and heated floor-tiles. Only a dung-fire and a horseblanket between them and the killing cold.

Their hearts soared like hawks, bursting with love for the land.

They surprised a black bear one day bumbling out of the woods. When they had speared her and rolled her over in the grass and prayed to the Little Sister's spirit for forgiveness, they found she had milk in her teats. She had hidden her cubs under moss, know-ing she must die that day. But they searched and found the cubs and killed them, too, their fur so fine a gift for a pretty girl. But one cub they kept alive, wet-nosed and wide-eyed, with huge and floppy paws, and he came along with them after that. They packed up the meat from the rest of the cubs and the mother and went on.

Little Bird carried the cub on his lap when he began to tire, and the cub slept and then urinated on him lavishly by way of thanks.

'Tell me about Rome,' said Sky-in-Tatters, lying back in the firelight after gorging too heavily on bearmeat. He belched and rubbed his bulging belly.

Attila sat cross-legged and looked into the fire. He spoke slowly and softly:

> 'By a King of Kings from Palestine
> Two empires were sown,
> By a King of Terror from the east
> Two empires were o'erthrown ...'

Despite his groaning belly, Sky-in-Tatters sat up, or at least raised himself on one elbow. 'Explain.'

'This is a prophecy, a Roman prophecy. The first lines refer to that fiery Jew they call the Christ, the King of Kings, who sowed the empires of Heaven and Hell. In the empire of Rome, he is their god.'

'He is a great warrior?'

'He preaches peace. Preached. He is dead now, though they believe he lives.'

'In heaven?'

'In heaven. Palestine is ... a desert country far to the south. The tribe there is called the Jews. Now this dead god-king is worshipped by all the empire of Rome.'

'Though they are not Jews?'

'No.'

Sky-in-Tatters was looking more and more baffled. 'But they in Rome – Romans ... ? They do not follow his preaching? They are great warriors?'

'Not bad.'

Sky-in-Tatters shook his head. 'My heart is heavy for them. They are confused.'

Attila went on, 'This Christ taught that we should forgive our enemies.'

Sky-in-Tatters threw back his head and laughed. 'When all men know that the sweetest pleasure in life is to destroy our enemies, rape their women, and steal their gold!' He reached for the flagon.

'It was the Romans themselves who put him to death.'

Sky-in-Tatters drank from the flagon and wiped his mouth. 'Now my head is beginning to hurt. And it isn't the koumiss.'

'They put him to death four centuries back, and then realised they'd killed God.'

Chanat said, 'No man is God.'

'There was a Greek wise man,' put in Orestes from the edge of the circle, 'who said that if horses pictured god, they would picture him as a horse.'

They all chuckled.

'These Greeks,' said Sky-in-Tatters, 'they are not the biggest fools I have ever heard of.'

'They are conquered by Rome now.'

Sky-in-Tatters pondered. 'And the other verse. This King of Terror from the east ...'

Attila's eyes shone and he said nothing.

Geukchu said, 'Perhaps he will overthrow even heaven and hell itself, Your Majesty.'

Attila didn't look at him. Geukchu shrank back into silence.

'Rome and China,' said Sky-in-Tatters, a slow smile dawning on his face. 'That makes two empires.' He raised the flagon of koumiss again and took a long, long draught.

A broad river they forded in silvery light, and a rocky defile colourful with larkspur, and then down another sunbaked slope of clattering scree and over a stony plain of malachite and slate, warm fumes of rosemary and lavender and chives rising amid the horses and the leather. It was summer now, sunbaked, and they had ridden the long trail back west for many months, the sun hot on their forearms as they turned and headed south amid a chorus of oxlips and cowslips and anemones and musk orchids, lilac cornflowers and yellow broom and white clover, white windflowers and purple pasqueflowers, with insects rising and falling murmurously among the open flowerheads.

There were silver poplars and rose-coloured rocks, rocks along the river valley, this river that ended at home. Rocks crumbling under the generations of ice and wind, brown earthbanks crumbling into the mighty river. Horses strained up the farther side, wagons clattered over the gravel strands and up shallow slopes to the plains again. The plains that hereabouts were dotted with mighty kurgans, the tombs of the ancient, bearded, blue-eyed Scythians, silent monsters asleep in the long grass.

As for Attila, the fierce joy in his heart was boundless. He could barely hold himself down in the saddle; he kept pushing himself up on his fists, looking afar off for the camp of his people. Orestes noticed and teased him for it. Only Orestes could. He even dared to mention the name of Queen Checa. But it was true. Their joy was boundless, their future without check or limit. They had done it. It was an unbelievable feat, this vast project of unification. They had ridden out across the steppes at the onset of winter, eastwards over the Iron River. They had ridden thousands of miles into the heart of Scythia, to the very shadow of the Great Wall itself. They had united Hun peoples, the Kutrigur and the Black Huns, and joined with another great people, the Oronchans. They had massacred an entire Chinese armoured column for good measure and good practice, and they had been joined by several thousand more nomad and distant kinsmen as they journeyed home. Ahead of them now, ahead of so great and powerful an army, lay only more conquest, and then the ultimate prize. None could stand against them.

Even in these last days, as they approached their homeland, more came to join them. Some had come before, a year ago, hearing of the finding of the Sword of Savash, and then drifted away disconsolate when Attila rode east. They came back, laughing with astonishment, those tribute kings and petty princelings, rulers over tiny, scattered bands of White Huns from the shores of the Caspian, under their king, Charaton; and Kouridach, the great, bow-legged chieftain of the Hepthalite Huns from beside the Aral Sea.

Charaton made to dismount from his horse when he came before Attila, by way of submission, but Attila stopped him. So Charaton sat his horse, and told him that he, even he, had had an embassy from the Byzantines. They had not dared to raise their eyes towards him, they said, for fear that they should be dazzled by his effulgent brilliance. And then the Byzantine ambassadors had offered him a bribe to ally with them, but Charaton had declined their offer, 'though,' as he admitted ruefully, 'it cost me dear.'

Attila told him not to repine. 'We will be before the gates of Constantinople soon,' he said, his eyes glittering. 'Then Constantinople and all its wealth will be yours.' He stroked his beard. 'Soon now.'

It was dawn on the last day of their journey, which had lasted two hundred days. By nightfall they would be back among their tents and their women.

Attila assembled them in their regiments and ranks and told them that they were the greatest army the world had ever seen.

'A great war is coming, and a great empire is falling,' he said. 'And all of you – Black Huns and White Huns, Red and Yellow and Hepthalite Huns, Kutrigurs and Oronchans, people of the mountains and the valleys and the plains – all of you will have glory for yourselves and your descendants in this war. Only follow me and you will be great. For the time of the Hun nation has come.'

The shout might have been heard in the camp. But they would be there by nightfall anyway. He looked over his ranks of men, tens of thousands strong now, and the wagons without number. Then he turned and raised his head high, and they rode on home.

Little Bird galloped half a day ahead, alone but for his bear cub.

The women clamoured round him for news when he rode into the camp, and he drove them almost to distraction by not answering a single one of their questions. Several even struck out at him in their anguish but he dodged them and skipped away, laughing.

When the sun went down, the women were still gathered around him in forlorn hope of news that made sense. He dropped down and sat cross-legged at the fireside and raised his eyebrows at them.

The earth was rumbling.

He leaned sideways at an extraordinary angle and put his ear to the ground. He waggled his topknot merrily and grinned, still canted sideways as if he were made all of flesh and had not a bone inside him. Then he snapped upright again and looked around at the troubled women, his hands resting on his knees where they poked through the ragged holes in his grubby breeches. They waited, fit to scream.

'These baleful *borborygmi* in the deep earth's bowels,' he pronounced, 'presage either the return of my mad-eyed master at the head of a million horsemen, or the end of the world.' His black eyes danced with malevolence. 'Or perhaps ... both!'

16

THE SICKNESS OF ELLAK,
THE POWER OF ENKHTUYA

But there was no celebration when the horsemen returned.

Attila rode first into camp, at full gallop, and made straight for the royal palace. Someone tried to hail him as he sped past, but he took no notice. It was Bleda, open-mouthed at his brother's return – he had been getting accustomed to kingship.

Attila pulled Chagëlghan to such a violent halt that the horse skidded forward several yards on its rump, and was off and striding away before the poor beast had its feet. As the king approached the palace, Queen Checa emerged. She was gaunt and hollow-eyed, and her face had the grey pallor of sorrow. He ran to her, but she could not bear to look at him, could not bear him to touch her, as if her guilt were a contagion.

It was Ellak, their second son. He was dying.

'We all have to die one day,' said Little Bird jauntily, playing with the cub nearby.

Attila stopped in mid-stride, and for an instant it seemed as if he might at last turn on the shaman and slay him where he stood. But then he walked on into the palace after his wife.

Little Bird pushed in between them. 'Let me see.' After a few moments of pushing and prodding he stood back again. 'The boy just needs rest,' he said, 'and boiled milk. It's something he ate.'

The bear cub chewed his finger. Little Bird set him down.

And then there was another figure in the shadows by the doorway. It was Enkhtuya.

'The child will die,' she said in a soft hiss.

Little Bird cuffed the cub away and stared angrily at the ground.

The witch glided over, her footsteps not making a sound. 'Unless he drinks innocent blood.'

Attila looked at her long and hard. Then he nodded. 'Take it.'

Bending swiftly, her long hand swooping like a falcon, Enkhtuya seized the cub by the scruff of its neck.

'No!' cried Little Bird, leaping round. 'She shall not have it, curse her and her stone-eyed snakes!' He rounded furiously on Attila. 'How dare you give her the nod over me! She is not our holy thing, she is no one's, she is unholy in her very soul, that cub is under my star and my protection, if she dares—'

Attila roared for silence.

Little Bird stood chewing his lip wrathfully, eyes darting.

Attila nodded to the witch. 'Take it,' he said again. 'Heal the boy.'

Little Bird stood aghast, mouth still working furiously. Then he said softly, 'You have chosen.' And he vanished into the darkness.

Enkhtuya worked her will over the groaning boy while his mother and father and brothers and sisters looked on, and in the shadows Orestes kept watch. She waved a smoking branch of fir over the perspiring, prostrate form, and she burned spruce resin on a flat stone, and made a maddening drone deep in her throat like a swarm of angry wasps. She grew frenzied and, rolling her eyes, began to flog the invisible demon out of the boy with ferocious lashes of the fir branch. In her other hand she produced a little knife with a point like a needle and she pricked the infected boy in the chest and belly, feet, head and hands. Ellak's lips turned blue even as they watched. He groaned and twisted, then struggled and arched his back and gasped for breath as his mouth filled with blood.

But it was not his blood. Enkhtuya had raised the bear cub high over his head, and with her little knife had slashed open its throat. The cub went limp almost instantly, and bright young blood cascaded over the boy's face. The witch let the knife drop to the ground and in her long, fleshless hands she twisted and squeezed until the last drop had been wrung from the cub's corpse. Finally the boy on the couch choked up blood from the back of his clenched throat, and then with a whistling wind from his lips the spirit of the demon fled. He sank back exhausted. Beneath the mask of blood, his lips began to turn a natural pink again. Enkhtuya dropped the bloody mitten of black fur to the ground, turned on her heel and walked out of the palace without another word. Only Orestes watched her go. Checa and Attila stood holding each other, looking over their living son.

The camp lay under an uneasy stillness all the next day. Towards evening the king reappeared from his palace and stood with his forearms crossed and without expression. Then he smiled.

The whole camp erupted into wild celebration, both of the return of the men and of the life of the king's son. Ellak would live! And a great host of kindred Huns had come to join them from the east! Everything was in a state of ferment and excited chaos. The enveloping darkness was warded off with fires burning everywhere, and a babel of dancing and drinking and rejoicing had errupted, with men retiring somewhat hurriedly into their tents with their wives, not to be seen for another day and a night. It was even joked, more by the women at the riverside than by the men, since men do not find such jokes so comical, that a number of passionate encounters took place that night in the fevered darkness between women and men not, by the strict light of day, actually each other's husbands and wives. In nine months' time, the women chuckled, there would be born a greater than usual batch of 'festival babies'.

When, after this night of reunion and celebration, the dawn broke there was a strange air of hesitancy in the camp. One or two early risers dragged themselves from their blankets and wandered among the last of the smoking fires. They stood a little wearily and looked out over the vast encampment, an hour's walk or more from end to end. Suddenly it all seemed unreal, insubstantial. A madman's dream ...

They had returned and gathered at the same time of year as they had left. It was nearing the end of summer. For tens of thousands of them came the question: what next? Talk of empire and conquest was all well and good, but ...

There was nothing but this man. Quite a man, they acknowledged, quite a king. But there was nothing besides him except a few square miles of scratched grassland, corrals of tired horses, summer's end, a summer passed so fleetingly as they had galloped home westwards that they felt they had hardly had time to warm themselves by it. A general lassitude and weariness of nature, the flowers already thirsting and drooping their overgrown heads, the very opposite and apogee to the youth and promise of spring. Impossible that one man's vision, however powerful and vivid, could energise and inspire a whole nation of kindred peoples. Not now, not at this sleepy, dusty end-time of the year, when the thoughts of men and animals alike were turning to the comfort of winter pastures, shelter from the coming winter blizzards, and long, long nights of sleep under dark furs.

Had they come all this way on nothing but a fool's errand?

It looked a great gathering. Ruga's tribe of Black Huns had numbered perhaps four thousand, with maybe a thousand warriors. With the coming of the kindred clans, they had been as many as ten or twenty thousand, and now, though no man could count, they were many more than that again, with tens of thousands of men-at-arms alone. A mighty army, but soon it would be a hungry one. Like the sheaves of an unimaginable harvest, the tents of Attila's many peoples stretched almost as far as the eye could see. A hundred thousand? Two hundred thousand? Who could tell? Who could number them? And they grew afraid of their own numbers.

So in the dismal dawn, the world looked very different to the revellers, the many chieftains and princelings, the captains of the bands and the bandit-kings, and their world-empire looked very far away.

Attila came out of his palace, folded his arms before him, and said that there was to be a great council, and he would speak to them. They asked when, and he smiled and said, 'Now.' He ordered that all the chiefs of the various peoples, Bayan-Kasgar, and Kouridach, and Charaton, and Sky-in-Tatters, and all his chosen men and the captains of his regiments, assemble before him. The rest of the people would crowd close as best they could.

There was a certain amount of covert grumbling at their host's lack of consideration. 'Much koumiss, much sleep,' went the Hun proverb, but this tyrant had allowed them no more than two or three hours under their blankets. He himself, Attila, whom they had seen with their own eyes the night before, draining bowl after bowl of koumiss and never wavering or slurring for one moment, was now riding around among the tents, apparently all the better for so little sleep, grinning, his teeth flashing wolfishly, his gold earrings dancing in the early sunlight, and calling out to them each by name, which he remembered perfectly.

'Empires are not won by late sleeping!' he roared at the tent entrances, leaning down from his saddle. 'Shake your old bones, Bayan-Kasgar! You will never become rich and beautiful by lying there in your tent breaking wind! To the council ring! There is war to be planned!'

Then he vanished in a cloud of dust to torment Sky-in-Tatters, who was still sunk in boozy slumber between his two favourite wives.

Poor Bayan-Kasgar, feeling very far from a beautiful wolf this morning, crawled out from his tent, ratcheted himself upright and looked blearily out on the world.

He gazed out over steppes with that burnished silver horizon, strange for late summer, already promising cold to come. Overhead the sky was slate-grey and heavy, bad for headaches. Amid the tents the dung fires still smoked forlornly, and in the corrals the horses stood with dew on their backs and their damp heads hung low. Everywhere, roused unwillingly from sleep by their leader's tireless and furious energy, men were awakening with foul tongues and parched throats, bitter stomachs, throbbing heads, as tired as men of a hundred. After less than three hours' sleep, tempers were frayed.

But they stumbled obediently from their tents nonetheless, knowing that this king's decree, of all decrees, would brook no argument. Within their tents, many wives turned over again and sighed with relief and slept.

17

ATTILA SPEAKS, THE COUNCIL LISTENS

He sat to one side of the council ring on his plain wooden throne, his great fists clenched round the carven horsehead finials, his eyes blazing. In the centre of the ring stood a dark wooden chest. The chieftains and captains sat round the circle, and beyond gathered more and more curious people. Sitting close to the king's right hand was his brother, Bleda.

Bleda had said little to him since his return, apart from a polite and formulaic expression of happiness to see him safely returned. But Attila knew why. His brother was complaisant about surrendering the throne to him for now, because he knew that before long he himself would occupy it, with the help of Byzantine arms. Last night, while Bleda lay sozzled in his tent door, a crust of vomit down his front, his unwatched wives mysteriously absent from his tent, Orestes had stepped quietly over the blubbery prostrate form and quickly searched within. He found what he wanted in moments. A little olivewood box, of pleasing Greek craftsmanship, he noted approvingly, containing four scrolls. Letters from the court of Emperor Theodosius, in the customary flowery and flatulent Byzantine style. The first letter began:

'To Our Beloved Brother, Bleda, son of Mundzuk, son of Uldin the Great, Our Most Favoured Confederate, Our Bulwark against the Eastern Hordes, Our Most Highly Esteemed Ally, Lord of All Scythia under Theodosius, Vice-Regent of Almighty God upon Earth, and Our Very Dear Brother in Christ. Greetings.'

So Bleda was officially a Christ-worshipper now, was he? Orestes grinned and returned the scrolls to the box. Wonders would never cease.

As the light-footed Greek stepped out of the tent-door, he had thought how easy it would be to lean down and open Bleda's throat. It could be blamed on one of his wives, tripping gaily back from her night with her lover, only to find this pig of a husband blocking the entrance to her tent and to her life. She could be lightly whipped and then pardoned. But no. The traditional fate for Bleda: an accident while out hunting, an arrow carelessly fired.

Attila glanced at his brother and smiled benevolently. The idiot. Who had fathered this grub? What rancid womb had borne him, this retard from the farrow of a retard sow? Bleda smiled blearily back at him. When would Bleda sit upon this throne?

When mule foaled, when foal flew, when an arrow drew blood from the moon.

He turned away from Bleda and began to unfold his plan to his chieftains.

No doubt, he said, as pasture was growing scarce under the mouths of so many horses and cattle and sheep, they should be thinking of breaking camp and turning south, to the winter pastures beside the Caspian Sea.

Grizzled, bow-legged old Kouridach of the Hepthalite Huns nodded and stroked his long, narrow beard. 'The Caspian winter pastures will be fine and green. These steppes are eaten bare. We are happy to serve, but we must soon return east, or go south for winter pastures.'

Charaton agreed. 'The Huns are not a people to live in clotted masses, like ants.'

Attila nodded slowly. 'Yet finer pastures by far await us to the west.'

The chieftains eyed him.

'By the banks of the Roman Danube, in the territory they, in their arrogance, call Trans-Pannonia, beside the Tisza river. The Hungvar.'

'Our people pastured their horses there before, in my youth,' put in Chanat from the other side of the tent. 'Long ago, when we were allies of Rome, in Uldin's day. When we fought against our ancient enemies, the Germanic tribes of Rhadagastus, and cut them to pieces on the plains of Italy.'

'That was long ago indeed,' said Attila.

'But since then they have driven your people back east,' said Kouridach.

'Driven?' said Attila. 'The Romans do not drive my people anywhere, like cattle.' Only now did he turn slowly to face Kouridach's direction, and the look in his eyes was pitiless.

Kouridach's gaze dropped to ground. In the voice of this king, this leader of men, there was the sound of a terrible fury under iron control.

'Under Ruga,' Attila said, 'as well you know, the Huns withdrew east in exchange for Roman gold, like slaves doing Rome's bidding in all self-abasement. When Rome wanted a troublesome, rebellious boy got rid of, that detestable Ruga did their bidding for more gold.' He glared around at them. 'But neither decree from Rome nor chests of gold will keep us from our chosen pastures. Who owns the earth? We Huns are a free people of the steppes and we come and go as we please.'

'And if the Romans think otherwise?'

'Then we should bow before them, yes?'

'Perhaps,' said Kouridach, shifting a little in his seat, 'perhaps this empire of Rome is appointed by a higher power. Is it not one of their myths that they are blessed by the gods?'

Charaton concurred. 'Surely so great an empire, which has lasted so long, and seen so many generations of men arise and pass – surely it must have the favour of the gods? Is it right to ride against it? Are their gods not powerful? Perhaps it would be wrong to ride against it. Perhaps the bounds of this empire are set for eternity.'

No one dared look at Attila. Not Chanat, not Orestes, no one.

His voice could have scoured the skin off a man. 'Then let us bow before Rome! Let us content ourselves with our permitted Caspian pastures. Perhaps in spring, we might make one or two little mouse-like raids upon the northern borders of Sassanid Persia, to remind ourselves that once we were warriors. Those Sassanid kings who mount to their thrones on golden footstools, and sit there dangling their divine feet in silver bowls filled with rosewater, chilled with handfuls of snow brought down by their numberless slaves from the Zagros mountains. How terrible they are, those Sassanid kings, and how right we are to fear them!

'And after our little mouse-like raids we should disband again. For this many nomads to flock together is bad wisdom. The wandering Huns were meant for the lonely tents and the wide spaces, but not for high ambitions or mighty conquests of nations! When the Huns flock together it is like the gathering of ravens by the winter sea. A storm is presaged. Is it not so?'

They hardly knew how to respond. One or two nodded in cautious and kingly agreement. Others murmured among themselves, putting careful points, attending politely to the elders, nodding in agreement, and many began to concur that perhaps there really was nothing to be done for now but go their separate ways, with hearts rejoicing inwardly at the marvellous discovery of the Sword of Savash, and at this newfound unity among all the tribes and kindred of the Huns.

Suddenly Attila was on his feet, the Sword of Savash in his powerful fist. He drove it daggerlike into the dusty ground. 'That is what I think of your wisdom!' he roared.

Not a few of his listeners pressed back on their stools in fear. The crowd beyond stirred. The sky above seemed to grow darker.

'I tell you, a storm is presaged! A storm such as the world has never seen. A storm from the east.' He flung his arms wide. 'We fellow Huns and brothers-in-arms, we are that storm. You say we are too many. I say no, we are enough. You say we ride south. I say no, we ride west, to settle back upon the Hungvar, where we pastured our horses in the proud days of King Uldin. But not as allies of Rome. Not this time. As enemies.'

He rounded on Chanat. 'You were within the empire once. You went there, to the emperor's court in Ravenna.'

Chanat cast his mind back to that long ride to Ravenna. He grimaced. 'I remember Ravenna. It smelt bad, like a camp ditch after a month without rain.'

'And are you telling me now that this rotten stinking cadaver of an empire still has jurisdiction over the Hungvar? You, old Kouridach, whom I took for a wise man: that Rome has jurisdiction over the whole earth? Who gave it jurisdiction? Who permitted it suzerainty?' His fury grew, and those closest to him felt it, like the dark, bruised sky overhead, waiting to burst.

'Who set the bounds to this vaunted empire that you hold in such craven dread? Him who laid the foundations of the earth? Did he set the bounds, as the Romans in their arrogance and impiety proclaim? No!' His great fist crashed down upon the lid of the chest with such violence that they thought it might splinter beneath that hammerblow. His voice roared out, and the very walls of the tents around the council ring seemed to bat in the wind of his passion. Their ears were seared. His voice was the voice of thunder and darkness. They listened in awe, pressed back into their seats. The people beyond were spellbound. He paced among them, his eyes burning into their quavering souls, his rage and power like that of an uncaged lion. It was as if someone had put a torch to a huge bonfire in the centre of the circle, and it now blazed up and threatened to scorch and then engulf them all.

'Who decreed that the Hun people should not wander the earth as they will? Who forbade their wanderings? Who set the bounds on where they might pasture their horses? Who set the fences? Him who made the earth? No!' Again that mighty fist crashed down. 'Astur the All-Father, who made the earth, gave it to us and to all men, equal and without distinction under the right and God-made Sun, as he gave us souls, as he gave us life and breath and freedom to ride the livelong day over the unbounded plains. He set no fences. He made no petty laws. He built no customs houses, established no river crossings and toll-roads and imposts, decreed no payment of taxes to idle parasites in their pristine white robes in their gorgeous palaces. He made us free as he made all men free. He forged no chains for us, his children. His delight is not in the lifeless laws of the Romans, in the debates of their senators and the petty decrees of their courts. I have seen these Romans myself, and I would have you remember it well. With the clear and undimmed eyes of my childhood I saw those contemptible pygmies of men in their cities. I smelled the stink of their fetid streets. How dare you conflate their pompous pronouncements in their courts of law, their paper bills and levies of taxation, with the will of the everlasting gods! How dare you!

'I have seen their chests and bribes of gold, my brothers!' He gave the chest a furious kick. Its ironbound lid flew open, and they

264

saw that it was filled with dully shining coins. His burning eye fell on Bleda, and Bleda looked away. 'That is all their power amounts to!' He slammed the lid shut again. 'I know all, all! Their bribery of Ruga, their collusion in the murder of Mundzuk, my father, this you know – you all know – as I, too, know the truth of it. Shuffle with guilt you may, but then cast it off! You wonder: do I not hate my people? Do I not scorn them for their cowardice and passivity? Where have been the glorious battles and triumphs of the Huns these past three decades, during my long and bitter exile when I laboured and suffered in the wilderness? No, I do not scorn them. I love my people as a king must love his people if he would lead them with all conviction. And I would cover them in glory. They are a great people. They are an untamed horse-people of the plains, and they will come down on Rome like wolves on the fold.'

His voice grew still more in strength, a booming, rumbling bass reverberating in every head there. Abruptly he took a stride forward, set one mighty hand round the throat of old Kouridach and shook him. The others were astonished but powerless, immobile. Even had he torn into the old chieftain's neck and ripped his head from his shoulders there and then, as it seemed to them in his frenzy he might do, none would move. He had killed many a man with his bare hands before. Now he shook Kouridach like a thing of rags, like an old pelt, words still pouring from him in violent oratory the while, and then let him drop back onto his stool and turned away, still ceaselessly carrying them all forward on his torrent of baleful words. Not persuading them by any sophistry, but battering them into submission with sheer rhetoric, with an almost divine anger at their stupidity, their smallness of spirit and pettiness of mind. Whether or not they agreed with him in their intellects, their hearts swelled and burned within them at his words. They would do his bidding. They could do no other but follow this storm-force of nature, powerless as husks of wheat driven before the wind.

He released the choking Kouridach and turned away.

'Do not mutter to me, old Kouridach of the once-proud Hepthalite Huns, that Astur the All-Father has pronounced and approved the imperium of Rome, or decreed that she was destined to decide the fate of the world since before the world began. Astur did not bid us obey Rome's paltry man-made laws, or hoard its gold in lieu of our own glory. Then who? Who is this power you so dread, which forbids us from pasturing our horses on the European plain where we have pastured them many a winter before as in my grandfather King Uldin's time?

'I will tell you of this power. I lived under its shadow, when I was a helpless child, and I have spied on and patrolled that power through the many eyes of my spies since my return. The power you dread is a whining puppet-emperor called Valentinian – the drooling offspring of incest and wine – and his mother, Galla Placidia her name, a cold, green-eyed monster with icicles for teats. That inbred buffoon, her son, I shall slaughter like a diseased sheep before his mother's very eyes. This royal family is my bane, they hunted me through Italy like an animal, they slew my father: my curse is upon them. I shall cut them and their seed off for ever, their blood and their lives are forfeit. You Hun princes who dread him, how dare you dread him! Him and his armoured footsoldiers who move like snails over the battlefield and are marshalled like so many performing beasts of burden. Who are these Romans to dictate to us where we may pasture our horses and pitch our tents?

'You speak of the Emperor of Rome as if he were Astur himself.

'Blasphemy!' The fist crashed down yet again. The voice scorched the air and their ears burned with his words.

'You sit and puzzle and ponder like old women over who made the laws and dictates of Rome. Who established it as lord of the earth, robed in imperial purple. You propose to settle on the Hungvar in all timidity, if at all, with the permission of Rome. And you will allow Rome to be your rule and ruin. To tax your kin and kine, as Rome taxes and leeches the lifeblood from all its subject peoples, using that tax to pay its legions to oppress you further! Do you not see? Do you not see a great evil? Yet you would bend your necks to this yoke? A tariff on your horses' every footfall, a capitation on every ewe in your flock, your very breath excisable. Because this is the fiat and firman of the gods?

'Blasphemers!

'It is Astur and the gods above who made the earth and forged the chains of the mountains, who established the bounds of the lands under the sun and poured in the tumultuous seas from their earthen vessels. Have you not heard? Have you not heard the poets and the shamans tell it often enough by the campfire in the night, or were you too drunk with koumiss to open your ears?

'Have you not understood the will of him who made the jaws of the leopard? Him who forged the iron hooves of the warhorse, who crumpled the Five Kings in his hand, who brought us into this world which he made from a clot of his own blood. Who stretches the sky over our heads as a canvas, who spits forth lightning, who roars in the thunder, whose tears are the rain that drums the plains into an impenetrable mist. Who set the stars to burn in the heavens, who cut the moon from silver and the sun from gold, who crushed the life out of the dead places of the Kyzyl Kum with his fists – you know them well, my captains, those red sands and those desert places, I have shown you them all! Who forged the chains of the Tien Shan, who breathed fire on the deserts of the Takla Makan and burned the life out of them, who tore up the earth and rent canyons with his claws, who laughed to see the raging lion in the waste places, who rejoiced at the stampede of the saiga, at the thunder of their thousand thousand hooves. Who moulded the untold deeps of Lake Baikal, and made creatures to dwell there, huge and silent and glassy-eyed, which no man shall ever see or dream of even in his wildest dreams or nightmares. All, all is for the joy and delight of God, who is vaster than you dare to grasp in your petty imaginings. You think the Emperor of Rome, that pocky, whining whelp, is appointed by him and so should command our obedience! We are the sons of Astur the Father of All! It is blasphemy so to tremble before any mortal man with the god of our fathers at our side. Dare, dare ... His delight is not in those who chain and punish and restrict, but in those who dare ...

'You have heard his voice in the beating of the shaman's drum, you have seen him turn the steppes to ice with one cast of his hand, and with another bring them to life again and strew them with all the colours of spring. Out of his hands came the sun and the stars, the constellations in their courses, the night time and the bright day. Can the Emperor of Rome, howsoever decked in majesty and arrayed in the beauty of gold and rubies, send forth lightning by imperial decree? Can he number the sands of the shore? Does the eagle mount up at his command, and the hawk stretch out her wings towards the south? Can he bind the sweet influence of the

Pleiades, or loose the bands of Orion? He is mere mortal flesh, and you dare to sit before me here and tell me that you fear him as if he were a god. Do you so fear man that you do not fear Astur? Do you condemn his ways, do you disannul his judgement?

'Blasphemers!

'He scorns the multitude of the city, and the range of the mountains is his pasture. The multitudes in the city know him not, because they have chosen to dwell in a little false world made by man. Who has given the warhorse strength, and clothed his neck with thunder? He scents the battle afar off, the thunder of the captains, the shouting of the gleaming battle lines.

'Where were you when he made the iron talons of the eagle, the curved yellow beak and the amber studs of his eyes, and breathed life into him and bid him go forth to be the terror of all birds under heaven? When he made the kicking hooves of the wild ass, the white teeth of the wolf, the claws of the bear, the tusks of the boar, the shoulders of the bison? Do you claim equality with their power? What folly, then, to claim equality with him who forged them in the furnaces of heaven before you were made! What were you then? You were less than a baby's cry.

'He made the tiger, the chief of the ways of god, with his bones of adamant and his sinews of steel. What can you compare to him? Will he make supplications to you? Will he speak soft words to you? And will he be a gentle plaything for your maiden daughters?' Attila laughed and the sound carried far over the heads of his numberless listeners and was terrible. 'Whatsoever is under the whole heaven is his. And he has given it to all men, equally and without distinction.

'Bounds and laws, degrees and distinctions, toll-roads and customs-houses, exactions and imposts, the law's arraignments and the court's decrees, the solemn pronouncements of kings and chamberlains and eunuchs and all the petty panoply of man's deluded government on earth – what have these to do with the high eternal ways of god? You fools! These arrangements and orderings of man, which seem so noble and grand, overawing all but the true rebels and sons of god, elicit nothing but scornful laughter from the throat of the All-Father. Do you not know? And the pompous articulations by which kings and governments tell the people that they are appointed of god – do you not know? These are the scandalous jokes of god. And this sword? Did it come from god? Did it so?'

He pulled it abruptly from the ground where it had stuck and tossed it clattering onto the chest with extravagant contempt. Then he glared around balefully, as dangerous as a maddened bull in the arena, challenging them to find the bright steel vein of truth in the tangle of his taunting words and contradictions, and to make sense of the rage he vented on them. Few now believed anything of that strange decorated sword. It was, after all, just a sword. But they believed all the more in him.

It even seemed to some of them there that the thunderous voice that filled the council ring and even the whole camp, a camp so vast yet barely big enough to contain him and his primeval fury, the voice that demanded Who, Who ... ? It seemed to some that that voice was the voice of Astur himself, and they feared him beyond the power of words to tell. All the rumours that he was as much shaman as king, as much wizard and witch-born spirit as mortal flesh and blood, filled them with terror and at the same time with growing elation. It was not only the power of his words, of his voice, of his blazing presence. It was the intimation that he was party to something that they dreaded and could not understand, but only worship.

With him at the head of their horsemen, nothing could stand ...

He dropped his voice, and said with a note almost of sadness, 'They have taken the earth from you, my people. And with it, it seems, your hearts. But I will win back the earth, and with it your wild hearts.

'The earth is the gift of the gods and everything that is in it, and not a possession since time before time of the Romans. It is not the great-hearted and eternal gods who bid men huddle in stinking cities and behind defensive walls and make laws and bounds and fences. The gods gave men the earth for their home. The wide green measureless inexhaustible earth! And the great sky above, look you, the measureless and eternal sky! It is Astur who forged it all out of a clot of his own blood, it is the Great Mother who bore the living creatures from her womb, She is the amber butterfly on the birch tree, she is the dewdrop in the early sunlight, there! There! You know these things in your hearts, why do I tire my voice in telling you? These are the wellsprings of power in the world, these are life, and kings and governments are something other than life. We shall ride west and break down the walls and fences of the Romans, my friends. That is our destiny. That is the decree of Astur. I have promised you gold, glory, empery, and you shall have them all, in abundance. In good measure, pressed down, and running over!' He laughed harshly, as if at some private joke. 'You have ridden with me this far, and you shall have your reward. Let the way of the Hun horsemen be the way of all the world. And as for those lawyers and tax-gatherers and senators and conniving politicking courtiers and murderous plotting eunuchs in those perfumed courts of Rome, may their throats be slit open by our very children! May their bloated white bodies be hung from the battlements of their burning cities and scorned even by the crows!'

Part III

THE HUNGVAR

1

RIDING WEST

He gave them three days.

Even during that time, as they hurried to pack, he ordered the warriors out onto the plain for ceaseless drills and exercises. Though they and their families, the women and the children, should have been weary after such long travels across Scythia, and so little rest in the Euxine pastures, nevertheless he urged them onward, still onward. Urging them with such zeal, like a contagious fire, that despite themselves they felt a surge of limitless energy.

Out on the plains he had his warriors gallop and wheel in huge formations, in battle lines over a mile long. He had them fire volley after volley of arrows at distant targets across the steppes. And he had them play the ancient games of the Huns with a new competitiveness and ferocity: the mad gallop towards a steep riverbank, the winner being he who was the last to pull up. A number of men pulled up too late and tumbled, still mounted, over the bank and twenty or thirty feet down into the river. Several arms and legs were broken, and at least two horses had to be killed, to their owners' great grief.

'Women come and go,' said one, shaking his head in sorrow, 'but horses ...'

There was also the perilous rope-walk among the knives, in which each warrior had to totter along a tightrope suspended several feet above the ground, in which were set dozens of knives and daggers, their blades glinting upwards. And of course there was the furious game of *pülü*, played out over the steppes with spearhafts and an inflated pig's bladder. Never before had one game been played with so many thousands of men on each side. Most never even got to see the object of all their strenuous efforts.

There were slower and gentler games of skill with their leather whips and nets and lassoes. And in the lazy mid-afternoon many of the young boys came running out from the camp, eager and red-cheeked, and their fathers went with them on earnest hunting expeditions among the reeds by the river's edge, their five- and six-year old sons armed with child-sized bows, hunting for small birds and mice. Attila watched them go, and joked to those near him that Bleda had still been hunting thus only a year or two back.

There were more martial games towards sundown, and it was during these games, towards evening on the second day, in failing light, that Bleda was tragically shot from behind. The arrow flew cruelly true, penetrated through his back, beneath his left shoulder, and pierced his heart. None could say for certain whose bow it had come from. His wives put on a good show of lamentation, and he was buried with full if expeditious funeral rites.

Later that evening, Orestes heard Little Bird singing at the edge of the camp, holding a small brand and waving it back and forth over his head as he danced with slow footsteps in the dust. The Greek remained silent to listen and heard the words of the low chant. Little Bird sang of great brothers of the past. He sang of two called Cain and Abel, and of another two called Romulus and Remus. In each case, one brother had killed the other ...

Orestes went over to Little Bird and warned him softly not to sing too loud. But the shaman in his gentle slow-stepping trance seemed hardly to hear him or to heed his warning. He only murmured that there would be many more such songs to be sung before this tale was over. And he continued to sing long into the night, long after his flaming brand had expired in a grey wisp of smoke.

At night the shamans maddened themselves with hemp-smoke baths in their sweat-lodges, and danced and clubbed their drumskins with the thighbones of goats. The dry ground lapped up the blood and the molten fat of the sheep led bleating to the sacrifice, and the flames towered into the sky from the pyres and the altars. Sparks flew higher still, the dark horizon of the steppes lit up for travellers to see from far off in the night. Any lonely travellers seeing that sight from afar off out on the steppes would have shuddered, and, hearing that sound, would have turned back and returned home another way.

For it was the sound of the Hun nation on the point of riding out against the whole world.

It felt like the first day of autumn, late on that dying day when they finally departed. The skies were low and streaked grey and harried with the wind.

Bayan-Kasgar was still having his armour polished by one of his women when Attila rode near.

'How far is this Rome?' the general demanded. 'How many days in the saddle?'

'Days?' repeated Attila sardonically. 'Weeks. Many weeks' hard riding, far to the west, far from your beloved homelands. And then there will be long wars, and dangers I cannot even describe to you.'

'You make a poor salesman,' growled Bayan-Kasgar.

'But honest,' said Attila, heeling his horse onward.

So the people loosed their guyropes, dropped their tents, dragged free the central tentpoles and packed up the smokey black felt walls in rolls bound with rawhide and stowed their tentpoles on their wagons. They drove their cattle and their sheep and horses together and began to roll off in a desultory column to the west that very day. With them went the wagons and their drovers: thirty feet wide from wheel to rumbling wheel, bearing barrels of salted meat, bundles of tentcloth and ten thousand arrows apiece. Those ships of the plains with their canvas sides billowing like sails, their huge axletrees creaking, the great wooden wheels groaning like beasts dragged unwillingly to work. As the camp emptied, Attila gave orders for the royal palace to be fired, none knew why. It was still burning, far away, low on the horizon, a strange second sunset, when the people vanished over the curved horizon to the west and into the sunset's silent holocaust.

So began the great migration of the huge new nation of confederate Hun tribes under the sovereign rule of Attila. They passed westwards over the storm-lashed plains of Scythia, fording the wide rising rivers under the rolling clouds of autumn. After many weeks they came to the Kharvad mountains, which the Gothic peoples call the Harvaξa, and the Romans call the Carpathians. In the first falling snows they came up through precipitous dark rocky passes, the drovers and cattlemen already complaining bitterly that it was too late in the year for such long journeys in such terrain, and they should have stopped and found winter pasture as best they could east of the mountains. But Attila and some of the men who had ridden with him on his legendary gathering of the tribes, into far greater mountains than these, only smiled. They had known worse. And he drove them on without mercy. Never a moment of rest, under the rule of his furious, restless, vengeful energy.

Cattle stumbled and fell by the roadside, and were either lashed to their feet again or abandoned there. The great column of men and women, children and animals, creaking ox-carts and mounted warriors, moved on up the passes under the softly falling snow, wrapped and cowled in their woollen blankets, passing in eerie silence, every hoof-fall and footfall and wagon-roll muffled by the thick snow. The passes behind them were strewn with the humped bodies of dying cattle like dark boulders, the soft flakes falling and melting on their still warm bodies.

2

THE IDIOT CHILD

At last they came down into the wide flat plain of Trans-Pannonia. They set fire to whatever forlorn, huddled villages they came across, and drove the wailing inhabitants away across the plain into the swirling snow. But most of the people of that country had already fled westwards, having heard dreadful rumours of the approach of fur-clad Scythians, appearing down from the ominous Kharvad mountains, the abode of witches and werewolves, hidden in mist and snow for half the year.

The Huns continued westward on the heels of the refugees, razing the villages and clearing the whole plain of the Hungvar. For they called it by this name again already: the Domain of the Huns, their home. They torched the pitiful reed huts, driving the bewildered and terrified Sarmatian or Ostrogothic villagers out from their firesides into the bitter winter nights, to flee half naked with their infants in their arms. There was no resistance.

One freezing dawn they returned from an all-night raid and saw among the ashes of a village they had burned the night before, an idiot child sitting there among the still smoking ashes to warm itself, quite naked, seemingly oblivious of its plight. The child was perhaps five or six years in age, its head too big for its body and misshapen, and its face covered in rheum and snot, but not it seemed from weeping. Its upper lip was scaly and crusted with dried phlegm, and the underlid of one eye was swollen with some infection. The sores on its face and body were painful to look at. The child shivered among the ashes, covered in their grey dust, as if tethered like a scapegoat, or like a tiny penitent or bedesman crouching there in atonement for the sins of the world.

If the gentleness of a people is measured by how they treat their sick, their crippled and insane, this had been a gentle village once. Not for them the swift despatch of malformed infants to the rubbish heap, as the Romans do with what they call a *koprios*: a dunghill child, stashed in an old winejar and buried in a midden. Or as the Spartans did with their unwanted and rejected. Their sickly whelps and weaklings cast into the ditch beside the road to Messenia that they called the Apothetae, the Dumping Ground, and left to die in that abyss among a litter of tiny bones, blinking and gazing heavenwards to die of thirst and unimaginable agony, bewildered from the moment of their birth to their innocent death. Not once in their curt and crippled lives knowing one smile, one touch of gentleness, one look of love.

What gods made such a world where such things pass?

Among the Huns it was at least customary for such as this idiot child to be quickly and mercifully slain, and one of the warriors was already drawing back his bowstring to that end, to despatch the pitiful creature as one would a sickly lamb. But someone darted forward from among the warriors. It was the witch Enkhtuya, and to their astonishment she plucked up the idiot child and set it on her horse, and climbed up again behind it. They waited a little to see if she would hold her snakes to the child's ash-grey flesh but she did not. The men exchanged looks as if to say that perhaps the witch had some kindness in her dried-out scrap of a heart after all. And then they rode back to camp.

Enkhtuya played with the child. She gave it all her attention, and lavished upon it her vast knowledge of herbs and medicines, and before long its sores healed. She shaved its scalp, and marked it with the image of two entangled snakes in midnight-blue ink. The child could not see, but it appeared very proud of this new decoration.

She could not make it whole, of course. Its head was too large and heavy a burden for its small sloping shoulders, and lolled at times when the child was tired, and its belly was always swollen. It never spoke, and one side of its face remained all wrong, as if collapsed from within. But with the other half of its face, when

Enkhtuya dallied and played with it, it smiled. It even laughed, an odd, hiccupping laugh.

One morning, Orestes went down to the sleepy banks of the River Tisza in the soft grey drizzle, though the day was promising fair. Among the reeds he saw Enkhtuya and the idiot child a little downstream. He stopped and watched, as was his custom.

She was bathing the child in the warm shallows, and at the same time playing with and teasing it, as was her custom. The child laughed. It loved to play. She stepped into the river, up to her shins, then her knees, and pushed the child a little further in. The child felt the waters deepening around it, but Enkhtuya smiled and made encouraging sounds, and the child laughed trustfully again.

Orestes wanted to turn again and go back to the camp. Something was not right. Something was happening here that he did not like, though it was not his business. But he stayed and watched. He could not turn away.

Now the witch Enkhtuya took the child's hands in her own long, lean hands, and lifted it high out of the water. She was much stronger than her fleshless frame suggested. The child screamed with delight and kicked its feet. Enkhtuya stepped in deeper, the river water up to her thighs now. She began to swing the child back and forth over the water, in wider and wider circles. Orestes looked down, as if ashamed, and then up again. The child screamed and kicked. It swung in one last great arc.

And then he was released, and flew backwards, and there was a big splash as the child landed far out in midstream, his oversized head bobbing amid the wavelets, the laughter choked off in his throat.

Orestes could not move.

The child was carried along by the rapid current out in midstream, crying out desperately, raising its arms, rising and sinking again time after time. It was not laughing or playing, it was drowning, and he watched with impotent horror. He thought of Little Bird's hysterical antipathy to this woman, this creature, and his mind gave him grim forebodings.

Enkhtuya, too, watched the child, and laughed to see it pulled away in the current. She stood tall, with her face raised to the rising sun, and held her long dark hands up to her chest, her neck. She softly caressed her throat and her gaunt, sallow face as she watched the child drowning before her eyes, those uncanny pale-blue eyes huge and rapt and moist with pleasure. The child was gone, it was drowned. The sacrifice to the rivergod was done. The witch had saved it and lavished care and affection upon it and made it a thing of value, and then she had tired of it, and offered it up to the rivergod, and very much enjoyed the spectacle of its destruction. She was almost gasping with pleasure at the child's final cries, her breastless chest heaving with deep sighs, her lips apart, her eyes half closed. The child gasped, too, its lungs filling with water, its arms flailing, not understanding. The big head bobbing beneath the water, bubbles erupting from its clenched lips, its small deformed body falling, falling through the clear sunlit water, descending down and down, dragged by the current still along the gravel bottom of the riverbed through tapered waterweeds slimy and emerald green until finally it settled there, insensible, lifeless.

And then there was a sudden backwash and a watery commotion and the spluttering idiot child was miraculously bobbing close to the bank, making a kind of paddling motion and pulling itself up onto the mud like a primitive amphibian.

After a moment of astonishment, Enkhtuya shook her head. The rivergod had rejected the sacrifice as unworthy. Then she went over to the child and pulled it to its feet. The child was blubbering and weeping, and she laughed and wiped the water from its naked body with the edge of her hand, and wiped the snot from its nose with the hem of her robe, as gently as a mother would have done. Then she took its malformed hand in hers and led it back to the camp.

Orestes looked back over the implacable and indifferent river that had played thus with the child and then cast it aside. Today the river had decided not to kill. Enkhtuya did not oppose the dictates of the river or the earth. But Orestes felt something coming off the surface of the river, as cold as an evening mist. The day was warm and promising fair. But there among the tall reeds and rushes, Orestes the inscrutable, imperturbable Greek, shivered uncontrollably, as if he had just been vouchsafed some vision he had rather not.

Later that morning, if any had been watching, they would have seen Orestes walk determinedly into Attila's tent. After a few minutes they would have heard the king's voice raised in wrath, and then seen Orestes emerge from the tent and stride away, white-lipped with fury.

Later, they might have seen Orestes and Little Bird talking privately together, over by the horses. Then after a little the two men falling silent, hanging their heads as if in sorrow.

Attila decreed that another fine wooden palace should be built for him and the royal family, and his people worked for many days and with great labour to that end.

Little Bird became more and more insolent. At the campfire one evening, with the king himself close by, he began to sing one of the tales of Tarkan, the ancestral hero of all the wide-wandering Hun people. Tarkan, he sang, was a man both foolish and wise, like many kings and rulers. At first he would live only in a tent. But then he became so mighty, and his fame so celebrated, that Astur his father made him a house to dwell in, built of fine wood, with lintels of purest gold, and walls panelled with ivory, and set with jasper and chalcedony and every kind of rare gem. A magnificent house, a palace, the equal of any that the settler peoples boast of. But Tarkan the Tent-Dweller lit his fire inside, in the middle of the house, and fell asleep beside it after too much koumiss, and woke up in the midst of an inferno! He ran out weeping and bellowing, falling into the rain and the mud and kicking his legs and complaining bitterly to Astur that he had given him such a death-trap for a dwelling. And Astur spoke to him out of heaven and said, 'Foolish hero, I gave you the finest house that god ever gave man. But like all the wide-wandering Hun peoples for ever after, you will have no house to dwell in, but be always a tent-dweller and a keeper of flocks and a nomad upon the earth, despising the farmers and the towns, and despised likewise by those who dwell therein.'

At which another voice cut in, and it was the voice of Attila. 'And they shall be your enemy, and you shall be their enemy. And there shall be warfare perpetual between nomad and settler across every part of the world and for all time until the war at the end of the world.'

As if he had won a round in a battle of the bards, the king vaulted to his feet, clapped the dust from his clothes and retired to his proud new wooden palace, unperturbed. The chieftains and the chosen men left around the fire laughed.

But Little Bird did not laugh. He said, 'And they shall take up snakes.' Then he added, so softly that only Orestes heard, 'And they shall make sacrifices of innocent blood.'

3

A PUNITIVE EXPEDITION

It was spring before the full impact of the news reached the courts of Rome and Constantinople. There had been a reshuffling of the distant, restless barbarian tribes beyond the Danube frontier, and now those wild Scythians, the Huns, were once again encamped on the Trans-Pannonian plain. The people they had displaced had fled westwards into Germania, or else over the river to seek refuge in the border towns of Aquincum and Carnuntum. But few of the refugees had any great tales of horror to tell. It seemed the inscrutable nomads of the steppes had simply decided to overwinter in the lush pastures beside the River Tisza this year. It was no great cause for concern. Those people were as drifting and aimless as leaves in an autumn wind. There was no reason to suspect any great plan, for those barbarous people had no capacity for making plans. They lived without reason and law, and knew only their own primitive customs and dreadful blood-red rites.

But one listener took it differently: Galla Placidia, in the court at Ravenna. She said there could be a plan. She said there could be a very great plan afoot. She wanted to know if the King of the Huns was the still the one they called Attila. The messenger did not know. She slapped him twice, but still he did not know. Galla angrily hissed something about the poverty of intelligence on the frontiers these days and swept from the room.

Later that day, Valentinian was in his private chambers, eating white truffles fresh from the woodlands of Umbria.

His mother entered unannounced, followed by a court clerk

bearing a large scroll on a long wooden pole. The birthplace of this court clerk was Panium, a humble and unremarked little town in Thrace. The clerk himself, through his diligence and trustworthiness over many years, had risen high in the echelons of the Byzantine administration, so high, indeed, that he was not infrequently seconded to the court of Ravenna in the west, as now. There were those who said that these frequent and seemingly quite unnecessary secondments and to-ings and fro-ings between courts were the means by which the Western and Eastern Empires kept an eye on each other; that such a civil servant, in other words, with a foot in each court, must needs be a spy. But the clerk always met such extravagant speculations with a polite little bow of his head, and recourse to that most trusty of friends, silence.

He had served for some time as chief clerk in the office of the Count of the Sacred Largesse, and also as a clerk-in-consistory, recording rank, until he had been appointed deputy chief clerk-in-consistory, a post, it may justly be said, of no little reach and responsibility.

But let me not be boastful. It is just that oh, how I wished my aged parents could have lived to see the day when I attended upon the Empress Galla Placidia herself! How proud they would have been, how they would have beamed and nodded their white heads, to hear their son tell of court doings and dealings, on my rare visits home on leave to that little town of Panium, there on the sun-warmed olive-green hillside. But it was not to be. Both my parents lay sleeping beneath that green hillside, and my family, if I had any, were the clerks and secretaries and chamberlains of the imperial court.

Thanks to my well-known trustworthiness and reserve, I was at this time as close to Galla Placidia as any commoner. This was doubtless a great privilege, though not always a great comfort. I often obliged to sleep at night lying on my right-hand side, my less favoured side, since my left cheek was stinging so much from her slaps and was too hot to put to the pallet. However, all agreed that the empress slapped her staff less often than she used to.

She was now an old woman, approaching her sixtieth year, and although she tried to maintain her regal bearing and hold herself rigidly erect she could not disguise a worsening stoop, as if she carried a great weight on her thin shoulders. Her skin was still very pale and pure, untouched by sunlight in six decades, but she had many fine lines round her cold green eyes, and her thin, hard lips were thinner than ever. It was long since a husband had shared her bed, and she had found motherhood a disappointment. What mother's breast could swell with pride contemplating such a daughter as the ludicrously named Honoria, or such a son as Emperor Valentinian III? A son who had on more than one occasion, it was said, tried to poison his mother, leaving her retching and groaning in her chamber for days afterwards. They never spoke to each other but to quarrel.

Valentinian born in the month of July, 419, was on the eve of his twenty-eighth birthday, though still without either wife or child. He was very thin, with almost no muscle on his arms and legs but with a distended little potbelly like that of an old man. His face was unlined and boyish, chubby and wide-eyed. When excited he dribbled a little. But the appearance of sottish, retard boy was deceptive. He was in fact exceptionally cunning, cruel and unscrupulous. And darker still were the rumours of his fascination with witchcraft and black magic, and what monsters that had brought forth, deep in the underground chambers of the palace kept strictly for his private use ...

Now he withdrew his right hand hurriedly from under his lavish robes and leaped to his feet with a cry of indignation. The golden platter of truffles shot from his lap and fell clanging to the marble floor like a dropped cymbal.

'Mother!' he cried. 'How many times have I told you ...'

She ignored him, and ordered me to unroll the scroll on a large oak table. I did so, and a beautiful map of our beloved empire was revealed, all illuminated in a gorgeous array of coloured inks on venerable ivory-hued linen paper.

Galla placed a cool forefinger somewhere beyond the borders, in Trans-Pannonia. Then she traced it south, over the Danube and into the heart of Illyricum and Moesia.

'Should an enemy army attack here, at this point,' she said, 'between Sirmium and Viminacium, say, whose responsibility would it be?'

'Enemy?' gabbled Valentinian. 'What enemy?'

Again his mother ignored him. 'Whose territory is it? Yours, or the Emperor Theodosius'?'

'I, I ...' stammered the emperor, staring open-mouthed at her. To my shame, I saw his right hand creep between the folds of his long robe, like a little boy clutching himself for comfort in a moment of anxiety. I turned my face away. God's appointed vice-regent upon earth. The Lord of Western Christendom.

'Here!' she cried icily, rapping her fingernail on the map.

Valentinian looked down where she pointed, his eyes swimming, uncertain.

'Sirmium is, is ...' he stammered. He couldn't think straight. His mind kept going back to his truffles. Where had they got to? It felt as if one had got stuck to the bottom of his sandal. 'Sirmium is mine, obviously. At the junction of the Danube and the, what is it? I can never remember. The ...'

'The Sava,' said Galla.

'Is it?' The emperor laughed, a manic, high-pitched giggle. 'But then after that, this bit ... I mean, it's a bit vague, it's ... Singidunum is theirs, isn't it?'

Galla Placidia looked at me for enlightenment.

'Singidunum falls within the prefecture of the Praefectus Praetoria per Illyricum,' I affirmed, 'and therefore is also under Your Majesty's rule.'

'Is it?' Valentinian looked like a child who had just been given an unexpected present. 'It's a while since we have toured our Danube borders, I confess.'

'And from Singidunum eastwards to Viminacium and beyond is under Theodosius?' asked Galla. She was talking to me. I nodded. 'Viminacium, at least, is strongly fortified, is it not?'

'Does it need to be?' asked Valentinian. 'Why?' He looked very anxious again. 'Why does it need to be fortified?'

At the risk of losing my head, I ignored the emperor and answered his mother. The words of the most recent report by the clerk-of-the-works at Viminacium still all too clear in my memory. Scarcity of funds ... months of back-pay still awaited ... consequent depletion of manpower ... numerous desertions ... labour costs and shortage of decent materials ... decay of the Danube fleet ... lack of communication with Aquincum ... walls in disrepair ...

286

gatehouse extremely unstable … bridge requires compete rebuild … crumbling river embankments causing dangerous subsidence of western walls … Nor was the story any better at Sirmium or Singidunum or Aquincum or Carnuntum or any other frontier fortification you cared to mention.

'I believe,' I said carefully, and truthfully, 'that the capture of Viminacium would still require skilled siegework.'

Galla understood. No mere nomad army, however numerous, could capture a Roman legionary fortress.

'And the Seventh is still stationed there?'

The Seventh. The once-legendary Legio VII Claudia Pia Fidelis. Like all the legions, it was a mere shadow of its former self. A handful of poorly equipped centuries, going to seed in a damp and decaying riverside fort. Playing dice, quarrelling, drinking cheap wine. No longer even able to seduce the local girls, not without their soldiers' pay in their purses. Five hundred men at most, in place of the old five thousand. Aëtius had done his best, but it was never enough. There was never enough time, enough money, enough urgency.

'Its numbers are not what they were,' I said. 'But yes, the Seventh is still stationed there.'

Galla knew it all. She also listed the XIV at Carnuntum, the I at Brigetio, the fierce IV Scythica at Singidunum, and the II at Aquincum, along with the Danube fleet, or the dispirited remnants of it.

She looked at the map again, and tapped the barbarian lands beyond the river, the rich plains between the Danube and the Tisza. On the map this land was still called by its ancient name, derived from the people who once lived there, and Valentinian, craning over, read it out loud.

'Sarmatian Jazyges,' he repeated slowly, almost lovingly. 'Sarmatian Jazyges. I like that name.' He looked at me and smiled in way that I can only describe as witless. 'I wish I had a friend called Sarmatian Jazyges.'

'It is right on the border,' his mother snapped at him, 'and for a reason. And that reason is called Attila.'

Valentinian stared at her.

'I have gathered the intelligence I required,' she said crisply. 'Attila is indeed their king. His brother, Bleda, is already dead, who would have been our ally, or at least our neutral feoderatus. Attila will not be our ally. Attila will be our enemy. That is why he has come and camped with his vast horde, in' – she almost spat the words at her startled son – 'Sarmatian Jazyges. He will invade across the river shortly, at the precise intersection between our two empires, to confuse us and set us against one another. I know that he is no fool. He is a man of the utmost cunning. He will attack here, at Singidunum, or close by. We will dither. He will ride on. He will ride at the head of a hundred thousand horsemen, and we had better be ready.' She was nearly trembling with suppressed rage as she looked her son in his quavering eye. 'Your Majesty.'

Suddenly Valentinian snapped. There was danger. He did not understand, he was bewildered and frightened. He even trotted round in a little circle, and when he spoke it was in something of a wail.

'Why? But why? Why do they want to attack me? Who are they? What do they want?' Then he grew angry and tyrannical, his abject fear turning to aggression and then to cruelty, as is often the case with cowards. 'We will attack them! We will march against them! See how they like it!' He tried to draw himself up, and he touched his fingertips to his purple stole and affected a grander style. 'How dare they insult Our Imperial Majesty or impugn Our Sovereign Territory!'

'We should recall General Aëtius,' said Galla Placidia, trying to remain calm, 'no matter what offence he has caused Your Imperial Majesty in the past. He still commands great loyalty among the legions, and he knew this Attila in boyhood. He was a hostage in the camp of the Huns. They are of the same age.' She tried to conceal her distaste. 'The general even speaks some of their barbaric tongue.'

Valentinian looked darkly at his mother. 'He is as much of a threat as any Huns.'

Galla shook her head. 'No, he is—'

Valentinian's tantrum was instantaneous. 'Do you contradict me, woman? Remember who you are! And who *we* are!'

Galla bit her thin lip.

'That Aëtius is nothing but trouble! He has never been anything

288

but brusque to me!' He slapped his hand down on the map. 'I will not have him back. I'll not!' He stamped his foot, and when he moved away again, a single white truffle remained behind, squashed flat upon the marble. 'Where is he now? With the Goths? With those great hairy lairy Germans he gets on so well with, who stink of onions and rancid butter?' He looked rapidly between the empress and me, his tongue stretched right out, for some reason, the tip almost touching his chin, and his forefingers waggling on the top of his head, perhaps to resemble horns. 'Hm? Hm?'

I tried not to betray myself. 'At the court of Theodoric, Your Majesty, that is correct.'

'They must be punished! And the Huns, too, they must be punished! They must be punished first. They must be warned – given a warning shot, like an arrow, like a flying arrow.' Valentinian was babbling now, pacing up and down the chamber, pulling the fingers of his left hand with his right and chewing his lips to ribbons. In a moment I feared he would start dribbling. 'We are not afraid, that is the thing. A punitive expedition, that is the thing. Eutropius!'

The chamberlain came bustling in from the neighbouring antechamber, from whence no doubt he had heard every word. He spread his golden dalmatic wide and knelt at the emperor's feet and kissed the hem of his robe – the hem, he noted, was splashed with blood, and a little matted clot, like a clot of human hair, was stuck to it.

'Send a message to the Fourteenth at Viminacium. Or is it the Seventh? Did you say the Seventh?'

I nodded.

'Well. Send a message out to the Seventh at Viminacium. They are to despatch an armed body of men, a cohort or something, however many they can spare, and make a punitive expedition, that is the thing.'

'Against whom, my lord?'

'Against the Huns, you fool!' Valentinian's fists were taut and white at his sides. 'Capture some of them, that's it! Put them in chains, old men, women, little children! Tie them all up tight like fowl on a market-stall. Tightly tightly!' Now he was dribbling. 'We must show the people we are not afraid! We will have a proper games in the arena, and the Hun captives will be savagely and mercilessly punished!'

'My lord,' said a voice behind him.

He turned, eyeing Galla dangerously. 'I trust you agree with our plan, mother?'

Galla's thin breast heaved. 'My lord, I beg you to reconsider ...'

Valentinian raised his hand to slap her, and held it there, inches from her cheek, as he yelled into her face, 'You are growing tiresome, mother! We are the emperor, not you!'

Galla did not flinch and she said nothing.

Valentinian turned and bellowed at the chamberlain, 'Well, get on with it! A punitive expedition. Those beastly barbarians in the arena in chains! Tightly tightly! See how they like that!'

He looked over the empress and myself one last time, puffed up his cheeks and made an odd, explosive noise. Then he picked up his skirts and hurried off into the antechamber.

I carefully rolled up the great map.

When I turned round, the empress was still standing there, her head bowed, her eyes closed, her small white fists clenched by her sides, not moving.

There was a circle of black tents beside the lower reaches of the Tisza, not far from where it flowed into the Danube, one of many such circles which spread over the plain amid a haze of campfire smoke. Women were stirring pots, or bringing water from the river in leather pails. Round-headed, red-cheeked children were playing chase and tag. It was a cold day in late spring, but very beautiful, the sky pale blue, the sunlight sharp, the green earth slowly softening after the night's hard frost.

A double ala of Roman cavalry, which is to say a hundred and sixty men, appeared in the west. They had ridden from the legionary fortress at Viminacium at dawn. They saw the camp from some way off and drew their curved cavalry swords.

The grass was lush and bright with spring flowers.

One of the children saw the men on their horses coming. She stopped and stared and put her thumb in her mouth. Then she raised her other hand and waved uncertainly.

The horsemen did not wave back.

There came the sound of two cheerful tuckets on brass bugles, and then the line of horses began to gallop.

The smoke was seen rising from the circle of tents from far off, and one of the Kutrigur chieftains rode out with his men to see. When they got to where the cluster of tents had stood, there was nothing to see but ashes, heads on stakes, and severed limbs.

The news was brought to Attila in his palace. He sat very still and looked into the fire, saying nothing.

Late in the evening, when most had fallen into an uneasy sleep filled with dreams of revenge, Little Bird came unannounced into the presence of the brooding king and sat cross-legged in front of him, his face streaked with tears. And he half said, half sang:

'The Song of Little Bird, Truth-Teller:

'News travels like a plains fire
And is as blood-red as a plains fire at dawn.
Over the river they rode, their swords bright silver,
Into the village, among the black tents they rode;
Ten in red cloaks, bearded, oh, noble white men!
Then over the river they rode, their swords bright red.'

When he fell silent Attila looked up and their eyes met.

'Vengeance travels like a plains fire,' said Attila, 'and is as blood-red as a plains fire at dawn.'

4

IN THE COURT OF THE VISIGOTHS:
A GAME OF CHESS

Far to the west, in a small arched courtyard partly shaded by the pale green leaves of young vines, two men were playing at the fine old Roman board-game of *latrunculi*, or chess. In the Visigothic court of Tolosa, in sun-warmed southern Gaul.

How elegant was the court of the Visigoths under great old Theodoric! What paeans of praise were written of it! It seemed to unite all the old Roman virtues, and none of the new Roman vices. Many looked towards the new kingdom with something like longing, or even expectation, as if they saw in Theodoric's kingdom, and in his six proud sons – 'the Sons of Thunder', they jokingly called them – the future of Europe: a future at once Gallic and barbaric, Christian and Roman. Theodoric and his sons were valiant in battle, they knew their Roman history and jurisprudence, and they spoke Latin and even a little Greek as well as Gothic. They knew their Virgil well enough to quote appropriately when occasion demanded, and their accent was such as would make only the most scrupulous Latinist wince.

Here at this court of supposed barbarians, wrote one admirer, the elegant-minded Sidonius Apollinaris, Bishop of Clermont, there was no heavy, discoloured old silver, but rather weight and value in conversation. Viands attractively cooked, not costly, and without ostentation. Goblets so replenished by silent slaves that both intoxication and thirst were unknown. There was Greek elegance, Gallic plenty, Italian vivacity. The dignity of state, the affection of home, the ordered discipline of royalty.

And there was great, grizzled, grey-bearded old Theodoric

himself, King of the Western Goths, the son of Alaric, the conqueror of Rome, glowering over the chessboard. It was said that when Sidonius played him at chess, the bishop always made sure he lost to the hot-tempered king. But Theodoric's adversary today was of a different stamp. He was a lean, grey-eyed man of some fifty years of age, a Roman of noble birth and ancient lineage, currently a guest at the Visigothic court on account of certain tensions arising between himself and the imperial family, certain jealousies and insecurities, the details of which amused old King Theodoric rather more than they amused the Roman.

The grizzled old Gothic king would slap his grey-eyed guest heartily on the back and tell him that he was welcome at Tolosa any time, any season. In fact, why not permanently? Quit the sinking ship of Rome for good. Get out while you can.

But that was not the Roman's way. His name was Gaius Flavius Aëtius. And he was determined to win not only his game of chess.

Not that he wasn't deeply fond of the gruff old king. Often grumpy and grouchy to a comical extent, Theodoric in fact meted out justice among his people with a scrupulously fair hand, and was revered by them in turn. Despite being powerfully built and as strong as an ox, he complained bitterly and daily about the evils of encroaching age and his failing strength. Such complaints earned him only wry looks and raised eyebrows from his family, especially his wife, Amalfrida, who knew him well enough after forty years of marriage. As he sat at dinner, loudly holding forth, before sinking his teeth into his third roast fowl of the evening, and draining his twelfth goblet of Provencal wine without the least sign of intoxication, it was hard to take his laments about waning powers too seriously. At one point during last night's dinner, Theodoric had leaned over to Aëtius, nodding down the table towards two particularly comely young Gothic maidens who had recently arrived at the court as ladies-in-waiting, and muttered, 'Strange how I stay the same, while the girls grow younger and prettier every year.'

Such a man was King Theodoric: quick to anger, quick to forgive, lusty, powerful, a little hard of hearing. Just, passionate, oddly sentimental over trifles, such as injured animals; a lover of hounds and horses and well-trained hawks, given to bemoaning bitterly the slightest ache, pain or sniffle, but never having spent a single day in bed since the age of eight, when he was confined with a broken leg after falling off his pony at full gallop.

Aëtius had a deep respect and affection for him, and sometimes wished that the book of history could have been written differently. But you are what you are. No man can change his tribe.

Whilst beating the Gothic king at chess this afternoon, Aëtius talked to him of the affairs of the world. Of the savage reign of the Vandals in North Africa. Theodoric only grunted. Aëtius told him of how the brutish King Genseric of the Vandals, having gained a taste for naval warfare, had sailed from his capital at Carthage – what irony there was there! – and sacked many of the islands of the Aegean. The inhabitants of Zakynthos had put up fierce opposition. When they were at last overwhelmed by sheer weight of numbers, Genseric had had every man, woman and child on the island beheaded, and the mounds of heads shovelled into the sea.

Theodoric looked up at his guest from under grey, bushy eyebrows. But still he said nothing.

It was during this game of chess that a messenger came with two letters for Aëtius. He took the first and tore it open. After reading it, he sat and mused for a long time.

'It is sad news?' said Theodoric.

Aëtius nodded slowly. 'And from a man whose name I had almost forgotten.' He stirred himself and spoke more briskly. 'From a Briton called Lucius.'

'A good Roman name.'

'He was a good Roman soldier. A good man. A lieutenant, as I recall. It was he who – yes, extraordinary to recall it now. It was he who accompanied the boy Attila on the great flight from Rome, back in 410, and who later made a great journey to the camp of the Huns, to find and buy back his own son. An incredible tale – I'll tell it to you one day.'

'What does he want with you?'

'What everyone wants from me, except Rome itself,' said Aëtius. 'Military aid. Which now I cannot give.' He scanned the letter again. 'He must be fifty – no, more. The father of good sons. The king of a little kingdom, as he ironically puts it, in the west of Britain, in Old Dumnonia. But the picture he paints is not a pretty one. The Picts, he says, are raiding further and further south, and the heathen Saxon raiders growing ever more bold. In the east of Britain, he says, Saxons invited over as mercenaries in petty wars have already settled and stayed. He is not optimistic.' The general shook his head. 'But I cannot help him. I cannot.'

'What of the other letter?' said Theodoric quietly.

Aëtius tore it open and read it, then slipped it inside his robe. 'How strangely news comes twice. This, too, is in remembrance of the Huns, and of a particular name among them. So suddenly he reappears. In a letter from Rome.'

'To say?'

'To say that the Hun nation has returned and is encamped across the Danube.'

Theodoric looked up sharply. 'Who is their king?'

'It is him,' said Aëtius, a note of wonderment in his voice. 'The boy has come back. Attila. King Attila.' He was silent for a while, then said, 'Galla Placidia sends me welcome. She bids me return.'

'And the emperor?'

He said nothing.

An unfortunate clerk chose that moment to come into the king's presence and request his signet-stamp upon a document.

Theodoric turned on him in fury. 'Out of my sight, wheyfaced ledger-slave!' The poor clerk reeled backwards in the blast, open-mouthed. 'Scullion! Fool of the counting-house! Come to tell me how much gold yet graces my treasury! What do you know but how to tell of gold! I'd see thy milksop temples furrowed with a man's cares, a man's burdens on your counting-house crouchback, see how you like that!'

Theodoric turned back to the chess game. He swiftly moved one of his pieces, and set it down with such force that the board shuddered and several more pieces moved in concert.

'The Huns,' he rumbled. 'Alliances. I know what you seek: a new alliance, my warriors to ride in Rome's defence. And this Lucius the Briton, he should be riding in your defence too.' He laughed harshly. 'Never mind your going to Britain to fight the Saxons for his salvation! We are all under attack in the Last Days!'

Aëtius studied the board.

'But I am old, my Roman friend. My old eyes weep and dazzle

under the sun. My ears, alas, hear less than they once did. Although they hear less folly too.'

He heaved himself more upright in his great wooden chair. 'Yet I think I do still bear me most royally in my hoary, rheumy old age, do I not? Eh? Eh? Though no more than a bag of old bones, held together by this kingly ceinture.' He slapped the great gold buckled belt round his broad stomach. 'A bag of ancient, mead-filled, boarmeat guts!' Suddenly Theodoric turned in his chair. 'Do you eye my throne, boy?' he roared.

Aëtius looked up. It was the king's eighteen-year-old second son, the tall, graceful Torismond, waiting respectfully to speak.

'May you suffer hell's own haemorrhoids seated here if you take your place before the appointed time!'

'Father, I—'

'Bring me a pot to piss in.'

Torismond obediently retreated, and returned a moment later with a pot.

Aëtius gazed away over the courtyard rooftops. Swifts were wheeling in the spring sky, their high-pitched screams swooping over the red-tiled rooftops of the city.

The poor clerk was scuttling along in the shade of the colon-nade, still clutching his unsigned document and hoping to pass unnoticed, when Theodoric saw him.

'Here, wheyface! Take this pot. Here man, take it from me! Damn thee for a fool to fear to soil thy hands with the royal piss, that daily soil thy palms with foreign gold.' The clerk retreated, stumbling backwards. 'Ledger-slave!' the king roared after him. 'Coin-counter! Now go spill it on the palace roses! They will smell all the sweeter for it!'

He looked back at Aëtius. He took a deep draught from the plain wooden cup by his side and smacked his lips. 'There can be no alliance between the Goths and the Romans, old friend. The past forbids it. The past makes a mockery of it, though there will be friendship until death between you and me. We are Christians both, are we not? Yet you call me an Arian, and a heretic.'

Aëtius shook his head. 'Christians both. I am no theologian.'

'Don't pussyfoot, man, I know you have a braver heart than those who hide their convictions like a bear hides its dung! Is the

Son equal to the Father? Is my son equal to me?' He looked round at Torismond, waiting patiently. 'Are you greater than your father, boy?' he bellowed.

The youth gave a graceful bow. 'I am not, my lord.'

'I am!' said a bright, girlish voice, 'and a deal prettier to look at too!' In a flash and blur of white robe and flying blond hair, a young girl tripped across the little courtyard and flung her arms round her father, bestowing a flurry of kisses on the laughing king. She was Amalasuntha, Theodoric's only daughter, some fourteen summers old and the apple of her father's rheumy eye. He doted on her. So did her six elder brothers, for that matter. A little spoilt she might be, but none of them resented it. Spoilt and vain and careless, she was also sweet-natured and full of spirit and laughter. One day she would make quite a match. But woe betide any man who dared to offend her honour or her name before that day. He would have Theodoric and his six sons to contend with.

There was no man on earth whom the king would not bellow insults at if he felt so inclined. But against women he was rather less certain of himself. And with his vivacious young daughter ... he was putty in her hands. Aëtius tried to hide his smile.

'What are you laughing at, General?' asked the girl archly. 'Do share your little joke. It is well known what a keen sense of humour you have – always laughing and joking as if you had not a care in the world.'

'Nothing, nothing at all,' replied Aëtius gravely, thinking what a flirt she was becoming already.

She tossed back her long fair hair and kissed her father sweetly once again. 'Well,' she said. And then she flitted away across the courtyard. Aëtius did not turn to watch her go. He knew she would be looking over her shoulder for him to do so. And he old enough to be her father – her grandfather.

'Hm,' murmured Theodoric fondly, his hand to his cheek. 'Well, then.' He sat up and returned to the attack.

'That Christ, he was a great prophet, a blessed one,' He turned back to Aëtius. 'but to say he was the same as the Aesir, and the power that moves upon the waters of the deep, or that brooded upon eternity in his vast and silent solitude, in the time before time was created ... that is folly. No man is God.'

Aëtius kept his silence.

'Christ told his followers to get themselves swords. That is good: he was no milksop!' Theodoric touched his hand to the hilt of the scabbarded sword that lay on a bench close by, even in this peaceful palace courtyard. It was the king's hereditary sword, called in the Gothic tongue Tilarids, Attacker, mysterious with runic silver set in beaten iron. 'That Christ, he said he came to bring fire upon the earth! To burn up the heathen and the unbelievers, and with them the accursed Huns, I would believe. That is good. That Christ, he was no wheyfaced ledger-slave, he despised the things of the counting-house, did he not? He was a man of war.'

Aëtius coughed. 'It is an interpretation that I—'

'And his Jewish forefathers, certainly, they were great fighters. As are we. We Visigoths. The Gothic People of the Plains. And I, Theodoric, son of Alaric, have played my part in our people's battles most royally, have I not? Nor cried out womanishly in the fight? And fought with that still undefeated power, the Most High God. All my fighting is done, but for that unending word-war, that ceaseless strife in the silence of my soul with that one ceaseless and undefeated adversary. Him I still find worthy of my sword-arm, the Lord High God! And may I yet hobble to my bed at evening undefeated.'

He bowed his old grizzled head. 'But O, my Roman friend, must there be more battles? "Hard is the gods' will, My sorrows but increase, And I must weep, beloved, That wars will never cease." That is an ancient rhyme, and an ancient truth. Never have I shirked a man's duty to fight, nor a king's, either. But now, must we ride out against the Huns, our oldest enemies? And in alliance with Rome?' He gave a bear-like rumble. Any moment he might give a bear-like roar. But still he spoke quietly, meditatively. 'History is against such an alliance, friend Aëtius. You know of what I speak.

'The Huns of Uldin – now of this Attila, whoever he may be – I have no love for them. They drove us shamefully over the face of the world, from east to west, and we fled, not knowing where we should go. Where we should rest our heads each night, nor where to take our stand, disarmed, desperate, pitiful refugees. How could we stand against them? We fled from under their rainstorm of arrows. Any people would have done the same. They were demons of the steppes.

'Ancient is the enmity between our people and those demons of the steppes.' Theodoric stroked his long white beard, still streaked with yellow. 'But enmity with the Huns does not necessarily mean amity with the Romans. My people still remember how we were treated by Rome when we were penniless immigrants, shamefully stripped even of our dignity.'

Aëtius said quietly, 'Rome is not without injustice. No city or empire, no civilisation or people, is perfect. Not even the noble Visigoths.'

Theodoric grunted. 'The Huns fought against the Goths under Athanaric. "*Ymb Wistlawudu, heardum sweordum*", In the Vistula woods, with hard swords. That day of sorrow lives on still in the lays of the people. By moonlight the Huns crossed the Vistula upstream, and fell on our flank like wolves. And many were the tall horsemen that fell that day.

'The lovers and the dancers are beaten into the clay,
And the tall men and the swordsmen and the horsemen,
    where are they?
And there is an old beggar wandering in his pride –
His fathers served their fathers before Christ was crucified.'

Aëtius listened patiently. He knew every detail of the story, of course. But it was a deep Gothic tradition to recite the lays again and again, until they became holy by repetition. Besides, it was good to sit in this sun-warmed courtyard, in this small haven of peace, and listen to the old king talk, even if the story he told did no honour to the name of Rome. And respite would not be long.

'Three generations ago it was now,' said Theodoric. 'Athanaric and his people fled south – though they were a brave people, do not doubt it.'

'I do not doubt it,' said Aëtius. He had seen the Goths fight.

'They fled south, across the Carpathians to the banks of the Danube. They stretched out their hands to Rome, and the emperor of those days, Emperor Valens, assented. Preparations were made for our many thousands to come into the empire. But then the Romans demanded we surrender our weapons, our swords. Once we were disarmed, they demanded payment. Your frontier lords, and the officers of your rapacious state, how they loved gold.'

Aëtius met the old king's eagle eye steadily.

'The noblest names among the people, even the red-cloaked Wolf-Lords of the Visigoths, were held at swordpoint. They were bargained with, they were exchanged like cattle. Still they were not permitted to cross the Danube. More came, more refugees from the north and the east. They were invited to sell their dogs, their own wives and children, it is said, to pay their passage into this coveted empire. They were starving and destitute. The bellies of their children sagged like the bellies of old men and women. Their cheekbones stood out from their young faces. Their eyes wept tears.

'Did you listen to their cries? Though they were not of your tribe, yet their cries were human. They were your fellow men: their children hungered and sorrowed like your children. Did you take them in? You did not. You looked out across the river to these pitiful refugees from the outer darkness, beyond the walls of your fortified Europe. And you saw only ... what? Enemies? Demons? Danger? A danger so weak it could barely walk. What danger is that? All men will be brothers. That is an old Gothic saying, and it is what Christ taught. 'Will be brothers': note well the future tense. It is prayer, a hope, perhaps a prophecy. It is certainly not a description of the way things are.'

Theodoric took a gulp of wine. 'Finally my people were pushed to despair, and then war. They seized back their swords and their horses and fled. And then at Adrianople, in the year 378, your Rome sent out a punitive expedition against us, to punish a starving and maltreated people who had dared rebel against Rome's inhumanity to man. Our generals, Alatheus and Saphrax, commanded our weary and emaciated horsemen and our spearmen, and against all expectation Rome was destroyed that day. Surely Christ fought with us then. Your emperor, Valens himself, was killed on the field, and the flower of the Roman army destroyed by our despised and wretched barbarian cavalry. And I do not think that the legions of Rome have recovered from that day to this.'

Aëtius suddenly leaned forward. 'Join with us now,' he said with low urgency in his voice. 'Rome has need of you, the civilised world has need of you. Whatever is past, Christendom has need of you now, the Last Kingdom in the West, and your Wolf-Lords in their red cloaks, with their long ashen spears. Who would you rather have triumphant over the world, the Huns of Attila, or Rome – Christian Rome?'

'For now,' growled Theodoric, 'neither. Let the Goths keep to themselves.'

Aëtius would not hear such an answer. He seized the king's wrist in a steely grip, his grey eyes suddenly burning with that passion which burned like a slow, inextinguishable flame deep beneath the cool, reserved and formal exterior. Now it was blazingly visible, like an equatorial sun appearing from behind cloud.

'My lord,' he said urgently, 'I do not flatter you, you know that. But this will be no ordinary skirmish between Roman and barbarian, I know it in my heart. For I know this Attila. He is the boy I fought with and played with in the camp of the Huns when I was a hostage, long ago.'

'Ah, I remember. You caught a giant boar together.' Theodoric reflected. 'It is strange. And now this boyhood friend of yours leads a hostile army to your borders.'

'And more,' said Aëtius. 'I knew him well. I know him still. Thirty years of exile, and now he has returned. I know how he hates Rome and dreams of its destruction.'

Theodoric shook his head. 'This is sad and strange, like an old ballad.'

Aëtius shrugged off Theodoric's musings impatiently. 'This is no mere chapter in the long history of Rome. This is the conclusion. Do you not see? Upon this battle, this war, depends the survival of Christian civilisation. I tell you the truth. Upon it depends the long continuity of our institutions and our empire. The whole fury and might of the enemy must very soon be turned on us. And if we fail, the whole world, including the Kingdom of the Visigoths, including all that we have known and cared for, will sink into the abyss of a new Dark Age.'

Theodoric smiled. 'You are a fine orator, no doubt, and I know you are a fine commander of men, but no, I will not sacrifice my young people to save old Rome. Nevertheless, I wish you well. I will have my priests and deacons pray for you in the cathedral, and that smooth-tongued Bishop Sidonius say a mass. And if either

Rome or the Huns must triumph, I pray it shall be Rome – of that you may be sure.'

With all his impetuous great-heartedness, he seized Aëtius' hand in his own huge paw. This Roman, his enemy. 'My brother,' he said, his voice thick with emotion, 'one day perhaps, if we do not ride with you, you will ride with us.'

'It will be a long wait, brother. You know I am a Roman.'

'I know. You fool.'

At that moment, an almost forgotten figure stepped forward from under the shade of the colonnade. It was young Torismond. Theodoric's second son, now in his nineteenth year.

'My lord,' he interrupted, his voice abrupt with excitement. 'Father.'

The king turned.

'Send me. Send Theodoric, your eldest son, and me with a band of men. Let us ride with General Aëtius against the Huns.'

Theodoric snorted. 'I'd rather send puppy-dogs against bison. Get you gone, boy.'

'My lord, I beseech you—'

Even Aëtius was rocked back by the blast of Theodoric's voice. Torismond departed.

Aëtius said, 'Your six sons, my lord. Fine lads.'

'Puppies.'

'Puppies improve with training.'

Theodoric glared at him.

Aëtius rode out at dawn, with the old king's blessing, and just two mounted Gothic warriors for escort. There was no danger in this quarter of the empire. The sleepy, sun-baked roads of the old province felt like the safe heart of empire now.

The gates of Tolosa opened and the three men rode forth. They had ridden only a few hundred yards down the road when there came a mighty trumpeting from the towers of the city. Aëtius and his guards reined in and looked back.

The wooden gates of the city swung slowly open. There rode out into the sunlight, in magnificent array, an army of as many as a thousand Gothic Wolf-Lords in their long red cloaks, their long ashen spears slung low at their horses' sides. Proud pennants fluttered in the breeze, horses were champing, white horses of the finest Gothic strain, high-fettled and glossy-maned. At the head of the majestic column were two youths, their long fair hair crowned with thin gold crowns, the princes Theodoric and Torismond, Sons of Thunder. Aëtius' heart surged within him.

From the top of the gate-tower, a voice roared over the departing horsemen, 'Go east and bash the Huns with my blessing, boys! And break their wicked bones for my old heart's sake!'

The ride back to Rome was peaceful. The news on arrival less so.

'A punitive expedition?' repeated Aëtius.

'Absolutely!' Valentinian was intoxicated at the thought. He beamed at the recalled general, quite forgetting his former mistrust. It didn't even occur to him who might have recalled Aëtius, behind his back and against his orders. He skipped gaily across the room and poured the general a glass of pink Alban wine with his own hand.

The general dismissed the proffered goblet. 'How long ago?' he demanded. 'Where is Empress Galla Placidia? What was the response of Emperor Theodosius in Constantinople? Is Trans-Pannonia not in his jurisdiction?'

'Flimflam and flibbertigibbet!' cried Valentinian. 'Theodosius is no warrior emperor, like Us! And so it was up to Us to deliver the knock-out blow. A short, sharp shock. An entire limb of their people cut off!'

'An entire ... ? Your Imperial Excellency, what form did this punitive expedition take exactly? How many were captured?'

'Captured? None! They were put to the sword like silly, yelping puppies! That taught them! Those barbarians wouldn't understand anything less. It's what they do to others.' Valentinian wagged his finger admonishingly. 'An eye for an eye, General, and a tooth for a tooth. You won't be hearing any more from that lot for a while, I can tell you!'

'Men, women, children ...'

'Vermin, the lot of them! Barbarians, beyond all law and reason! Onions and rancid butter! They must be told. One has to be cruel to be kind. A pre-emptive strike, General Aëtius.' Valentinian was positively bubbling with martial confidence, his pallid cheeks aglow.

'A few must die so that a far greater number can live. It is in the nature of things, and especially in the nature of war. It is a kind of sacrifice at the Altar of Peace!'

Aëtius begged leave to depart, his teeth gritted.

Gone were his plans to take command down at Ostia. Gone were his great ambitions to rebuild the Mediterranean fleet down there at the decaying shipyards, and then to sail for Carthage to retake the African grainfields from the Vandals. Such plans had been burned up as surely as if someone had put a torch to them.

He would be needed elsewhere soon, he and his Gothic Wolf-Lords. They would be needed on quite another frontier.

EPILOGUE
The Crossing

A boy was fishing on a small tributary of the Danube, that great river of ever-changing colours, now a warm and limpid green in the early summer sun. He was not fishing very hard. The river was so beautiful, nature at the full, a peaceful pastoral scene. He trailed his hand in the clear water. Among the reeds, a dabchick was sitting on her floating nest, incubating six neat white eggs. Surely they would hatch soon. The boy wondered if he would see it. Everything was being born today, everything was coming to life. The dabchick's partner was diving for stickleback. Trout were jumping, and the air was full of waterflies and of butterflies of brilliant yellow and blue. A ladybird was a splash of blood on reedmace close to, spoonbills swept the shallows farther off. House martens were coming down to the river's edge to pluck up little beakfuls of mud and fly back to build their artful nests under the eaves. Marsh marigolds nodded their great golden heads at the water's edge. It was such a peaceful scene.

The boy was almost asleep, face turned upwards to the sun, when a kingfisher flashed past in a dazzle of emerald and blue, and he lifted his head. And then he stared, open-mouthed. He might be dreaming – he wished he was. But he felt the wooden boards of the boat hard enough beneath him. He wasn't dreaming. This was real.

Then he was reaching for the oars and tearing at them in pure panic, whimpering to himself under his breath.

No more than two hundred yards upstream, having already crossed the great Danube, the Hun army was fording this tributary to fall on the town of Margus. There was no numbering them, nor describing the way they looked.

At their head rode Attila, face set like stone. Not far behind him rode the witch Enkhtuya. On a leather thong round her neck hung two small severed hands, and from her saddle, tied by its hair, hung the head of the idiot child, eyes closed and mouth agape.

'Sir, the Huns have crossed the Danube. They have fallen on Margus Fair.'

'Very well.' Aëtius nodded and turned away.

All was now ready. It was time to begin.

It was time for the End to begin.

LIST OF THE PRINCIPAL PLACE NAMES
mentioned in the text, with their modern equivalents

Modern equivalents marked with an asterisk* are approximations only

Altai Mountains – mountain range in western Mongolia, holy to
    the Huns and to many other peoples
Aral Sea – in present-day Kazakhstan/Uzbekistan
Aquincum – Budapest
Borysthenes – the River Dnieper, Ukraine
Byzantium, Constantinople – Istanbul
Carnuntum – Hainburg*
Chersonesus – Sebastopol
Chorasmia – Uzbekistan/Turkmenistan*
Dzungarian Gap – between the Tien Shan and the Altai
    Mountains, straddling present-day Kazakhstan/China
Euxine Sea – the Black Sea
Kharvad Mountains (Hun), the Harvaǧa (Gothic) – the
    Carpathians
Hippo Regius – Annaba, Algeria
Hungvar – the Hungarian plain
Illyricum – Croatia/Bosnia/Serbia/Albania*
Kyzyl Kum – the Red Sands, desert in present-day Uzbekistan/
    Kazakhstan
Leptis Magna – Labda, Libya
Maeotis Palus, the Marsh of the Scythians – the Sea of Azov
Margus – Pozarevac, Serbia
Massilia – Marseilles
Mauretania – Morocco and northern Algeria*

Mediolanum – Milan
Moesia – northern Bulgaria/Macedonia*
Narbo – Narbonne
Numidia – Tunisia*
Ophiusa – Odessa*
Panium – a humble and unremarked little town in Thrace
Parthia – Persia, Iran*
Qilian Shan – mountain range in northern China
Scythia – Russia, Ukraine, Kazakhstan, and all points east*
Sea of Ravens – Caspian Sea
Singidunum – Belgrade
Sirmium – Sremska Mitrovica,* Serbia
Takla Makan – a desert in Xinjiang, China
Tanais – Rostov-on-Don*
Tavan Bogd – the Five Kings, the highest peaks in the Altai
Tien Shan – the Celestial Mountains, stretching through
    Kyrgyzstan and Northern China
Tolosa – Toulouse
Treverum – Trier
Viminacium – Kostolac, Serbia

Acknowledgements

Among the many books read and consulted, the most useful were two recent studies, Peter Heather's *The Fall of the Roman Empire* and Bryan Ward-Perkins's *The Fall of Rome and the End of Civilization*. Both scholars agree that Rome really did fall, that the West thereafter collapsed into a terrible Dark Ages; and Heather argues that it was the Huns who were largely to blame.

The verses on the ancient Irish King Goll are taken from *The Madness of King Goll* by W. B. Yeats, while the verse on p 299 is from *The Curse of Cromwell*. Claudian's hymeneal hymn is genuine. The other verses are my responsibility.

More personal thanks to Jon, Genevieve and Angela at Orion for all their enthusiasm, encouragement and patience; to Lizzie Speller and Bywater for help with my small Latin and less Greek; to Patrick Walsh, best of agents, as ever; to the helpful staff of various libraries, including Shaftesbury Public Library and the London Library; and to Iona, for great forbearance, and for everything else, too.